TERRORIST

BABE

Ernie & Wanda Moore

Printed by InstantPrinter.com
For additional copies of this or
other books go to:
www.BarnabusPress.com

Shalom Shalom
Love & Prayers,
Wanda

EDM - Author's Note

I grew up without a father. In his place I had two wonderful role models. My grandfather, Ernest Hunter Crabtree, a blacksmith with simple ways and country learning. He transferred some vital foundations to me. One was the absolute necessity that family was not conditional. You kept your word, loved your family, protected them and there were no exceptions.

The second male role model I was blessed with was my uncle. Donald Eugene Crabtree. Fourteen years my senior, Jake as he is called, took me everywhere when my father deserted us. Spoiling me, loving me and taking time to provide the security I desperately needed as a little boy, Jake was the light of my life. He still is. When I was six – to the dismay of my mother and grandmother – he taught me to shoot. First a BB gun which he secretly purchased and publicly transferred to my overjoyed hands.

He took me hunting, taught me tracking, safety, respect for the environment and the game we pursued. When Jake enlisted in the Paratroopers during the Korean War I was devastated. When he returned I was ecstatic and relieved beyond words.

Jake wrestled with me, loved me, came to my rescue during family crisis and was a friend and example of integrity and honor as I grew older. When I enlisted he saw me off with manly words of caution and love. When I returned from Viet Nam he welcomed me home as Uncle Harold (who served in the Marines in the Pacific during WWII) had welcomed him. As a beloved comrade. We had served our nation during a time of war, faced the danger and come home. Mission accomplished.

When I got the idea for this series about some of America's heroes the names of my main characters were never in doubt. This is my way of paying respect to the man – the men – who were and are precious to me in ways others can only imagine.

For our Fans

We work hard to give you ever better reads.

OTHER BOOKS
BY ERNIE MOORE

One Time Messengers
(First in the Jake Crabtree Series)

Traveling Israel With Your Bible
(For Anyone who wants to see Israel on Tour)

Get Both Books on Amazon.com or
www.Barnabuspress.com

ONE

Richmond was astir. This old southern city was no sleepy backwater, but neither was it the hottest spot for front line entertainers. Oh, Johnny Cash had been to the fairgrounds a few years ago. Bruce Springsteen's plane once made a forced landing when it developed engine troubles. He'd happily signed autographs at the main terminal for an hour and a half then gratefully beat it for taller cotton.

There is no Carnegie Hall or Radio City Music Hall here. Not even a Grand Ole Opry wannabe. The rock groups who play the Coliseum are mostly head-bangers with a cult-following. They tour the country after their record sales are in the toilet deceiving themselves with autographs and photo ops.

When the announcement that Babs was going to tour the "second cities" of America in a "Thank You Tour" and Richmond was on the list her fans went crazy. The tickets sold out by dinner time. At a beginning price of one hundred dollars each that too made news. Her flight landed at Byrd Field and everyone wanted a photo or just yelled her name and caught a glimpse of that crooked nose that helped create such an unforgettably beautiful sound.

Her limo was sandwiched in between six police cars with flashing light bars and wailing sirens. The Diva made the quick ride to the beautiful Jefferson Hotel downtown; one fading light housing another.

Waiting in the lobby was the Mayor and the Governor. She greeted them like they were muddy-booted stable servants then made her way up to her suite. One of her staff tried to smooth their ruffled feathers. *You understand, she's a diva*, and all that.

They didn't understand and left angry.

In a rundown motel in Mechanicsville, just a few miles northeast of Richmond were more fans.

"Why you reckon they wanna whack Babs? Gee, I like her sound. You hear me, Hon?" The speaker tenderly worked on a 308 caliber Winchester Model 70. There was a 4x10 Unertl scope on the bed beside her. A butter yellow, microfiber cloth was caressing the bolt assembly in her hand.

Roxanne looked up from the spotting scope and tripod. She had just polished the lenses and prepared to put it back in the hard-side case.

"Way I figure it is that she probably made somebody mad in Vegas or maybe even out on the Island. You know her rep for spittin' on people one way or another, Val."

"Well, we got it to do," Valerie sighed, rising smoothly. "Let's load up and ride. You think we really have a security team to run interference or are we on our own?"

"My thinkin' is that we better not plan on any help. That Maxine was a real pro, but I glommed onto those two in the van and they looked like scut workers to me. They be our security, we gonna be in a shoot-out for sure!" There was no humor in Roxanne's voice.

"That's how I see it too, Kid. Why I said we better do it as she gets to the car. Downtown ain't gonna be that easy to shutdown, what with I-95, I-64 and the other main highways running close by. And we'll be on none of them. Closing all the streets in town won't be happening."

At four that afternoon, the Babs parade was about to leave for the Richmond Coliseum. Rehearsal.

"Harriett! Where are the *@%&# police cars? I told you we had to have a police escort from here to the Coliseum! Where are they?!

"Call somebody. RIGHT NOW!" Babs wasn't shrieking. Had to protect the vocal chords, you know. But she was irate and there was fire in her eyes and a snarl on her lips.

"They pulled out right after the Mayor and Governor left. I saw the Mayor talking to one of the officers and he said something in his radio. That was it." To herself, she said, *Right after you treated them like jerks!*

Babs and her lap-dog-husband moved through the hotel's revolving door, him pushing; her cussing the cops.

A sparkling white stretch limousine waited a dozen steps away. The driver, outfitted in a burgundy uniform complete with hat was bowing and holding the rear door open.

Suddenly everything just slammed to a stop. There was a red mist behind her like a pink halo in the sunshine and she went down like James Brady in that Reagan assassination video. Harriett was sprayed by some of the gore. The husband caught some and stood there looking at his shirt while a rifle echo bounced around the brick and concrete walls of Richmond.

The chauffer was right there beside her on the paving bricks. He had spent some very educational time as a lance corporal with the Marines in Iraq. He didn't need any instructions when somebody went down. And he well recognized a rifle shot. If he could have fit, he'd have been *under* the Lincoln.

Scrambling off the roof of the elderly but genteel rooming house across the street two ladies from Long Island didn't wait to say goodbye. The irony of their being tasked with Babs' demise didn't occur to them until late that night as they drove through South Carolina listening to one of her CDs.

As the screams of bystanders echoed down Franklin Street, an old Jeep Waggoneer literally drove up onto the trunk of a Chevy Geo. The driver got out, circled around behind his Jeep before the stunned compact's driver could respond.

He smoothly opened the door of a gray Dodge of indeterminate age as it glided to a stop beside him and then drove away. The Geo driver stood beside his ruined car looking all around, cursing and shouting into his cell phone at a 911 operator who was distracted by the woman at the next desk screaming that somebody had just killed Babs down at the Jefferson!

TWO

Maxine Bates moved with the light step of the perpetual jogger. Long, tough muscles, a boyish chest, and slab-thin sides that make female joggers barely noticeable as they take their daily trips to nowhere. When men do notice them, it is usually because of the tight attire, the well-defined shoulder muscles and flat tummies, but mostly such joggers are like street lights and mail boxes; part of the scenery. In Maxine's case they could not have been more wrong.

Her short, brown page-boy cut bounced with each step, reflecting the hot sun. Maxine has covered three miles and has two more to go. Her hazel eyes are the best feature in a face detractors would call "ferret-faced." She is buck-toothed, with a recessive chin and a fairly long, thin, bony nose with a break mid-point. It is a weak face until one looks into her eyes. Then they see nothing but cold steel.

Sweat paints a "V" on the front of the light blue tank top. The waistband of her spandex shorts is dark with more of the same. Her heartbeat is a steady ninety-seven beats a minute. Maxine is singing a Jerry Garcia song in her mind, keeping time with the "plop, plop, plop" of her Nikes as they raise El Paso's reddish dust.

She runs on the track built for U.S. Army Patriot Missile teams to take PT. Her accent, though Middle Eastern never raises a curious glance. After all, many of these soldiers have wed dusky-skinned ladies who speak English exactly as she. The soldiers' tours in a number of Arab lands and Israel have provided a safe haven for Maxine. Her concealment is complete among the enemy.

She is not exactly a happy woman, but she is content. Like an alligator on a Mississippi mud bank, Maxine Bates aka Basma Barghouti is biding the time until her next kill.

At age twenty-nine she knows that she is a valuable asset for Al Qaeda. The sniper training she received in Jordan's army was intensive. She finished at the top of her class in spite of the rough treatment from the sexist male instructors. The experiences which followed took her from a sniper with the appropriate military code and skills to an Al Qaeda assassin.

Maxine is no longer a military sniper; no longer a weapon in Jordan's arsenal, used to protect her fellow soldiers' lives, or shorten a battle or a war. Maxine has regressed from the honorable profession of soldiering down into the darker more unexplainable area of murdering for a mad cause.

Regardless of the nation they serve, military snipers share certain common distinctives. They are supremely proud of their training. Not just exactingly accurate trigger-pullers, the best are experts at concealment, movement – even in open environments, woodcraft and study of the environment, range determination and target acquisition.

If the uninformed should speak of them as "killers" he is firmly corrected. They are neither killers nor murderers though they certainly bring death to the enemy. Their tradecraft saves lives – their own troops and sometimes captives. It often shortens armed conflicts by removing the enemy's leaders or a unit's will to fight. They are in the business of soldiering, not murdering. For Maxine, that was how it began. Then, one day it all changed.

Transformed from the young girl who followed her brother into the army, she became the terrorist's tool. Twelve previous missions, at places ranging from the Syrian border to Europe, and even once in Uzbekistan, were all one hundred percent successful.

Now she is restless, but still supremely patient. It has been eleven years since she was that innocent girl hoping the Jordanian Army would offer her a better life.

Born in a sleepy village on the outskirts of Amman, she enlisted in the army at eighteen. What promised to be a boring existence took a turn for the better when the truck she was driving broke down at the Royal Jordanian Army's armory. Maxine had just delivered a load of ammunition. It was offloaded, but the truck would not start when she prepared to leave. Waiting, – the primary task of soldiers in every army – Maxine strolled over to the block building housing the armory and peeked in the door.

After ten minutes in which the senior Sergeant neither invited her in nor scolded her she stepped inside into the shade.

A private at a table was attempting to disassemble a well-used American-made M-60 machine gun. On his third try to extract the bolt, he huffed in frustration and muttered a curse.

"Having a difficulty?" she asked mildly mocking.

"If you can do better, I'd like to see it!" the private shot back. Maxine stepped to the work bench and gently nudged him aside. With flying fingers she removed the bolt, and then continued to break the weapon down, placing each part in order on an oily rag laid on the table to facilitate easy reassembly.

The four other men in the cement block building were watching – at first with amusement, then with amazement. The Senior

NCO walked over, nodded and smiled. Never let it be said Arabs don't have a sense of humor.

"And you learned such a lady-like skill where?"

She picked up a rag and began to wipe the stubborn bolt. "My brother has one just like it. He is a Corporal in this unit. I learned from him. I am faster than he is now. Even blind-folded," she grinned an impish grin.

"Can you shoot it, too?" the stunned Sergeant asked.

Lowering her chin she replied quietly, "Sergeant, I do not wish my brother to be in trouble for an aggressive sister."

"Private, can you shoot the machine gun?" The Sergeant asked firmly but not roughly. "No trouble will come to your brother."

"Yes, Sergeant, I can shoot it also, but not as well as he. Of course he has more practice. I only fired it once." Maxine presented a hesitant smile. In a nation where women could be murdered for "honor crimes" – causing the family to lose face due to immorality or a host of other offenses – all sensible females tread cautiously.

The Sergeant asked about her present assignment, her commanding officer's name, and other pertinent information regarding her posting. He walked to a telephone and called someone. In a few minutes, he was laughing and nodding to the person on the other end of the phone.

As he was speaking, the repair crew arrived to get the truck going. Maxine started out the door, but he called her back and spoke to the private she had challenged.

"You! Go drive the truck back to the warehouse. She has your job and you have hers." The flabbergasted duo looked at the sergeant, then one another. The private with murder in his eyes; she with a downcast face. That had not been the intent, but one does not challenge authority in the military – or ignore good fortune.

Maxine was now in the Armory. She loved it. The gun oil's warm scent, the beautifully machined steel of the weapons, and the shared expertise and friendship of the armorers who repaired and fine-tuned the rifles, pistols and machine guns of the battalion all provided her a place to serve with joy and fulfillment.

During any repair process, there is a testing phase. The various armorers went to the firing range and test fired the newly repaired equipment. Then the day came when the Senior NCO had just replaced the telescopic sight on a Remington 700 sniper rifle. It had been the gift to one of King Hussein's personal body guards by a friendly American President. Such a beautiful weapon! And it could shoot the fleas off a camel without making the beast flinch!

"Private, come with me. We are going to fire a Crown Jewel!" With that Maxine and her boss headed for the nearby rifle range. At the fifty meter bench he removed the bolt, squatted down to gaze through the barrel, and silently adjusted the rifle on the sandbags. Then, holding the rifle in place, he moved the adjusting screws on the scope. They were finally centered on the bull's eye on the target. At last satisfied, with a grunt so saying, he began to fire it repeatedly, each time adjusting the settings on the scope and allowing the barrel to cool before the next shot. Cold zeroing.

Finally, he said to Maxine, "Your turn. Move to the 200 meter target."

She had never touched such a fine weapon in the six months she'd worked in the armory. She looked through the ten power scope and was stunned at what she saw. The target was unimaginably close and clear!

She withdrew her eye and looked at her mentor. He nodded, and she resumed her firing position. He made some suggestions regarding grip, placement of her cheek on the comb of the stock – touching her right thumb just so, and breathing. She carefully followed his coaching.

The first shot was dead on, and a star was born. She fired four more shots, all interlocking and able to be covered by a ten piaster coin. The Sergeant was also head of the Long Distance Rifle Competition for the Division, and knew he had just found a champion.

Maxine had never fired a rifle of any kind before joining the Army. Of course she *had* shot her brother's machine gun. Even after enlisting and enduring the prejudice of the male soldiers, she'd only been allowed to fire one thirty round magazine from the American made M-16 the instructor placed in her hands and said with a smirk, "Try not to kill any of us." He had somehow forgotten to advise her that the selector switch on the side of the rifle was set to full automatic fire.

Maxine was startled at the vibrating shock of constant recoil and the string of brass cartridges flying to her right. Releasing the trigger, she then fired the remainder of the magazine in short bursts. Her brother's coaching paid off. She gazed coolly into the eyes of the shocked instructor. The 100 meter target was stitched and the other recruits were disappointed that they could not laugh at her.

The instructor yanked the rifle from her grip and called for the next shooter with a growl. Maxine went to the motor pool and a driver's assignment.

That had all now changed. After watching her with the Remington, her Sr. NCO soon found its twin. In somewhat rougher condition, but equipped with a matching 10X (ten magnification power) Unertl scope and with all the Match Grade ammunition she could shoot. *AND* he found plenty of time for her to shoot with a good instructor who recognized a natural when he saw one.

Maxine responded to the training and loved the whole package; the challenge of exceeding her last best effort. The relentless push to perfection to incorporate her lessons; the blast of the rifle, its recoil shoving her bones backward, and the constant improvement that came with time, so much so that all the doubters and scorners became not only silent, but eventually unashamed supporters. Maxine would put them on the Arab Rifle Competition map. They knew it and she knew it.

Then, as everyone sooner or later experiences, what was "known" was no more. Jordan had a new king. Abdullah II, the son of King Hussein was young, dashing, American-educated and with a modern Palestinian wife. Like all First Ladies, she became involved with "causes."

The old-fashioned Arab men sat around tiny tables in the small coffee shops, drank their "mud" Turkish coffee, pulled on their hookahs and cast questioning eyes at the newspaper reports. They shook gray heads but mostly kept silent. Kings, alas, could do one damage and how does one say anything unkind about a powerful man's wife?

Princess Aisha took an interest in women in the military. She even marched with special units of women soldiers, as her husband did with the men. Not happy with just truck drivers and cooks, she --- she wanted combatants! One of those units would be snipers. Women shooting!

It seems that the lovely Princess had been watching American television one night and saw a program on the History Channel about the 2000 women who served Mother Russia as snipers in WWII.

She spoke to the King. He spoke to the Generals. They spoke to the Colonels, and so on. Finally a Captain received the message and the Jordanian Women's Sniper Platoon was created. Thirty women. A special barracks. Male instructors. The best of everything.

Maxine was promoted to Corporal and released from Armory duty. Life was good. Shooting every day. Learning the art of concealment, stealth, movement, distance evaluation, and all the other traits that make snipers a dangerous weapon and keep them alive.

The Jordanian instructors had attended training in England under some of the best in the business. They were demanding but fair and they too, saw the promise in the skinny brown-haired girl who could turn a rifle into a magic wand out to a thousand yards and more. It first turned targets, then moving goats, into rags in her hands.

Being able to hide herself in camouflage and creep slowly within range of an instructor who was expecting her was her great delight. The men were armed with powerful spotting scopes and years of training. To close on them then fire a blank cartridge was a real rush for her. She was invisible. She was a *jinn* sent to deliver death to Jordan's enemies.

She was a natural, and as her training continued week after week, she increased in confidence. Where once had been a backward village girl who tried to live in the shadows and remain unnoticed, Maxine became a woman who realized that, though far from beautiful, she gained the attention and respect of her male counterparts due to her professionalism. Like many before her, she had found her calling in the military.

Her cause was Jordan's defense. Though a Muslim outwardly her god was not Allah. It was the twin deities of Remington and Unertl she worshipped. She became known in the platoon as the Death Angel. And she had yet to fire a shot in anger.

That all changed her third year in the army. She had trained until she could not be found in the ingress or egress modes of a mission even by three teams of observers. Her favorite spotter-team mate was a husky young man who was as ugly as a camel, but floated over the ground like smoke on the wind. He could read shades and textures better than any other man in the sniper school, and because of it he could also hide better than anyone. Once he even located a grenade pin hung on a bush at two hundred yards! Whereas the women snipers had their own unit, it was not so with assignments. Mixed teams were the norm.

The Old Man, actually a Captain who had just celebrated his thirtieth birthday, came to the valley outside of Amman where the teams were working and blew a whistle. All teams were called in and gathered around their instructors.

The handsome, raffish Captain stepped before them and said, "The dogs to the North are killing some of our people and taking their livestock, their vehicles. Their daughters, even. A couple of young boys have been kidnapped and murdered. Apparently diplomatic methods have availed no relief from this deplorable behavior.

"We are going to deal with them a bit more firmly. I want two teams for a month's duty on the Syrian border. You will be free-ranging, on your own, and with permission to kill anyone harming the villagers in your sector. Of course this will not be known to the general public. If you are caught or captured, do not expect to survive their interrogations. These are Syrians and no friends of ours."

Every hand flashed up, including all the instructors. Boredom is a great motivator for soldiers. The Captain smiled and said, "I think only four of you will be enough." He called the Sr. NCO aside and in a few minutes Maxine and Hamir her spotter were chosen, along with another team.

Four days later, Maxine and Hamir found themselves on the east side of the Golan Heights. West was Israel. North was the Syrian border. The land was green and lush as a result of the recently finished winter rains. Farmers were tilling crop plots, fruit trees were blooming and the earth was rich with promise.

Their Sergeant left them with supplies in a small shepherd's cottage, handed them the key to the door, and wished them good hunting. Inside was a radio, a cell phone, food, bedding, water, and most importantly, ammunition.

For a week they never fired a shot. Rather they crawled all over the mountains, inserted themselves into crevices of rock and draped vegetation and burlap covers over themselves as they watched for Syrian invaders from the north, much as the Israelis must have a thousand years earlier.

This time it was not hordes of Assyrians. Rather, it was a tan jeep jolting down a dusty mountain trail they watched. It arrogantly rode the crest of the ridges, stopped occasionally as the passenger in the front seat scanned with binoculars, then moved on.

Such fools! Reflections, noise and worst of all – total visibility. And they were in Jordan, not their own Syrian lands! Even the United Nations' eunuchs stationed at the juncture of the three countries – Israel, Jordan and Syria – were more circumspect.

After watching it was time to move. The team returned to the cabin and spent one day working up a plan, packing their necessities and sleeping in rotation. During the night they moved to a rock outcropping that overlooked the jeep trail the Syrians always traveled.

They had watched them scout a small village of perhaps six homes. There were sheep and goats; a cow even. And there were two nubile teenage girls. The team had watched as the Syrians glassed the *kfar*, or village, tracking the girls with their binoculars and elbowing one another in unheard jocularity. Maxine said nothing, but inside it made her furious. It might just as well have been her young sister back home they lusted after.

She and Hamir dug into the side of the ridge. It was tiresome work, and all the harder since the place was so rocky. *Had Allah dumped all the rocks he did not need in creating the worlds in the Middle East?* At last satisfied, they climbed into their "hide," fixed the cover just right, and began the hunt – the waiting part, at least.

A day passed with nothing but hot dust and eye-numbing glare. A sip from a warm canteen. Snipers, once in place, do not leave their lair.

Then they could both hear the jeep grinding gears before they saw it come around the gigantic gray boulder below. According to their laser rangefinder it was exactly 826 meters to the village. Six hundred to the area the Syrians had parked previously. Today they chose the same spot.

One had an AK-47 with a banana clip and the other a baby Uzi, the small, vicious Israeli sub-machine gun. One of them stretched then grabbed his groin. Hamir muttered, "Michael Jackson," referring to the same gross movement by the alleged-pedophile American rock star.

Maxine never said a word. She was in her shooting groove. Cheek nailed to her right thumb on the stock; the same place every time. Breathing and heartbeat and grip identical with the thousands of shots she'd placed on ranges. Then the tightening of the trigger and the rifle roared and bucked in her hands. Her shoulder took the jar of recoil. The rifle lifted a bit then settled back on its bipod.

Hamir said – as quietly as if he were speaking of a bug on a peach – "One down." By the time he'd uttered the words, Maxine had worked the bolt, retrieving the spent brass with her fingers lest it rattle on the rock beneath her. She then smoothly moved another round into the chamber.

Below them, over a quarter of a mile away, the 165 grain, .308 caliber bullet had entered the cranium of the soldier who stood on the opposite side of the jeep from Maxine. It was travelling about one-half mile per second, spinning and slamming through the skull as if it were papier-mâché.

The soldier dropped backward, dead already, with a reddish spray of blood, brain and hair blooming from the back of his head. There was just a thump of impact then he was hurled back and down. Not like one sees on television or the cinema, but with a collapsing of all nerves making the action more like a marionette whose strings are simultaneously cut.

Before he was completely down, there was a report from the rifle above the Syrians. As the dead man hit the reddish-orange dirt beside the jeep, his fellow soldier, spun and crouched. Disbelieving for an instant, looking first toward his compatriot, then for the source of the shot, he was rooted to where he stood. It was his last mistake.

He should have taken cover behind the jeep. Maybe – just maybe – he could have survived. Probably not. Stupidity and arrogance often combine to create death.

Instead, there was an instant replay of the "thump," the same spray – this time splashing the jeep as well as the dust with gore, and the man fell from his crouch into a lump of former humanity as his still-beating heart pumped his life-blood from the massive wound in the side of his skull. His hands fluttered briefly, then stilled. Almost immediately from above, a second report from the Remington.

Up at the hide, Hamir said, “Down and out.” Maxine’s heart was pounding so hard she was certain her observer could hear it as she worked the bolt, again trapped her warm spent brass with her fingers then loaded another round.

“Are you all right?” Hamir asked, looking at her. A sheen of perspiration coated face. Her skin was pallid and she was breathing fast and shallow. “Slow down your breathing. It will be alright. You did it perfectly.”

“Hamir, I’m fine. Keep watch! There may be others just out of sight. We cannot move from here until dark.” Maxine knew Hamir was concerned for her, and certainly she knew she must look shaken. She *was* shaken!

For the first time in her life she had caused another human being to die. Two of them in mere seconds! The mechanical parts of her training were fine, but nothing could have prepared her for the emotion of it. The *enormity* of it. Even the sergeants who talked of combat and stress had not made it real enough to prepare her for this. She consciously lowered her head a bit, slowed her breathing, and willed herself to think of something besides the bodies dropping.

She had not seen the blood-bloom of the bullets’ impact. The recoil had moved the scope off target while that instant played out. Hamir had though, and it was engraved in his mind’s eye for ever. This was a first for him as well. He had come from an artillery unit before sniper training, and lugging shells was far removed from this. Unbelievably removed!

At dark, they packed up, finally satisfied that no more Syrians were nearby. Two hundred yards from the village, and not one Jordanian had walked up the path to the jeep. In fact, no one had come out of any of the poor hovels below. They saw nothing, had nothing to report. They were blind and mute regarding the dead Syrians.

Maxine and Hamir walked carefully down to the jeep. There they inspected the bodies. Dead-center where she had aimed. They piled their equipment into the jeep and left the bodies lying. Hamir called down to the people below to hide the bodies. The Jordanian Army had removed their oppressors.

No one answered, but both soldiers knew by dawn there would be no blood in the dust. They drove the jeep back to their cabin and parked it. Much easier than the day’s walk to the killing ground. Once there, they rotated watch and slept like logs. One day more and the hunt would move to another part of the border.

They killed two more Syrians in the next ten days. When they returned to their cabin, the jeep was gone, removed by one of their support troops, but their Sergeant was waiting with a lorry to haul them and the remaining supplies back to Amman.

It was a long ride, and he never once asked how they faired until they were back at camp. Then he said, “Report in the morning for de-briefing at 0800.” They unloaded the truck and returned to their respective barracks until morning.

That was eight years ago. Maxine had her first four confirmed kills. The total would climb in the next two years. Then came Iraq. Oh, she hated Iraqis! Unbeknownst to her, America was on her horizon three years after Iraq. That she would hate even more.

THREE

Jake Crabtree woke up wondering where he was. It was not a new experience for him. For years now it had been that way. He always came instantly awake, but it sometimes took him a moment to recall his cover name and identity; where he was currently sleeping.

He lay perfectly still with his eyes closed, using his other senses to probe for danger. Outside a cardinal called for a mate and a farm tractor moaned under a burdensome load. The smell of coffee wafted faintly across his consciousness. Somewhere downstairs he heard the low rumble of men's conversation. Occasionally a woman's voice joined in.

He opened his eyes and looked around. Sunshine flooded the room from two east-facing windows. The room was well decorated, but like a hotel room, in that it lacked the personal touches which bespoke one's home. Jake realized, though, that he *was* home, at least for now.

"Home" was thirty eight acres just west of Elizabethtown, Pennsylvania.

Solutions.com's headquarters was at Harrisburg International Airport but until it was totally complete, they had established its base of operations on what had been a boarding school for horses and a pseudo riding academy. The farm included a large farm house, caretaker's cottage, hay barn, granary, chicken coop, stable/barn and a farm implement shed complete with two tractors.

One ground floor bedroom was already an armory with shelving, rifle and pistol racks and work benches.

Jake, his father Harold and partner Larry Fielding shared the farm house. George and Helen Allen, the caretakers, lived in the cottage. Their pilot Tex and his wife lived nearby in a home of their own..

The farm was situated atop a long narrow hill overlooking the Susquehanna River, Harrisburg International Airport and the infamous Three Mile Island.

Jake liked the eight acres of hardwood timber and the remainder in hay fields. It wasn't home in Illinois, but it was out of the city, and that was great.

Solutions.com, Inc. had begun as a cover for Jake, Larry and their team. Originally agents with the Defense Intelligence Agency, they had been tasked with pursuing a female Al Qaeda operative (who, unknown to them, was the daughter of Osama bin Laden). Her name is Raquel Linden.

Just months ago, as the noose tightened – more from blind luck it seemed, than expertise – she had bolted. In the process she shot up the Solutions office, killing a young secretary and wounding Larry and Oleg Gregori Nabatoski, AKA – Elvis, the team's electronics genius. Both were recovering well.

She also torched her own office building and home, then hid out in a cabin in the piney woods near Chancellorsville, Virginia. When a forest ranger stumbled upon her there and called for reinforcements, she burned that place to the ground too. Escaping through a tunnel she had ordered built years before, she was now the most sought after fugitive in America. Alas, her trail evaporated like dew on a July lawn.

In the mean time Jake's team went through some major changes. The farm was only one, and a minor one at that.

After a quick shower Jake descended the stairs and walked into a large, friendly country kitchen. A trim-looking woman with gray hair pulled back into a bun smiled like she was gazing on a favorite child and said, "Ah, the son also rises!" As she spoke, she reached for a cup and filled it from a pot of dark, strong brew.

Jake accepted it *and* the kiss she gently pecked on his cheek. Inside, he was touched by the greeting. It had been many years since he had received a loving touch from a woman who mothered him. His Grandma Crabtree was long passed, and his Israeli-born mother had been killed by a drunk driver ten years ago.

Helen Allen's husband George was last posted in the Midwest. A federal agent posing as an illegal gun dealer, providing weapons for a variety of White Supremacists and other thugs, he had reported to his bosses in D.C. He was sixty-one, medium height, but slight of build, large of heart and courage. He was also very happy to be "retired."

Helen had lived a lonely life up until recently. She'd raised a boy who died in the jungles of South Vietnam, and loved a man whose best traits were utilized combating America's enemies. First in the military then for two different government agencies, George had taken the fight to them.

He was a kind and gentle man toward his family and friends, well knowledgeable in farm-craft as well as the warrior skills. For years she'd watched him leave and wonder if, like her son, he would never return. She hadn't whined. She had prayed without ceasing for him, knowing he was doing God's work in the way for which he was fitted.

As time passed she'd watched him return home a bit more soul-weary and hopeless. Wondering if America could ever be safe. After the attacks on 9/11 George had seemed to burn with a righteous indignation toward the evil that was striking his beloved nation. The near-hopelessness was submerged by a rage that refused to let such a thing happen again. Yet when Jake had called him and offered him this position as caretaker Helen had been shocked that he'd accepted. *George – a farmer not a fighter?*

Then one morning while they were packing to move to Elizabethtown, George sat down on the sofa and patted the cushion beside him.

"You don't know why I'm doing this do you?" he'd asked, and then continued without waiting for an answer as she sat beside him.

"These boys – you'll see when you meet them. They're different. I talked to Tex about them after they called me. I'm getting slower, Helen. I forget things. And, to be honest I'm tired. Truthfully, I know it will get me killed if I don't do something different.

Jake said they needed someone to "take their backs." Someone to watch over their home so they would have a place to come to and restore themselves.

Helen, you remember when I'd come back each time? How emotionally spent I'd be?" There was almost a pleading for her to understand that he wanted to continue in the fight, but not on the front lines.

Helen reached out and took his hand. Raising it to her lips she kissed the back tenderly. This hand that she was sure had slain many of America's enemies was the same one that could touch her with such gentleness and love. A tear tracked its way down her cheek.

"George, anything that will give us time together and lift your spirits is heaven to me," she said leaning her head on his shoulder.

George's eyes too were moist. For a moment he couldn't speak for fear of weeping. Finally he said, "I just want you to understand that I'm not quitting the fight, just trying to help these boys do their job without having to worry about home. That and trying to give us a home together for whatever time we have left."

Helen's new duties entailed housekeeping, cooking and mothering the men at the farm. In a few short weeks she was already taken with them.

On her priority list was a new vegetable garden in the spring, a chicken house full of Plymouth Rocks, and the imminent purchase of a Labrador retriever. George maintained the large yard, a quarter mile of paved road, parking area, and the three nags that had come with the farm. The thirty acres of alfalfa would be harvested by the Miller brothers across the road.

The previous owner had been a wretched woman according to the nearest neighbors. When she had expired from a massive coronary and fallen face-down in a pile of horse manure the most outspoken among them said it was her due.

George and Helen considered this the perfect life. Together all day and night; with good men to serve; peace and quiet for a change. There was productive work to do without having to worry about getting shot or blown up. That would soon change, but they were not yet to know it.

Harold said, "Yossi called about an hour ago. He's in J'burg. Said that the final piece of the financial puzzle is in order and that Zulu is officially and totally ours. Kurt's guess was a bit short. It totaled out at one-point-one billion in current assets. He also said that soon after the signing of the final papers Kurt Mullenberg went out, sat down on his veranda and quietly expired. That day he was cremated and his ashes spread over his estate."

The room went silent. Every person at the table knew they owed their current circumstances to this man's faith in them to combat some of the world's evil. A man whom they had never met. "He will be missed, that's for sure," Larry said.

Jake said, "I still have a hard time believing what he did. We owe his memory our best efforts."

Helen was stunned. Had she heard Harold correctly? *Did he say these men were worth over a billion dollars?!*

Harold was sitting at a seven foot long oak kitchen table that gleamed from applications of lemon oil polish studiously applied by Helen. Before him was a plate, yellow with drying egg yolk and garnished with a crust of whole wheat toast. An empty glass that had held ice cold whole milk was standing sentry.

Helen moved to him and refilled his coffee cup, took the plate and glass, then returned to the sink, and began to prepare more coffee.

Larry Fielding leaned over a plate four eggs – sunny side up, barely cooked ("raw!" as described by Jake), toast and bacon, accompanied by the same coffee and milk as Harold. He was carefully elevating a piece of Stroemann white toast on which was balanced some of the runny egg. He ducked his face toward it and virtually nabbed it as it began to slide away toward his lap.

"Nice catch," remarked Jake drolly. Larry nodded in agreement and grinned while he chewed. Humor to break the mood was their *modus apperandi*.

"I hope Ehud knows what he's doing with all this. It is sure that I don't have a clue," Jake continued. Larry nodded agreement as he chewed.

Larry had dubbed them the "odd-trio." Of Arab origin, big as a lumberjack, teamed with the compact but snake fast American-Israeli Jake, and now joined by Ehud Palmach who gave the impression of a light-skinned but hairy gorilla, they were indeed odd looking when together.

Helen had remarked to George one evening as they sat together watching Jeopardy, "These men are not the dry-as-dust, somber kind you'd expect when combatants are discussed. And they're not the James Bond types, or bullies. They look like young executives, athletic, healthy, handsome and strong. The kind who are up-and-comers in some international corporation. I understand your feelings for them." George reached out from his recliner and patted her hand.

"I liked them when we first met. They instill confidence even in a wary old dog like me."

"Speaking of dogs, Hon…" Helen began.

"Yeah, I know. A Lab. I'll talk to the vet in E'town next week."

Helen watched the men as she prepared a fresh pot of coffee. She could see Harold in the son. *Jake's solid,* she thought.

There was a disarming openness, quickness in his smile, and the dark brown hair with a slight touch of a wave to it. His intelligent brown eyes were anchored by grin lines. Still and all, he could walk into a crowd of people and no heads would turn. George had had that same handsomeness but not such that it would draw undue attention when he was young.

Harold was, well… comfortable. Or perhaps *comforting* was a better description. At fifty-eight and well fit, he missed six feet by a couple of inches, but seemed taller due to his bearing. With thinning gray-brown hair, the same friendly eyes as Jake, a nose that had been broken a few times, and the exact look of what he had been just six months ago – a college professor. He tended to plaid long sleeved shirts, expensive wool slacks and sweater vests. Those in the know understood that since the events of the recent past the sweater was a cover for the .45 auto that was always on his belt.

Yet unknown to Helen, Harold was a warrior from another era. Like her son, he had seen life in the jungles of Viet Nam. Serving as a coordinator with the Army Security Agency's Special Operations Group he'd encountered and worked with Navy Seals, CIA, DIA, and NSA operatives. Harold had eventually been recruited by the Defense Intelligence Agency.

He met Jake's mother and married her while stationed in Israel. Her family had moved from New York the year before Israel became a nation.

After surviving a plane crash in Athens, with injuries that forced his retirement, Harold moved his bride back to Southern Illinois, bought the old family farm and started teaching at MacMurray College. He completed his Ph.D. in International Relations shortly thereafter.

When Jake recruited him to oversee the operations side of their crackdown on an Al Qaeda operation, a dormant drop of adrenaline had surfaced. When soon afterward there had been some gun action in Illinois, then again in Virginia, Harold had proven equal to the task.

Jake pulled a chair out and sat down. He glanced at a clock that hung over the sink – 7:30AM. The sun was bright. Birds were shoving each other around at the big round feeder outside the kitchen door. As he looked further out, he could see George with a white plastic five gallon bucket heading into the stable.

"What else did Yossi say? Did you tell him we are bored with settling in as gentlemen farmers?" Jake asked as Helen motioned to him and pointed to an open egg carton beside the stove. He held up three fingers, and she turned to the task of making another breakfast. These boys could eat!

Harold stood and took his cup for a refill then returned to the table. "I told him that I had met with enough lawyers and builders and township zoning officers to fill a lifetime. That I was thinking of heading to Israel for some peace and quiet," Harold laughed as he blew across then sipped from the cup.

"Don't do it!" Larry quipped. "First of all, there ain't no rank to be had. They're on a budget squeeze, and there's peace coming down the road. Peace time armies are lousy duty!"

All three men laughed. They knew that the only peace that Israel would likely ever really know would come when the Messiah established it. That could not be soon enough for them.

"The Solutions.com Swiss *and* US company charters are filed and approved. World headquarters in Zurich, same as Zulu. If we need to go to any of the Arab countries it will be better for us if we aren't known as American or Israeli."

"French would be the best as far as the Arabs are concerned, but right now I can't stomach the idea of being French," Jake added only half joking. Larry nodded, but said nothing.

"Well, none of us speak German fluently except you Jake, and that not with a Swiss accent."

He was fluent in Hebrew, European and Arabic languages and dialects. Harold and Larry had some Hebrew but needed much improvement. Jake and Larry were fluent in Arabic, both Palestinian and Saudi dialects.

It was discovered early in his life that Jake has some sort of "supernatural" ability with languages. He could listen to it spoken, and in a short period of time and almost no effort attain a fluency that was stunning. He spoke Arabic, Hebrew, Italian, French, Spanish and German. He wanted to learn Chinese and Russian, but there was just no time it seemed.

The other partner in the company, Ehud Palmach, had served as Yossi Cumi's executive assistant. Cumi, Harold's late wife's brother, was for many years now the Director of Israel's Mossad – the Israeli equivalent of the CIA.

Ehud was built rather like Magilla Gorilla, with round rolling shoulders over a tiny waist and short powerful legs. His arms seemed too long for his frame, and it seemed surprising that his knuckles didn't drag the ground as he walked. His chest and stomach were both full, giving image to the "barrel-chested" phrase. Coarse, curly black hair coated his arms, hands and even knuckles. More sprouted thickly out of his open collar.

A pair of soft blue eyes peered intelligently from under the expected simian forehead. Large floppy ears, full lips, and a nose that was somewhat like a squash thanks to meeting gym floors too often belied an off-the-scale IQ. Ehud looked like a former wrestler in the heavyweight class. Which, not surprisingly, he had been in his college days at Stanford University.

He was American-born, thirty-eight years old, and single. He'd been married, but it had ended with a bottle of pills, a two AM ambulance call and lots of tears. Too many ghosts from her hometown somewhere in New Mexico.

Prior to that he had served in Army Intelligence as an analyst. Upon completing the four year enlistment with the rank of First Lieutenant, he decided he wanted to go to Israel. Ehud made *aliya* – the Hebrew word for ascending, but in current Hebrew vernacular meaning moving to Israel and becoming a citizen. That was ten years ago.

He joined the IDF, did two years, got out with his Israeli citizenship and began to teach at Hebrew University in Tel Aviv. One day, a pair of Yossi's people paid him a visit. *Voila* he is at "the Institute," as that organization is known.

Ehud speaks Hebrew, English, Spanish (California neighborhood kids taught him), a smattering of Arabic, and can drive a Mercedes like Richard Petty used to push the Mo-Pars. His shooting skills are horrible, but he has nearly instant recall of anything he has ever learned.

Ehud adores Yossi Cumi. Called him the 'little guy' when out of ear range of the Director, and "Boss" when they're together. Leaving Yossi's side was a personal tragedy to Ehud.

Ignoring the wealth attending his new role, he had bedeviled Cumi for a release from the deal. He respects the other agents, believes the cause is just, and the duty promises to be both pleasant and exciting. He just didn't want to leave Yossi Cumi's side. Even the Boss can't understand that.

Jake likes Ehud – the little he knows him. Moreover, he respects his Uncle Yossi's judgment. If Yossi said Ehud needs to be on the team that settled it for Jake.

Ehud had faxed a partial agenda for their meeting:

- The exchange, storage and analysis of intelligence from the US and Israel
- The recruiting and hiring of other agents for America and overseas work – primarily deep cover intel gathering – HUMINT
- The recruiting and hiring of an intel analyst to coordinate the product from all sources
- Further physical training, including Krav Maga for Jake, Ehud and Larry in Israel from Global Security's "hard man camp" near Caesarea.
- Finally, where Ehud will live; America, Israel, Europe – or all three.

The men finished the fresh pot of coffee, discussing more details for the house and office, determined that they needed Yossi and Ehud on the phone for clarification of some major points, and prepared to go their separate ways for the remainder of the day.

These past months have been very busy. Just before Raquel Linden, the "Terrorist Babe," escaped (Larry's name for her) – twice – they were living on a farm near Gainesville, Virginia.

Yossi Cumi shocked them at a dinner meeting with a discussion of making their DIA cover as a security company a reality.

After the attempted capture of Raquel "went south," things became a whirlwind. The same week she took off, the farm where they were living was sold, and the three men found themselves homeless.

They also found themselves out of work. Jake and Larry resigned DIA – for real this time, and Harold was paid for a month's services as a consultant. A high-level meeting took place in a Willard Hotel suite where Jake, Larry and Harold took up residence after leaving the farm.

Attending besides the three worthies were Secretary of War Donald Rogers, the President's National Security Advisor Leona Johnson, the Director of the Central Intelligence Agency, Harvey Reed,

AKA "The Tortoise," and Ehud Palmach, in his last Mossad duty, formally representing Director Yossi Cumi.

At said meeting a brief awards ceremony was held where Agents Larry Fielding and Donald "Jake" Crabtree were presented the State of Israel's highest "foreign-national award," The Ben Gurion Medal for Civilian Warfare. Then Don Rogers stood and gave them both National Service Award Medals for Meritorious Service to the United States.

Immediately afterward, they signed formal resignation forms, were handed envelopes with all the endless government forms saying goodbye, and their final pay checks.

What followed then, was a sometimes heated discussion (usually between the three high government officials) regarding what role Solutions.com would play, what intelligence would be transferred to them, and how. The primary concerns seemed to be Harvey's, since his house would be the primary provider of same.

He was not exactly the most thrilled to have Ehud in the room. Israel was – in his opinion – a very self-centered nation. They would take and take and take and only say, "Thank you very much, but we don't feel it's necessary to reciprocate."

Jonathan Pollard's spying for Israel was a prickly point between the U.S. and Israel. Israel wanted the American Jew released and sent to them. Thus far no U.S. President would pardon him. One might have thought Clinton would, what with the full load of good and "crooked" pardons he issued his last day in office, but Pollard was not on the list. He was still too furious with Arafat and Barak for denying him the Nobel Peace Prize to do any favors for either one of those rats.

The six hour meeting finally ended. Everyone was in agreement, if not particularly thrilled.

Solutions would contract for both Israel, the United States (primarily the CIA), and for individuals, where that could be beneficial for their cover.

Surprisingly not a single media source had tumbled to the fact that they were more than next door victims of Raquel Linden. In fact, the national search for her was as a crazed murderer, not an Al Qaeda terrorist. The major crimes of blowing up the Seattle Space Needle, four theme parks in Orlando, Florida and Giant Stadium in Hershey, Pennsylvania were never publicly attributed to her.[1]

---

[1] See *One Time Messengers* for more details of Solutions.com's establishment, the referred to attacks – and more thrills. Available from Amazon.com.

As he was leaving the suite, Don Rogers handed Harold a large manila envelope, gripped his hand warmly and said, "A little going away present for the team. Go with God."

After closing the door, Harold slid the papers from the envelope onto the large shiny mahogany table in the suite. There was all the documentation for their vehicles, a GMC Envoy, and a Yukon.

But Santa wasn't finished. All the computer and electronics equipment in the building was listed with a bill of sale noted "paid in full." Same thing for all the furniture, telephone systems, everything, including the front door mat.

Finally, Jake pulled a registration and title for the brand new Beech King Air 350 they'd picked up less than a month earlier in Boise, Idaho.

"Whooo! I can't believe it! They even gave us the plane!!" Jake stood straight up and waved the title in the air.

"Can they do that?" Larry asked. "I mean legally? Can they just write all this stuff off and give it to us?" He was looking at Harold.

The professor was as amazed as the other two. "Larry, you're asking the wrong guy. I don't have a clue. I guess when you look at all the stuff the government wastes every day; the one hundred dollar hammers, and all that, this list of materials is not so much.

"Still, my guess is that they look at it as equipping an ally. And, actually it was titled to Solutions.com as cover." He grinned then chuckled, "It's a lot less than they give either Egypt or Israel every year – or the PLO for that matter!"

"The rich get richer," Jake said quietly. "Here we are, holding these papers and thanks to Kurt Mullenberg we could write checks for all of it and have millions left over." It was evident that he was still suffering reverse-sticker-shock. Having so much money and so many assets suddenly available was stunning.

"Speaking of which," Ehud said, "Money is on deposit for each of us, disbursed to our personal accounts in the amount of five hundred thousand dollars. We have to account for none of it. Taxes have already been paid. It is our beginning salaries. Expense accounts are on the credit and ATM cards.

"The gnomes in Zurich are already at work. We are all officially rich beyond imagination.

"Solutions has just under one-hundred-fifty million in available funds at the same bank. All this stuff is already in the company's name, I see."

He opened a brief case and dealt out envelopes, this time large green-bordered white ones, keeping one for himself. Deposit slips, account documents, bank cards, etc.

There was a final envelope. This one he unceremoniously dumped on the table. Inside were Swiss diplomatic passports for each of them as well as supporting documents. At the amazed questioning looks, he responded, "Yes they are absolutely real. No I don't know how Yossi did it. Yes, you may keep your US ones. No, you don't owe me undying gratitude. A large meal will suffice."

They ordered dinner sent up to the suite and continued to plan throughout the evening. Occasionally one of them would look around the group, and say, "Millionaires." Not in a maniacal way, but sort of stunned. For the first time in their lives they had a whole different set of options and responsibilities.

"Yossi says that we should all seriously consider buying better wardrobes. Including shoes." At the stunned looks, he smiled and continued.

"He says that most of the people who have wealth or work with those who have it will immediately pick up on us if we continue to wear K Mart styles." He grinned, and looked at Jake and Larry, but said no more. Both agents looked at their clothes and shrugged. They'd listen to Ehud and do some serious shopping, but keep their jeans close, thanks.

The men, in essence, now had only themselves to answer to. No worries about finances, buying clothes, cars or plane tickets for personal travel. They had no schedule established by anyone else. The missions dictated everything now.

Larry looked at his ex-DIA partner and grinning, said, "Jake, no more sorry reassignments."

Jake nodded, then paused, smiled and said, "Well, Lare, now we have to give *ourselves* the rotten reassignments."

It was then that the reality of it all struck them. Even Harold had not totally soaked it all up until that time. They needed a plan of action. Priorities.

They needed to manage this company, to work out assignments on the war against terrorists, and even to prepare their move from this suite to a headquarters. So many details. So much management before they could really go operational. It truly seemed overwhelming. And to Jake and Larry, boring.

A couple of days later Leona Johnson called with information on a beautiful farm that was coming up for sale in south-central Pennsylvania. A friend of a friend, etc. Networking at this level was new, but they were certainly used to the concept.

The team flew up, met the realtor and visited the property. They drove around it in her SUV, poked through the out-buildings, toured the gigantic farm house and small cottage.

Then they excused themselves and stepped out into the yard for a private conversation. The place was truly lovely. It sat on a hilltop overlooking a wide tree and farm-blanketed valley. A creek meandered its way to the Susquehanna River, just visible in the distance. It was centrally located between Harrisburg and Lancaster. Minutes from Philadelphia, Baltimore, D.C. and New York by plane.

Suddenly there was a tremendous roaring whine overhead and two gray A-10 Warthog tank-killer jets banked into final approach for Harrisburg International Airport.

Jake grinned and said, "Well, any place that has air cover like this should be all right for us."

The others laughed, and Tex, who was standing by the realtor a few yards away gave Jake the thumbs up signal. The team agreed. They could live here.

Negotiations took only a few minutes, a price was offered, a call was made, and a deal was secured. The farm was theirs. Thirty-eight acres of fields and timber, two tractors, some implements and the afore-mentioned three nags.

When the realtor asked about financing, and was informed that their bank would transfer the full amount to her escrow account tomorrow, if that was agreeable, her eyes went wide. This was a first. They would settle in four days and arrange construction changes in a week. She knew just the perfect Amish crew who could build a whole town in a month if they wanted.

They didn't want, but they did desire some major renovations and some new features. Like a gym and indoor swimming pool to help the men stay in peak condition. The renovations and re-wiring were done in three weeks, but in no time the rest of it was also underway. A call from Washington had instantly seen to the Lancaster County building permits.

That afternoon they met with the man in charge of airport facilities. Harrisburg International was undergoing massive renovations too. Vertical parking, more apron and terminal space. Baltimore and Philadelphia and Allentown airports were in for some competition.

On the south end of the airport was a Pennsylvania Air National Guard Wing that flew C-130s on psy-ops missions all around the world. They were being relocated to an ultra-secure base. Massive renovations would see it become Solutions' office-hangar combination.

No sign would identify the Solutions building. A tall chain link-razor wire with twenty-four hour professional security would keep the curious or worse out. Unless someone was looking for them specifically, it would look like more military facilities.

That was then and this was now.

Before the men left the kitchen to go their separate ways the telephone rang, Jake answered it, listened briefly, then said, "Just a minute." He reached to the sideboard, and punched a speakerphone button. "Go ahead, Yossi."

"Good morning men. I have a little detail I feel we should discuss. It was on my list earlier, but we never got to it. Airplanes. I know you have a nice twin prop, but that will just not do for international travel. You need a jet."

Just before he said that, Tex, had strolled into the kitchen, and was approaching the coffee pot. When Yossi said, "You need a jet," his hand stopped in mid-reach. He was literally spot-welded to the floor.

Then before anything else could be said, he muttered, "Yup!"

"What?" Yossi asked, hearing him on the other end.

"Nothing, Yossi. Continue," Harold said, looking curiously at Tex, who now was pouring coffee and giving Jake the eye. It was obvious that Tex believed that he had certainly grabbed the brass ring when he gave his life to Jesus, sobered up totally and came to work for these boys.

"I'm calling at this time because the State of Israel has, in its perfect wisdom, decided to bestow on its beloved Director, a new airplane. Actually, they ripped my previous one off, which is fine, because it was a Lear and had to make multiple stops to travel any great distance."

Tex nodded his head in understanding of jets and their ranges.

"There is a dealer in whom I have great faith who happens to have a brand new Dassault Falcon 7X coming online in a month. This is their newest model, is literally still in the factory, but which he would like to place in my needy hands. For the right price, of course. While discussing this purchase, he mentioned a Gulfstream V…"

At this, Tex did another of his freezing acts. His head popped up, eyes wide, and mouth open, and there he sat like he'd been hit with a baseball bat.

"… and I asked if he would be willing to negotiate a truly deep discount if I could take both at the same time. I gave him the numbers and when he recovered from his shock and awe act, he came to the table.

"What he did not know, and I failed to mention, was that I had previously learned that this particular Gulfstream V had been ordered by an animal in Iraq named Quday, who will not be needing it. He had already put a million and a half down on it. My suggestion is that you purchase the G-Five and I will take the Falcon. All right, questions?"

They all looked at Tex like he was the Chairman of the Board. Even Harold was waiting for a response out of the little man with the faded denim shirt with mother of pearl snaps, scuffed cowboy boots and old blue jeans.

"Well. What do you want me to say?" he looked around the table. This was way out of his league.

For her part, Helen was at the sink scrubbing some vegetables, trying not to listen, but so stunned that this group of men could be discussing the purchase of two executive jets at "her" kitchen table. She looked like a Mennonite farm wife, but had a masters from Texas A&M (as did George), and was a bright blade when called upon.

Not only were they talking about *two* jets, but discussing it on the phone with the Director of Israel's Mossad!

She was a Christian and well versed on Israel – Biblical and current affairs. She'd heard these men discuss Yossi and Ehud. Knew about their Israeli employment. But who would have thought six months ago she'd be here?! It seemed this whole household was asking that question a lot recently.

"I say buy it if Yossi thinks it's smart," Larry said abruptly.

"Larry? Is that you?" Yossi asked.

"Hi, Yossi. My thought is that you likely know more about this than any of us, and you are on top of the money. Speaking of which, how does that work?" Larry responded.

"We do the deals separately, Solutions of course, getting their money through the Zurich bank. Actually the dealer will make a three year contract, half the first year, then twenty-five percent a year for the next two. Zulu titles it.

"This is a brand new plane and the asking price was thirty-eight. We will settle for thirty-six-five. The down payment having been already paid!" He laughed – an unusual sound for him. "Do we have a consensus?" Yossi wanted to do business, but still not push the men into anything against their will.

Jake looked at Tex with a question mark in his eyes.

"Hey, Jake! I ain't tellin' you boys to spend no thirty-seven million bucks!" It was then that Helen almost cut herself with the paring knife. She hadn't consciously registered the "millions" when Yossi had said thirty-six-five.

"Yossi, if you think it wise, then we bow to your expertise. This is not your first dealing with such things, I take it," Harold spoke now, and the others nodded.

"Thank you, Harold. I am not a novice here. I believe it to be a wise purchase. The plane is fully outfitted, beautiful, and in fact can be seen on the internet." He then read off the web address, which Jake jotted down quickly.

"We are agreed, Yossi. Do the deal, please," Harold said firmly.

"It shall be done! I will make arrangements for taking possession of the jet. Is your pilot rated in a G-V?" Yossi asked, covering all the bases.

Tex shook his head no.

"No," Jake said. Tex had sort of lost his voice, and his face was pale.

"Then you might be interested to know that you can contact Flight Safety in Savannah for that. If there is nothing else, I will say *Shalom*."

"*Shalom, Lihheetrahoht*, Yossi," Jake answered for them all. Goodbye, see you later.

Where everyone was silent for the most part during the phone call, now they were all talking at once. Finally, Tex seemed to surface above all the rest.

"One thing you might consider, fellas. We gotta have another pilot. That G V is a big beauty of an airplane, and it requires two full-time pilots. I'm not even rated in it. I got no business bein' the chief pilot."

"So what do we do first?" Jake asked, with real excitement in his voice. Harold looked at his son with pleasure. He knew how Jake loved flying, and how much joy he had taken in the beautiful King Air 350 when he'd flown them to Detroit and back. Now there was a new girl in school and she was also Miss America.

Before Tex could answer, the phone rang again, and they all seemed disgruntled by the interruption.

"Hello!" Jake said.

"It's Yossi, Jake. I wanted to tell you something important. I just ordered the plane, and added something. It will be flown to Israel and be fitted with a special threat radar, anti-missile flares and chaff to ward off any Stingers or enemy fire. Shalom plus a couple of extras from a friend of mine who used to be Chief of Staff of the Israeli Air Force and now heads his own company near Tel Aviv." Then he was off the phone.

The silence hung in the air. All celebration died. Helen, standing at the sink, suddenly felt the tears flood her eyes. These wonderful boys were not just college students gathered around the kitchen table talking football. They were at war, just like her George had been almost all his life. They were in danger of being shot down even as they flew somewhere.

Oh, God, she placed both hands on the edge of the sink and silently prayed so fervently she almost sobbed aloud, *Keep them safe and in the hollow of your hand!*

"Well, he coulda sure said a lot of things beside that!" Larry remarked dryly. "He knows how to shut down a celebration, that uncle of yours," he smiled a mock-serious smile at Jake.

"At least he's not only thinking, but he has the people to see it through," Harold said.

"I just hope I don't pop any of them things off on final approach around here. Set Helen's chickens right off their nests, that would!" Tex said with a glint in his eyes. He too, was a warrior, and knew that black humor was the best way to diffuse fear and worry.

FOUR

PREVIOUSLY

The Taurus had been waiting like a spacecraft escape pod. She'd moved it to the gravel lane where the tunnel exited into the woods upon arriving from Manassas. Three years ago she bought the land, had the cabin renovated, and added the tunnel through one of her Al Qaeda sleepers who owned a construction company in suburban Washington, D.C.

At least monthly she visited the site, saw that it was not broken into by robbers, had utilities and generally looked to the Park Rangers like someone who used it as an occasional weekend retreat.

In the trunk two suitcases were packed with her disguises and supplies for a hasty retreat – along with lots of cash. Up until recently she had maintained the plan like someone sends in their homeowner's insurance premiums. Disbelieving that it would ever really be necessary. Now she was very glad she'd kept to the plan.

The cabin was aflame and Raquel was moving. Coming out of the tunnel she peeled off the muddy outfit and moved quickly to the car.

In the distance she could hear the roar and crackle of the inferno. She smiled and climbed behind the wheel of the Ford, then headed north on Route 3 toward Culpeper. After about five minutes, she met a fire truck, lights and sirens screaming to clear a path to the action.

"Take your time, boys," Raquel laughed, her tongue caressing the chipped tooth in the front of her smile. "You're not going to put that thermite out."

Three miles further along, she pulled off at a pre-planned picnic site and moved quickly to the trunk. She grabbed a white plastic trash bag. Opening it she lay out her new identity. First a medium-length brown wig in a popular flip style. She had already cut her beautiful raven tresses and burned the hair in the cabin's fireplace.

Removing her blouse and jeans she donned a full slip and flowered cotton dress with buttons up the front and a high neckline. A pair of cheap K Mart sneakers, white anklets and a pair of plastic framed, clear eyeglasses and a plastic black imitation leather purse completed the transformation.

Raquel Linden, twenty-five, a close duplicate to the famous movie star of yesteryear, Raquel Welch, with the long golden bronze legs, amazing figure and magnetic face was no more. Certainly no one in Manassas would recognize her. Into the bottom of the purse she placed the Ruger 22 with the barrel changed from the silenced model to a standard four and one half inch one. False IDs and a pile of normal looking chick-junk were already inside.

Finally she bagged her original outfit and stuffed it into the nearby trash can, then poured a large baggie of chicken entrails over the top of the can. No one was going to poke around in here once they ripened.

Looking around and satisfied, she moved back to the Taurus. She smiled as she glanced at the blue-gray infant seat fastened to the rear seat, and then pulled back onto Route 3. Great camouflage. *Here I come, Memphis, El Paso, and Tucson.*

The first day she drove all the way to Memphis. East of the city, a rest stop restroom on I-40 provided opportunity to wash up, and then a bit refreshed, she moved to the other side of town and got a room at the Marriott across from the Convention Center. No meal, just a quick shower and sleep. No one paid the plain-Jane any attention, and the Do Not Disturb sign on the door kept the maids at bay. Finally rested, Raquel arose, showered again, and flipped on the TV while she ordered room service's biggest hamburger plate. Fries, salad, iced tea, the works. Big girls have large appetites.

Occasionally on the way to Memphis she had listened to the radio. There were constant news bursts of the search for a crazed, murdering woman from Manassas. What amazed Raquel was the fact that nothing was mentioned about any terrorist ties. Surely by now someone knew she was involved in the attacks in Seattle, Florida and Pennsylvania. Zip. Nada. *What was going on?*

The lurid details of how she had set fire to her offices killed one woman and wounded two men in a neighboring office building were repeated until she was sick of hearing it.

She smiled the first time she heard that the men were alive, though. Actually when she'd flipped a shot up the stairs she had no idea who was yelling and coming down after her. She's just seen legs and wanted the pursuit to stop.

Raquel was the daughter of Osama Bin Laden. Born in 1957, he was the 17th child to a father of 52 children! In 1979, Osama'd known his upcoming plans to capture a major mosque in Saudi Arabia would bring danger and likely death to his first wife if things went badly. Fatwah was a striking half-Iranian, half- Saudi woman whose father was a wealthy businessman. He was also a distant relative to the Fahd family of the Arabian House of Saud, the family that has ruled that land off and on since the mid 18th century.

The plan was sprung and Osama was part of a "fundamentalist Islamic" uprising that invaded and took control of the Sacred Mosque at

Mecca on November 20, 1979. 350 zealot followers of a man named Muhammad ibn Abdullah al-Qahtani. They declared him to be the Mahdi – messiah – prophesied by some sects of Islam.

The ruler of the mosque refused to turn it over to them and so, as those things go, shooting resulted. There were some 50,000 worshipers celebrating Islam's 1400th year there at the time. The rebels were led by a man named Juhaiman al-Utaibi and his lieutenant, one Osama bin Laden. It may or may not have been his true name, but it was his *nom de guerre*.

The 26 gates of the Sacred Mosque were slammed shut and bolted. The zealots stationed snipers in the minarets, and a standoff was underway. For two weeks it lasted. The House of Saud – shaken to their core by the revolt and embarrassed by the loss of face, first attempted reason. The leaders of Mecca would not allow the Sacred Mosque to be defaced by a gun battle.

The rebels demanded changes in Saudi Arabia and all of Islam. They hated the government in place for its weakness in dealing with the Western nations and for allowing all the "defiling" industrial development that was taking place. For instance they said, soccer, television, telephones, and education of women had to stop immediately. Ultimately they wanted to return Islam to its tenth century greatness.

Finally, with no injuries to the Kaaba (mosque area) or the hostages, the standoff ended. Victoriously for the Saudis and ruinously for the 350 rebels. Many of them were killed "trying to escape the area." 63 were beheaded and three fled the country. Bin Laden was one of those whose escape was purchased by his and his wife's families.

His pregnant wife was already in the United States. It is ironic that with such a hatred of western ideas and ideals he would want his child reared there, but he felt the child – a son, he prayed – would be safest from reprisal if his upcoming enterprises failed. And, he felt America's freedom of movement, money handling and education would better prepare the next generation to carry on his jihad.

So… the mother arrived, the baby – sadly a daughter – was born. Without his knowledge, the mother legally changed her name, and applied for citizenship. When the child was born, it was under the name "Linden." Father deceased. No one in Manassas cared, and so Raquel Linden, the Terrorist Babe, is a United States citizen.

Her father has visited many lands. He has been in Algeria, Syria, Uzbekistan, Indonesia, Lebanon, Iraq, Iran, Kosovo, France, Chechnya, Gaza, Egypt, Pakistan, Afghanistan, the Philippines, and Libya (where he was trained in terrorist tactics and weapons). He lived in Sudan for a number of years, establishing and operating cover businesses while training agents.

President Bill Clinton sent Tomahawks after him there, managing to blow up a powdered milk factory. Sudanese government officials took his money then tried to capture him to curry favor with America. He murdered four of them in one night and fled to Afghanistan.

During her formative years Raquel was taken to Europe for regular clandestine meetings with her father. Fatwah obediently raised her to be a jihad warrior against her nation of birth, and to worship the father who spawned her (and who actually cared nothing for her).

The warrior training sprouted in fertile ground. An amazingly high IQ, a mind which could conceptualize and memorize staggering amounts of detail, and an unruled arrogance had created a Jekyll and Hyde personality in Raquel.

To her classmates throughout high school and college she had been a wealthy, pampered beauty whose smile was a ticket to the most popular circles and whose intelligence greased her way through George Mason and Georgetown Universities. What was not known was that she was also masterminding networks – organized by her uncle Amir (her mother's brother and Osama's chief of staff).

Amir loved the girl, protected and guided her in establishing both Muslim networks in America and – a stroke of genius he said when she suggested it – White Supremacist organizations to do much of the early terror activities, keeping their people in reserve.

Utilizing voice-altering telephones, the latest in computer technology – ironically bought through CIA provider-companies – Raquel moved "pieces" like a chess Grand Master.

Finally word had come that Osama was ready to strike at America again. The September 11, 2001 attacks were fading from the memory of Americans. They were not yet frightened enough. Their leaders were posturing and threatening and the little Christian Cowboy President was crowing about defeating him. Let the weak Americans taste real panic. Saddam had not proven so strong but Osama would give them something to make them quake and fear in the midnight hours.

Osama had turned Raquel loose on America's playgrounds. Retired American soldiers, bitter from imagined wrongs, used a tank to blow the Seattle Space Needle to the ground. Then multiple explosions had reduced the most famous theme park in the world into fiery rubble. After that a little creep who liked to blow things up personally dropped a new sports stadium on its twelve thousand rock concert fans. In total, over thirty thousand people were dead or wounded and America was going crazy with panic.

Raquel was in the final stages of blowing twenty school buses in twenty cities to smithereens when it had all come crashing down around her.

As all this was occurring and unbeknownst to her, she had brushed up against total insanity. Killing the "one time" messengers sent by her father to prevent any leaks had set her off on blood lust. She began to travel to nearby cities and kill men for the thrill of it.

All of that culminated in a burst of destruction when her provider of arms and explosives, one Tomas, had warned her to flee, that the Feds were on to them both. It was then that she had destroyed her own property and shot up the next door neighbors for good measure.

Accidentally discovered hiding in a cabin in the Virginia woods, that place too had gone up in smoke, and Raquel was retreating to Arizona to rebuild and begin anew her personal war with America.

The hunt was on for a beauty who was a crazed murderer, not an Al Qaeda terrorist. *Why not tell the whole story? Had Tomas been wrong about the Feds closing in on them? Was she too paranoid?* She had considered it all – first in the three weeks of seclusion in the woods, and now as she drove down America's central highway.

Finally the realization surfaced that she had been very close to losing her mind. At first she had resisted the idea out of hand. *Me?! Mad? Never!!*

Then as she used that brilliant-if-warped mind to review past events, even drawing them out on a legal pad, the truth persisted and finally won out over her ego. She had indeed succumbed to emotion and bloodlust. That must never happen again. *Be a Professional, as you were raised*, she chastened herself all across Tennessee.

Then she began refocusing on her cover; getting across the country and establishing a new hide from which to operate. Raquel was getting well, and would be more dangerous than ever before.

Rested, she left Memphis, changed her mind about El Paso, and stayed on I-40 to Albuquerque, then up to Santa Fe. She sang along with the Bellamy Brothers' love song to the famous city as she drove on.

She took up residence in a motel on Route 14 across from a small park. There she donned loose fitting shirts and jeans, slept late, took walks in the late afternoons, and soaked up the laid-back atmosphere of the city.

The artsy community was everywhere, and she looked at some horrible paintings by too-cool artists. No *discipline, no real development, but there ya go*, she thought one day as she strolled through a festival of colors.

She bought a burgundy Dodge Durango with twelve thousand miles on it. Parked it away from her motel and locked it tight. At four o'clock the next morning she took the Taurus to a neighborhood just beyond where she'd parked the Dodge. The place was up to the brim with misery and crime. She'd completely wiped it of all fingerprints, vacuumed it for loose hairs, etc. at a car wash. She parked the car, driver's window down and the keys in the ignition, then walked quickly to the Durango.

She would get to Tucson in style. The Taurus was someone's Christmas present.

On her last night in Santa Fe she decided to treat herself to a steak dinner. Living like a rat, hiding, not speaking to anyone, waiting to hear a harsh voice proclaim her "under arrest" was frustrating Raquel.

At a local saloon and steak house she sat in a booth and enjoyed the rare porterhouse, onion rings and fresh baked bread.

A short, wiry man stepped to the booth and then slid into the bench across from her.

"Well, well, there, Darlin'. Ain't you lonely sittin' here all by yerself? Why don't I just join ya?" His small teeth were furry and green. Stubble of gray and black whiskers over his rat face, and mean little blood-shot eyes squinted against the smoke rising from a cigarette drooping between his lips.

Raquel was disgusted by the sight and smell of him. "No thanks, I'm meeting someone," she said curtly.

"Naw ya ain't, Darlin'! Ya come in alone, ordered alone, and ye need me ta keep ya company." the scrawny interloper persisted.

Raquel looked up, caught the eye of a waiter and visually pleaded for some assistance.

He was happy to respond, and the "problem" was ordered not only away, but out of the restaurant.

Raquel finished her meal, glad to be rid of the rat. Thinking of the Ruger in her purse, *Pa'dner, yer jest lucky I'm reformed,* she mentally mocked her nemesis as she walked to the Durango. She took in the parking lot at a glance, even looking under the vehicle before she approached it. A girl can't be too careful.

Rat Face wasn't a total fool, though. He was posted at the back of the lot, watching from the shadows. When Raquel climbed up into the SUV, he trotted to his rusty old pickup truck and fired it up, sure he could tail her just like the TV hot shots.

She spotted him by the time she was half a block away.

Driving away from the restaurant she picked up Route 25 and headed east. Outside of town, she took Exit 297 and in a short while was on a jeep trail into the hills. Sure enough Rat Face was right on her tail, no doubt pleased by his expertise.

Finally satisfied that she was out far enough, she spun around in the dirt, faced her back trail and parked. Rat Face jerked his wreck of a truck up near the Dodge, stomped his brakes, rolled out and swaggered quickly up to Raquel's window.

"Well, Darlin' do ya think ye got fer enough outta town?" he grinned a lustful smile and laid his left hand on the window sill, reaching for the door latch with his right.

"I think this will do nicely," Raquel flashed a Hollywood smile, quickly raised the Ruger centering the barrel on his forehead and squeezed the trigger. His head snapped back, and he fell backwards with fear and amazement in his eyes just before the lights went out. He now had an Eastern Indian beauty mark.

The noise of the .22 was deafening inside the Durango. The spent cartridge was automatically ejected inside the SUV and glanced off the windshield. She turned on the interior light, searched for and found it, placing the warm brass between her lips. Nice smell, gunpowder. Then she drove back to I-25, and just before exiting off the highway, spit the brass out the window.

"Dinner *and* entertainment. That was fun," she said aloud as she hopped from the vehicle and strolled to her motel door. By daylight she was off to Tucson.

Raquel found and bought a conservative, but very comfortable home along the mountain range northwest the city. Nearby and just over the ridge lay the western movie lot called Old Tucson. She established a high speed internet connection, sent Uncle Amir an encrypted email message to advise him that she was safe and regrouping, then began to familiarize herself with her new hometown. It was a place of danger and beauty. *Kind of like me*, she thought one afternoon when she heard a news reporter use the phrase.

Giant rare steaks, red beans and salsa at Li'l Abners gave her evenings a new flavor. The occasional knife fight by black top cowboys out back added zest. She spent hours walking the desert trails to keep in shape. Drives further out to Tombstone, Cochise's canyon hideout, Bisbee and Wilcox then down toward Mexico and into the Chiracahua Mountains refreshed her. Cochise and his Apaches had been her heroes ever since she'd learned he was the only Apache chief never to surrender to American cavalry units. It was fun to take in the breathtakingly beautiful haunts where he had ground down the pony soldiers. *Apache Jihad.*

Hmm. Maybe I could organize some of those guys into some raids. They got no love for the government, seem pliable. I'll check into that.

She shopped for stylish, conservative outfits. Often dressed as a highly successful business woman, with suits and outfits like the clothes she saw on some of her neighbors leaving for work in the mornings. Raquel fit into Tucson like a hand in a glove.

She dyed her hair strawberry blonde, had it cut a stylish length and loved her new "cute" look. She exercised hard, ate wisely and kept her 5'10" frame tight and healthy. She loved the black mountains, flat white sunshine and heat of the desert. She laughed at the "dry heat" idea and said to herself. "*Hot's hot*," but understood what they meant.

This was her first real taste of desert living and she reveled in it. Her forebears, after all, were desert people and she felt she was born to it. Life was good.

She was beginning to re-establish contact with some of her American Al Qaeda leaders by email. Not one word to any of the red-necks, though. They were far too hot, if the TV news was to be believed. Homeland Security was rolling them up like biscuit dough.

Hardly a day passed without a report of another group being rousted by the cops. She had no idea that her computers in Manassas had been compromised before she torched them, and just figured her exploits had put them under tighter scrutiny and brought about their arrests.

She was happy, though somewhat restless to get on with the war. She had some ideas that were beginning to bubble like the rich spaghetti sauce she occasionally made at home.

Uncle Amir advised her of the strange companionship her ex-neighbors kept, namely one Yossi Cumi. Further, he told her that he was moving people into position for when she was ready to resume her operations, and institute the sniper plan they'd previously developed.

He would configure the teams. A trainer was in the pipeline. He wished her well, told her he loved and missed her and bid her goodbye. Raquel misted up at this last line, and touched the screen of her monitor as she thought of the only person in the world who truly loved her. *Uncle Amir.*

FIVE

Rain pounded the galvanized roof of the machine shed with a sound like BBs being poured onto it. It was at once comforting to Jake and reminiscent of his childhood in Southern Illinois when he would climb up into the hayloft on days like this.

"How old is the Farmall, George?" he asked as he perched on the tongue of the hay wagon.

"I looked the serial number up on the web. It is either a 1976 or '77. Couldn't find the exact number." George was using a Crescent wrench to loosen the plug on the bottom of the crankcase. A plastic five-gallon bucket was directly below.

"Pipsqueak had one of these. I guess I must have ridden it half way around the world if the miles were all added up." This farm wasn't really the home place, but he was so happy just to be out of a city environment that it would do.

"Jake, I need to talk to you about what's happening to you all. Me and Helen are happy here, but I always have the feeling that I'm waiting for the other shoe to drop. It's just in my mind and I can't get rid of it."

"What do you want to know?" Jake asked as he watched George jerk his hand holding the wrench back and deftly snatched the crankcase plug with the other before it plummeted into the bucket. Warm black oil poured down with a plopping and gurgling sound. Like the rain on the roof, Jake was very familiar with this sight and sound. He had changed the oil in tractors many a time as a boy on the farm.

Pulling a red cotton shop rag from his back pocket, George first wiped the wrench clean and then the plug. He placed both on the tractor's foot platform beside a new oil filter in an orange box.

"See, Jake, that's the problem. I don't know. I asked Tex a few days ago and he said I'd better check with you. He wasn't goin' to spill any beans, was the way he put it," George finished up with a chuckle and a grin at Tex's high regard for security.

"I understand. Let me start at the beginning." Jake walked over to the green thermos he'd earlier set on the work bench. He pulled two metal cups from the pegboard, wiped them with his shirt tail and poured steaming black brew into both, handing George one and returning to his seat.

"Larry and I were in Israel with the DIA. Dad was teaching at an Illinois college. We were called home for what we thought was to be a security detail for the Secretary of War. We hated the idea of nurse-maiding big shots. We'd both done it but neither one of us enjoyed it.

“After we got back we were told it was a ruse. We were tasked with putting together an undercover team to hunt home-grown terrorists. They were going to set us up as security experts so we could move around the country and do our job. Solutions.com was the name they gave the company.

“We added Tex when we learned we would have a “company” airplane. I have a license, but he would be the chief pilot. Then we added a computer geek, Sarah and an electronics expert. A character named Elvis.” Jake grinned thinking of George and Elvis’ first meeting.

George turned from his task of replacing the oil filter at that and met Jake’s impish grin with a look of disbelief.

“Truth.” A wider grin. “You’ll meet him before long. You gotta see this guy. His name isn’t really Elvis, but when he talks you’d swear it’s the King himself! That is if you aren’t looking at him.” Jake hammed it up a bit.

“He’s a Polish Jew, tall and skinny as a straw. Can’t sing a lick, but he can make about anything electronic stand up and march in a straight line. And he’s way ahead of the technological curve, though I don’t know how he does it. Just says he has lots of friends who tell him lots of things.” George nodded.

“Anyway, I got Dad to join us as the office boss and intel coordinator. We actually got the SecState, SecWar, and the DCIA all on board, which is in itself some kind of miracle.”

“You got that right,” George added, pointing a screwdriver at Jake to make his point.

“Then three things sort of happened at the same time. First of all, I stumbled into a gang back home in Illinois that was dope dealing and on the fringe of some terrorist activity –“

“That’d be the ones tied to the feller in Omaha got what he had comin’, I’m guessing,” George added.

“Right. Then back in Virginia where we were setting up shop somebody started popping people with a 22 Ruger. That’s the one Larry lovingly refers to as the ‘Terrorist Babe.’ She shot him very close to home plate.” Jake laughed. He could, now that Larry was all right.

“She’s the one that disappeared, right?” George didn’t need Tex on that. He had Fox News.

“Right off the radar. Lots of people are still looking for her.”

“So what’s number three?”

“Number three is complicated. A billionaire from South Africa got terminal cancer. He wanted to help Israel (he was Jewish), and he wanted to fight terrorism, not just see his money make strangers richer. Larry and I had been in Israel when terrorists killed his nephew. We helped kill one and capture the other. Anyway this guy contacted my uncle who is the head of Mossad and put it to him that he wanted us to take the inheritance and fight terrorism. It's literally billions of dollars." This last was said with a sense of awe that Jake still could not eliminate.

"Billions?!" George turned from the tractor, eyes wide.

"Billions. So there you are. We left the DIA, folded a now-real Solutions-dot-com into the companies that Kurt Mullenberg left us – me and Dad, Larry and a man named Ehud Palmach. You'll meet him too, but no tellin' when.

"Now we're at the beginning stages of establishing a headquarters at the airport.

"By the way, the SecWar, Don Rogers and the DCIA, Harvey Reed, the guy the President called the Tortoise are both on board with this. Reed was sort of negative at first, but I guess he's gotten over that.

In fact I think he plans on sending some real business to us now and then. I don't know what it will be, but we aren't going to do any black-bag jobs, or work we don't like.

"As Dad said, being billionaires can let you be a mite choosey about the jobs you take on."

The rain stopped. Mud puddles scattered the back farm lot where new gravel needed to be applied. In the western sky, a tiny strip of blue was slipping over the hills and a breeze freshened the air.

George tossed the last empty oil can into the big trash barrel. He started the tractor, let it run for a couple of minutes, then shut it off. A bit later he pulled the dip stick from the tractor. Wiping it, he reinserted it and pulled it out once again. After a quick inspection, he nodded his head to himself and replaced it. Job complete.

"Jake, I got one more question. Exactly where do Helen and me fit into all this? I mean as far as long range plans."

"Pretty much where you did when we first talked. We need someone who can look after the place – farm and house. And we need someone with enough training to keep his eyes open, and maybe deal with anything around here.

"Honestly, we don't foresee any real danger. But we want someone here because there will be times we will all be gone, and we want the place kept up. Your jobs are taking care of our home place.

"But… just to be on the safe side, I want to put some weapons around the farm in locked and secure places. We need a dry, gun safe for a shotgun and semi-auto rifle of your choice. More than just a ground hog rifle. One here, one in your house and one in the barn. We'll get whatever you want. You take care of placing them.

"Truthfully, I think we might be over cautious, but I'd rather be safe than sorry."

George nodded and didn't say anything. He already had some hardware in the cottage and he carried his .45.

Jake would later look back on his last statement and wonder how anyone could have been so very wrong.

SIX

Maurice Kleppman didn't look like a warrior. Five foot eight inches tall, two hundred pounds, bald as an English walnut, with a great pot-belly and a sunken chest, he walked with splayed toes and a waddle that said he'd never been on a Marine drill team.

In his day, he was really something, thought his wife, Tilly. She was sitting on the floral sofa in the salon watching her man fiddling with the radar or something. *When he was in the navy during Korea, he was a knockout*, she grinned.

They met in San Diego. She'd told her friend, Judy, "I'm gonna marry the guy and make a success outta him when he gets out of the navy." *And that she had*, Tilly nodded to herself, remembering. Maurie had gone back to college in Boston, finally graduated as an ophthalmologic surgeon and moved to Galveston to practice with his uncle. That was long ago and far away.

Well, Tilly thought, *not so far away. But sure long ago.*

"Maurie, what's the weather forecast looking like?" she called to her husband. "Would you like some iced tea?" before he could answer.

He turned and smiled, "That'd be nice. And the weather is going to be hot and calm for the next three days. Smooth sailing."

"Except, we ain't sailin'," Tilly called back as she rose, walked to the refrigerator and pulled a peach Snapple from the shelf.

Maurie laughed at the joke and held the cold bottle she handed him to his brow.

It was hot. The windows on the 1985 53 foot Hatteras power yacht were open to any breezes, there just weren't any.

They'd bought the yacht used a few years back. Had it refurbished from top to bottom and stem to stern last spring. Maurie had finally retired. He had invented some equipment for eye surgery in '64 and one thing led to another. He was a millionaire a few times over, but just kept working.

Both of them loved boating – usually by themselves, and both could run the Hatteras single handedly. A year on the boat was what they'd talked about. A month was what this trip was about. *Just head out into the Gulf of Mexico and tool around. If we want to go into a port, great. If not then we will drop a line, and try to catch our dinner.*

Tilly had said with a leer, "Maybe try some of that nude sun bathing we hear about." Maurie grinned and patted her ample rear, but thought to himself, *Hon, we'd have to gather skin up and clothespin it to keep from getting zebra striped where the wrinkles meet.* He was a very astute man, however, and did not even think this for an overly long time, as Tilly could read his thoughts fairly well.

This was their second week out. The box of books each of them had brought along was getting a dent in it. Maurie had a shelf in his study at home filled with books for pleasure reading when he had the time. As the years had passed, the shelf filled up, and another was begun. When they left the Port of Galveston, he'd brought the ones on the full shelf. Tilly had gone shopping for some of her own. They spent time outside on deck enjoying the breeze, sunshine and quiet of their own company. They read, sunbathed, and reminisced, enjoying one another's company.

"I thought you'd go nuts by now, Maurie," Tilly said as she reached out to touch his forearm. The skin was creped, tan and tattooed with liver spots. Still, she loved to touch him. He was hers. Always had been from that first night they met at the USO.

"Honestly so did I. I couldn't imagine not having a calendar to answer to. This is nice though. But I do think we ought to build some kind of itinerary before long. Some places we want to visit. Some people to invite out for a few days then dump them ashore and get back to being alone. You know."

Maurie was looking to port. He thought he'd seen a reflection above the horizon for a moment. *Guess not.* Still, he picked up the binoculars and scanned the sea. It looked like there might be something, but it was just on the edge of reality. Mirage, sea movement. No telling.

"What's for dinner? Or do you want to get some sun?" He leered theatrically at Tilly.

Tomas was like a tiger in a cage. When the ATF had grabbed him and slammed him into an interrogation room back in New Orleans, he'd been cool, calm and collected. He *was* Tomas, after all. The Jamaican boy who came to America with his mother and her brother had landed in free enterprise heaven.

For seventeen years he had worked the New Orleans underworld like a board game. First as a runner for black crime bosses who liked his great white-toothed smile and quick wit. The onyx eyes that sparkled with intellect and mischief seemed to know the boss's every thought and desire.

Tomas, with the musical patois that was touched with mangoes and warm tropical breezes. He was handsome enough to attract the ladies yet so masculine that the men liked having him around too. The lad watched, listened and learned.

Busted by a street cop for selling cocaine to tourists when he was eighteen, Tomas got the last laugh. When they tested the white powder in the glassine envelopes downtown, it didn't flash the royal blue everyone expected. The cop licked his finger and dipped it in, coating the fingertip lightly, then touched it to his tongue. Powered sugar! He first flashed fury then looked at the imp watching him.

Finally he smiled. The other cops were grinning. A couple of them had grabbed Tomas before today. "Get outta here, before I change my mind and bust you for ugly," the big black cop had said with grudging admiration. *How was this kid's con any different from the fortune tellers and card sharks in the French Quarter?*

Tomas had come criminally of age not long after that when he killed a competitor with a machete. No anger or malice in it, just a roundhouse swing to the back of the neck, and he had enlarged his territory. The body never turned up, and there is no vacuum in leadership.

Tomas sensed the weak and like a shark, and began to feed off the old-timers in drugs, loan sharking, fencing stolen goods. One of the bosses would get careless, anger a bodyguard, or step on a competitor. Tomas would have a word, offer a reward, and strike like lightning.

An empty car would be found with bloodstains on the upholstery. Bones would get dug up at a building site a year later. Occasionally putrefying gases would float a corpse that had fed too many catfish and turtles to be recognized, but New Orleans would know. Tomas had enlarged his operation, adding men – and women – to his coterie.

His one true love was selling arms and explosives to the "clod-kickers and red-necks." Intense survivalists from Idaho or someplace where the buffalo roamed. Good ole boys with their white sheets from the South. Virulent militia from the upper Midwest. They all came to Tomas sooner or later and he loved the hammering of their hand tooled cowboy boots on his sidewalk.

No money ever changed hands. Wire transfers moved money to accounts offshore where upon arrival, another transfer immediately occurred. Trucks, vans and sometimes containers aboard eighteen wheelers were loaded, hauled and hidden. Then the neighbors heard midnight gunfire, and explosions shook the hills.

The fact that all those racists needed his black hide kick-started a chuckle deep within his chest which rose to his thin cheeks and full lips. Soon a bellowing roar of laughter erupted under dancing coal-black eyes. Good ole boys, indeed! He threw his head back and laughed deeply like that guy in the old 7 UP ad. Among his own men he called it "reverse affirmative action."

Then a certain woman in Manassas, Virginia with a most seductive voice had kicked over the stove. Tomas had delivered her all kinds of materials. The last order would have been the best. Twenty twin-sets of C4 with radio detonators and transmitters. Trucked to twenty cities in twenty states. A cool million dollars profit. Money already in the bank.

What was she going to do? Blow things up, obviously. Tomas didn't care. It was what certain people did. He was just a facilitator. Theirs was the guilt. If *he* hadn't provided the wherewithal, someone else would have.

Ah, but the ATF grabbed his boys outside of Houston. They hadn't talked, but things being the way they were in New Orleans, the Feds brought him in and sweated him for a while. Finally, thanks to a good lawyer, they released him.

Tomas expertly evaded the surveillance they had on him and headed to the marina.

There, fully outfitted for a day such as this, was a 52 foot Najad (pronounced Ni-add) sailboat. Low slung, single-masted and luxurious. Tomas had won her from a rich kid from San Diego in a poker game about two years ago.

He loved boats but up until the Najad had never owned one. He hired a good captain to teach him how to run the boat, and, like all his other education, proved a worthy student. In no time, Tomas was taking the boat out into the Gulf alone. He loved the tranquility, and nimbleness of the lavish Swedish sail boat. The center-mounted open cockpit with it's big chromed wheel thrilled him when he hit the strong winds and the sea mist sprayed him as he let her race full out.

Below deck, the teak and mahogany salon, stateroom and galley were finer than many nice homes in New Orleans. Speed, comfort, style, and opulence – Tomas loved his boat.

Then he sold it. To a company headquartered in Iowa. A meat packing firm. Of course there was no meat packer. It was all a lawyer's paper ruse to protect the true identity of the boat's real owner.

Tomas never approached the Najad again. A company that makes a good living off absentee boat owners kept it maintained to the highest demands of its "rich Midwestern owners."

They also saw that it was provisioned with a certain list of foods – replacing any that reached expiration dates – and that the water tank and fuel tank for the 150 HP Volvo Penta Diesel engine were both full. Tomas had a bolt hole no one in New Orleans knew about. Not even a single one of his bodyguards. When he wanted to fine-tune his sailing skills, he rented a boat.

Then, one day he began to learn another skill. Running power yachts. His men thought he'd lost it. He didn't even own a boat! Seldom even swam in the turquoise Olympic size pool at his home. But, of course, they never questioned him. Just waited in the shade until the giant motor boat came burbling up to the dock, and watched as he passed a line to the boat boys and nimbly stepped onto the dock with a ten-spot for each of them.

He nodded to his men with an ebony-eyed look and they snapped-to like the best of Dobermans and headed back to the little run down restaurant where Tomas held court. *Who could understand the Boss?*

Four days had passed since Tomas had boarded the Prejudice. That was her name. Don't ask why. Someone said it was bad luck to change a boat's name, so Tomas, not wanting to anger the sea-gods, had left it. *He didn't need no stinkin' bad luck.*

Three days of sunshine, and one of gut-wrenching fear as horrible gales and rain hammered him, demanding more of his boat and his skills than even he thought possible.

Still he was prepared. His instructor had mandated that he must learn and practice in all kinds of weather. Now the storm had passed, finding him out in the Gulf still afloat. And he was coiling like a cotton mouth on a Mississippi levee.

Tomas needed a new ride. There was, alas, the chance that the ATF boys were sharp enough to check the marinas as well as airports and bus stations when they discovered he had split. This sail boat would turn up missing sooner or later and they would nab him with Gulf over-flights. Even this large body of water was not big enough to hide in when the Feds wanted you.

That little chickadee in Virginia had indeed stirred up a hornet's next! And she was a looker. WHOOOEEE! That girl sure enough matched her voice. The television news he caught on the dish mounted atop the mast said she had shot up her neighbor's office, killing one and wounding two more then disappeared. Burned down her own office building AND her home! The newsies were not reporting any motive. "Undetermined at this time," they kept repeating.

Tomas knew *why*, though he did not know exactly *who* Raquel was. Only that he hoped she made it. Still, he had a million of her dollars and she hadn't received the plastique, so he didn't want her looking for him. *Just fly away little Chickadee*, he thought with a pensive smile.

By mid afternoon, the Hatteras was large in his Zeiss binoculars. He watched an old couple sitting on the aft deck alternately reading and napping. This looked like his boat. He'd checked out others but they did not fit his plans. Some were too small. Others too big for one man to operate smoothly. A couple of others had too many people aboard. Not that he was adverse to killing lots of people at once. It just meant he would have to use a lot of rounds and some of them would mess up the boat. Repairs were not his strong suit. The Hatteras would fit in without marking him as wealthier than he wanted to seem. And it was not so sleek and fast as to draw the attention of the DEA.

"Well, my little chickadee," he again mimicked the old W.C. Fields movies he enjoyed, "I think you were made for me." He lowered the flaccid sail but did not secure it. Firing up the diesel, he moved closer so he could hail the other boat.

"Halloo the I See U," Tomas called using the name he read on the stern of the boat. He was standing in the cockpit, a black baseball cap with the "Budweiser" emblem of the Navy Seals on the front. He was bare-chested, in a pair of iridescent blue boxer style swim trunks, and grinning like he'd just been told his mare had foaled.

"Hey, Maurie, wake up!" Tilly reached over and poked him in the ribs, at which he jerked like she'd slapped him with defib paddles. "We got company."

Maurie was instantly awake. Straight out from their stern was a beautiful white single-masted sail boat. A lithe, light brown man stood in the cockpit grinning and waving in a friendly way.

Maurie stood and waved back briefly. "Howdy," he called across the thirty feet of water separating the boats. The sail boat was being kept in place by the adept manipulations of her captain.

"It's nice to see a friendly face," Tomas said, though Tilly was not smiling, and Maurie's face simply reflected curiosity. "I been out here for a month and you're the first people I've spoken to face to face. My puppy fell overboard in the storm two days ago." Tomas was good.

At the reference to the puppy, Tilly spontaneously erupted with an, "Awww." The man could not have known how that would strike her emotions. They had to put their wonderful black Lab, Tootsie, down only six months ago, and neither of them could speak of the old good friend and pet without shedding tears even now.

One thing led to another and the introductions led to conversations of pets, occupations – Tomas was the beneficiary of a deceased uncle's love and largess. He had inherited some money that allowed him to leave his accounting job and sail for six months. He had not realized how lonely it would be.

Eventually, with his deft leading, the boats were secured side by side, cushioned with bumpers. A dinner aboard the Najad was scheduled for twenty minutes later. The old folks went to freshen up from their nap.

Tomas went to prepare for their demise. He placed his metal baseball bat just inside the door to the dining area. He then fixed a pitcher of iced tea with lemons and carried three glasses up to the cockpit.

The Galveston couple went like sheep to the slaughter. First Tilly, then Maurie entered the lower level of the boat. He smashed Maurie, then before he'd fallen completely, was on Tilly like a cougar. It was over in moments. Their blood splattered Tomas, the walls and pooled on the teak floor. The Kleppmans were united in death.

Tomas moved quickly to get his suitcases up to the Hatteras. Then he muscled his weapons, charts, and finally a large box of cash. Hundred dollar bills. Ten thousand of them, all used, no numbers in sequence. Clean money. Stashed for flight, and now in motion.

He then grabbed Maurie's and Tillie's things and lugged them to the sail boat. He couldn't just toss the stuff overboard. Floating debris would look suspicious.

Finally, satisfied, Tomas loosed the Najad, pushed it off with a rod, went below deck and opened the petcocks in the bilges. The portholes were already open courtesy of the aforementioned baseball bat. He secured the door to below deck so the bodies could not float to the surface, and then gracefully dove overboard.

It was a short, refreshing swim back to the Hatteras. He drank a dark rum drink and chewed the fruit he'd sliced into it while watching the bubbles erupting at the final sinking of the lovely sail boat. He raised his glass in a final toast, and smiled, "And to your dog, too."

Then still laughing, Tomas evacuated the bilge of fumes, fired up the yacht and moved east at a sedate fifteen knots. After a while, he became familiar with the Hatteras' equipment and set the auto-pilot for a heading of 185 degrees. The GPS said he had 650 miles to go. He had 43 hours at a constant rate of 15 knots, but, with any luck a good tail wind would push that up a bit.

He would stop at Ft. Myers, Florida to do a bit of business with an old pal before heading due south to his final destination, Key West. Tomas took in a large breath and let it out slowly. Things were moving along just fine. *Too bad about the old folks*, he thought, then shrugged and went to the galley to check out their food supply. *What does one do with gefilte fish?*

SEVEN

New York has two Senators. One is a chameleon and the other is a snake. The chameleon once lived in the White House, then reverse-carpet-bagged her way into the US Senate from New York.

The snake is a native New Yorker. He is smooth, congenitally liberal (which he must be to survive New York politics, of course), and a shameless manipulator of the highest order.

These thoughts were running through the camera man's mind as he awaited the cue to begin filming. The Senator's people had called all the networks and announced that he was going to make an announcement about the travesty of Wal Mart dropping its gasoline price below every other station in the metropolitan area.

The result of the Wal Mart price war was predictably lines of happy consumers reaching out of sight in all the boroughs.

What is this jerk going to do now, claim Wal Mart is being unfair? the camera man wondered as a black Town Car pulled up next to their Explorer with the red WGAB logo on the side. A cop stepped from the front seat – plain clothes, but with white socks and oxford shoes on.

Plain clothes, right! grinned the camera man.

The back door opened and out stepped the Senator. His receding hairline was almost surrendering to baldness but his smile was radiant as he noted all the people rubber-necking the camera crews.

Guess who we saw today. I wonder if I'll be on the 6 o'clock news tonight? they wondered.

The Snake walked purposefully toward the bank of microphones his advance girl had organized so neatly. Just behind him and across the street was the Wal Mart gas station. Lines of cars flowed in and out, but it was the sign and a few of the people pumping gas that he wanted in this shot.

"Thank you, ladies and gentlemen for coming out today. The Senator has noticed something that is grossly unfair to New York's business community. He is about to address it in Washington later, but wanted to give you an opportunity to have some early video." She was good, this media girl who worked for the Snake.

Right. No video, no news. No news, no face time, thought the cynical camera man.

The Senator glided to the microphones, stood still and smiled for the still shots. Then he began to speak without notes with the gleeful sadness of a mortician in the middle of a flu epidemic.

"There is something tragically unfair about a gigantic corporation undercutting the small businesses of New York – and for that matter all across the United States.

"You are aware I'm sure that the price of gasoline has skyrocketed. There are many reasons for this raid on the family budgets of America which I am currently addressing in Washington.

"Now the struggling gasoline station owners are being hurt right along with the consumers.

"This very company," he pointed over his shoulder at the large sign on the canopy behind him, "is undercutting every station in the New York City area. Reports are flooding our offices and those of other Senators as well. It has to stop…"

Before he could continue, one of the men with a microphone in his hand said, "Sir, Rush Limbaugh says you're pandering. He said if Wal Mart could save Americans even one dollar on a tank full of gas, it was a good thing." There was a murmur of agreement from many people around the speaker.

"Excuse me, I was not finished. Furthermore, who really cares what a flak for the Republicans says?!" fire was flickering from the Snake's eyes. Whether it was because of the mention of Rush Limbaugh or because he had been interrupted no one knew.

Suddenly, the Snake's face seemed to disintegrate right before their eyes. The camera man saw it in his viewfinder, but it did not register on him like it did on the people watching in real live, vivid color. There was a gush of red spray, and the Senator crumpled forward like a string of wet spaghetti.

Somewhere off in the distance there was a report that might have been a car backfiring or a cherry bomb. Men and women screamed all around the cameraman.

Beside him a man groaned, "Ahhh," and folded forward to the ground, then rolled onto his side, hands grabbing his stomach.

Ricochet the cameraman instantly realized as he squatted, but continued to pan and shoot video.

The off duty cop had his pistol out waving it around at the media crowd, then turned and pointed it toward where the sound had seemed to originate. There was a large building off in the distance. He was shouting, "Down! Down! He's down! NO!"

He needn't have said "down" but once, because the media-types were getting exactly there quickly as the reality struck them.

It was bedlam. The cop was on his radio calling in the shooting. The media girl was at the Senator's side weeping. She grabbed the shoulder of his jacket and rolled him onto his back.

Shouldn't a done that, the camera man thought in a double entendre as the girl vomited onto the Senator's suit then began a keening wail with mindless fear and grief. There was simply no face where one had been only moments ago. Ruby red blood pooled quickly around what was left of the Senator's head.

Inside a seventh floor room, Juan and Miguel were quickly but expertly packing up. Miguel had just closed the window the rest of the way. Earlier he'd raised it about six inches to allow the shot. Miguel had been sitting about six feet back from it so that nothing would show to any passerby. Now no one from the outside would be able to tell they had ever been here.

"Ver' nice, Miguel. I think I coulda done it, Compadre, but ver' nice.

"*Gracias,* Juan. I thought it be right fine, myself. Now let's skedaddle. Ain't that the word that old boy in Kentucky used? Skedaddle? Nice word."

"You t'ink we have security on this job like we was promised?"

"Ha. Vamoose! Ain't gonna matter. We be like smoke..."

He was twisting the scope quick mounts from the rifle action and storing it in the hard side gun case. Next he lovingly laid the broken down rifle's two pieces in the black aluminum case. Velvet compartments had long ago replaced the eggshell foam it had originally contained. He pocketed the warm, just-fired brass. No ballistics ejector marks to trace the gun that way.

Juan peeked out the door. *Nada. No one around.* Empty warehouse. No street traffic.

They'd been in a Long Island hotel for three days. Then they'd driven to this area as soon as the call came in yesterday. Juan dropped Miguel off. Miguel picked the lock. Then as he moved inside with their gear Juan located a place to park their van so it wouldn't get towed.

Inside they'd found an old crate to use as a shooting bench and lugged it up four flight of stairs. Then they just hunkered down, napped, drank bottled water and ate from a can of pork and beans, cheese, and saltines, while they waited to see what happened next.

"Jew know we have to play it cool here, man. No telling where they gonna put the Senator," Juan said peeking out the dirty window. He was the planner. He worried a lot about stuff that they couldn't handle until the time came, but it gave him something to do. His English pronunciation suffered when he was deep in thought.

"We see the way they put the microphones and stuff, then we know can we make the shot or not. Maybe we move. So I gotta shoot off the windowsill or back a ways; I can do it on my knees. You seen me do it before." Miguel grinned and comforted him. They had been lovers for years, and Miguel babied him.

The deed was done and now they were headed quickly down the stairs. The electricity was off so the elevator didn't work. Behind them they could hear the flames devouring the dry wood of the crate. It had made good kindling. Big fire; no evidence.

They would be heading east and north to the ferry, then over to Connecticut. *Another day's work done. Maybe a bit of gambling to relax them. Them Indians really knew how to put up casinos. Even if they were Indians.*

EIGHT

"…. second person to be assassinated by a sniper in the past four weeks."

She was angry with herself for missing the opening of the show. She'd been certain that since the hit on dear Babs, this one would make Brit's show. What a doll he was!

I can't believe I can run the best computer equipment and I cannot get a stupid VCR to record right! Raquel ranted at herself.

"First of all, is there any proof that the same person killed Barbara Steinfeld and Senator Schumbler? Charles what do we really know about this killing?" Brit nodded to Charles on his right.

"There is no evidence either of the shooter's identity or that the same person did the shooting. A high powered rifle was used in both cases. Both people were hit in the head – which my military sources tell me is a very good indication that professional or an ex-military sniper or snipers are at work. The first target was over 350 yards away, the second almost 100 yards more."

"Fred, who wants these people dead?" Brit asked, skipping the obviously antsy Mort.

"Well it's likely that lots of conservatives are glad both are silenced, but that's not to say they wanted them dead. Barbara was sort of the Hollywood kook fringe, if I may speak ill of the dead. Her far left political proclamations kept her from being taken seriously, but she was not a threat. And – "

Mort couldn't wait and broke in. "The Senator had multiplied times more enemies on the right, and they did take him seriously on the Hill. Maybe Hillary is right. There could be a vast rightwing conspiracy out there, and they finally got a sniper on the payroll!"

Charles interrupted the interrupter. "That's utter nonsense," he said in that calm, dismissive voice that verbally head-butted Mort regularly. "The people in the political arena are not killers. These killers are not politicians.

"This pair of killings – and I am convinced they are connected – has taken out two people who played the media for all it's worth. They were grandstanders for the left. The Senator also had the power to poke a stick in the administration's spokes and that made him lots of conservative enemies, but not to the point of wanting him dead. In fact he helped some conservative fund raisers.

"If a Democrat were in the White House, then Schumbler would have been the lead man for many of their worst legislative ideas. As it is, he was mostly just grabbing headlines for his own fundraising efforts. No one in their right mind wanted him or the diva dead."

"Obviously someone wanted them dead," Brit said with that sorrowful, serious look that was his trademark.

Mort wasn't finished. "Well, they were both from New York. They were both liberals. ..."

"And they were both Jewish," Fred added.

Raquel reacted physically but didn't say anything. Was Fred onto her already?

"This is not a racist thing! They were not in the same circles socially. They were neither one religious. They were not in the forefront of the Jewish movement except at election times." Mort argued.

"What do you think, Charles? Is there a Jewish angle to the killings?" Brit asked.

Charles was famous for his love and dedication to Israel. He was the recipient of untold awards from both Israel and Jewish organizations.

"There might be. Obviously the Islami-fascist Muslims are in the hunt for anyone who opposes them, and both Steinfeld and Schumbler have spoken out strongly against Muslim radicalism.

"She was the prototype Jewish girl from Brooklyn. The Senator was also very obviously an ethnic Jew, and had the quote – New York Jew – mannerisms that identified him with that group. Remember too, there are still people – aside from the Muslims – in this country who are very anti-Semitic. Having said that, my guess is that any Jewish connection is a reach. At least until we see if the killings continue."

"With that we'll take a break and when we return, answer the question, 'Why is this White House so ineffective in presenting its good side to the American public?"

Raquel sat still for a while, running her tongue over the chipped front tooth and thinking. That someone was already wondering about the killings being directed towards Jews troubled her. She wanted many more to go down before that flag went up.

She grabbed her purse and dug around inside. There was the phone card she'd bought at the 7-11 earlier in the day. "Untraceable Telephonics." She laughed as she read it. *What were Americans thinking?!*

She left the apartment and headed for a pay phone at a nearby hotel. *Let's throw dear Fred off the scent,* she thought as she drove to the Windham.

NINE

Four hundred acres at the foot of the Appalachian Mountains is enough space to hide a lot of activities. The large farm house had been changed into a barracks. The red hip-roofed barn was used to hide the numerous vehicles. A car and three vans were currently inside, one being dirty white with a dent in the left rear.

Back near the foot of the mountain, rifle and handgun ranges had been established. Beside them and alongside the lovely meandering trout stream was an obstacle course including a rope climb, swamp swing and all. Lacking a swamp, however, the creek would drench anyone who lost their grip.

An area was cleared for hand to hand combat training. On the other side of the farm was a hay field. In the summer it had grown up and fallen over, having no one to mow and harvest it. Among the brown confusion stood new man-shaped silhouettes at three hundred, five hundred, eight hundred and a thousand meters. Finally out at fifteen hundred meters was one last silhouette. All were unmarked by bullet holes.

Inside the house Alex Tort was on the telephone. "I just want to know when they're coming! I have a schedule to keep here." He listened for a while then hung up without another word. He was a slat of a man; strong like a swimmer or marathon runner. At thirty-five, the lines in his face from sunshine, cigarettes and seeing too much of life told their own story. Still, he was oddly handsome with the sharp-edged hook nose and tanned skin of his ancestors. The beautiful head of white hair was flecked with black specks like gold flakes at the bottom of a Colorado creek.

Across the kitchen table sat a thin woman with dark hair cut in a page boy style. She sipped a cup of tea and watched. There was a lizard-stillness in her demeanor as if she could have sat there for the rest of the day and neither spoken or even moved.

She made Alex nervous. Real nervous. It was like there was something missing in her. Like she was some kind of swamp-thing, rising from the primordial soup with slime hanging from her shoulders, batting reptilian eyes, and just watching – motionless – for the next thing she would eat. Like one of those Schwarzenegger movies. She looked like a human being but with a difference that was indefinable until it was way too late. She had shown up yesterday, identified herself, and just moved in.

Alex had lived at the farm for three years. He bought it with money not his own, set it up with more of the same, and overseen the training of the men and women who arrived with their leaders, stayed for a month or so and left. Most of them came from mosques in New York and New Jersey.

He himself had been recruited from a mosque in Paterson, New Jersey. Born Alex Bensaad, an Americanization of his family's Arabic name, changed by his grandfather when he came from Libya many years ago.

His father worked for General Motors, his mother for Fisher Body. Growing up he'd expected to do the same – and hated the idea. That was where the Army came in. The recruiter said he could see the world as one of Uncle Sam's airborne soldiers. And he *had* seen a bit of it. Ft. Benning, GA, Ft. Polk, LA, and lots of sand in Saudi Arabia, Kuwait and Iraq.

It was during his time in the desert that he'd met men – soldiers like himself – who read the Koran, and taught him the magnificent history of his Arab forebears. One thing led to another, and after receiving an honorable discharge from the military, Alex Bensaad ended up in Paterson studying the perfect path for one such as himself. The enlightened leader had noted Alex's background and eventually led him into the system of helping to bring back the glorious reign of the Magnificent Arab World.

At the mosque leader's suggestion he had legally changed his name to Alex Tort and moved to Harrisburg, Pennsylvania. It was a misleadingly sleepy city along the banks of the Susquehanna River. What looks like a small city, with clean streets, modern downtown, and nice people, is actually an interesting place for a number of reasons.

Its highway hub makes it a natural distribution center for drugs. With Interstates 83, 76, 81, 80 and 70 either intersecting there or nearby the opportunities are endless. Pittsburgh, Cleveland, New York City, Philadelphia, Baltimore, DC – all are just a short hop away.

Meet me in Harrisburg. They're small change, not too sharp in the cop-shop, and we can be in and out before they know anything. That was the criminal mind-set on Harrisburg.

The constant competition to rule the local drug scene made the city's poverty areas a shooting gallery. On a regular basis some brown man was murdered on the streets of the city to settle a border infringement. Typically the police had the perpetrator within hours. He was seldom ever more than a soldier for the powers that be and therefore expendable.

That is not to say that metropolitan Harrisburg is a bad city. On the contrary, it is a lovely place to live, work and raise a family. If one chooses to stay away from the wrong neighborhoods and criminal elements.

Alex arrived on a mission. Find and purchase a farm. One with outbuildings that are in good shape, a certain lay of land for training soldiers, and get it set up with as little attention to yourself as possible.

He soon discovered Perry County. On the west bank of the Susquehanna, it is rural, remote and an area where people are friendly – read that naïve. They mind their own business, and gunfire is common!

It didn't take Alex long to learn that the sound of a gun going off was not something most folks in Perry County worried about. They own and carry guns – on their belt or in their purse, and certainly in their pickup trucks.

These people set up shooting benches in their back yards and exercise their Second Amendment rights. They're proud of it. When the neighbors do a lot of shooting, they consider that he's likely "working up loads" for his new rifle, just poking holes in paper or groundhogs for the fun of it. And they leave him alone.

Alex purchased the farm, erected a steel pole gate across the gravel road that led back into the farm, and got to work.

A call to the mosque brought a small army of workers who drove the three and half hours to join him. They turned the house into a barracks. Then the stalls in the barn were removed so vehicles could be kept out of sight from the air. Additionally, there was an arms room and shop established in a tool shed near the house. They built out-houses, in direct violation to both local and state sanitation laws. Considering that they were about to train an army of terrorists, that didn't place too high on the list of concerns for Alex.

Perry County is a bastion of old-fashioned values. Filled with people scornful of the "big cities" of Camp Hill and Harrisburg, many of the local citizens work in town then race home to the country at the end of the day in all kinds of SUVs and four-wheel drive vehicles.

Church, little league, high school football, deer hunting, fishing and gardening are important activities in this enclave of truly decent people who want to be left alone by the government and one another. They wave when they meet on the curving county roads. At the grocery store they discuss the news – mostly local, cuss the latest idiocy in Harrisburg or Washington, and thank God in church on Sunday that they live in a different world.

Sadly, that world is creeping up on them like some of the creatures Alex Tort contended with at Ft. Polk. In fact, Alex Tort was *one* of those creatures.

Minding one's own business comes high on the priority list for folks who themselves want left alone. Even the ones who came in contact with Alex gave him a pass when they noted that he was sort of aloof, didn't explain his strange purchases at the hardware store, like ten rolls of barbed wire (setting up an obstacle course), and figured him for somebody who'd had it with most of society. They understood and even sort of envied him.

"So when will the shooters arrive?" Maxine asked it softly and non-judgmentally. She was here to sharpen up some sniper teams. Six shooters and spotters who would fan out across America. She had received orders to come to this farm and teach. She would do it, of course, but knew that unless these six were already trained professionals she was not going to fine tune them in three weeks.

She could teach them to shoot. Perhaps they were already able. Who knows? But a sniper's art could not be transferred to even willing students in such time. What her leaders had in mind for these, she had not a clue. Did not want to know, actually. She would just do as ordered.

Maxine had come a long ways since Jordan. Not all of it pleasant.

"He said they will be here when they get here. He laughed and said to send all but the one pair away then go to Hershey Park."

Alex spoke this last with amazement. He did not know the man on the other end of the telephone. So many unknowns. Too many for him.

First he'd received a call about this woman. Then she arrived and had given him the first twinge of fear he had known in years. This morning he had walked upstairs to her bedroom to awaken her and found crumpled up newspapers filling the hallway.

When he kicked them aside and started to her door, she'd flung it open and stuck a Glock 9mm in his face and asked what he wanted. When he calmly replied that he had made coffee and wanted to know if she would like to join him for breakfast, she nodded, said, "Make me tea," then slammed the door in his face. Ten minutes later she was sitting at his table saying nothing, just looking out the window.

A *woman who doesn't talk. Spooky.*

She looked out the window as Alex bustled around the house, frustrated that the people in charge seemed so haphazard about schedules. *Like the Army- hurry up and wait.*

As she watched the tree limbs bend in the breeze her thoughts returned to her introduction to Al Qaeda.

Maxine returned from her first mission on the Syrian border a sort of hero to her sniper company. None of them had ever fired at a human being. They wanted to know what it was like to pull the trigger and extinguish a life. They wanted to ask – but they did not.

She had changed somehow. They sensed more than knew it. Still they watched and listened for some indication of how the mission had gone.

For her part Maxine had matured. Significantly she felt no remorse. The Syrian soldiers were dishonoring their profession. They had become kidnappers, rapists and murderers. They deserved death for what they were doing. Had her village been up there in the mountains it might well have been she who was their victim rather than their executioner. They were dirt! It was not tribal or national, but more visceral as a woman.

She trained, exercised, ran endless miles in her off duty time, and put it behind her. She knew that some of the others in her company wanted to speak of it but she never gave them an opportunity.

She sensed that, for the most part, the woman sniper company was a political thing. Her instructors had inferred that she was the only member of the group who was *really* a sniper. She alone took the training and developed the proper level of skills to stay alive in combat. She alone worked with her weapon and other equipment to reach the fine-edged expertise necessary to fire and hit targets at ranges beyond imagination.

She had the mindset necessary to experience the hours of stillness and tradecraft a true sniper needs in the field. The others were here and they went through the motions, but Maxine was special. This was not said in a verbal manner as much as the instructors worked to refine her training and abilities.

They expected so much more of her. Demanded so much excellence! She responded to it with self discipline, and joy. Maxine shut out everything but the computation of mil-dots, range, ballistics and bullet drop. She was a professional. Not a killer. Not a murderer. She was a soldier. On equal ground with a jet pilot or a tank commander. She was special. She knew it, and they knew it. Life was on the ascent.

Three years after her first experience at the Syrian border, Maxine was ordered to report to her Company Commander. "You are being asked to travel to Iraq for a mission. I say 'asked' because it is a live fire mission. I will not order you to go.

"You will be under the command of the Iraqi army. They have a problem with Iranians encroaching on their northeastern border. Bands of them are killing villagers and stealing vehicles and the occasional woman. Like the Syrians, they consider this fair sport.

“Do not ask why they cannot deal with it themselves. I do not know. Only that the request has come to me. If you say no, it will not be held against you, Sergeant.”

Maxine stood at a relaxed attention before his desk. She considered it for a moment, then nodded her head and in a monotone said, “I will go.” No questions, just the simple answer. It was what she did.

Two hours later she, her gear and Hamir were aboard a military aircraft headed for Iraq.

They finally landed at an army camp east of Baghdad. When they landed the first thing she saw was a trio of white Mercedes and a cluster of officers. And one other.

He stood taller than the group who were spread out around him like a human fan. He addressed them with scornful looks and motions. She heard the tone but could not make out the words. Apparently he was here to bring order to this riff-raff. That was what she saw. Their sins were unimportant to her. And every sergeant knows that officer territory is best avoided if at all possible.

She and her spotter reached inside the plane to retrieve their equipment. When she turned to walk away she literally bumped into the tall man who had been reviling the officers. He had close cropped black hair – who didn’t? – a rough beard and moustache, a bullet head, and sharp black eyes.

“I could tell the way you looked from the back that they’d sent us a woman!”

There was a smirk on his face. *Uday*!

“Don’t the Jordanians have any men who can shoot?”

The officers were gathered at a respectful distance watching the arrogant man in casual civilian dress..

Maxine looked him in the face and responded in a respectful voice, “Don’t the Iraqis have anyone who can shoot Iranians that they need me at all?” She dropped her pack at her feet and stood straight, the rifle case in her left hand, the right relaxed near the holstered Beretta 9mm at her side.

As one the officer group recoiled a half step. Their faces were ashen at the idea of ever speaking such words to the “great one.”

“Do you know who I am?” he asked conversationally. His face was poker plain with a slight trace of a smile on his lips. The eyes were not amused.

“I know only that you are in civilian clothes, and insult someone who comes to Iraq in an act of friendship at the request of your country.”

“I *am* my country. I am the son of Saddam!”

"Congratulations. I'm sure your father is proud of you. I cannot imagine he would insult a friend who is in the process of doing him a kindness. If I have insulted you, I apologize. I came only to do a service to your nation." Maxine was not really afraid, but common sense told her that she had not been wise either.

The man did not speak. He looked into her eyes, and seemed to be deciding on his next course of action. The silence stretched to a minute. It seemed an hour to those watching. On other occasions some of them had stared in shock as he had personally pulled a chromed Walther and murdered men who insulted him far less than had this woman soldier.

Finally he smiled a tight smile, nodded and said, "Of course. You are here to do us a kindness. And so you shall." He turned and the green sea of officers parted as he walked to the idling middle Mercedes and sat in the rear seat.

The door slammed, then the black tinted window hummed down electrically and he pointed to one of the officers. The man ran to the car, leaned forward at the waist, nodded his head a few times then turned and double-timed back to the others. A call went out to a group of enlisted men and NCOs. One of them broke off and trotted to the officers, came to attention and saluted.

The three Mercedes departed in a cloud of sand and dust. All the people seemed to take a deep breath. The man who had gone to Saddam's son gave instruction to the Sergeant. He nodded, saluted, and trotted to Maxine and her spotter.

"You will come with me," he sneered, and turned toward a white ¾ ton Toyota pickup truck. The sniper team followed, placed their equipment in the back and climbed in after it. The sergeant took the right front seat and a soldier drove them off the base.

They traveled the rest of the day, stopped along the highway that night and were on the road again for the major part of the next day. They halted only for gasoline and food at way-stations manned by run-down groups of soldiers whose campsites along the road looked more like hobo jungles than anything military.

Finally the truck came to a stop at a small outpost of perhaps fifty soldiers. The geography was now mountainous, rugged peaks and valleys with a scrabble of villages and goat trails. The sergeant stepped from the truck, walked directly into the camp, and left Maxine and Hamir to fend for themselves. The driver trotted to catch up with his sergeant.

The Jordanians looked at each other, shrugged, and moved to the camp. No soldiers spoke to them. None offered them water or hospitality. They were pariahs. The sergeant had made it so in the brief time he had preceded them.

The camp was a shambles. Litter, empty food tins and trash littered the ground. Even piles of human waste were everywhere. One simply stepped around it and walked on. Maxine could hardly believe her eyes.

She and Hamir finally moved outside the camp to a bare piece of ground and that night slept with their heads on their packs, huddled beside one another for warmth under their ponchos.

At daylight they were up, ate some rations from their packs and drank a cup of weak tea they heated with a piece of C4 they burned beneath their canteen cups. The camp was still asleep. Finally well past daylight the Sergeant and his ever present private approached the snipers.

"You will go onto that mountain to hunt. There is a village on the other side. It is there the accursed Iranians come, often one in a little green car. That one you kill first." Motioning to the private, "He will drive you out and come for you at night."

"He may drive us out, but leave us there. Do not come for us. We will fire a flare when we want picked up. We will stay on the mountain until we take them," Maxine responded. She was also a Sergeant, and considered herself in charge of the mission.

The Iraqi's face turned to granite. He was not about to take orders from a Jordanian woman, sniper or not.

"YOU WILL DO AS ORDERED! WE WILL COME FOR YOU AT NIGHT!" he shouted, spittle flying from thick lips.

Maxine considered this for a moment, shrugged and agreed. "Fine. Send the truck an hour after dark. We will meet it at the drop off place. Do not go near the village. That could be dangerous."

They loaded up and were off to the mountain. That day Hamir and Maxine moved carefully around the ridge. They watched the village and sought a place for preparing a "hide" or shooting location. One with acceptable egress and ingress. Sniping is not a suicide mission.

There was no one to provide security for their back, so they wanted a location that would give them some concealment from observation, at least. Finally they chose a spot, then a secondary location to fall back to. It had taken most of the first day, and they were back at the pickup spot at the appointed time.

The ride back was uneventful. The arrival at camp the same. No one greeted them. No one shared food – thankfully as far as the team was concerned. Anyone who relieved himself in the midst of his living space was worse than a pig and they chose not to dine with such.

On the second day, an hour before daylight their driver was not there. Maxine and Hamir took the truck, drove away and heard an angry shout from behind. They moved to their second hide and spent the day watching the poor village, waiting for – what? A parade of Iranian tanks? A lone soldier afoot? Who knew? They saw nothing that was a target, and stayed on the mountain that night.

The third day there was movement. A small green car drove into the village around mid-morning. A lone man climbed out and entered a house that was little more than a hovel.

"Is this our Iranian?" Hamir asked quietly.

"Let's just watch," Maxine said. She had a feeling of discomfort, but could not actually say it was from what was happening in the village. She just had a sense that someone was watching them.

"Hamir, move very quietly backward. When you are in the shadow of the overhang, begin to scan the area around us with the spotting scope." A sixty-power scope can count the fleas on a dog's back at two hundred yards, and Hamir was good at seeing anything unusual. Finally he called the short distance to Maxine.

"I see nothing. What did you think you saw or heard?"

"Maybe it was just this whole mission. So little briefing. The animosity. Starting with the crazy son of Saddam. Come back up here."

Below no one had emerged from the house where the stranger entered. Life continued normally. The village baked below. The snipers baked above.

Night fell and they continued to watch. Taking turns sleeping and watching. Dawn found things as before with the green car unmoved.

BLAAM!

Hamir hunched up as the round struck the base of his skull. Maxine began to roll onto her back, turning with her rifle to face the enemy behind.

"Do not move!" It was the Iraqi sergeant's voice, as flat as the rock she lay on.

She lowered the rifle then looked over her shoulder where she saw the sergeant, pistol in hand, and his aide who held an AK-47 with smoke tendrils rising from the barrel.

"Move back from the rifle – stay on your belly!" growled the sergeant. He looked slightly mad with white drool in the corners of his mouth. His uniform was filthy in the front from climbing and crawling. He rose to his knees as Maxine obeyed his command.

Her mind raced as she tried to think of ways to defend herself from these two. The aide also rose, keeping the rifle aimed at Maxine.

"Stop! Now stand up – slowly!" ordered the NCO. He was smiling – if that was what it could be called. Maxine knew what would come next. She turned to look at poor Hamir, lying dead in his own blood with flies already congregating on his ruined skull.

Looking back at the Sergeant she was struck in the face by his fist and fell backwards. She struck her head on the mountain rock stunning her and firing flares of yellow behind her closed eyelids.

Next he grabbed the front of her uniform jacket and yanked her roughly to her feet. She stood only five feet six inches tall and with the NCO another four inches taller and nearly twice her size he had no difficulty jerking her lithe frame around. Slapping her on both cheeks with a back and forth hand movement he spat into her face! His fetid, garlic and beer breath sickened her.

"Whore! You think you can speak to Uday in such a manner and go unscathed?! You think you will not pay? He gave you to me with very clear orders!" His voice dropped to a quiet whisper and came like a razor wrapped in velvet, "Orders I will love to obey. And then the idiot there," nodding toward his aide, "will have his way. Then he will shoot you in the crotch and stomach. Finally, we will watch the buzzards pluck out your eyes and unravel your intestines as you scream." He struck her again. Then he stepped back.

"Take off your clothes! DO IT!" he moved to a rock outcropping and sat on a large stone, crossing his legs and lighting a cigarette. He was panting from exertion and excitement, the whites of his eyes showing all around the pupils like a crazed horse.

Maxine began unbuttoning her uniform jacket. One piece of her uniform followed another.

"ALL OF IT. HURRY!" the private shouted like a maniac. From the look in his eyes as he shook the barrel of the rifle, Maxine was certain he was exactly that.

The Sergeant stood shaking before her then abruptly stepped forward. He moved so fast Maxine had no time to dodge as he kicked her in the stomach, forcing all air from her lungs. She fell backwards, again slamming her skull on rock.

CRACK! CRACK!

The sergeant began to fall toward Maxine. She shoved him aside with both hands, a disgusted grunt coming from her lips. He toppled beside her onto the rock. She saw a trickle of blood leave his lips as his head lolled sideways.

Maxine rose up and looked toward the aide's location. He was on his face in the dust, the rifle by his side. He too was leaking blood, and the pool of crimson enlarged as his wounded heart continued to pump out his life.

She quickly retained her garments. There was no one visible, and it had been difficult to guess where the rescuer had fired from.

"The worst is over now." The voice was well modulated, had a peculiar accent, and was not at all full of excitement. Another day at the office.

Maxine moved to reach for her Remington 700.

"Ah. Ah. The handgun in your holster will be enough for now. Just stand very still." Obviously the man could see her, but still she had not located him.

He moved into view finally and kept a dark revolver in his right hand, though pointed down and not at Maxine.

He was dressed in a light blue long sleeved shirt and loose tan trousers. Like most men his age in the Middle East he was black haired, dark eyed, and had a moustache. His was neatly trimmed in a British Military manner.

His face was pockmarked with scars from acne, smallpox or both. Still he was handsome in a darkly dangerous way. Rudolph Valentino, from the old movies she had seen on Jordanian television as a girl.

He smiled a small smile and said, "I am Hisham Hatef at your service. My last name means guardian angel in Farsi, you know." There was a hint of a bow at the neck, and then he moved more into the open, looked at the sergeant and the private then walked further over to note Hamir.

He clucked his tongue, "Such a mess. I hate this. This makes it very difficult for you now doesn't it?" He holstered the revolver and looked at Maxine who was getting herself under control.

She was so angry at the Iraqis. *Why had they asked for her and Hamir in the first place? Who was this man? Handsome and at such ease under these circumstances. How had he found them all so quickly after the first shot?*

"You have questions. Let us move from here to a more peaceful location and I will try to answer them." The man moved to Hamir's side, picked up the spotting scope and his M-16 rifle. Then he scooped up the day-pack with rations, ammo, etc. Maxine stood stock still and watched it all.

"Get your case and put the rifle in it," he said tenderly, as one does to a serious patient in a hospital. She moved wordlessly to obey. It never occurred to her to do otherwise.

When they had their arms full, and she had shouldered her own pack, they moved down the mountain, this time circling around toward the village below. When they were on the outskirts a dog barked. Its owner scolded it and the people moved to their houses and went inside. Maxine thought, *This is someone important.*

They reached the little green car with its chalky paint job and a few dents. Halawi opened the back door on his side and unburdened himself. Motioning to the seat, he said, "Put the rifle and pack in here too." She complied.

As he closed the door, he motioned toward the house she had watched him enter the previous day. Inside the darkness it was cool. He sat on a modern, though poor, couch, patted the cushion by his side and said, "Sit."

Maxine sat, as far from him as possible, but turned slightly so as to see him. A middle aged woman who had suffered a difficult life by the looks of her carried a tray with glasses of hot mint tea and small sesame seed dessert cakes. She looked fleetingly at Maxine, gave her a glimpse of kindness, and then quickly departed.

"So tell me all about it. You have nothing to fear from me. I am the commander of the Al Qaeda training camp located northwest of here outside Mosul. She," he nodded toward the room where the woman had just gone, "is my sister. We are Iranians. I visit here and bring some small items and a bit of money to them. It is the least I can do, and I enjoy seeing her again. I will be leaving before long and we may never see one another again.

"Now tell me. Why are you trying to kill me?"

His manner was anything but threatening but Maxine knew the exterior meant nothing. He reached for the tray and handed her a glass of the hot tea infused with a sprig of mint, added a cake to her other hand and took more for himself. Then he sat back, sipped, nibbled and waited.

"I was not trying to kill you. At least not personally. We were ordered by the Iraqis to kill the person in a green car. That would be you, though, it seems.

"It was all a bungled mess from the beginning. I am a sergeant in the Jordanian Army. The man on the mountain was my spotter." She sipped the sweet tea and continued, starting with the call to her Company Commander's orderly room. When she finished, she said, "How did you get here so quickly after the first shot?"

"I was already here. At least almost here. I thought I saw movement not far from your location the previous day. A glint of light, perhaps a shadow out of place. Before daylight I left the village and began to move upward. Then the first shot gave them away and I moved toward it. I would likely not have been able to stop them from killing your spotter, at any rate.

Maxine nodded. They had been friends, she and Hamir. Soldiers together. She hurt deep inside for him. Suddenly the dam of control broke and she began to sob and shake.

Hisham Hatef, rescuer, warrior, terrorist, guardian angel grasped the glass and took it from her. She moved to his embrace and sobbed. As he cradled her in his arms, she continued to release all the tension and passion so long held back. His sister moved silently into the room, clucked her tongue, as their mother had once done, and smiled the sad smile of understanding so many in this land knew. *Insh'allah.*

Finally the sobs subsided. She was embarrassed and began to wipe tears, stood, moved to a corner, facing the wall, and leaned her forehead against it.

"It is not shameful to find relief after so much trauma. You were victimized." He sat still, and sipped a fresh glass of tea his sister had placed beside him.

"Will you go north with me? You can hardly return to the Iraqis and tell them what happened. You say you believe the young Saddam plotted this. You are already no doubt reported dead to your army.

"We will be in Germany in a month. Your training will be very helpful to the cause of Allah. You will become someone important to his jihad."

"What of the two trucks and the bodies up above?" she asked, thinking for a moment of the people in the village when other soldiers arrived looking for their sergeant.

"They will be moved to another mountain miles from here. The bodies will disappear. Your man will be buried today, the others to the carrion eaters. When they find the trucks they will wonder, but no one will come here looking. These people have allies among the Iranians and Bedouin alike. They live by *baraka* – divine grace – and can survive more than the Iraqi army can deliver, trust me.

So Maxine joined Al Qaeda. The coming years would see her in Germany, but also in Yemen, France, Turkey and Britain. She learned to speak English and sounded like a long time immigrant to American ears when she arrived in Texas.

To Texans everyone from any place else always sounds like a foreigner anyway.

TEN

Larry was laughing so hard that tears filled his eyes. George, for his part, was grinning and enjoying the story teller more than the tale.

"We pulled into the parking lot of this athletic club. Walking out of the entrance to the gym was Man Mountain McGurk. At least that's what he looked like to George.

"Six foot eight, bald as a cue ball and with this big white beard that looked like someone hit it with about two hundred volts. The guy truly is a giant. Massive thighs, a tiny waist cinched with a wide black belt and a chest popping out of a spandex shirt with crude words on the front. Earring made him look like Mr. Clean!

"He was headed for a purple Harley chopper. When I honked he stopped and gave us a look that could freeze steam heat. I got out and when I was about a yard from him, he put up his dukes. I swatted his hands aside and grabbed him in a bear hug. Man, he busted that and reversed it faster than it takes me to tell it."

Jake and Harold had been to "Larry's story telling time" before. They smiled and waited.

"That was when George came to my rescue.

"He leaped from the Jimmy and reached under his bibs. Out he came with this antique Colt 45 1911. Two steps and he was in front of us. I didn't even know he had a piece under there.

"'Okay, Tiny! Put him down or I'll put you down!'" He yelled, in a perfect Weaver stance, both hands rock steady and in Condition One.

Willi turned me loose – IMMEDIATELY, and I shouted, "No, George! It's all right! Don't shoot him! We're just horsing around!"

Willi gave out with a giggle like a ballerina and said pleasantly, "Well, Tiny yourself, big guy. You can shoot me, sure, but it's been done before. I take tree 9mm hardballs in Lebanon and walk to de medic." His speech was English but with a European accent.

"George clicked the safety on with his thumb but he didn't uncock it."

"Willi and I were laughing and slapping each other on the shoulder. George just watched without a word."

Jake was grinning when he turned on the bench toward George. "We met Willie Knaustler in Israel. He was in their army for a while during their little trip into Lebanon in the 90s. He's actually from Egypt though. His folks were German diplomats."

Larry continued, “He went to fight with Israel because it was there and the Israeli cause was just. He was in our Special Forces but before I was. Now he’s in the arms business.”

Harold, who was driving, weighed in. “Actually, George, he’s in it exactly the same as you were. None of us know which agency, but along with the hardware, ammo, night vision equipment and all were the necessary forms, licenses and IDs. For all four of us. It was handled through Don Rogers’ and the Attorney General’s office.”

George was a good sport and enjoyed Larry’s telling of the tale. It was even pretty close to accurate.

Larry, Jake, Harold and George had their hardware spread out over three shooting benches. Two Kimber custom .45s, a Ruger Mark II with 4.5 inch barrel, then another with four more inches of suppressor/silencer, the M-4 frame, suppressed 9mm with six twenty round mags, three FN P90s and three 9mm baby Uzis, each with six mags. Extra ammo for all these was in two tool boxes on another bench. Ear protection and shooting glasses of various kinds lay scattered among the firepower. The men had actually brought a red Western Flyer wagon to haul it all from the parking lot to the benches, laughing as Larry pulled it along behind him, about how it would look to someone just driving up.

They were at a typical small town gun club range. Nearby sat a clubhouse and behind that a 200 yard rifle range. Occasionally a loud report from there made all four men jump inside.

At the other end of the line of pistol range benches, a very fit, salt-and-pepper haired man of around forty and a blonde young man were working with a Sig Sauer 2022 40S&W. Both were handsome, athletic and shooting at twenty-one yard targets.

Outwardly the two groups seemed totally unaware of the other. Actually both were *very* aware of what was happening at opposite ends of the range.

“Maybe we better not shoot the P90s or the Uzis till they leave,” Harold suggested nodding sideways toward the pair down the line.

“Well, we got ID if they ask. The Police Chief got us our memberships, and they could be here all morning,” Jake responded logically. He wanted to bust some caps. “And when we rip off a silenced magazine the jig is up anyway,” he grinned a silly grin at Larry, who nodded agreement.

Harold shrugged a surrender, smiled at George and said, “Let the games begin.”

Larry stepped between two benches, raised the silenced M-4 carbine to his shoulder and fired three rounds single fire. Sub-sonic rounds created a low cracking sound which joined the clacking of the action as it ejected the spent brass and moved forward to reload the chamber. Suppressors *reduce* the sound they don't eliminate it like the movies show.

Next he flipped the selector switch on the side of the rifle and sent a string of three three-round bursts down range. Holes peppered the target. The only ones near the center were the first three single-fire shots. When he fired the bursts the dark-haired man and his son instantly turned to watch.

Curiosity is common at shooting ranges. A new or different looking gun draws shooters' attention. Super accurate hits on a target do the same thing as the competitive spirit and respect for excellence combine. A drop of testosterone leavens the elixir.

Most Americans – courtesy of the liberal media – are greatly un- or misinformed regarding firearms. True automatic guns – machine guns – have been regulated since 1934.[2]

An automatic weapon fires for as long as the shooter keeps the trigger depressed, until the magazine is empty or the gun malfunctions. A person can still buy a full-auto gun. The same is true for a silencer or sound suppressor.

They must undergo extensive background checks and pay a two hundred dollar license fee, plus the cost of the item. As far as Harold could remember (and he tried to stay abreast of it) only one person who was licensed to carry a concealed firearm, much less an automatic weapon had ever been convicted of a firearms offense – and he was a police officer from north central Pennsylvania.

As mentioned by Harold all four men were licensed to own and carry the weapons. Granted, these permits were abnormal. Few people had letters and photo ID cards signed by the Attorney General of the United States.

Nick Lawson walked casually toward the team leaving his son at the other end of the row of benches. He was a Pennsylvania State

---

[2] It has been unlawful since 1934 (The National Firearms Act) for civilians to own machine guns without special permission from the U.S. Treasury Department. Machine guns are subject to a $200 tax every time their ownership changes from one federally registered owner to another, and each new weapon is subject to a manufacturing tax when it is made, and it must be registered with the Bureau of Alcohol Tobacco and Firearms (BATF) in its National Firearms Registry. To become a registered owner, a complete FBI background investigation is conducted.... Since the Firearms Owners' Protection Act of May 19, 1986, ownership of newly manufactured machine guns has been prohibited to civilians.... but those manufactured after the ban cannot ordinarily be sold to or owned by civilians. http://www.guncite.com/gun_control_gcfullau.html

Police Sergeant and a part of Governor Red Endreling's executive protection unit. He stopped a bit behind and to their left.

Larry continued to fire until the magazine was empty. He laughed, set the safety, pulled the magazine from the rifle and handed the warm gun to Jake. "That was fun. I see I tore the bull's eye right out," he mocked himself. There were about ten holes scattered over the whole silhouette target.

Jake passed the gun to George. Harold gave him a full magazine. The small man in his bib overalls looked out of place with the rifle, but held it like a friend's hand. He moved to where Larry had stood.

"Which one should I take?" he asked referring to the targets.

Jake said, "The one to the left of Larry's. Or you could take his or mine. We didn't hurt 'em!" Everyone laughed, including Nick.

George did not place the gun to his shoulder. Rather he locked it in the crook of his arm with the stock resting firmly into his bicep and fired a three round burst. Almost immediately there followed a string of more bursts until the magazine was empty.

"Whoooee! Would you look at that!?" Larry roared. Indeed, *everyone* was looking. The center body mass of the silhouette target was in tatters. A couple of rounds had struck the right shoulder. The rest could be covered by a paper saucer.

"Well, George, we see what *you* did while the other kids were takin' piano lessons," Jake dead-panned.

Harold took the hot-barreled rifle as oil smoke rose from the juncture of barrel and receiver. He gingerly dropped the magazine and laid both on the bench beside him.

George smiled coyly but had a difficult time being humble as Jake and Larry praised his skill. He had actually built one of the first suppressed 9mm rifles on an M-16 frame, but they didn't know that and he didn't mention it.

"Okay, Dad. Try the Kimber," Jake was the emcee for this outing. He started to speak again when a light touch came to his left bicep. He already knew the man was there but wanted to see what would develop.

"Pardon me. I'm Nick Lawson. PA State Police," Nick said and badged them.

"I'm sure you fellows are legal, but, you don't mind if I verify that, do you?" There was a firmness to the way he said it. This policeman was not some pus-gutted backwoods hillbilly. He was on the front line from the cut of his jib and they recognized one of their own kind.

Harold spoke immediately, and everyone kept their hands empty, open and visible. Not that there was any threat. Rather as a common courtesy everyone involved with threat situations appreciated.

Nick noted it, and felt good about that.

"We're legal. Let me get you some documentation. He reached into the pocket of one of the black Cordura tactical rifle cases. Withdrawing an envelope, he pulled a letter from inside, unfolded it and handed it to Nick, who scanned it, his eyebrows rising when he saw the AG's *and* the Secretary of Homeland Security's signature.

He easily recognized the latter, having been the leader of his protective detail when he was Pennsylvania's previous Governor. Nick folded the letter, handed it back to Harold and visibly relaxed his posture.

"Thank you, Sir. Now I have more questions than before, but perhaps I shouldn't ask them," Nick smiled with friendly blue eyes.

"Ask," Jake said. "Maybe it'll help if I tell you we're on the same side, only we're doing it as civilians now. All four of us are former DIA agents or something like that," he grinned at George and continued.

"How about you? What do you do for PSP?" He said it all with a friendly manner, and the team realized he'd deflected the direction of Nick's questioning. It was sparring. Sort of one police dog sniffing around another.

The conversation continued for a while, Nick motioning his son to join them. Introductions were made with Nick getting all their names right the first time.

Larry said, "Marcus, want to bust a few caps?"

He obviously did, but looked to his dad for approval. Nick nodded.

"Sure!" said the young man quietly but enthusiastically.

"Larry inserted a fresh mag, handed the rifle to Marcus with some brief instruction on the safety and selector switch. "Fire away."

A quick learner, Marcus flipped the safety off, fired a couple of bursts at the target, holding the gun as he'd seen George. He managed to spray splinters from a cross-board on the target frame and get two onto the paper, neither in the black. He returned the gun to safe then handed it over to Larry who inserted a fresh magazine. He pointed to Nick who grinned, took the gun and stepped up to the firing line.

Nick had been there before. He caressed the trigger, quickly sending separate three-round bursts into his target. He didn't match George's expertise but he was good. Jake whistled his appreciation.

"Well, Nick, I gotta be goin' now," Larry joked as he accepted the rifle from the policeman.

“Actually *we* do have to go. I have to go on duty soon,” Nick said. Everyone shook hands and Marcus went to pull their targets and box up the gun and ammo. Jake and Nick swapped phone numbers and discussed getting together again.

When they’d gone, the team continued to break in their new equipment. It was a fun day, as they all enjoyed shooting, competition and fellowship. Underlying all this was the fact that all four knew from experience that their excellence could save lives – theirs or someone else’s.

When he arrived at work in Harrisburg, Nick tidied up some loose ends then closed his office door and dialed a number in Washington, D.C.

“Chet, this is Nick. I need some information. Yeah, he’s different. I guess it will work out. You know how it is. Thanks for asking.” A pause.

“I ran into some guys today. I’m faxing their names and address. Said they are part of a company called Solutions.com. They were at the range shooting some silenced and full auto stuff. Truthfully, they seem like straight arrows, but it’s close to home.”

He listened a moment longer, then, “Thanks, I owe you one.”

An hour later Nick’s phone rang.

“Well, Nick, you hit a home run. Seems like your buddies know all the brass. National Security Advisor, Secretaries of War and State, even the DCIA.” Chet continued to fill Nick in on the team’s adventure in Virginia. Then he cinched it and straightened Nick up in his chair. “Seems that the one named Jake Crabtree is the nephew of Israel’s Mossad Director. Let me tell you, that bird is all crust, but he’s one hundred percent for the kid from what I read.

Well, You got a good bunch for neighbors, Nick. Make friends. Never know, they might want some protection of their own. Hey! See ya, buddy.”

Nick hung up then spent the next ten minutes in deep thought making doodles on his note pad.

ELEVEN

By the time Tomas arrived off the coast of Sanibel Island he was more than ready for the sight of land. His trip had taken far longer than he'd expected. Initially upon escaping New Orleans he had figured to make a bee line and get off the Gulf. Then after taking the Hatteras the idea occurred that not only might the police be trying to find him, but that there might be people seeking the couple he'd murdered as well.

For that reason, whenever he spied other boats he slowed his progress to give them time to avoid him. He felt changing course might be too overt, so he just reduced speed and let them pass. This was frustrating to one who was used to getting his way immediately. Patience was not Tomas' strong suit.

The killer spent a lot of time cleaning the boat. Wiping every surface for fingerprints was first. Then he tossed the remaining murdered couple's personal items into garbage bags, weighed them with fishing weights and other metal items and dropped them overboard. By the time Sanibel was visible he was certain no embarrassing materials would be found should he have visitors.

When he was still about seventy miles offshore he made his call to Bobby in Ft. Myers. "Are you able to do some painting for me and do you have the papers we discussed?"

"You betcha, Man. Just tell me when you want me there and I'll motor out and we'll get started."

They discussed details and times. Bobby showed up as requested in a beautiful Bertram. He offloaded a blue Zodiac, and buzzed over to the Hatteras. Bobby was from the same island village as Tomas. Another Island boy who came to America and made good. His area of expertise was art and forgery. Lettering boats was just a passing hobby that made him some extra loot. A mutual contact had put them in touch a couple of years ago, they discovered their common roots, and Tomas kept the relationship alive by phone calls and a couple of gifts sent when requested by Bobby. Gifts that go boom in the night. Today was a favor. A simple kindness returned. Maurie would have called it a *mitzvah.*

Bobby listened to what Tomas wanted, returned to his boat for a while, then zipped back to the Hatteras with some cans and brushes. In no time he was on the swim platform at the stern, then hanging from a harness he slung from the bow.

Voila! the Hatteras had a new name, new serial numbers, and Tomas had title, registration and other miscellaneous pieces of paper that would serve to prove he had owned the boat for just over a year, a gift from his uncle. Bobby was given a package of Semtex, detonators and a warm embrace. What he was going to do with the explosives Tomas did not want to know.

When Bobby was out of sight, Tomas went to sleep. He had cat napped on the way across the Gulf, but now he lay down in the main salon and dropped into a deep sleep. For his part, Bobby returned to Ft. Myers, docked his boat and took his package into the old downtown area with its pastel stucco buildings and narrow streets.

There he turned it into a nice chunk of change, then went to his favorite bar to court some of the local female talent. Life was good when one did not get overly curious and had a useful profession.

Tomas awoke, if not refreshed then at least rested. He bathed, ate the last of the canned fruit – he chastened himself for not asking Bobby to resupply him. Then he made his way down the Gulf coast of Florida. He would stay just out of sight of land and take his time getting to his new home.

When he motored into Margaritaville's home island, the Hatteras was making no wake and burbling that lovely throaty growl larger boats make. He'd watched the news on the satellite television channels. There was nothing reported about a search for a missing couple from Texas or any hunt for him. That did not mean that he was fat and happy. Both stories were likely still local news.

Just be cool, man, he thought as he idled the boat up to the public landing and tossed a line to a skinny youth in shorts with a perfect tan and a scruffy blonde beard. After the tie up was complete he made his way to the Harbor Master's office, paid the appropriate fees, made arrangements for refueling and filling his water tank, then asked about a good place to eat. He was sick of his own cooking.

Tomas was dressed expensively, but conservatively. After all, he wanted to make a good impression on this small community. Under his blue, green and white flowered cotton shirt was a stainless Colt and five rounds of Hydra-shock ammo. Friendly isn't contradictory to careful.

He walked down the boardwalk along which a wide variety of boats were docked. Fishing rigs, sail boats, and yachts, both sail and power, were mixed together in a democratic batch. Even a few skiffs which likely belonged to citizens of the big yachts tied out in the basin. *Resupply and dining excursions*, he thought.

As he walked behind one medium sized fishing boat, a thin dark-haired young man looked up from cleaning his boat, smiled and said, "How ya doing?"

Tomas slowed his pace and answered, "As soon as I get some groceries in me I'll be fine. Where's a good place to eat?"

"Just up the walk another fifty feet. The Rusty Mussel. I eat there a lot. Good service, decent prices and plenty on the plate. You just get in?"

"Yeah. Came down from Charleston. I'm sort of new with the boat thing. My uncle passed on and left it to me. This is only my second real cruise. First one any distance from home. I tell ya, I did pretty good but it takes some getting used to, living in a small area like that. And my cooking ain't to be eaten for more'n a couple of meals. I'm going to get supper then buy some groceries."

"You're standing in front of the closest grocery store," the man on the boat pointed behind Tomas. It was true. A general store was directly behind him.

"My name's Dave. Captain Dave's Fishing Tours," he handed Tomas a card, and they shook hands.

"Leon Smith," Tomas responded. "I owned a computer company. Started it from scratch. It took off, and I sold out before the 'dot.com crash," he grinned.

"Been thinking about what to do since. Then my uncle left me the boat and I'd always wanted to come down here and live after I visited a couple of years ago. Here I am. Hey, gotta move." Tomas waved.

Dave returned the wave and returned to sloshing buckets of water on the deck and scrubbing fish blood.

Tomas found the Rusty Mussel and dined well if plainly. He returned to the grocery store, bought three bags of supplies and walked back to the Hatteras.

The blonde guy was sitting in the Harbor Master's chair with his bare feet up on the desk reading a motorcycle magazine. "You're berthed down the way," he pointed a thumb over his shoulder. "Slip 16B. I took her down there for ya."

Tomas' heart skipped a beat. He'd had no idea that this stupid kid would go aboard his boat while he was gone. Had he discovered anything Tomas had forgotten? Was there any evidence like that? He thought he'd cleaned everything up well, but … What was he to say?

"Thanks. I guess. You always do that? Move someone's boat without telling them?" he asked sharply.

The kid sat up, plopped his feet on the floor and looked at Tomas. "Gee, Man. I thought you'd appreciate it. You looked beat, and I figured it would make your life better. Sometimes I move them when the folks look tired like you do or when they aren't true blue sailors.

"The way you came into the dock, well… You were okay, don't get me wrong. But you didn't slick it in and grin. Ya know what I mean?" The kid could see his tip evaporating.

Tomas relaxed. He better learn to be cool here. There weren't ten minions to protect him from life's little exchanges like in New Orleans. He was out of the habit of dealing with people on his own. Back home he was feared, insulated, and liked it that way. Here he was just a *tourista.*

"It's cool, kid. I was just surprised at that kind of service. Kinda like valet parking, huh?" he grinned and the kid relaxed.

The tip was reviving. Tomas reached into his pocket and peeled a twenty off a nice wad of bills, then handed it over. It disappeared into the faded blue shorts like magic.

"Thanks. Let me help you with the groceries and show you where she'd tied up. She's a nice craft, but Mister, seems kinda old fashioned for a mellow dude like you." The kid wasn't trying to pump Tomas, he realized, *Just be nice.*

"It is a good boat. Probably wouldn't have been my first choice, but, you know, don't look a gift horse in the mouth, huh? I'm thinking of living down here. This is only my second trip out.

"Is this the best place to keep her, or are there better marinas to stay long term?" Tomas would do his own survey, but the kid was a talker, and none too subtle, so why not?

They walked on the wooden dock, down toward the old fish processing plant, and the kid began to jabber on and on about locations, local people and places.

Then he said, "Don't get to wandering around the western part of the island between the Hemingway House and Ft. Taylor. You could find yourself disappeared. There's some tough customers down there, for sure. That neighborhood used to be populated by the escaped slaves – nothing against Black people – don't misunderstand," the kid looked at Tomas to see if he had stepped on his own tongue, and seeing no malice, continued. "There's a lot of drugs and crime, and tourists really do disappear in there now and then. Just a warning."

"Thanks, I'll remember that," Tomas said sincerely with a warm smile, and thought privately, *This sounds like a place I need to investigate.*

They arrived at the boat, the kid handed over the two bags of groceries, and returned to his motorcycle mag with a wave.

Tomas went aboard and stowed his fare, then inspected the boat for any signs of snooping by the kid. Finding none, he retired to the main cabin and his first real night's sleep for a long time. It was ten AM when he awoke.

He was padding around in the galley, idly watching Fox News and making some key lime tea from a tin he'd purchased at the grocery.

"A lot of people are relocating to Arizona, John. Seems like the dry heat agrees with them. And what with Florida getting more crowded every day, there is an influx of senior citizens finding this a wonderful place to retire."

The news chicky was reporting from some kind of upscale shopping mall. The camera man left her and tracked a woman coming down the wide expanse of mall toward him. He tightened up the shot, and Tomas could see why.

This one was a rare beauty indeed. She was strawberry-blonde, long-legged, stacked and graceful. Then she smiled, not knowing that she was on national television, and unconsciously touched a chipped tooth with her tongue. Just an old habit, caressing the flaw in an otherwise perfect smile. The camera closed in at that moment, and framed her face perfectly.

Tomas' heart stopped beating. He knew that face!

Couldn't be, he chided himself, as the report ended, and the news turned to Jerusalem for a report of more fruitless peace talks.

When Tomas had split he kept up with Fox News. The reports of a beautiful crazy woman who had killed a secretary, shot some men and burned her home and office was big news for a couple of days. Police were looking for this killer with a vengeance. Her picture was constantly plastered on the television. It was a good story, but the fact that she was a dead ringer for Raquel Welch really got her lots of face time. In fact that was what they used; old pictures of Raquel Welch in her prime. There was only one of the killer; a driver's license photo and like most of them, it was lousy. Tomas finally had a face to go with the voice. And did they ever match!

His mind was racing but he paced his activity. He placed his tea on the table, peeled a grapefruit, then sliced the skin off the segments and gushed the pulp into his mouth for a full impact of the tart juice. *The best way in the world to eat grapefruit.*

What should I do about the chickadee in Arizona? Am I even really sure it's her?

Absolutely! It's her. I just know it. Where was she? It's a big state. Should I turn her in, or tip her off again? Maybe just let sleeping cougars lie. Naw, that wasn't Tomas' way.

He finished the fruit and tea, cleaned up after himself and went up top. It was a beautiful day in paradise. Hot, clear and dazzling. People were bustling around the docks, gulls were doing aerobatics, and the pleasant salty, fishy smell of ocean filled his nostrils. He grabbed a bucket, sponge and towel and began cleaning the salt residue from his chrome work.

As he labored he turned the situation over in his mind. Stripping his shirt off, he garnered some admiring looks from a few women – and men – as his muscles ripped under the café au lait skin with the action of a shark moving through the water. Tomas was a perfect example of what good genes and hard work outs could produce. He knew it, and liked showing off, but then remembered that he definitely did not want to attract attention here.

Finished for now, he went below, stowed the materials, showered, changed into dressy shorts and a shirt, re-holstered the Colt and walked toward the public phones he had noticed the previous night.

He pulled a prepaid card from his wallet and called Fox News in New York City. Finally he got through, learned that the reporter was in Tucson and hung up. So the beautiful lioness – that was how he thought of her after watching her walk through the mall – was in the desert. He made evening flight reservations for Tucson. A little visit to his new best friend was in order.

Returning to the Harbor Master's office, he informed the man in charge that he was called away and that the boat would be locked up for a week or two. He paid the appropriate fare for berthing and care of the boat, then walked back to pack a bag.

Flying out of New Orleans would have been dangerous, but the odds of any watchers here were slim to none. He had all the appropriate false IDs, including real, legitimate credit cards, with real money behind them. His checking account was in his new name of Leon Smith, with a Charleston, South Carolina address. An empty lot, but hey, the maintenance was low.

The plane lifted off, Tomas sat back and was instantly asleep. The blue-haired lady beside him thought it was so nice that he neither drooled nor snored. This nice young man was not at all like that tourist she'd sat beside on the flight from Tel Aviv not long ago. A layover in Dallas-Fort Worth followed by a mid-morning landing at Tucson International Airport brought the trip to a close.

Stepping out of the terminal, Tomas was amazed at how crystal clear the air was. The jet black mountain peaks looked as if he could reach out and touch them. He amused himself by asking, *If so many people fear flying, why do they call the place they leave from a terminal?*

He rented a car and reserved a room at the Hampton Inn & Suites Mall, located in the Northwest part of town. The name Mall being the deciding factor when he chose his hotel.

He registered for a week then went mall-walking. Once there, he called the Fox affiliate and asked about the news piece that ran on national TV the day before. Sure enough they were thrilled about their local girl hitting the big time. And guess what? He was standing in the very mall from which her report emanated. Tomas was on a roll.

He strolled the mall sipping an iced coffee. Now that he was in the right jungle he needed to set his trap. Then he needed the Lioness to come calling *and* for him to be able to catch her without getting himself killed.

Tomas wracked his brain for the names of stores in the screen shot he'd seen on the news. Unable to remember any he did the next best thing. Struck up a conversation with one of the maintenance men. That gave him what he wanted – the spoke of the mall, if not the very spot. There was a fern and potted palm coffee shop just inside the hub. Tomas went to a book store, purchased a notebook, a couple of novels, a pen and a small tote bag. He was going to kill time reading, writing and trying not to look like he was in the hunt.

It took three days. Then the Lioness stepped into his trap. She walked with that long-legged rolling gait that he remembered from the television. Right towards him swinging a large bag from a national chain. Tomas' heart slammed in his chest, at first being afraid she would recognize him, then quickly remembering that they had never met.

He rose and began to walk behind Raquel. Finally, as she approached the set of glass doors leading into the parking garage, he stepped past her and held the door open for her. She smiled a thank you, and he said lowly as she began to step forward, "Be careful, Chere, it is a dangerous world for the likes of us."

Raquel was good but not good enough. She snapped her eyes into his face and her hand began to reach inside her large Dooney & Bourke handbag.

Tomas' grip was like steel on her wrist. "Now, now. You are in no danger from me, Chere. Let's just walk into the parking garage."

She tried a bluff. "I don't know you, and if you persist, I'll scream for security."

"Won't work, Chere. You are wanted just like me. After all, it was I who tipped you off. Let's don't be catty now." Tomas was smiling like he was discussing where to get a mint and endive salad.

Suddenly Raquel seemed to click into focus. She smiled, relaxed her posture, and Tomas released his grip on her wrist.

"Tomas," she said with recognition and surrender. "Where shall we go?"

"Your car or mine?" he asked, and she suggested hers. He walked her to his rental, and they exited the mall.

Tomas had lightened her bag by removing the Ruger, then inspected it. As the rental pulled onto I-10 and headed west they were thinking an identical thought. *That is one beautiful person. And dangerous as a snake.*

"How'd you find me?" Raquel asked, leaning against the car door and searching Tomas' face for any indication of his intentions.

"Don't lean against the door. If it pops open, you will be dragging your brains out on the highway, even with your seatbelt on." Tomas spoke sternly but quietly, as if to a small child.

Raquel responded to the command in his voice without thinking, and swiveled around in her seat. Then realizing what she had done, became instantly angry, and with white circles on her cheeks jerked herself back against the door. Tomas smiled but said nothing.

"Answer me! What do you want?" she persisted.

"Well, first of all, I was taken by your awesome beauty, Chere. Beautiful women have been a part of my life for many years now, but none who are also as dangerous as you. Besides, because of you my industry in New Orleans is over. I have had to relocate and must now begin again to establish an honest trade." He smiled at her, inwardly loving the white circles of rage on the beautiful cheeks. *Ah, she is such a lioness.*

"It was your men who were caught and led to your downfall!" she fired back.

"And they were on your fool's errand!" his instant calm rejoinder kept the fight going. He was enjoying just looking at her. It generated a feeling like when one is close to the big cats in one of those safari parks, knowing that the bus offered a margin of safety.

"I saw you on the television. This week! On a news report about Arizona. You were walking through the same mall where I found you. It was kismet. We were meant to be together. Bonnie and Clyde. Dale Evans and Roy Rogers. Bert and Ernie."

Raquel laughed in spite of herself. *He was charming. Like watching a panther.* Anyone could see he was constantly coiled for a lightning strike if necessary, but there was a languidness in his speech tempo and even in his posture. He was so absolutely confident in his ability to strike first that he gave away some points to prove it.

"How'd you find me?"

"The same way a good FBI agent could have if he were watching daytime television instead of working in his little government cubicle. You must admit your face is rather famous. And not forgettable either. I called Fox. They directed me to Tucson. The local affiliate told me which mall. The maintenance man told me which part of the mall, and here we are! Together at last." He chuckled that deep barrel chested sound.

Then he smiled a fetching smile reminding Raquel of what he must have looked like as an innocent little boy asking his mamma for a frozen fruit bar. She liked him in spite of how upset she was at this very moment.

What was she to do now? She was just about to begin operations once more. Was the government at her house? Had they also seen the broadcast? How could this have happened? She had been so careful. She hadn't seen the television crew until she was almost past them, and even then wasn't sure they had her on film.

Oh, what now? Could she kill this killer of others? Was he better than she? Was he going to kill her? What to do?

Raquel watched as the western edge of Tucson passed them by. They were climbing gradually, heading for desert. Cactus and sagebrush replaced taco joints and apartment complexes. *Was the idea to take her out there and kill her?*

"I'm not going to kill you. Relax," Tomas said, as if reading her mind. She slowly looked into his face as he drove just at the speed limit and with casual grace.

"What is this all about, then?"

"I want you to get out of here. In fact, I have the perfect place for you already established if you want it."

"Where would that be? Let me guess. With you?" she asked mockingly.

"Exactly. But not New Orleans. That is no longer an hospitable environment for the likes of me – or you, I dare say." Tomas smiled.

"If you want, I have another spot. One where most people have a laissez faire attitude and will pay little attention to us."

"And that would be?" Raquel asked searching for any indication in Tomas' intonation, mood or words for a hint of his motive.

"First, my lioness, we will discuss our future together. Then we will talk location. Where do you live?" He looked across the car and noted that she had moved her back away from the door now and was sitting properly in her seat. Inwardly he smiled, but only reflected a question on his face.

"Why do you want to know that?" she asked, still not ready to give anything away.

"Because I plan to take you back to retrieve your car, then drive to your house and approach your door like a salesman of household goods. See if there are any watchers nearby. If not, you can pack some clothes and leave this lovely desert town with me."

"Why not just tell you good-bye, thank you for another timely tip, and we part company?"

"Because you still need a supplier, no? And I still need a customer. Especially now. And who can overlook kismet?" His raised eyebrows and glittering eyes were intent on her face.

Raquel didn't comment, but it made sense. Tomas took an exit, circled under the highway and re-entered I-10 headed east now.

"Just take me to get my car. I have been very careful about tails. There are none. I agree with you about leaving. And about my car? I think we can take it. I bought it in Santa Fe. Used. Cash. It is clean. Where will we go?"

Tomas had considered all this during his vigil for Raquel. In fact, he reached into his tote bag and handed her the spiral notebook. In it were pages of notes on what to do exactly. The route to drive, when to stop. Raquel read the first page, raising her eyebrows, flipped to the second, read, and then to the third. By the time she had finished the four pages she was impressed. She was an expert at planning missions. This was well done, she admitted.

"Tomas," the first time she had used his name and in a friendly manner. "I agree. What makes either of us sure that the other will not later simplify his life by just killing the other and walking away? I don't want a partner. You likely don't either. So why should we pair up?"

"Chere, it is as I said. Now listen closely." He spoke as if to a slow child. "There are two very good reasons. First, I believe you are not finished with your business in the United States. I am no patriot. I am a business man. My business is weapons, drugs, and the like. You are a good paying customer."

"And you owe me one million dollars!" Raquel seemed to remember at that moment.

"Let us table that discussion for another day, Chere," he smiled and then continued.

"Secondly, I have plans to bed you, for you have taken my eye like none other. Beautiful as a thoroughbred and as dangerous as a lioness. It is truly irresistible "

The honesty of his intentions stunned her. Prior to this time, Raquel had always done the choosing, though letting some of her suitors think otherwise. This time a man had taken the pursuit to insane levels of danger for himself. She was anything but piqued by that.

"Well that is not going to happen! Business maybe, but never mix the two! It is a rule I have never broken, and never will!"

"Perhaps. So do we have a deal? Will we travel together, you and I? Will you be my Bonnie?" Tomas laughed that deep rolling Island laugh that he utilized like a surgeon did a scalpel, to cut away disagreement.

What was he doing? he asked himself. *Was this going to cost him his million dollars? Not likely.*

Was it for her beauty? Tomas had seen a handful of women equally as attractive as she while cleaning his boat a few days ago.

They would be less trouble, more easily had and not as dangerous. *What was it?* he wondered. *Ah, I am bored,* he thought.

They discussed immediate plans and finally he took her to her Durango then followed her to her home in the hills. *This is mad,* he thought but took her word for the security.

Once there she went immediately to her new bedroom office. She loaded her laptop, some CDs, a couple of external drives and other materials.

Then to her closet. She was going to miss some of these new clothes. She put Tomas to running refrigerator foods down the garbage disposal. Then she called the realtor she had purchased the home from and asked if they had a rental service. Finding that they did, she requested that a cleaning crew be dispatched.

Her mother in Spain had just passed away and she was required to go there immediately to deal with the estate. It was large and complicated. She would no doubt be gone at least for a year. Maybe more. Would the woman see that the house was cared for, rented to a good renter, and depending on the future, perhaps liquidate it for her? She would contact her later with more details.

She gave the realtor the checking account number to deposit rental fees, determined what was necessary for the maid service, and promised to leave a check on the dining room table for that amount. The realtor could retrieve the back door key from under the potted cactus by the carport.

On the other end the woman shook her head at the rich and thought, *They are different than the rest of us.*

Just before they left the house Tomas said, "Before we leave, there is something we must deal with." He removed a small package from his pocket and handed it to Raquel. Inside was a dental appliance. It was usually sold for novelties with grotesquely formed teeth, or as in this case, not grotesque, but different. They are also used by film and theater make-up artists. Along with the appliance were two tubes of paste. He showed her how to mix the two-part paste and fit it into the appliance.

As it was setting up, she asked, "Why is this necessary?"

"When I watched you on the news, you used your tongue to touch the very attractive chipped tooth in your smile. I watched you do it three times already today. No doubt others will have told the authorities about the gesture as well. Now you will not do that."

She realized with a start that he was certainly right. And so touched it again, nodded and went to the bathroom to fit her new, slightly buck-toothed smile. *At least it isn't bubba-weird or with a gold tooth,* she smiled inwardly.

They would drive in two cars because, said Tomas, in some places people may not take well to one such as he traveling with a woman like Raquel. No need to draw untoward attention.

They went back to his motel where he checked out. Once they were on I-10 headed east, he called the car rental company, advising them that he was extending the rental to be dropped off in Tampa at the airport. They could have cared less. From there they would travel in the Durango.

It was ten o'clock two nights later when they arrived in Key West. He found a parking lot not exactly close, but yet not far from the boat, and they carried his case and hers to the boat. The rest remained in the SUV. Lots of people were about on the boardwalk. The party never ended it seemed at some of the bars along that stretch.

As Raquel stepped up onto the boardwalk a small man of obvious Spanish decent stumbled toward her with a beer bottle in his hand. He slurred his words, "Hello, Conchita. Whass you say we do a leetle loavin'?"

He reached for Raquel's chest with his free hand. She had one foot up on the boardwalk, the other – her left – on the ground. The suitcase was in her right hand, and she dropped it instantly. With her left hand, she grabbed her molester by his belt and simultaneously reached across with her right, grasping his encroaching wrist, and yanked him hard off the boardwalk. Tomas was about ten feet ahead of her, and heard, then saw, the beginning of the altercation. He was turning to help her, when it became obvious he was too late.

Once she had the small man moving, she took his right elbow in her left hand and shoved it very hard. It was easy – either he went with the shove or she dislocated his elbow.

He dropped the beer with a crash of breaking glass, stumbled forward, and went with the flow – out, and downward.

As his heels hit the ground – hard, Raquel swept them out from under him with her right ankle then dropped both knees into his back at the base of his rib cage, bringing his wrist and arm into a very smooth half-Nelson.

"OOOPH!" The air left his lungs as his cheek scraped on the sandy sidewalk, his head snapped back and upward in bloody shock and his glassy eyes went wide.

He was sober enough to know not to move – if he indeed could have. There was a small stainless steel stiletto just barely piercing the skin at his jugular vein and a very angry woman leaning down over him and looking into his eyes from about a foot away.

"You want some more?" she hissed.

Tomas lifted her by the upper left arm, nicking the man's neck with the knife as he changed the angle of it in her hand.

"Chere."

The drunk whimpered, she growled at the intervention, and then realized that Tomas was the only cool head on the dock at that moment.

"All right. Let's go," she said, releasing her captive.

TWELVE

"Dear Most Honorable Sir:
"This humble missive is directed to you as per our instructions and understanding regarding anything we perceive to be of major interest to your efforts.
One of our members has been employed as a clean-up man, also called 'bus-boy' at the Willard Hotel for over two years as of this writing. He is well-versed in the English language as well as French, Arabic and German.
Said young man reported to his leader that the despicable Jew Israeli Yossi Cumi and a very large young man were in residence at the Willard Hotel for a four day period in the very recent history.
On the last evening of their stay they attended a strange meeting. A large round table was established at the rear of the primary restaurant. Only round table ever used at same during clean-up man's working there. The two Jews were met by three other men, one older and two younger. One of the younger looked to be of possible Arabic decent, but could not establish this beyond doubt.
No conversation was to be overheard by clean-up man. When he attempted to discuss the members of the table, Maitre 'de scolded him unreally totally firmly.
Dinner was followed by extended conversation by all attendees, and eventually warm handshakes were shared by all and three left.
The next day, Jew Cumi, whom we determined is the Director of the Israeli Mossad intelligence organization, dined at breakfast with American Secretary of War, Donald Rogers. The two Jews then left the hotel for unknown destination.

“Were this all the information we ascertained, it is likely that we would not have humbly submitted this report, for we are sure others could have done a better and more complete job of informing your worthiness. However, the three men – one older, two younger – who were at dinner with the two Jews from Israel later took up residence at the Willard.
It has been learned that their names are Harold Crabtree, Donald Crabtree and Larry Fielding. These men are known to owner a company called Solutions-dot-com. We are attempting to learn the activity of said enterprise, but have sadly failed to date.
“Said three lived here for an extended stay, then quit the premises. Their conversations during meals were sometimes overheard, and consisted of such topics as pursuit of a woman who apparently killed one of their employees and fled the area; of the sale of a farm they previously occupied; and of a move to another farm in a location known only as Elizabethtown.
We could not confirm that their exit from the Willard was to this Elizabethtown. There is an Elizabethtown in the state of New Jersey and one in Pennsylvania as well as most other States in America.

“Most Honorable Sir, we pray in Allah’s name that this information will prove profitable to your enterprises, and that you will kindly think on us if so. It is our great pleasure to serve you and our cause. It is with utmost regret that this is arriving lately to your notice. Events denied us the ability for more timeliness.

“Respectfully,

Ahmed Aziz”

The encrypted email was sent to Amir. It would reside in that mailbox for three days until retrieved by "Uncle Amir" and read with real interest.

Since the days after the foolish attack in Mecca in the 70's, Amir has served Osama as Chief of Staff, strategist, advisor, and only trusted friend.

He doted on and guided the girl, and now sends loving and kind encrypted emails to the woman. Her activities in northern Virginia were of great concern to him. The idea of killing the messengers sent by her father, and the additional killings of "civilians" worried him beyond words. Her ranting emails bespoke a person reaching the outer edges of reality, and made him want to order her out of America and back to his personal company. That was overruled by Osama.

Willing to sacrifice the child that he numbered among his many progeny, and a female, after all, Osama saw her more as a useful pawn than a beloved child. Amir never let this be known, rather telling her of her father's adoration and pride in her accomplishments.

When she fled, Amir lost touch with her. Their pre-conceived plan was for Raquel to go to the Southwest area of the United States, but even he was not privy to the details.

There would be no leaks. She would log onto the internet someday, locate the website established to communicate with her. In this case, one selling saffron, cooking ingredients and kitchen utensils. She would initiate an order and leave her message in an encrypted email. The order would never be filled, and the email would be decrypted by Uncle Amir then he and Osama would know Raquel's location and condition.

They would begin the new plan to undermine America. Amir was already moving people into position just as a chess master begins an attack before the queen ever initiates movement.

This current email was interesting to Amir. He had read all the news reports of Raquel's attack on her neighbors. Rumors said they were a high-priced security company serving the ultra-rich in America. This news of a meeting with the head of Mossad, however, shed new light on their activities. *Had they been working for Israel? For the American's? Both perhaps? And did such men really have the audacity to locate their offices right beside Raquel's own office? Amazing?*

Had she deduced she was nearing capture and initiated a pre-emptive strike to enable her escape? Amir shook his head in admiration, if that were so. He smiled and felt his heart also wither just a bit at the danger – she would likely call it excitement – that his beloved niece was experiencing. *Where are you, girl?* he asked himself as he began to copy the email and add it to the text of his own.

This one would await Raquel's contact then go out immediately.

> "Dear Raquel,
> I have followed your exploits in Northern Virginia with great interest. I pray this finds you well and comforted from your travels and travails. Your father sends his love and admiration for a true jihad warrior. He is well pleased and proud of you.
> It seems the people whose offices were beside yours – the ones you attacked when leaving Manassas – are more than even you may have known.
> Below is the text of a report I received through channels from a cell in Washington, D.C. I know you will find it interesting.
> Also, we are searching for the location of their new farm. Why, Niece, would they need a farm, do you think? At any rate, when we find this place, it is possible that we will take the jihad to them once more.
> You need not trouble yourself with such activity. We have many who will be gratified to receive such orders. I will keep you informed.
> Now, to other matters: I recall that you had an interest in sending out teams of riflemen for the purpose of killing well-known American Jews. The great singers, musicians and politicians you said. I have a suggestion. (Raquel would know that this statement was, in fact, an order from her father.)
> The shooting of American Jews is fine, but let's refine it and in so doing accomplish more terror, more for our cause world-wide, and well, more personal satisfaction. I have ordered people for this next mission, and will keep you advised."

Amir's email continued for four more pages. He gave concrete details on a plan he and Osama had worked diligently to polish. Contacts had been made. Arrangements for travel and funding of others who would be involved were in the works.

All that awaited was Raquel's tapping into the website and letting them know she was again operative. Amir saved his work, transmitted it, and turned to other activities. He was again in Beirut, a city that was indeed schizophrenic in light of its first becoming a

Phoenix, rising from the ashes of virtual destruction, and then a second visit of destruction by the Israelis.

Beirut was alive. New, modern hotels were alive with activity. The curving white sand beach was again pristine and filled with sun worshippers. The markets had fresh food and vegetables and customers bustled as in the old days when Beirut was known as the Paris of the Middle East and the wealthy flocked there from all over the world.

Bashar has pulled his soldiers back to Syria. Life could be good here, if Nasrallah would only calm down, Amir thought as he sat on the wide window ledge enjoying the morning sunshine and watching the street below with its swirling traffic and pedestrians in western and traditional Arab garb.

That was when he heard and felt the rumble south of him, and then saw the oily black smoke rise into the beautiful clear blue sky. *Well, perhaps Beirut was only partially repentant,* he thought ruefully, as he peeled a ripe orange, tossing the peels down onto the street below.

Hezbollah will be the destruction of this nation or I will be shocked.

THIRTEEN

Maxine was frustrated. The equipment she wanted was held up, the last telephone message had said.

That day the shooters arrived.

She assembled her troops the next morning. Alex took off for the gun stores in and around Harrisburg to put together three rifles, ammo, scopes and spotting scopes. He returned by mid-afternoon.

"How many of you have any sniper experience?" Maxine asked the four men and two women. She was pleasantly surprised when all six raised their hands.

"How many in the American military?" Two hands. Both men on one team.

"How much training?"

Howard was tall and thin. From Brooklyn by his accent. He was dark skinned, almost Negroid in his features, and with angry, brooding eyes that always looked like he'd seen way too much of the world and been disappointed by it all. He spoke with a reedy voice that sounded like it should be coming from a scrawny Italian.

"Well, ya know, Gerold and me went through the school together. We flunked out for smoking some weed, but it wasn't our fault. The sergeant hated us 'cause we was 'darkies,' as he called us.

"We got kicked out, but we're still good! We've done some missions since," he grinned at Gerold, who nodded affirmatively and looked at Maxine like he wanted her to pat his head. These two were not impressing her. She decided to move on and later see how they did with weapons.

"In some other army?" Two more hands. The other two men.

"Training, or actual military sniper experience?" she asked.

"We got sixteen kills," the one named Miguel said proudly, not really answering the question.

Medium height, a burr haircut, and swarthy complexion. He looked sixteen, pimples and all, but with the nasty streak associated with Tijuana pimps and switchblade knives. He was leaking "macho" from every pore. He didn't like Maxine and it showed.

His partner was short, stocky, and pleasant looking. He kept squeezing a tennis ball, Maxine guessed to pump up his arm muscles. She had no idea which was the shooter here. They sounded Mexican to her, not Brazilian but that was what they claimed, so that was that.

The other one, Juan, offered, "That's sixteen *confirmed* kills. We prob'ly nicked as many that got away into the jungle. We was hunting *insurgentos*. Only got paid for the heads we turned in."

Their *compadres* – the other two teams – in unison snapped their heads around to stare at Juan and Miguel. Cashiering heads for payment was a bit much even for them.

She looked at the women and said, "Ladies, How 'bout you?"

The medium-sized woman, about thirty with brown frizzy hair, dark eyes and pouty lips answered for them both. "We worked for some Italian businessmen outta Long Island, Hon. One of their organization guys trained us both.

"I shoot, Roxanne spots. And before you ask, Hon, we got six kills. Six shots, six kills. All on the left coast," she smiled a cocky grin, amused at her own cuteness.

"And how many of you are aware of who you are working for?" inside her head Maxine was amazed at this mix of shooters. *Where did they find these guys – whoever "they" are?*

The six all looked at each other like this was a game show and no one wanted to answer first. Finally Roxanne took a chance. "Hon, we don't care who we're working for!

"Why's it important? They paid us to be here. When you set up the target, we go get it. You pay us more. Honey, we don't give a rat's tail who we hit, who pays; only that we do hit the target and that the check clears." She grinned at her shooter, Adele, who nodded. *Well done, Kid.*

The four men nodded agreement. Get on with it.

Maxine would have preferred real jihad believers. Still, she had learned that all was not as it seemed in Al Qaeda. The organizations and their people she had so far brushed up against in various countries held a wide degree of fervor. Alas, many were just stone killers who liked the pay and cover of having a cause célèbre. If this bunch could shoot, then she would do her job and leave it at that. She was actually disappointed that she was not going on a mission herself.

The next day the teams worked on the rifles. There were two used Winchester Model 70s and a new Savage 110 – 30-06s and a 308. Four to twelve power scopes and three different kinds of spotting scopes completed the equipment. Alex had brought six boxes of ammo for each gun – one hundred twenty rounds each.

They stripped and cleaned the rifles. Next they sighted them in for two hundred yards. That took a bit of work, because they had not all been well cared for.

Finally, on the range Maxine had each team shooting at three hundred yards. The shots were all in center-body-mass, but she would have to cover them with a basketball, not a tennis ball.

She saw that all three teams had not been well chosen. They each worked well as teams, the spotter calling hits; the shooters familiar with rifles and scopes. They were just not going to be able to go up against any serious security on high-profile targets and make an escape. She had to admit that better equipment would make for a better result, but this was not equipment. It was professionalism that was her main concern.

Sure, they could take a dope dealer out from an upstairs window across the street. Everybody nearby would dive for cover. Not so with high profile hits. Their security came after you before the echo died.

At the beginning of the second day, Miguel looked at his scope and scowled. "Maxine, this scope's for junk! How 'bout I get our gear outta the trunk and use that?"

Maxine stood stock still. How stupid of her not to ask about their own gear?! She wanted to walk over to the nearest oak tree and bang her forehead against it until the tree fell over. *Speaking of unprofessional!*

"How many of you brought your own stuff?" she asked looking around. Part of her wanted to shoot them all for not volunteering that fact when six hands were lifted and six heads nodded.

"Go get it," she said resignedly, with a long drawn-out breath. "Hurry up."

The shooting improved remarkably, calls, hits and a drop in excuses too. She would have to do some classroom time to see about their mental abilities, but she wasn't holding high hopes in that area either.

They worked for ten straight days. Rain and shine. On one day, lying on the bank with their feet in the creek for three hours until they got the command to take out their target – a water melon hidden in a weed pile at two hundred yards. The women had a six foot black snake crawl lazily over their sandbags, glide silently beside the shooter and then slip silently into the creek and away.

Neither of them moved, though the spotter looked like she would pop both eyes out of her head. The shooter smiled and kept her mind on the task at hand, repeatedly and soothingly muttering, "Be cool, Hon."

They were the superior team of the three, Maxine decided, when she tallied her work reports.

The last night they had a little cookout with steaks Alex grilled on an old charcoal grill. Maxine praised them and away they went. Report back to the people who sent you to us. Wait for the call. It will come. Just be ready. Speak to no one.

Maxine was ready to return to El Paso the next morning when Alex's cell phone rang. He answered it, listened a moment, and handed it to her.

A soft, Middle Eastern voice asked, "Have you been to Iraq since we were last there together?"

Her heart stopped, and then leaped into her throat. How many lifetimes had it been since she'd heard that voice?

"No, and this would not be a wise time for such travels, I believe," she answered with longing in her voice. This man she loved. Not just as a woman loves a man, but as a soldier who has found that special calling in life loves her recruiter and most professional trainer.

"I agree, though there are many of us there, and we are scoring, if you watch the news. You have been ordered to stay in the area. Find a hotel and go sightseeing.

"How were the shooters?" he asked with genuine concern for her rather than them.

"They were dismal. Do not send them after anyone important. Perhaps back country policemen. Never let them be captured. They can shoot, but they are primarily stupid. They are not believers and profess to be ignorant of who pays them. I doubt that too."

"When I studied the files on them, I reached the same conclusion," he agreed. "And the man, Alex?"

Maxine did not look around so as not to give away the subject of her answer. "Adequate, I suppose. I cannot really tell."

"All right. I will take this into consideration. It is likely we will sacrifice these six to mislead the authorities. Either there will be better ones coming or perhaps you will be called upon to work your magic. Be patient.

"You should find an apartment nearby. Move from the farm. Tell Alex that you are going to Canada. I want you safe. Give me your cell phone number."

Maxine provided it, then hopefully asked, "Can I see you?"

"Not at this time. I am nowhere near. Let me speak with him."

"I understand. Goodbye." Sad. Her life was lonely and sad. She handed the telephone to Alex.

"Alex."

"Maxine is a special person. I would not be pleased if she is captured. Under no circumstances should you cause her any discomfort. But, alas, we cannot allow her to survive if she is about to be captured. Do I make myself clear? She will be moving to the city near you. Follow her and give me the address when next I contact you."

"Yes sir. I understand," Alex said, with the same distant look Maxine had used when speaking of him. She noted it and wondered what her mentor had said about her.

"Goodbye." The phone was dead.

Maxine moved out that afternoon, found an apartment in downtown Harrisburg, and went to tour Chocolate World. Each day she ran the lovely trail along the Susquehanna, watched television news, and walked the streets of Harrisburg, enjoying the beautiful weather and scenery.

What a place. So open! They are totally vulnerable. A warm and friendly people. Why must we make war on them? she wondered often, then chastened herself for such seditious thoughts.

FOURTEEN

Raquel ran up the beach, sweat pouring from every pore. Her shoulder length now-brown hair was stuck wetly to her neck and cheeks. Her full figure, tanned a golden bronze, grabbed the attention of every man she passed. Of course they soon moved on to the next beauty to come by. There is no shortage of lovely women on this island.

At the Route 1 marker on the southwest end of the island she slowed to a walk and cooled down, laughing at some of the graffiti scrawled on the thing. Her apartment was near mid town and she would take her time getting there.

Once home, she showered long and luxuriously. With her hair still damp and tied back, she sipped a strawberry yogurt smoothie and clicked her computer mouse, opening and reading emails. She'd been in Key West only two weeks, but the flood of correspondence was already staggering. She was again in the game. Uncle Amir had written three times. *Well, he's missed me,* she thought gratefully.

The information coming in on Elizabethtown, Pennsylvania was interesting. *So the hunks next door were really after me*, she'd thought when she read about them. She was glad her hunch had been more than validated. And tied to Israel?! *How did they get on to me in Manassas?* she wondered.

"I need more information on this Solutions.com bunch," she'd stressed to Uncle Amir.

Even more interesting to Raquel was the idea of the sniper teams. They'd been in some of the correspondence from a couple of years ago, but she had not really focused on them. The kill ratio to time necessary had seemed so small compared to what she was doing with the rednecks. When Amir jogged her memory, though, she'd immediately written back requesting permission to take over the entire operation. There had already been two hits, another was planned, and more were in the system.

His response was just as quick. Names, telephone numbers – even two email addresses – were provided, along with access to another bank account if she required it. Raquel was ecstatic! She loved making war!

"Tomas, I may need some equipment. Soon! Are you still in business or just lying in the sun?" Raquel played with her glass of raspberry tea, using the bottom dampness to form interconnected circles like an Audi emblem. They were sitting at an outdoor restaurant on the docks. Not fifty feet away rose the sheer white cliff of a cruise ship. Blue skies dotted by puffy clouds and caressing breezes stirred the hair of ladies as they walked by to see and be seen. Tourists strolled, strode and ran outside the white picket fence around the dining area, jabbering about their next stop. Each time a camera pointed in their direction both diners adeptly turned away or casually raised a blocking hand.

"Chere, of course I'm in business! Anything you desire – short of Russian anti-aircraft missiles. That is a business attracting too much attention currently."

Tomas was bored. He missed his daily business, his servile bodyguards stepping and fetching. Too, he missed the fear he generated with a scowl – even a raised eyebrow. Power. He'd been a powerful man and it was an addiction not easily laid aside. Now, in this place, he was just one rich brown man among many.

He watched an attractive brunette. "I wonder if I snatched her, and took her for a boat ride if it would be worth it, Chere?"

Raquel looked at him in amazement. "You're thinking of kidnapping a woman when this place is full of available ones?! Are you mad?!"

"Take care, Chere. We are friends, but do not speak so to me." His face remained placid, but there was death in the eyes. Raquel noted it, filed it, but showed no fear of her own.

"As for madness, what of one who shoots men outside of bars for entertainment? Is that not madness?" He smiled, turning his eyes to neighboring tables to watch for eavesdroppers.

Raquel was stunned. *How had he learned that?!* She *had* momentarily forgotten that this laid-back man with the sweet Island speech was as dangerous as a jungle krait. *Willowy and smooth, but poisonous and quick as a cobra.*

"I may need to gather some implements of the trade and have it delivered to Harrisburg, Pennsylvania."

As she said it a bell suddenly sounded loudly in her mind. *Harrisburg. ELIZABETHTOWN!! Could those men of Solutions somehow have learned about the training camp near them? Why else would they have gone there? I wondered why they wanted a farm? Is it connected to the fact that our people are on a farm?*

"Come back, Chere," Tomas was tapping her hand with a forefinger.

"Sorry." *I've apologized to him. I mustn't let him feel he's superior.*

"You can take the cost of the items from the million dollars you owe me," she said with a cold smile.

Standing at a food counter watching them, their waitress thought, *They smile, but not with their eyes. There is lightning crashing between them, but it is not love. They look like two gators meetin' on a mud bank measuring each other.*

"Chere, your last order left my control complete. Its loss coincided with your own operational collapse. Who can say it was not caused by your own hand? And it was me, you recall, who warned you of clouds on the horizon," he smiled and pointed toward clouds to their west.

As Raquel drew herself up to remonstrate, he raised a restraining hand. "Nevertheless, if you need something I will indeed halve the cost. You make a deposit to this account, he wrote a series of numbers and letters on a slip of paper, "and delivery can be made within ten days. I'll give the amount when you provide the list."

They soon finished their drinks and parted; she for some downtown shopping. He walked back along the docks, past the parking lot and toward more watering holes for tourists and locals alike. *This girl is a killing machine. More Americans are going to die. Watch the news. Film at eleven*, he smiled.

Suddenly he turned the wattage up and directed a dazzling tooth-filled look with lustful encouragement at a red haired vixen in skimpy shorts and halter. *Almost as good looking as Raquel*, he thought. She returned the steamy look, invitation for invitation, and Tomas said in his best basso-profundo, "My, my, what an orchid you are, my dear."

"Oh, I love your accent!" the girl responded giddily and stepped close. "Are you just visiting or do you live here?"

"Looking, Chere. Only looking."

"At me? Or at what?"

"Looking to see if I want to live here. Right now I live on my yacht.

"Say," he smiled a more seductive smile. "Would you like to join me for a noonday orange juice – and maybe an afternoon nap? I always take a siesta, you know." He said it jovially as a self-protective means in case the red-head rejected his invitation.

They moved off hand in hand through the foot traffic toward the Hatteras.

In a blue mini-van the ugliest couple in the world watched through binoculars. Her hair was a combination of the yellow in rancid margarine streaked with the dirty brown of wet sand along the banks of the Love Canal. There was no combination to it, just a ratty intermingling and intertwining of dirty strands. It appeared that it hadn't seen a comb, brush or shampoo since she was ten and she was now old enough to have voted in two presidential elections. Her whole face and neck were pockmarked like she'd had terrible acne at one time and used the round part of a hair pin to press the pus from every infected pore, leaving cratered scars. In high school, taunters said her face had caught fire and someone used track spikes to slap out the flames.

Her eyes were watery-looking blue with a spray of arterial veins in the corners. The bodice of her wrinkled blue velour dress was as flat as a run-over plum, and she was as listless as slave labor.

The boy with her looked young enough to be her son. He had a copper hog ring stuck in the flesh between his nostrils. The one-eighth inch thick brass kind farmers squeeze into the snouts of swine to keep them from rooting up the ground. Maybe it was some kind of an identity thing. If so, it was working. His identity was now perfect. Filthy swine.

He was about five feet six with scrawny shoulders that bowed forward – what your mother called a slump. This was a major tuberculosis-class slump. Ugly swollen red pustules drained clear and yellow seepage across his cheeks, nose and forehead. He constantly used dirty fingernails to scrape the yellowed skin off any acne sores that didn't burst on their own. Sandals that dated back to John the Baptist, with feet the same shade of grayish-brown as the straps, and a sagging, below-the-belt potbelly that looked like he'd had a soccer ball transplant. He was quite a specimen.

Actually twenty-seven years old, he had seen a hundred years of bad living, and his aura was as wasted as his karma. There *was* no *chi*. The mini-van was far too nice to fit these two, but this was a rush job.

"She's got him!" the mousy blonde haired girl said to the pimple faced driver. "That Tonya could talk the Lone Ranger into shooting Tonto!" she whined jealously.

Her partner laughed and nodded his head, then pulled the van right onto Simonton Street. The girl picked up a walkie talkie and began speaking into it.

"Cheryl" – she insisted it was "kismet" that Tomas had called her "Chere" right off the bat – would take residence aboard the yacht two days later. She could cook both Creole and Cajun style like a native – said she'd attended Paul Prudhomme's classes in New York City. It wasn't the only way to Tomas' heart, but neither was Cheryl without a multitude of charms. They would both be very happy.

At the corner of the plaza in front of the cruise ship, Raquel stood in the shade watching everything. Cheryl's "surprise" encounter. The people in the van watching through binoculars. Tomas stretching himself like a fool rooster waiting for the axe.

She felt the familiar stirring in her chest when she was facing danger. It was familiar, friendly and yet stirred an alarm that drove her home to pack yet again. This time the Durango would stay in Key West. *THAT STUPID TOMAS! I SHOULD KILL HIM MYSELF!*

Certainly he'd served her well, but he was a danger. *How had he been caught so quickly?* She did not know about the stopover in Ft. Myers and his "friend" the boat painter. That cretin was sure that trading Tomas for preferred treatment by the Feds would benefit him. Tomas' gift of C4 had blown his carefully crafted cover.

There was work to be done. Raquel was busy at her apartment tapping into her network. Intelligence agents were re-activated. Moles began to send in reports to email addresses long slumbering. She asked for specific dates, travel arrangements of certain people. Their public appearances, homes, working hours. She began to amass the enormous amounts of data from which she formed her exquisite plans of destruction. This time the number of deaths would not be in the thousands but the impact would be as shocking. Buildings would not fall, but giants would.

Then she packed a bag, sent a final email to Uncle Amir through the secure internet connection, and rented a car to be dropped at the Miami airport. Carrying personal weapons was not appreciated by TSA. When she was able to replace them, she'd dump these since their history would blare the fact she was back.

At Miami International Raquel turned in the rental and grabbed a taxi to North Miami Beach. There at a Ford dealer she bought a 2005 Saab Linear for seventeen thousand dollars cash. The salesman was sure to remember her with the copper-red hair, skimpy clothes and wrap-around shades. Just another bimbo connected with the Colombians out for new wheels.

From there she drove across Florida on the Gator highway, I-75 to Naples where she rented a hotel room.

She dumped the wig, trampy-looking clothes and shades into a trash can. Slept until two AM then headed north. At Ft. Myers she got off at a truck stop, visited the ladies room, bought a giant cappuccino and returned to the highway.

Raquel's new look was such that even her friends would not recognize her. She'd reinserted the upper plate that gave her a noticeable overbite, now had plain brown hair done in a short, modern cut. Loose fitting clothes that effectively masked her great figure and aviator shades to let everyone know she was just a bit unaware of new styles. She was the every day housewife, right down to the plain gold ring on her left hand.

Interstate 75 took her from one Flying J to the next as she headed north. Ocala, Valdosta, Georgia, then Macon where she got a room and slept for twelve hours. Atlanta, Dalton. Chattanooga, and Knoxville where she picked up I-40 east and more hours of sleep. She stopped at the Pigeon Forge exit. After a big breakfast at the Perkins, she drove to the Cabelas. In the parking lot she used a throw away cell phone to call a local number.

Fifteen minutes later she had directions and drove toward Pigeon Forge. Just before entering the town, she turned right and passed over a small stream. A stone crusher and cement works on the left was closed. She drove into the parking lot. Walked to the bathrooms situated in a separate building behind the office. Inside was a Cordura gym bag. She picked it up, placed twenty one hundred dollar bills inside the towel holder and returned to the Perkins parking lot just off I-40.

There she inspected her new bag. Careful to keep everything below window level, she laid it out on the seat beside her. A Glock 27 in 40 S&W with two extra magazines and a box of Federal ammo. A Spyderco flip open knife with a 4 ¾ inch blade. A Ruger Mk II, 22 caliber pistol with two extra magazines and a box of 100 Hornet extra-high velocity ammo. *And now I have stingers,* she smiled to herself, and then repacked the items carefully wrapping them in the towel they had come in.

Further east she turned north on I-81. Roanoke was her stop that evening. Near the airport she found a Golden Corral buffet and put a dent in their profit margin. The next morning at sunrise she dined at the K&W Cafeteria seated beside a covey of Baptist preachers.

At Front Royal she diverted onto Rt. 66 and headed for Manassas. It was fully dark when she drove down Rt. 234 toward town. The KFC provided her some chicken and coleslaw. *The old boy was right. The spuds taste like wallpaper paste.* Once she'd eaten her fill and then some, she drove on until she was at the ruins of her former office building. No one had done more than clean up the debris. The neighboring building now sported a real estate sign.

She pulled on a pair of gloves, grabbed a hand trowel she'd bought at Lowes in Roanoke and walked to the rear of her property. Back into the weeds there rose a single three foot piece of half-inch rebar, that kind of steel rod used to strengthen concrete.

Raquel knelt and began to dig around it. When she had gone about ten inches into the rocky red soil the trowel clinked on something. Quickly finishing the digging, she lifted a handle and tugged a cylindrical aluminum box about ten inches wide and that long from the soil.

Brushing it off, she held it up to the dim lights from the buildings behind her. The seal seemed intact. She wrapped it in a piece of newspaper and returned to the Saab.

An hour later she was in a hotel room in Leesburg, Virginia.

The box she'd dug up sat on the counter. All the dirt was washed off, leaving red bits of sand and soil still in the bottom of the sink.

Using a nail file to pry a flap up Raquel spun the dials beneath it until they agreed with the code she had two years ago programmed. There was a whooshing sound as a vacuum was released from a hidden vent. Now she spun the top off the box and looked inside.

"And my farmer friends, I will give you a few surprises with this, no doubt," she whispered as she smiled and lifted the contents onto the counter beside the box. C4, a detonator and three blasting caps.

Raquel didn't know it but they would never explode.

FIFTEEN

Jake and Larry moved to the office to discuss weapons acquisition and scheduling with Flight Safety. Harold left the house and began his rounds of the construction site. Life was moving faster than anything he had yet experienced. From teaching in a sleepy Illinois college to being Chairman of a billion dollar multi-national corporation – corporations actually – he mentally corrected himself. Not to mention being the intel officer for a spy outfit.

Zulu Holdings, Ltd. was a conglomerate built by the late Kurt Mullenberg, a South African businessman. Near the point of his death he had contacted Israeli Mossad Director Yossi Cumi and explained that he had decided to turn over the nearly one billion dollar (U.S.) annual business to the men of Solutions.com.

Using the assets developed annually by the corporations they could pursue freedom's enemies without political considerations or limitations. Being a devout Zionist, Mullenberg had indicated that targets should particularly include any of Israel's enemies.

Stunned, pleased and able to see significant benefits to his own organization, Cumi had flown to America and presented the idea at a sumptuous dinner at the Willard Hotel in Washington. Not surprisingly, all the others had responded with shock, but curiously without doubts. They were men of action, confident in their ability to adjust to about any circumstances and wanted to be in the hunt without considerations always tied to government operations.

Cumi had returned to Israel and then to South Africa to coordinate the details with Mullenberg's people. Kurt Mullenberg's death had reverberated throughout Africa and the entire diamond world. Mullenberg was second only to DeBeers. Leviev was a distant third. His holdings were managed, by pre-arranged decree, through men and women who had proven themselves loyal and trustworthy over the years. The profits would reward the employees, educate their children and grandchildren, support many of South Africa's natural parks and ecosystems, and – here the river of wealth turned underground – provide for the Mullenberg Company's intelligence network, which would secretly be run by none other than Yossi Cumi. Said network would provide valuable and timely information for every Mullenberg company, with a slice for Israel, of course.

Zulu Holdings, Ltd. headquartered in Zurich, Switzerland had a new owner. That being said, nothing would change at the corporation level. Yossi would deftly insert certain expert individuals who would oversee the management for him and for Solutions, whose international offices would be in the Zulu-owned building. One more piece of the conglomerate. Most outsiders or insiders would never suspect that this piece owned the larger.

The principles of the team somehow now had legitimate dual citizenship. They already had their Swiss diplomatic passports. Yossi had argued long and hard for this strange move with the Americans, finally won, then had done some absolutely legitimate deal of untold value with the Swiss government for the courtesy. Additionally Mossad would produce many other false identifications for the team's members.

Mullenberg had been planning this move for well over a decade. He did not know who the principals would be until Jake and Larry popped onto his radar during a combat operation in Israel when his only surviving male relative – an Israeli officer – was killed. Jake and Larry had taken command of the situation. The report reached Karl and the rest was, as they say, history.

Now Harold was Chairman of the Board, Jake, President, Larry and Ehud were Directors. Yossi Cumi was a very special sub rosa advisor. Executive Vice Presidents would handle day-to-day management. Privately held corporations had benefits that publicly traded businesses lacked.

Harold was currently tasked with overseeing the construction on both the farm and offices. Many changes were taking place, but most were not evident to the Elizabethtown neighbors. Some were electronic, some on a comfort level. One of the major ones as far as Jake and their pilot, Tex were concerned was the acquisition of a new Gulfstream G V.

The farm was becoming home. Harold had missed his Illinois farm while they were in Virginia. As he turned toward the stable, he was greeted by George Allen.

If anyone has bloomed, it's George, thought Harold. Living in someone's crosshairs had been part of his life from age nineteen. He was older than Harold with thinning gray hair and deep facial lines.

George was soft-spoken, but had lived a very difficult life. That life had hardened his resolve, but not his heart. He walked quiet as a cougar, had a slump-shouldered gait that fit the faded blue bib overalls he always wore. Clod-hopper shoes, a straw cowboy hat and a short sleeved light blue cotton shirt completed the picture. He looked as innocuous as could be. The custom Kimber 45 always in condition one[3], inside the bib overalls would have stunned most of the people in

---

[3] Condition one means a round is in the chamber, the hammer is cocked and the safety is on. This is <u>not</u> a practice for novices. Credit gun expert Jeff Cooper for "condition" numbers.

Elizabethtown. Harold chuckled as he thought, *Especially the old timers at the feed store.*

George, too, loved the hilltop farm. Yes, the horses were nags, but they were easy going and daily he saddled one of them and rode over the farm, noting the condition of fence rows, ground hog holes, and the readiness of berries, bird nests, white tail population and the alfalfa crop. Occasionally Helen rode with him, and they could be seen holding hands while watching a brilliant red sunset over the distant Susquehanna River.

"It's coming along fast, Harold," George said, nodding to the construction site where the rec center was being built. "How long do you figure until it's complete?"

Harold turned back to the job site, "The foreman says about six weeks. The big stuff will finish up in a couple of weeks then the bulletproof glass people, plumbers, electricians, and all the rest will pounce on us like Attila and his Huns."

"I need for you to come to the barn with me," George said, with a strange inflection in his voice. Harold turned to look into ice cold blue eyes that reminded him that this man was more than just a farmer. Without a word they turned as one and walked at an even pace toward the two story white barn/stable.

Once inside, George walked to the vertical ladder leading up to the hayloft. As he reached it, from a nail driven into one of the upright poles he snagged a pair of binoculars in a beat-up brown leather case and carried them aloft with him. Harold followed immediately, though the ladder was more difficult for him than he liked to admit as a result of the plane crash injury from years gone by.

George walked to the north end of the dimly lit loft picking his way through bales of hay. He gently pushed a door intended to allow hay bales to be sent to the loft on a metal farm elevator open a crack. George liked to stand and gaze at the distant valley watching for deer, Canadian geese and airplanes on final approach into Harrisburg International from here. Earlier he had caught something that raised the hair on the back of his neck.

"There, along Hess road. The dirty white van." He handed Harold the glasses, and stepped back to allow him a clearer view.

Harold moved forward, focused the binoculars on the van and experienced a sense of warning similar to that George had felt. Parked alongside the road, a bumper jack on the back lifting the van a few inches off the right rear tire, it looked like a break down. Until one looked at the side door. It was only open a foot or so, but the morning sun was reflected off of a telescopic lens. It was focused on their farm. A passenger in the front right seat was turned toward the inside rear of the van like he was talking to someone.

"How long's it been there?" Harold asked, trying to keep his voice level, and not seem too concerned. It might be a very innocent breakdown. He just didn't think so.

"Don't know. I came up here at daylight. Been watching a doe with two yearlings. Hoping they survive the hunting season this year. They come up from that draw below the van. It was there at first light. Door open just like it is now. No one was in the front seat then.

"I watched them for an hour, went out and did some chores, came back and they was still there. What do you think?"

"I don't know, George. The odds on anyone besides nosey neighbors paying us any attention are pretty thin. All the construction and cars in and out will get them wondering, but we've visited with some of them, and they seem okay with us.

"Most prefer us to the previous owner," George chuckled.

Harold backed further into the barn and handed the glasses to George. He had been very careful to stay away from any light that would have signaled his presence to the van's occupants.

"Want me to drive over and offer them some help?" George wasn't looking for any "action" but he wasn't running from it either. Harold lifted an eyebrow and George smiled. "I wasn't planning to ask Helen to go with me," he said, knowing what kind of reaction that would earn him.

"Now that we know they're there we'll keep an eye on them. I met the Regional Police Lieutenant the first week we were here. Former Marine. Has three like him on the force. Nice fellow. I indirectly briefed him that we were a security company, worked with intelligence systems some.

"I gave him all our backgrounds, and he grinned and said, 'Rent-a-cops you ain't, Mr. Crabtree.' I shrugged and left it at that. He was the one kind enough to get us all memberships to the local gun range just down the road.

"Maybe if the van is there in a couple of hours we'll call him and ask him to check them out."

"Good enough. Well, I got work to do. Thanks," George said, closed and hooked the door, then descended the ladder and went outside. Harold followed and returned to the house.

Entering, he poured a cup of coffee then walked to the formal dining room which had been converted to an office/meeting room for the team. A long oak table similar to the one in the kitchen, but with comfortable rolling executive chairs dominated the large room. There was a desk with computer, phone, fax-scanner-printer and filing cabinet near the large windows. A satellite phone rested on the desk beside the computer. Two smaller desks were on opposite sides of the room with laptop computers on each. He didn't know where Jake and Larry had gone.

Harold began a list.

1. Schedule training in Israel and see about Zulu Board Mtg. in Zurich on same trip.
2. Have weapons room secured with vault door and frame next week.
3. Check on dates for Jake and Tex to be in Savannah at Flight Systems.

He had just put the pencil between his teeth in concentration when there was a loud BAROOM! outside the window where he sat.

Suddenly Harold found himself on the floor. Outside he could hear shouts and cheering. Sheepishly looking around to see if anyone had seen him take his dive and being relieved that it seemed they had not he rose and walked quickly outside. Near the Grove crane stood a construction worker with a bolt action rifle in his right hand.

He was grinning widely and watching another worker run over to the tree line about a hundred yards distant. Harold too watched. When the man reached the trees, he stooped and lifted the bloody carcass of a ground hog into the air. The construction men cheered again. The rifleman turned toward them, carefully kept the bore pointed safely upward and took a deep bow.

Harold walked toward the back door. He remembered that George mentioned giving them permission to kill hogs in that area of the farm. His heartbeat was now almost back to normal. Before entering he walked to the corner of the house and glanced toward the parked van. There were two men trotting toward it from Black Swamp Road. He smiled. *Didn't like the gun fire, eh, boys?*

In the kitchen, Jake and Larry were draining the remains of a gallon jug of milk into two glasses, and grinning conspiratorially.

"What's up, Dad? Did you wet yourself a bit when that ole boy lit up the .270 out there?" Jake asked.

Before Harold could answer, Larry crowed, "Man I hit the deck so fast I almost went through it!! I forgot all about those hammer swingers shooting hogs. Whew! I think they should ring a bell or something before they blaze away again." He laughed self deprecatingly and both men looked at Harold.

"You hit the deck, didn't you?" Jake smothering a laugh.

"What makes you think so?" These two would give no quarter. Especially since Larry had also taken a dive.

They bantered back and forth then walked into the office. Harold informed them about the white van. The younger men had been roaming around without any sidearms since coming to the farm. It looked like today would change that.

All three had seen the cartoon of the deer hunter squatting in the woods with his rifle leaning against a distant tree while a large buck stood nearby. They didn't plan on such a thing happening to them. A favorite saying of all three was, "Even paranoids have people out to get them."

Returning to the "To Do" list, Harold covered the initial points, and the three added the following:

4. Larry and George work up armorer tools and supplies.
5. Check with Elvis on equipment for HQ. See to final install at his shop.
6. Sarah co-ordinate final installation in her shop.
7. Harold – plan final move from Illinois. (He would turn the care of his small farm in Illinois to his friend Melvin Barrow, oversee the movers loading his personal items, then secure the place.)
    a. Tex fly me out; I'll drive my Explorer back.
8. Begin search for Analyst and for G-V pilot. Ask Miss Frances for help. (Mrs. Frances Huffman was Sec. of War Don Rogers' personal secretary).
9. Give George go ahead on buying chest freezer, half beef and whole hog from Groff's in Elizabethtown.

Midnight in Harrisburg.

At Sixth and Maclay, a dirty white van with a dent in the left rear corner panel sat waiting for the light to change. Once it went green, the van proceeded on toward the river. Before it reached the Governor's Mansion it turned onto Orange Street and pulled to the curb. A dark-complexioned man with an unruly mop of hair stepped out and stood at the corner. A woman silently moved from the shadows and approached him.

"Lookin' for a good time, my man?" she asked in a sultry voice.

"I'm looking for paradise," he responded.

"Follow me," she said and walked down Maclay toward the river. He walked behind her a few feet, looking to the left and right, feeling exposed and vulnerable. He did not know this city but the neighborhood looked like somebody could get cut here if he wasn't real careful.

The woman disappeared, and the man, not paying close attention to her, stopped abruptly and looked all around.

From an alleyway between two buildings, she whispered, “Come on, Braveheart!”

He jumped at the sound of her voice right behind him then followed her deeper into the darkness.

“Well?” she asked, one hand on a plump hip.

“We watched them from daylight til mid-morning. Then there were shots fired and we took off!”

“They shot at you!?” the woman asked, the whites of her now wide eyes reflecting the street lights of Maclay.

“We don’t know where the bullet went. But when the gun went off, so did we.” The man told it simply. “We didn’t take the job to get shot at.”

“Did the bullet hit the van? Did it kick up dirt near you? Do you even know for certain it was a gunshot?” This broad was asking questions a man doesn’t like to have a woman quiz him about. Especially with that tone of voice!

“YOU GO WATCH THEM NEXT TIME!” he shouted, then caught himself. “Sorry,” he said quickly in a hushed voice when it looked like she was going to stab him for terminal stupidity.

“We paid you to get information on them. Get it. Don’t call me again until you know their pattern, how many there are, and everything else you’re supposed to learn. Now get out of here.” She turned and walked away like he had already disappeared.

The man was furious. At himself for looking like a fool. At her for noticing. He stomped back to the van, climbed in, and it drove away, headed to Perry Country.

SIXTEEN

He came calling one morning about a month after the headquarters was up and running. Just walked up to the gate and told the former Uniformed White House Secret Service man that he wanted to speak to Mr. Crabtree. A quiet man. Small, formal as an organ grinder and including the moustache, but there the similarity stopped. He was not at all obsequious and he spoke with a cultured voice salted with a bit of an untraceable accent.

"Mr. Crabtree, please."

"Sir, this is a private compound. Any entrance must first be requested by telephone." Immovable object meets irresistible force.

"And will you please tell Mr. Crabtree that a friend from his past has come to call?" responded the man. He had apparently not heard the guard.

"That will not be possible, Sir," insisted the guard in a commanding deadpan from the other side of the gate.

"Captain Snyder you and I both know this could continue for quite a long time. We also know I could have called at Mr. Crabtree's Elizabethtown residence, but since I am here please return to your station and ask Mr. Crabtree – Senior please – to come to the gate.

At the mention of Willy Snyder's name and his former rank at the Secret Service Willy was shaken. He wore no identifying name badge. Only a few minutes ago he'd relieved the guard normally on duty for a short break. *Had this man observed the routine and come when Snyder was there*, Willy wondered? As the hair on his neck stood on end he reached for the telephone in the booth.

Inside the Control Center officer listened, moved his hand to the control and magnified the image of the dapper man at the gate. A video recording was made as a matter of routine.

As the well camouflaged camera magnified the man's image he took a half step to the side and smiled benignly. He knew he was on Candid Camera.

Inside the officer picked up a phone and punched a button.

"Mr. Crabtree I think you better come in here, please."

Harold Crabtree was proud of the Solutions.com compound. The former headquarters of the 197th Pennsylvania Air National Guard was purchased by Solutions even before the Guard had moved to another base.

From his third floor corner office he was looking out the window at the runway of Harrisburg International Airport. The glass in the windows still amazed him.

A product of Cardinal Glass it was not only bullet proof, but one way. At the touch of a button it went from crystal clear to absolute black or any degree in between. And looking through it to the outside there was none of the "fish tank" feeling when it was in the clear mode. It was as clean as a picture window in a suburban home. From the outside the glass looked glacier green and was impenetrable – by sight, sound monitoring or gunfire.

Since purchasing the compound it had become an ant hill of activity. Populated by workers from corporations that normally provided services to the Central Intelligence Agency, these outfits had basically gutted the office areas, installed the latest in static and active security measures, bug-proofed the place, installed top equipment (all with CIA endorsed back-doors that would allow their snoops in without telltale signs.)

What the Tortoise didn't know was that Yossi Cumi's folks knew those backdoors and more. They showed up a day after it was online and did their magic. Voila. Clean computers, etc.

Never one to take anything for granted, Harold then brought his own people online to find the traps that Mossad had dropped while denying the Tortoise's people entry. Snooping on the snoopers. It was a never-ending game. And this was just his friends, Harold laughingly told Jake one day at lunch.

In the snooping department, one Oleg Gregori Nabatoski, aka Elvis, was not only one of the best, but dedicated himself to mastering the impossible. His shop was a theme park of the latest Sat phones, crypto-communications devices, his own inventions and twists on current developments. Never before had he been the King of so many gadgets, gizmos, and gewgaws. Not only that, but he and Sarah Longstreet had conspired to use their latest equipment to take Solutions.com into the next millennium of snooping. They were going to give their team the edge in spying and at the same time keep their agents and bosses safe anywhere in the world.

The compound was at the southeast end of the long HIA runway. It included a hangar large enough to hold three business jets if necessary. Tex was in the process of vetting a full time mechanic to handle the Beechcraft King Air 350. There was a Gulfstream V in the system somewhere, but it was yet to be delivered. Outfitting a shop, keeping up with Federal maintenance demands and the fastest changing events he'd ever faced kept the small Texan hopping.

He even had his own glass-walled office just off the hangar floor. First time for him and he was working in his spare time searching for a genuine cow skull with the horns on it, a saddle to fit on a saw horse and some appropriate rodeo paintings, etc. An office of his own. What was next?!

Harold looked at his watch, checked the Outlook schedule on his monitor and was reaching for a telephone when the intercom buzzed discreetly.

He entered the comm center and looked at the bank of monitors.

"What's up?"

"Sir, this man approached the gate a minute ago and asked for you. We have no record of any appointment. And he shook Willy. I could hear it in his voice. The guy called him by his name and old rank."

Moving closer as the officer twisted a knob and the face filled the screen, there was no hint of recognition to Harold.

"Send a back up out to Willy. When he gets there, ask him to frisk the man. I'll go out."

Harold arrived just as the new officer completed his search for weapons. He turned to Harold and shook his head in the negative to indicate that the visitor was unarmed.

"Hello, my friend. I assume you do not recognize me. We have both changed much in the years since we first met in Viet Nam."

"Let's take a walk, shall we?" Harold began to stroll up the road from the gate to the street leading back toward the airport proper.

Keeping pace, the dapper man looked at Harold and smiled. "You are a very cautious man. Good.

"I am the Russian officer who had the Viet Cong release you those many years ago. And in answer to your question, I have not tracked you since then. Until your company came to my attention recently I honestly did not know what had happened to you."

"Assuming that you are the man you say you are then please describe the events of those days."

The heat was stifling. Green was the world and wet was the air. Insects buzzed and bit every exposed part of his body. A bullet wound seeped pink fluids through the dirty field dressing on his shoulder. His eye sight was blurred. Something in the food to keep him compliant perhaps. Or just exhaustion.

A cramp knotted his left calf muscle. He thought it ironic that as wet as his body was from sweat and the humidity his mouth was like sandpaper with thirst.

Laughter drew his attention through the fog surrounding his mind. A Caucasian in tiger-stripe fatigues and the commander of his Viet Cong captors walked toward the cage imprisoning Harold. They each had a Baumi Bua beer bottle by the neck and the white man's arm was around the shoulders of the Viet.

"You look," said the VC and un-holstered the pistol from the rig around his shoulders.

Taking aim at Harold he squinted down the sights. The Colt 45's grip was too large for the Asian's small hands and the gun wavered. The Russian reached across and forced the gun upward with his hand holding the beer bottle.

"No! No!" he laughed to take the sting from the command. This was, after all, not his army.

"He is mine. You heard the Colonel," reminded the Caucasian. Both men laughed drunkenly at this.

Harold had no idea what it all meant but he was waiting for the crash of the 45 round to lift him from this life. Earlier the VC chief had fired off a clip of seven rounds all around Harold while he and his men drank beer. That had been before the Caucasian entered the camp with two other Viet Cong officers. Things had changed dramatically then.

One of the Viet officers had stood the whole squad at attention and harangued them for about five minutes. He introduced the Caucasian then he and his compatriot had left as quietly as they had arrived. The others disappeared inside the hut.

The Caucasian walked to the cage and undid the lock and clasp. He threw the bottle away, reached inside and took Harold under the arms and helped him stand straight. For three days he had been squatting. The cage demanded it.

Harold's leg muscles rebelled and he staggered. The other man helped him shuffle along. Then he leaned him against a wall and spoke quietly in very good English with no drunken slur.

"What's your name?"

Harold looked at him and did not answer.

"This is not an interrogation. I need something to call you."

"Crabby," Harold gave him the name he was most often called by his fellow Special Forces soldiers.

"Of course. A nickname. Crabtree," he said reading the name tape above the shirt pocket. I am Mikhail. But don't call me Mickey." At that the man laughed. He cracked himself up.

Harold smiled then winced as the pain in his legs multiplied.

"I'm Russian, you know. The very one your government is worried about. Right here in living color, flesh and blood. Mikhail to the rescue.

"Just stand there and don't move. I'm going to give you a couple of pills to help you. One is a very strong antibiotic and the other is to restore your clarity. You call them "speed" I think."

Mikhail then took the canteen from his hip and poured some into the cup. Harold noticed that it was GI not foreign. *Some soldier's who died here*, he thought.

He swallowed the pills and before long did begin to feel better. Mikhail helped him walk in small circles as the Viet Cong frowned and swung the Colt back and forth at his side as if trying to decide whether to shoot both Harold and Mikhail or follow orders.

Finally Mikhail said, "Stand here. When I motion to you, join me. We are going to walk out of the village together." Harold nodded.

Approaching the Viet, Mikhail reached into his pocket and withdrew a wad of American hundred dollar bills. He counted off five and offered them to the officer as he spoke quietly. The VC shook his head and backed up a step.

Mikhail advanced a step and spoke in articulate and commanding Vietnamese. The VC's eyes widened in surprise. He dropped his eyes toward the ground, slid out of the shoulder holster. He slipped the Colt inside and offered it to Mikhail. The cash disappeared like virtue on To Do Street in Saigon.

With a hand gesture, Mikhail indicated Harold should follow him. Together they walked slowly to the edge of the village without looking back.

When they had gone about a kilometer along a vague path Mikhail stopped to allow Harold to rest.

"For a while I thought I might have to kill him. That would have been rough. No telling which way his squad would go. The Colonel told everyone that I was in charge of you, but you know how these things work."

Harold did indeed know. He had led both Vietnamese and Hmong warriors as an advisor in South Viet Nam and Laos. He much preferred the Montagnards. Better fighters, more loyal and disciplined.

As the two men shared a ball of rice and some "mystery meat" Mikhail had pulled from his pack, Harold spoke.

"First of all, where are we headed? Second, thanks for the rescue, if that's what this is."

"Why, we are going to your base camp. A-334 isn't it?"

"No it isn't. Who are you and what's going on?"

"I am a Russian intelligence officer, like you are an American intelligence officer. Harold Crabtree, assigned simultaneously to 5th Special Forces and the 21st Radio Reconnaissance Unit, US Army MACV.

"I am here aiding my side in this war as you are your side. We are not so different. These little yellow people are murdering each other for power, money and occasionally for their beliefs. Also because that is what they do. Fight, follow orders. Or die. Sometimes all three.

"Where we are going is to the road that leads to your base camp. You don't have to give me the number. I know it, certainly," Mikhail chuckled. "And the names of your team members. In fact I know both the Army Security Agency team members and the regular Special Forces team members. Would you like me to recite them for you?" Mikhail put his canteen away and smiled as he said this last. Rising from his squat, he motioned along the path.

"Shall we go?"

They walked the rest of the day, resting when Mikhail could see Harold needed it. Though he never mentioned it, he was amazed at the strength Harold displayed after being a captive for a week, three days of which were in the tiger cage, and wounded at that. Simply being locked inside the "tiger cage" sapped a man's strength. The superficial bullet wound was red and swollen, obviously infected.

Strong and resilient, Mikhail thought as they walked.

They arrived at the red dirt road just at dusk. Mikhail stopped and turned back to Harold. "Do you recognize this?"

"Yes," Harold answered. He still wondered what was happening.

"I will leave you here. And in answer to your questions – our government felt it was important for your side to absolutely know that we are here. Chinese too, though certainly not at our request. They and Ho don't trust or like one another, but they are here. More to compete with us than help the Viets.

"This war will not get easier for your country, my friend. We will arm them better, and eventually will bring in North Vietnamese Regulars. A few are already prepared.

"You should take this message to your leadership. Tell them for us that you cannot win. You do not have the heart for it.

"We already know that democracies cannot successfully combat guerrilla armies. Their civilians have no stomach for the losses and your generals think that conventional forces can overwhelm them through massive numbers and firepower. It does not work. Ho's victory over the French should have taught them that, but your American arrogance dismissed all that as French weakness. Nonsense. The Legionnaires fought well and bravely.

"When you master killing shadows then you can win against our proxies. Until then you are futilely splashing youthful, innocent blood on the jungle floors and city streets. Tell your generals. Convince your government officials.

"We will not go away and we do not need the support or cooperation of our population as you do.

"You have already lost." With that Mikhail offered his hand and Harold shook it. "Thank you." He then stepped out onto the road and began to walk toward his camp wearing the unloaded Colt. Earlier Mikhail had removed the shells from the magazines and then smiled. "I am still a soldier and we *are* enemies, after all."

Harold had not looked back and as he walked away he wondered just how much of this dream was real. He began the day a prisoner and now he was a messenger for Moscow's government.

They were at the road where Mikhail had parked his rental car.

"Do you remember what I said to you when I returned your weapon?"

"You tell me," Harold answered.

"I said that I am a soldier and we *are* enemies. That was after I emptied the rounds from the magazines." He reached out and dropped a shiny brass 45 caliber "hard ball" round into Harold's hand.

"Yes, it is one of those I liberated from your magazines that day. My experience with you was a once-in-a-lifetime experience. I wanted a memento. But I meant it when I said I never followed up on our meeting." Mikhail smiled at the wonder on Harold's face.

"I can't invite you inside, but if you don't mind a short drive, we can have some coffee in town."

"Guide the way," Mikhail swept a hand toward his car.

At the diner in Middletown the waitress brought their coffee, two glasses of ice water and departed. Mikhail stirred in cream and three sugars. Harold dropped an ice cube into his.

"What's this all about?" he asked quietly.

"There are two aspects. First, as I said, one of our sources presented information that you were once again actively involved in intelligence work. It drew my attention when I read your name. The second thing was that your brother-in-law was involved. I am well acquainted with him.

"There is one other thing. I believe that you and your people may be at some possible risk from the same woman who killed one and wounded two of your associates in Virginia. That, by the way, is not verified. Consider it a rumour." Mikhail sipped his coffee-flavored syrup and purred his appreciation.

"You have dumped a lot of information in a couple of sentences. I suppose there is no reason to suspect you will enlarge on any of it?" Harold smiled a look that clearly indicated he wanted more details.

"Tell me, Harold. What is your son like? I know he is a professional through and through, but what is he like as an individual?"

"He's a lot like I was at his age. Courageous but not reckless. An idealist while being cynical at the same time. Hoping his cynicism is misplaced, but having serious doubts.

"Do you have a family?" Harold asked in return.

"Once. My son was an Army officer. He was killed in a training accident. My wife never recovered. She fell into a vodka bottle and I was not there for her. I wonder if it would have mattered, but I fear it might have and I lost the opportunity. She stepped into the path of a Stalingrad bus one day. Just an accident, they said." This last was delivered in a sadly wistful voice that brought a lump into Harold's throat.

"I'm sorry."

"Thank you. That unfortunately is the plight of many in my profession. Sorry when all is said and done. Would that I could have been a priest or discoverer of a cure for cancer. Of course many of the priests are as corrupt as my KGB and I fear the one who could have conquered cancer has been murdered by an abortionist in your country or mine." Mikhail's eyes were downcast, but his face showed the futility of a life spent stealing someone else's secrets and ending the lives of people just like himself. It was a sad countenance.

Harold had by now recalled a semblance of his rescuer back then. The years had added a patina of latent power and cosmopolitan grace along with the creases. They were the lines of a man who had indulged in too many cigarettes, too much alcohol and two few friends.

Mikhail revived his spirits with an obvious force of will.

"But now I must return you to your compound. Duty calls." With that he rose and dropped a five dollar bill on the table.

As they drove back to the airport Harold asked, "What is your real name? Your whole name. I will pray for you."

"Mikhail Nikolay Ivanovich Lobachevsky. I was named for a famous mathematician. Hope by my parents, perhaps. Someone once said that hope is adolescent faith. In their case it never passed puberty I fear.

"But thank you for the prayers. Though it is my concerted belief that such are purely subjective." He smiled that sad smile again and Harold wondered how many graveyards he had filled over the years.

When the car stopped, Mikhail reached out to again shake Harold's hand. They nodded one to the other and Harold rolled the shiny .45 bullet between his fingers as he walked back to the gate where the guard was waiting to grant him entry. He still had not the slightest idea of the real reason his old rescuer had visited.

SEVENTEEN

Howard walked around the blue Aerostar van as the salesman watched him. He hummed and kept his hands in his pockets. Blue, with bad carpet, seats that had been detailed but not enough to get the kid stains all out. Seventy thousand miles and some dents. He tried the side door. It opened and closed smoothly. It would do.

"I'll take it." The salesman's day was improving when Howard said that. His boss had screamed at him last week for not dumping the van at the auto auction.

"Great! Let's do the paperwork. C'mon inside," the salesman said.

"Ain't gonna be no paperwork. I got no driver's license or insurance." Howard sneered like a rodent. The salesman stopped in mid-step afraid he was about to be robbed at gunpoint.

When he turned slowly back to Howard, he saw that the man's hand was full of hundred dollar bills. *Well, that beats a Saturday night special,* the salesman thought.

The lot was in downtown Baltimore in an area where street crime was high. The salesman figured this set of wheels was about to be the newest coke mule on the street.

"But, sir, we have to do the paperwork," he tried to do things right.

"Yeah. You said you wanted just under three grand for this piece a junk." Here's thirty-five hundred. You do the paperwork. Just gimme the keys." Howard knew how to close a deal.

Howard drove the van for a block with a piece of advertisement stuck in the back window like a new license application. Then he stopped and screwed a set of Ohio plates he'd liberated from a green Volvo just up the street from the car lot.

From Baltimore he drove to a little house in Ono, a country village near Harrisburg. Concrete block painted a cancerous green with attached garage.

When he walked into the shabby living room Gerold was sitting at a chrome and red Formica dining table with a piece of white butcher paper laid out before him. Pencil marks showed streets, distances and angles.

"Get it okay?" he didn't even look up. A legal pad was riddled with numbers and more diagrams.

"Got it. How'd yer day go? Get everything you need?"

"Yep, right down to the traffic cones. I lifted them off a city truck while the grunts was piggin' out at a Mickey Ds. Got a pair of coveralls too. Made the measuring lots easier. But that boy I nabbed 'em from sure needs a bath. Whew!"

Howard chuckled as he stood at the stove and dumped a can of Castleberry's Chili into a pot. It sizzled as it hit the bottom in a glutinous blob. He smeared it around the bottom of the pan and it's aroma immediately began to waft throughout the kitchen.

Howard started opening and closing cabinet doors. "Hey, where's the crackers! I told you to buy Keeblers!" Howard was having a moment.

"On top of the frige," Gerold didn't look up from his work.

Howard looked at the doorless refrigerator. On top was a little red box of Cheezits.

He grabbed it, ripped the lid off, and hurled the crackers at Gerold. They hit him in a yellow blizzard. Face, hair, table and paperwork.

Instantly Gerold was out of his seat with a Taurus revolver pointed rock solid at Howard's face. A face white with fear and instant remorse.

"WHATCHU DOIN'!!" Gerold screamed.

Howard's hands were out toward Gerold, palms toward him. "Whoa, partner! I'm sorry. Don't shoot. C'mon, man. I just hate chili without saltines. You know that." Said chili now being fully scorched. You have to admit gas *does* heat faster.

Gerold's finger was tightening on the trigger. There was no hammer. This puppy was going to go off with just a bit more pressure. Howard sure knew that. And Gerold always hit what he aimed at.

"Okay, Gerold. Okay. Enough is enough. Put that piece away before somebody gets hurt." Howard was trying to figure if he could yank the Ruger out of his coat pocket and get off a shot before Gerold killed him. It wasn't lookin' good.

"Howard, you are a mouse-brained retard! I have carried you for years and the only reason I ain't already shot you and left you beside a highway like road kill is that you run errands good and leave me alone to do the heavy lifting. I'm thinkin' I could get a deaf-mute girl to do that and have benefits I ain't got with you.

"I'm tellin' you now. Clean up the crackers. Eat every one that's on the floor. Your chili's ruined. You jerk! Shut it off. It stinks.

"Ah! Ah! Don't move yet, I ain't done.

"After you clean up the crackers," Gerold swept the table clear of crackers and Howard winced. That floor was pig pen filthy. But he knew he was going to eat every one of them. Gerold was really mad.

"Personally I wish he would send them a roast pig and call it a day." Corporal Ted Jackson was seated at the desk in the converted pantry at the Governor's Mansion on Front Street in Harrisburg, Pennsylvania.

The mansion is a large two and half story brick. Wrought-iron-fenced, complete with security cameras, guards, sensors, the works. Even fake cut-out people at places. Those had really freaked out the State Police Executive Protection Detail officers when the landscapers first erected them. One nearly got shot on a dark night when the Governor was entertaining and decided to show a guest around the grounds. The detail still laughed about that now and then.

"Ours not to reason why…" Nick started to say.

"Don't finish that sentence. I hate that 'do or die' part at the end," laughed Jackson.

"Look," Sgt. Nick Larsen began patiently, "he started this during the first campaign and now it's part of the routine. The bikers wanted the helmet law abolished. The Governor felt that it would be a good chance to look like 'one of the great unwashed' and at the same time help get rid of the idea that the Democrats were trying to protect everybody from themselves.

It played good with the Viet Nam vets too. So he went down there and waded in among the Harleys and leather, shaking hands and promising to get rid of the law as part of his first legislation.

"When he won, he kept his word.

"I don't like it either, but it's what he wants, and he already hates it when I tell him about security. Drive a hundred miles an hour on the turnpike. Snake in and out of traffic with sirens blaring. He already made me replace Shelly because she didn't drive aggressively enough."

Nick had worked for the previous Governor and loved him. A conservative who had been a good governor, he was a family man with decent manners and respect for people. Ridge had been picked as the President's first Homeland Secretary after 9/11. For a while Nick had entertained thoughts of asking to go with him to DC but the idea of living there and being forever away from his family had killed that idea.

This Governor was foul-mouthed, crude and a crook in many minds. He kept company with people that Nick would like to slap the cuffs on. His deal-making on the phone and in person while he ignored the fact that police officers were standing beside him made Nick sick to his stomach. Nick, a Bible-Believing Christian who takes his faith seriously, also takes his work just as seriously, so he tamped down his own feelings and did his job to the absolute best of his ability.

"Did Trooper Adams complete the pipe-and-drape inspection at the Capitol?" Nick was referring to the shielding used to protect a subject from sniper targeting which was put up and taken down around entrances with too many possibilities to realistically cover. Governor Red Endreling hated it too. Kept him from getting his face on the front page he told the detail every time they insisted on it.

"Yes, it's up. But he said it was a waste of time if The Man was going to go Harley hopping on 3rd Street before we haul him up to the Capitol entrance." Corporal Jackson answered while scanning the security monitors.

"When Trooper Adams is responsible for the Man he can determine the levels of security we use. Until then his job is not to ask why, but…well you know." Nick shot back, only half joking. He ran the job by the book, and took no garbage from anyone but The Man himself. Even then Nick was known to get a bit red in the face and debate certain issues when security was concerned.

"The standard coverage?" Ted asked.

"Almost," Nick said paying attention to the screen showing 2nd Street. A young man with a dark, baggy jacket was leaning on the fence. He had a sock cap pulled low over his head, a bottle of something in his left hand, and dark trousers. His head seemed to be scanning the mansion and grounds.

"Have one of the guards run the guy off on the 2nd Street fence," he instructed, and Ted spoke into the mike with directions. In less than a minute a uniformed guard was moving toward the man at the fence who immediately felt a need to move on before the guard arrived at his location.

"You pick up something?"

"Not really. He's not the first one to lean on the fence and gawk. I just have an uncomfortable feeling today. Not spooky. Just an itch in my brain," Nick said and walked out of the little room.

At six AM the morning of the "Bike-In" a Ford Explorer with blacked out windows pulled into the west end of South Street. Howard jumped out and placed orange traffic cones at the outside edges of the end two parking places. He ran yellow "Police" tape between them. Finally he taped plastic bags over the parking meters for those spots. His Explorer was in the right hand spot. He crawled into the back and went to sleep.

Ten o'clock found him wide awake and sipping a cup of coffee he'd copped from a restaurant a couple of blocks away. Already the roar of motorcycles filled the air as the eclectic blend of bikers began to wrestle their steel steeds into position to welcome the Governor. Third Street was closed off from Walnut to North except for bike traffic.

Gerold arrived in the blue Aerostar van at eleven. Howard leaped out and placed two more cones and tape closing off the eastbound lane of South Street. They were inside the kill zone now.

A week ago at three in the morning they had come here with Gerold's laser range finder. It was 471 yards from the street behind where the blue van now sat to the steps where the Governor entered the Capitol Building. Thirty yards closer marble steps ended their rise from Third Street and a small open plaza area ran from there to the Capitol entrance.

Intelligence provided to them said that platform was always cleared but that the Governor usually rode from 3rd up to the entrance in a police car. Didn't matter, 441, 471 or a thousand yards. Gerold could hit an orange with his Remington every time.

There was a rub though. Tree limbs extended out into the line of fire from the parking spot. That meant that Howard would have to back the van out into the closed off street to give Gerold a straight line of sight to the target. Ole Gov Red was dead meat.

At high noon the three car procession was let through the road block at North Street. Traveling directly to the area roped off for the motorcycles, the first unmarked police car turned into the circular drive leading from street level up to the Capitol and stopped. Three plain clothes troopers got out and moved quickly to the Governor's car still on the street. The three took positions and the man in the front seat moved to open the rear door while the Governor's exit was blocked from sniper sight by the others.

Red (short for Redlin) Endreling exited like a bull out of the chute at Calgary. He was into the crowd of adoring misfits astride their bikes. Leather-clad bearded men and nearly naked women were everywhere. The smell of marijuana was clear to Nick who had busted his share of druggies during his time on highway patrol duty.

Soon the Governor had moved out of the protective cordon provided by the officers. He was, after all among his own kind. *Ruthless, reckless and ridiculous*, thought Nick in a moment of personal opinion as he moved a large rider in a greasy cowboy hat and black leather vest with no shirt underneath from his path. His hairy chest was surpassed by the enormous gut hanging nearly to the gas tank on his Harley.

The Governor was having a field day. He laughed and took a hit on a hand rolled cigarette offered him by the ugliest woman in the pack. Finally he had circled the wild bunch enough and Nick took his elbow and shepherded him back to the cars.

As they whirled upward and stopped at the pipe-and-drape area leading to the Capitol entrance they did the door-opening drill again and the Governor moved out, still laughing.

Instead of quickly going inside to address the legislature as planned he stepped away from his guards and strode to the edge of the marble plaza area above the steps leading down to Third Street. His adoring crowd below cheered and revved their engines. A few bikes backfired.

Nick spoke quickly into the mic in his sleeve and kept pace with the Governor. A second and then third officer came along. One at the Governor's right shoulder, another with his back to the Governor.

"They love me!" Endreling exulted turning his head toward Nick and laughing.

At the exact moment the governor entered the car below on Third Street, Gerold's Nextel beeped and a woman's voice said, "He's in the car."

Howard smoothly backed the van into the street as Gerold slid the door open only a foot. Dressed in black, the windows painted black inside and a stool and tripod set up he was ready for business.

Howard killed the engine, exited the van leaving the door open, and tossed a lit highway flare into the front seat of the SUV, then moved the cones and tape which now opened South Street onto Front.

When the Governor barged out toward him Gerold couldn't believe his luck. He was sure he'd have to take the shot at the man's back as he entered the building.

BLAM!

Howard was back in the van and backing out against traffic on Front Street even as Gerold was closing the side door and the Governor folded like a Case knife.

"They love me!" he said but before he'd fully turned his body back to the adoring crowd below the Governor's head exploded in a mass of brains, blood and hair.

At the same moment he heard the report of the rifle, Nick Larsen was punched in the right trapezoid muscle and went down. He scrambled for the mic in his sleeve but couldn't seem to function.

"GUN! GUN! THE MAN IS DOWN!" Corporal Ted Jackson heard it on the special monitor in the little office at the Mansion. Stunned, he hit the button that would sound an alarm on the radio of all the protective detail at the Mansion. Shut Down.

Next he radioed a broadcast to all police and emergency frequencies in the Harrisburg Area. They were to be ready for an emergency broadcast as information came in. Alert City, Capitol and State patrol cars. BOLOs (Be On The Look Out) would soon be forthcoming along with details of anyone on foot, everything and anything that could help catch the shooter.

At the Capitol controlled madness reigned. On the street below, there were lots of fat guys down. Not astride their bikes. Literally down on-the-street. Lying flat as they could get, with their heads scanning for any shooters that might be aiming at them. Many of these guys had once been young and soldiers.

Some had been looking up when the Governor and the cop beside him went down. They knew from the pink splatter that Red at least was dead.

Troopers and Capitol Policemen were fanning out, weapons drawn. Not waiting for an ambulance, three troopers grabbed the Governor's body and none too gently tossed it into the back of the gray Crown Vic. Nick went in on top of him and the cortege screamed toward Harrisburg Hospital, lights and sirens blaring.

Below, a phalanx of Harley's came to life in a majestic roar and brought up the rear. Honor Guard or funeral procession. They didn't know and didn't care. It was how they operated.

EIGHTEEN

"There's been another sniper shooting. This time it was in Harrisburg, Pennsylvania and the target was Governor Red Endreling.

"That makes three of these killings. All by a sniper. All the targets were famous political liberals – Barbara Steinfeld, Senator Schumbler of New York and now the famous or perhaps as some say, infamous Governor Endreling. In this case a state trooper was also shot but not killed."

The ever-sad looking commentator looked at the panel of three newsmen and asked, "Do we have one crazed sniper or a team like the Washington killers? What's happening here? Fred, let's begin with you tonight."

"Brit right now there is no way of telling if it's the same person or not. We do know that there was likely only one shooter in Harrisburg. Apparently there was a big motorcyclist gathering with the machines backfiring right before the hit. But unlike the grassy knoll of the Kennedy assassination, witnesses agree that there was only one rifle shot.

Mort couldn't stand it any longer.

"The same bullet that struck the Governor in the head apparently was deflected by his skull and hit the officer.

"There was one clue. A burned out stolen Ford SUV was found at the far end of the street that leads to the Capitol. Traffic cones were placed there though no one in the city government ordered that.

"I think it is some lunatic right-wing group trying to scare off liberals from speaking out before the Presidential election."

Charles smiled his "second mouse gets the cheese" look. The camera backed off and showed Brit glancing at him knowingly.

"Mort, the elections are two years away. Do we have another 'right wing conspiracy?'" Charles rebutted.

"People in Pennsylvania police circles are wondering if this is tied to some of the Governor's deal making. It's no secret that his friends include any number of organized crime figures. He almost bragged about the relationships.

"As to who the shooter is or who sent them nobody knows. What *is* interesting is the total lack of rumors. Usually when these things occur if there is a criminal association it is only a short time until whispers provide leads.

"The DC shooters had none of that because they were two madmen with no ties to a criminal element. They were lone wolves."

Fred interjected, "What about an Islamic connection? Charles you have some good contacts in foreign intelligence circles. Have you heard any stirrings in that direction?

"Actually, I spoke with some of them today. They've heard nothing regarding snipers.

"One thing I will say. There has been no real evidence left behind at any of the killings. No spent cartridges. No fingerprints. Nothing to trace the shooter or shooters. Nothing to connect them to any kind of organization. Even the vehicle was torched."

Brit did the wrap up. "Okay, then the next step is to wait and see if he or they strike again – "

"Or she!" Mort offered. Brit was surprised and it showed.

"The sniper could be a woman! Don't forget the Russians used dozens of women in Stalingrad in WWII. They were amazingly effective. They took out some of the Nazi's best soldiers," Mort hit a homer with that bit but a hard break forced Brit to only nod and the segment closed.

"YOU GO MORT!" cried a female voice with a Long Island accent, from a Montgomery, Alabama motel.

NINETEEN

Raquel slept until mid morning. The driving was wearying her beyond expectations. She longed for exercise, fresh air and action.

Before she left her motel room she booted up her email program. "Here it is," she mumbled, when the info came in from Uncle Amir. He'd sent her Alex's name and phone number. Along with that he'd said Alex would be informed that she would contact him. She was more than happy she would not need to place an order for weaponry from Tomas. *Good,* she thought, *for I have a feeling he will not long be free.*

She dialed the number.

"Alex."

"Camel," Raquel said immediately. There was an extended pause. Dead air.

"Dung," he said finally, with a tone of uncertainty. "I hate this spy idiocy," he added.

She laughed in spite of herself. "Who thinks these things up, anyway?" she asked, agreeing, though it was she who had set up the code words.

Raquel had seen Alex's photo in her email. He had, of course not seen her.

"Describe yourself," Raquel said it as a mild command. The soldier in Alex responded immediately.

"Yes, ma'am. Gray hair, brown eyes. One hundred seventy-five. Five ten, a bit more. You?"

She laughed again. "You wouldn't believe it. Brown hair. Your height and one thirty. Wait a minute." The food had arrived. When the waitress departed, Raquel said, "Okay. I need directions to the farm."

"You running? Hot?"

"No."

"Where are you?" he asked.

"Just do what I say! How do I get there?" spoken in a low voice because of her surroundings, but the anger came across. Raquel was grouchy as a bear with a sore tooth. *Just follow orders and answer questions!*

"Listen," Alex began again, in a tone worthy of a first grade teacher with a slow student. "For me to give good directions it is helpful to know if you are north, south, east or west of here." He changed his tone to a more militant one. "Want to try again? Where are you coming from?"

"I'm outside of Leesburg, Virginia." She felt like a fool as Alex gave directions.

"When you get to the little grocery store, I'll be there. What are you driving?"

"A black Saab."

"See you there. About two hours from now probably." Alex disconnected. He looked out the kitchen window and watched two camo-dressed men come from the barn where they'd parked the dirty white van. He despised these two clowns. They were slobs, stupid and always irked him when they arrived at the farm. Someone had sent them to report on people near Elizabethtown. Alex wasn't sure they even knew where it was.

They entered the kitchen and the slower of the two opened the refrigerator, slammed the door and said to the other, "Nothing! Yogurt and vegetables. I said we shoulda stopped in Harrisburg!" He was hungry for American belly bombs.

Alex asked the other, "Anything new?"

"We don't report to you!" Harry snapped back.

They slept upstairs, hid the van in the barn, and apparently took orders from someone in Harrisburg. The men thought she was a prostitute. One wanted to ask her. The other, Harry, was flat out scared of her. The Al Qaeda groups in America were very compartmentalized. Alex was somewhat surprised this dirty duo had been sent to the farm for a hideaway, and that they were so careless about talking in front of – but not to him – of their actions.

Later he drove to the mom-and-pop grocery store he'd described to Raquel. Inside he bought a diet soda and returned to his truck. It was raining again. Had been for most of the summer. *Hot and as humid as a Louisiana swamp.* He cracked his windows and enjoyed the rain drumming on the truck roof.

When Raquel arrived, he definitely was not prepared for her. He stepped out of the truck and approached her car. She buzzed down the window, smiled a radiant, movie star smile and said, "Hi. Let's go. I gotta wee-wee."

Alex's jaw dropped. He was rooted to the spot. This woman was so beautiful it almost hurt to look at her.

Raquel had experienced this before. Brunette, red head or blonde, it was the same. "Are you all right?" she asked, with a mock-serious look.

Alex visibly gathered himself and said, "Yeah, follow me." He spun on his heel and walked back to the truck thinking, *Okaaay. My lucky day.*

At the farm he opened the barn doors and motioned for her to drive inside. She parked beside a filthy, dented white van and popped the trunk. Alex reached in and pulled a large suitcase out easily. She stepped beside him with a small smile and a computer case in her left hand.

"Nice place," she said as she looked at the decrepit barn and unpainted house. Weeds were tall from the heat and rain. Alex didn't answer, just led the way to the front porch.

When they entered the living room, the two men, "Harry & Company," Alex had mentally named them, were slouched on the sagging couch watching Nickelodeon. They leaped to their feet when they saw Raquel and began a failed attempt to make themselves look more presentable. They stared at her like she had materialized right before them carrying a magic wand. Fairy Princess. They followed her progress through the living room google-eyed and open-mouthed.

Alex laughed to himself. *At least I kept my cool better than this when I got my first look at her.* He continued down the hallway toward the kitchen. He pointed to a door on the left, he said, "Bathroom."

Wordlessly, Raquel entered and locked the door behind her.

Alex made a pot of coffee, found a hidden package of cinnamon rolls and tossed them on the table. He added a cup, knife and fork, napkin and saucer.

"Who are those two?" Raquel joined him and took a seat at the place setting.

"They were sent here to spy on some people in Elizabethtown. I don't have a cl…"

"Get 'em in here!" Raquel was no longer tired. Alex was stunned.

"Now!" Raquel commanded. There was no doubt who was in charge here. Alex stepped to the hallway and called to them.

The dirty duo stood at their idea of attention before Raquel. *What was going on?* they wondered. Both instantly glommed onto the cinnamon rolls.

"You're watching people near Elizabethtown?" she asked kindly.

"Yeah! Got the bug bites to prove it," Harry said, nodding his head in the affirmative quickly. "Prolly gonna get Lyme's Disease we got bit by so many ticks!"

"Tell me about the people," Raquel said, and pushed the cinnamon rolls and knife in their direction.

"We must not that!" the other one said. His speech identified a mental slowness. His English was broken. Raquel could not identify its origin.

"Where are you from?" she asked quietly.

He looked around suspiciously, lowered his head and his voice and said, “Afghanistan.” He looked around again then added, “I am Taliban. Najjar is my name.” His smile clearly showed he was taken with Raquel.

Raquel about fell out of the buggy. “Taliban?!”

“Yes, Miss. My mother, she live here. Washington, D.C. She very sick so I come here three years ago. She die. I live with Harry. End of story!” The last was spoken with a beatific grin and in such a way as to show he thought it very clever. Alex, leaning against the sink, just shook his head. *Taliban. Right.*

“Tell me about the people in Elizabethtown, Harry,” Raquel tried again.

“Never!” Harry shouted and Najjar jumped.

The Ruger materialized in Raquel’s hand, drawn from her purse lying beside her on the table. She fired instantly, sending a bullet near – but not at – Harry’s face. He dropped to the floor like she’d pole-axed him. Living in D.C. teaches that move at a young age. Najjar wet his pants. Alex stood like a stone, controlling the fight or flee impulse that had been finely honed over the years.

Raquel screamed down at Harry, “Get up! Talk to me! Now!” Najjar started for the hallway.

“Freeze!” He froze, turned around with eyes nearly matching her saucer in size.

She looked at Harry. “Get up!” she repeated only a decibel quieter. Raquel was in command and her large brown eyes fired lightening like lasers.

No one here wanted shot. Harry got up.

That 22 is LOUD! Alex thought but said nothing. A bit of plaster was drifting in the non-existent air of the kitchen, and gun smoke added an acrid scent to the cinnamon of the rolls.

“They have two houses and barn, more. Much building going on. A couple lives on the farm in a small cottage. Three horses. An older man and two young men live in the big house. One is very large. The other two look much alike. They go to the airport often. We cannot follow there. That is all.” Harry was very ready to please. He’d forgotten all about mission security, *and* the cinnamon rolls.

“Okay. Who knows you’re here?” Raquel asked casually.

“In Pennsylvania? Well, there is …”

“No! Here. At this farm. Who knows you live at this farm, or have ever been here?” she tried again. She still had the Ruger in her hand, but it lay in her lap, out of sight.

No one had forgotten about it.

“Okay! No one,” Harry was now the spokesman. “Not even my own wife. My instructions said come here and spy. I received four hundred dollars in the mail after the telephone call. There was a map to Elizabethtown and a number to call to meet a contact in Harrisburg. I met her two times and reported. Not much to report. She does not know about this farm and we did not advise her of it. There was a map for getting here too." He was jabbering, his hands flittering like a moth around a lantern.

"Where are the maps, the envelope and the money?" Raquel asked kindly, the concerned nurse or caregiver.

"The maps are still in the envelope. Above the visor in the van." Harry did not mention money.

"And?"

"And? Oh. My wife got two hundred. I got eighty dollars left. In my wallet," he patted his left hip.

Raquel looked at Najjar. "Can you bring me the envelope?" He nodded, but did not move. "Go on, it's all right," she nodded and smiled. He ran from the room, eager to please. The front door slammed behind him a moment later.

"And no one knows you're here, or about this place?" Alex knew what was coming, and steeled himself for the noise.

"No one. I swear!" The last word was barely out of his mouth when the .22 was up and a hollow-point bullet entered his mouth. Its whirl inside the cranium nicked the medulla oblongata. Harry was dead instantly, with very little sign of injury. He tottered for a moment then crumpled to the floor.

Steps sounded in the hallway. Najjar was back with a crumpled envelope in his right hand.

"What happened to – No! No!" he put his left hand up to ward off the blow, but it did not stop the bullet, which passed through his palm, then entered his chest. He fell backwards, his heels drummed on the linoleum floor for a bit then stilled.

"Well you sure know how to impress a guy," Alex remarked dryly. "You gonna shoot me, too?" It was clear he was considering the odds of it.

"Get serious." Raquel put the pistol back in her bag. "We bury these two here?" she asked.

"I don't think so. I don't feel like digging. We'll take them to the river. If they *do* float to Harrisburg, the cops'll think it was drugs. Harry smoked some weed here 'til I stopped it." Alex had seen enough dead bodies and had made his share of men dead that he was not spooked now that he knew she wasn't gonna shoot him, too. *Man she was cool about it, though!* he thought.

"I'll bring their van up. Empty their pockets," he turned and went out the kitchen door rather than step over the bodies.

They dumped the bodies in the Juniata River. Ripped the bloody carpet out and threw it off the bridge too. Water, fish and turtles are a killer's friends.

Denny's is open all night. They sat in the middle of the smoking section and Alex offered up one burnt offering after another. He lit one off the embers of the last. Raquel hated cigarette smoke but knew he was dealing with stress and said nothing about it.

They'd just loaded two dead bodies into the van, dumped same into the shallow Juniata River and then driven over to this greasy spoon that Alex liked. It was well used, drab and populated by the detritus of Harrisburg's worst bars.

Three AM. The coffee was strong, and one customer was at the counter. A fat balding man in a shabby black overcoat sat at the counter talking to himself in a constant and strident argument he'd never win. It was raining again. Lightening sent occasional signals as if from one ship to another in the inky blackness.

"Sometimes I wonder if the jihad is real, or are we just thugs like the Mafia or the Israelis," Alex said, sipping his coffee.

"Defeatism. I would have expected better of you," Raquel said, almost teasing, but also wanting to judge his commitment. Keep him talking.

"I mean it. When I was in the desert we talked endlessly about the world's grandeur under Arab rule. In Moorish Spain the arts and science flourished. The Arab rule in the fifteenth century improved every nation they conquered. The Catholics murdered and killed our people reclaiming Europe – to what end?" he sounded like a true believer.

"I look at the kingdoms of the Arab world today and they are nothing more than a bunch of pompous windbags established by British oil companies decades ago. Not one of them has elevated the level of his people. Most of their people still live like their families did a hundred years ago except for the satellite dishes. The only democracy in the Middle East is Israel and they couldn't survive without America's welfare," he was looking into Raquel's face with another part of his mind thinking, *This woman is so beautiful*.

"Egypt gets their US welfare too. And Jordan. Oil poor countries. And they made peace with Israel. U.S. dollars can buy peace." Raquel said, goading him a bit.

"True enough. But look at what's happening to the Arab lands. Western television has degraded their societies. The leadership is filled with boozers, whore-mongers, and perverts. They hustle kidnapped girls and boys for sexual thrills, bow and scrape at the American President's photo ops, and then bank their fortunes in the Caymans.

They're becoming as politically correct as the ivory tower college professors in the U.S. or the Democratic Party leadership. I watch the news and think, 'Am I the only sane person alive?'"

"Then what will the jihad change?" Raquel asked, thinking to herself, *Nothing*!

"I thought it would change America's influence in the Middle East. I watch the fat slobs in this country and think, 'Go on, eat yourselves to death, you pigs!' but 9/11 didn't discourage them. It inflamed and incensed them. Look around at all the flags and posters that are still up everywhere. 'United We Stand,' 'Support Our Troops,' that kind of stuff.

For a while I believed Iraq might break them, but the soldier in me knew that Saddam would eventually get his head in a basket. I think now that we might have done the same thing the Japs did at Pearl Harbor.

"Really ticked off the biggest sleeping giant in the world," he shrugged his shoulders, "Honestly, I want to keep moving against them in hopes that history will turn the tide, but I don't know."

Raquel remembered then that he truthfully had no idea who she was, what her relationship to her father was, or what she was up to. He was an idealist, but his juices were drying up. Perhaps he needed an infusion of hope.

"Alex, what do you think of Osama bin Laden?" she asked, pouring a thousand volt look of sympathy into his eyes.

"I think he's a genius. His attacks were remarkable. Not just 9/11 but the previous ones and the ones since. Al Qaeda is a thousand splinter groups but he's the focus for them all. He and Iran are obviously behind all the fighters pouring into Iraq to battle the American troops since the 'great battles have ended.'" He said the phrase mockingly.

"And the Pacific Rim bombings have shaken Australia. I watch the news. People are asking if it is worth it. Should they just give the Middle East up to the Arabs? Iran is taunting the US but they're painting targets on their own chests.

The other day I listened to a couple of sod-busters argue at the little store where I met you. I'm standing there thinking, 'Yes, and when we take our countries back from the fat little kings, you'll deal with us for oil. We kick the British and Americans and the faggoty French out of all our oil fields and close your countries down."

Raquel looked at him in a new light. This ex-soldier was more than a trigger puller. He was a thinker. And he had been taught philosophy by someone who was the same.

"Alex, I'm bin Laden's daughter." She said it as calmly as she might have said, "Pass the sugar." She watched his face change.

At first it hadn't registered. Then was denial. Then the mocking about to surface. He studied her face to see if she was teasing him or simply insane. Finally came wonderment.

"No." he couldn't keep from saying it.

"Yes." she said. "Born to his first – and only true – wife. He sent my mother here while she was pregnant with me. Just before the first move against the Fauds in Mecca. That failed, and his and her families purchased his escape from Saudi Arabia. I was born here, to a woman who said she was single and didn't know the father's identity. Who would doubt that in America? I've been trained to wage jihad from childhood.

"I'm here for two reasons. I need a place to operate and I need help. Someone who is committed to the jihad, to my father, and ultimately to me," she hoped she wasn't being too corny or laying it on too thick.

Alex felt like someone had a wide belt wrapped around his chest and a giant was tightening it until his heart would actually implode. *She couldn't be bin Laden's daughter. Why not?* his head asked. *You were an American soldier and now you are fighting America. Why can't she be who she says she is*?

"Where are your from? What are you going to do? Why do you need my help?" his voice had been gradually rising in pitch and volume as he asked the questions.

"Shhh," Raquel said quietly and he brought it all under control.

"All of that is unnecessary information. What you need to do is decide if you will obey my commands unquestioningly and quickly." She sat back, crossed her arms and watched him.

"Or what? You'll shoot me like the other two?" Alex asked with a smirk on his face that said it would not be so simple to take him. Raquel believed it, but also knew that she would kill him as quickly as squashing a bug and with as little thought if she wanted to.

"Yes. I will kill you if I believe you are a threat. And you would do the same to me. We are jihad warriors, you and I. We wage a holy war." She said it with what she hoped was sufficient fervor that he would be convinced. She had plans that would necessitate a command post. This one seemed to fill the bill of manning the phone, dealing with surprises and keeping local things under control. When she was done with him, he could join the other two swimmers.

For his part, Alex was divided. He had had girl friends over the years, but they were absolute dogs compared to this woman. That was the masculine side of his head. On the operational side, he feared her. Not the gun so much as her impulsiveness. He knew that kind of behaviour costs lives. There was one life he was particularly fond of – his.

Killing the two watchers was stupid. She didn't learn anything about what they'd actually seen at that farm. Was anyone expecting them to check in? Stupid.

Distractions caused by unexpected events were bad enough. Being so close to this chick would be constantly on his mind. *Should I just kill her now? Who even knows she's here? Can I get her romantic?*

He jumped inside – calm on the outside as a turtle, though – when she said as if reading his mind, "Alex. Don't even think it. You need to respect me. Fear me. Obey me like I was the Queen of the World, but do not – EVER – think an amorous thought about me.

"I am the ice maiden as far as you are concerned. It will get you eliminated if you even once break that rule. Are you with me?" Then she smiled this sexy smile as if it were a test and Alex swallowed – his pride, his masculinity, and his smart aleck retort.

Then he nodded.

"Now, where is the sniper instructor?" Raquel asked quietly. "It is my understanding that she is very good, and we have work to do."

"She's nearby," Alex answered, his voice still sort of choked off from stress.

"Call her. Tell her to be at the farm at noon tomorrow. I'm going to be her new best friend." Raquel rose from the table, walked to the register and paid for their meal as Alex walked a half-step behind like a good Arab wife, and furious with himself for realizing it.

TWENTY

"Harold, Don Rogers. How are you?"

"I'm fine, Sir," Surprise was an inadequate word for Harold's response at hearing the voice on the other end of the line. "And yourself?"

"Same here. Retirement's a little boring. I miss the fights and backstabbing," he chuckled. "Seriously, I am enjoying some time with my family."

"How is Mrs. Rogers? I understand she is facing some health challenges."

"Not well, I'm afraid. Thank you for asking. It is only a matter of time, but she is a champion in spite of everything." Roger's voice changed as he fought to keep from choking up.

"We are all praying for the both of you, Sir." Harold understood losing a loving partner and friend and his heart went out to this man he liked and respected.

"Hmmph," Rogers cleared his throat and continued.

"Miss Frances' husband passed away a couple of weeks ago, I'm afraid. She said she didn't call you and I was out of the country at the time. Although that isn't the purpose of this call."

"I'm sorry to hear that. How is she holding up?" Harold liked the spunky former secretary to the Secretary of War.

"She's doing well. Living with her son near Atlanta. She says she's itchy to get out of there and do something productive. She is a wonderful person, Harold.

"She left the government when I retired."

"The boys and I all think of her as a part of our family. Could you send me contact information for her, please?"

"Of course. She will be glad to hear from you all.

"The reason for my call is to let you know that Harvey Reed is retiring this week. We spoke just a moment ago. To quote him, 'I thought this President had what it took to withstand the thought-police and really fight a war.'

"He's not bitter. Just frustrated that politics has nearly eradicated the fact that we are at war with the jihadists. He's a legitimate patriot but he won't break the law regardless of the justification. Some of his predecessors played fast and loose with the system, but you already know that. He is convinced that the President is wrong-headed on tactics.

"Harold, he will not call you and ask for a job, and we did not discuss this exactly, but I think he might be a very good asset for Zulu. We both know that the corporation already has an intel section that feeds Mossad and will certainly feed you. Still, there are things Harvey could bring to your organization that will not cause him to compromise his government security pledge."

"And you believe he would work for us?" Harold asked skeptically.

"I'm relatively certain of it, if you are willing to live with his independent streak. You might even consider using him as a contract worker. Help him set up his own group perhaps. He is used to being the boss. But he knows where all the bodies are buried in DC and his touch in intelligence – operationally and administratively – is renowned.

"Thank you, Sir. Perhaps you'd better fax me his contact info too. And I do appreciate your thinking of us. We are still in the foundational stages and it's sort of driving the boys crazy. Me, I'm used to admin, so it isn't so bad."

"I'll include something in my fax that may help them as well." Don Rogers chuckled. He knew the former agents would not be much for waiting around.

"Good bye, Harold. God bless you all. Stay safe."

"Our prayers are with you, Sir. Goodbye."

"Actually, Harold, I was thinking of taking a small vacation now that I'm unemployed. They say the stripers are six feet long up at Raystown Lake. That's only about an hour and a half from you," Harvey Reed was famous for his success at bass fishing.

"Give me the date that you'd like a little company and you'll get three visitors. Jake and I used to do quite a bit of cat fishing. Ever eat them?" Harold liked the Tortoise, though he was not at all sure the feeling was mutual. That name was secretly given him by the current President. The man had the decency to be truly embarrassed when Harvey showed up at an Oval Office meeting wearing tortoiseshell glasses and a smile. There are no secrets in the Capitol.

A Casper-Milquetoast-sort of persona was the genuine Harvey. He was quiet and unassuming in public but a steel rod in frozen ground on intelligence matters. Soft spoken but a zealot for the fastest automobiles he could get his hands on. An expert driver, knowledgeable on engines, fine tuning and racing, he scared his passengers with a glee far surpassing the most rabid roller coaster fans.

Harold had the impression that he was neither pleased nor trusting of Solutions newest move into fighting terrorism. This move out of government stunned Harold, who believed Harvey would be the DCIA until some very foolish President played politics with the job.

"You know, I have eaten catfish. You cannot go to Alabama without enjoying that delicacy. My late mentor and I went on a number of fishing trips there. Do you fry them in cornmeal breading or flour?"

"Ha. Ha. Only cornmeal is proper on catfish. Any other coating would get you run out of our county! Though it's actually a combo of cornmeal and flour."

"Well, I prefer my blue gill the same way. I'll lay in supplies and be prepared for a good fish dinner when you all come up. And seriously, bring some tackle and plan on staying a day or two. More if time allows." The joy in Harvey's voice was genuine, Harold could tell. This might turn into a fun day or two.

"Harvey, I should tell you that Don Rogers called a moment ago."

"I knew he would. I got a lecture about being too young to waste my talents. He mentioned your name in the next breath.

"How is everything going? I got a report that all your technical installations were up and running."

Chuckles escaped Harold. "I suppose they told you we erased your back doors, too?"

"Wouldn't know a thing about that. Just so you're happy with the stuff. It really is the latest and greatest, you know."

"It should be. I could wire a city for what we paid for everything. And then the software bills were nearly equal to the hardware." Harold was sure there was a mistake on the invoices until he'd checked with Elvis and Sarah. They'd just shrugged and said it was about right.

"Harold, I have done lots of thinking about your situation since our last meeting at the Willard.

"Don and I truly thought that the current administration would be different. It seems that Reagan was the last man who was strong enough to withstand the slings and arrows hurled by the sniffy elitists in and out of government.

"Are our leaders so egotistical and insecure that their legacy means more to them than governing well enough to protect the republic?

"I watch some of the movies about how abusive the Agency is, usually thinly camouflaged by some innocuous name, but still the Agency. The plot goes like this – weak national leader, firm somewhat radical DCIA[4], gutsy agent who agrees, and they take matters into their own hands to save the world.

Of course in the act, they break every law on the books, kill a few innocents, and then somewhere toward the end, the agent gets religion and wakes up to the wickedness of the DCIA. Turns the tables on them, saves the nation anyway, and kills a few hundred bad guys just to make it interesting.

---

[4] Director, Central Intelligence Agency

"One of the worst nightmares for me is that I should ever become like that. I know that one does not make an omelet without breaking eggs but our nation is a country where law matters.

"Your entity is – in my opinion – bordering on an outlaw bunch. Perhaps you can dissuade me of that idea. Truthfully I hope so, because I see so much that needs to be done and so few politicians or bureaucrats who have the lead in their keel to keep them stable when the tough stuff begins. 9/11 was only the flamboyant part of the war by the jihadists. Your boys know that as well as anyone in the world." Harvey was talking plainly, so Harold figured it was time for him to do likewise. If he was being recorded on the other end then so much the better.

"When I was operational I watched good men be abused because they didn't play politics. Some were in your agency, some in mine, and of course others with different units or organizations. I watched more good men burn out and become hopeless due to political appointees or boot-lickers rising higher and faster in the system. Men on the front lines need to know that the people sending them into danger are equally as courageous in their own way.

"Then there is this cold fact. There are people so evil in this world that killing them is the only answer. Talk, patience, negotiations are all tools they use only to gain advantage. They never plan to make peace. Ultimately they must die for civilization to progress. For real peace to ever be achieved. It isn't enough to be strong. There must be the will to use that strength in defense of freedom.

"There are pacifists in this world who believe that if you kill one then ten more will rise in his place. Others believe that if we just cut the greenhouse gases, act harmless and don't insult any of these jihadists they will leave us alone. I don't believe that for a moment. Bullies and fanatics don't go away in the face of pacifism, they become worse. Hitler, Stalin, Pol Pot, Saddam and the current batch all make my point.

"Furthermore, I don't believe you can just kill the shooters. You have to go after the money men. The major players. Even if they are at the very height of government, business, whatever.

"Just as the kamikazes were stopped by stopping the rulers in Japan, these terrorists will someday stop, but not until their leadership pays too high a price to fund, lead and motivate them in their horrific practices.

"As an example, Hamas grows in Israel because Abbas is so corrupt and weak. Western governments want to elevate and strengthen him. Their lap dog.

Arafat controlled the terrorist groups because they knew he was ruthless. Hamas knows Abbas' politicians are weak and they think ours are naïve compounded by weakness.

"When it costs the top leaders more than they are willing to pay, then they will make peace – or they will be killed. Simple. Cold, but simple. And someone has to do it.

"And someone needs to be confident enough to stand up and publicly espouse this idea. Over and over until it takes root in the hearts and minds of free people all over the world.

"This effeminate, humanist idea that all thoughts are of equal weight is nonsense. There *is* a right and wrong. A good and evil. When people or nations lose that concept they soon lose their nation, their freedom, and ultimately their lives.

"Solutions plans on stopping these power brokers. Take their jets away. Stop their lavish lifestyles, corrupt practices and expose their hypocrisy. Make them wake up in a cold sweat in the middle of the night. And we plan on using other tyrants to do most of the dirty work. We are not Murder, Inc. But we will maintain the right to defend ourselves and to act in our own best interests, and in the interests of freedom. That may be for America, for Israel or for some other nation if it genuinely wants peace and freedom for its citizens. We are Americans first but we know that no nation is perfect. We just want to do what we have been equipped and tasked to accomplish.

"That is neither Pollyanna nor prudish. We just won't get caught up in excusing stupid, corrupt or vain politicians – from any nation. We are going to be in the hunt using technology, massive redirection of corrupt money, and planting subversives within their own organizations." Harold suddenly realized that he had been preaching from his heart about why he was involved with Solutions.

"Sounds like fun, Harold. I am very pleased and interested in what you're saying. Let's go fishing and talk some more."

"Send me the information. We'll see you at the lake." Harold hung up and turned to the already humming fax.

After he replaced the phone Harvey Reed sat at his desk quietly doodling on a scratch pad and smiling like a Sphinx. Was he about to take the ride of his life in a juggernaut or climb into a new sports model that will go mach 2 and set his hair on fire?

He reached in his desk drawer and pulled out a personal phone book.

TWENTY ONE

Nick Larsen sat very still as the young doctor peeled back the dressing on his trapezoid muscle. The area was black and blue, with interesting shades of yellow, purple and green. A raw chunk of flesh was closed with sutures.

"How does it feel? Any muscle twitching; contractions? Like you're having a Charlie-horse here?" he probed gently with a forefinger.

"No," Nick started to shake his head in the negative. That action brought severe pain in the wound area along the top of his right shoulder.

"Probably shouldn't do a lot of that," the doc said soto-voce and grinned as he worked with a pair of tweezers and a magnifying glass. To his right, alongside the bed stood a nurse with a plastic dish about the size of a coffee saucer.

Nick silently agreed.

"There you are!" still quietly speaking to his work area, the doctor raised the tweezers. Between the tips was a piece of copper jacket with a bit of lead attached which he dropped into the dish.

"These will work out for the next year or so, most likely. Won't be enough to stop you at airport security, though," he smiled.

"We got everything we could see, but what with swelling and bruising we don't go digging. There are no major pieces left. Just these little boogers.

Still Nick was silent.

The doctor decided it was time for his anatomy lecture.

"The functions of the *Trapezius* muscle include scapular elevation – shrugging, scapular adduction – drawing the shoulder blades together, and scapular depression pulling the shoulder blades down.

"I'd suggest you not do a lot of pull-ups, chin-ups, or push-ups for a while. By the way the fact that you're already an iron man kept the damage from being more serious. "You'll be here for two more days, mostly for us to watch for infection, and take the stitches out. You can go home and then a week later follow up with your family doctor. No active duty for two weeks after you leave. Limited duty for a month after that. Any questions? No? Okay. Just take it easy." With that he and his silent nurse headed out. She flashed a sweet, sympathetic smile, and followed the doc.

Nick got out of the bed and gingerly walked to the window. Ten floors up, he could see a wide panorama along the Susquehanna River. The narrow strip of park on this side, Wormleysburg and part of

Camp Hill on the far bank. In the far distance the Allegheny Mountains were blue-green.

He idly re-buttoned the pajama shirt and considered what the future held for him. No one he knew had ever lost their primary[5] before. He'd talked with Secret Service men though and knew in their ranks once that happened you were whale dung. The lowest thing on the face of the earth.

It wasn't that you got fired. Just the opposite. You had a job for life if you were wounded. That job just stunk. Desk duty. Telephones, paperwork, details. Advanced secretarial trash. No longer a cop.

You needn't have done anything wrong. The Secret Service people said it was like you bore the "scarlet letter" on your forehead. *He lost his primary. Don't get too close. There's a pox on his house.*

So what do I do now? I'm forty years old. Twenty-one years on the Job. Too old to go back to patrol. Elizabethtown has a regional police force. The Chief is a good man. I don't want to put up with all the baloney necessary to run for Sheriff. No Thanks!

The Pennsylvania State Police Commandant, Colonel Kryder had departed just moments before the doctor came by. He was nervous. Not that anyone was to blame. The team had done their job correctly. Security was a nightmare with the Governor and everyone knew it.

Nick's reputation was stellar. If he'd had a college degree and played the political cards that came with it he could have ended up high in the system some day.

It was just that, well… no one quite knew how to handle him. He was wounded in the line of duty. Not exactly a hero, but a man of note. Still there was the fact that the governor was dead. Couldn't very well promote the lead man.

"Nick, I know this is tough on you. You're one of our best. Still, we will give you a good job. I'm thinking Assistant Commandant of the Academy. You were great there before. If you want to handle the special ops training along with your administrative duties that would be fine. Get you out of the office. I know you like the field." Kryder had looked away from the view he'd been surveying as he spoke. *Help me here, Larsen,* was written in his eyes. He was a decent man. Liked Nick, detested this part of his job.

"Yessir. What ever you think is best. I just want to stay in this area. I have a home here. My church is here. Family. You know I have roots here."

---

[5] The subject of the protection detail. In this case the Governor of Pennsylvania Red Endreling.

"Of course," relief flooded the Colonel's face. This was going to work out fine. Larsen was a good soldier. He would do his duty and not make any waves about the move out of Executive Protection. The Colonel grabbed his hat, gently shook Nick's hand.

"Oh, Mrs. Endreling asked me to tell you that she knows you did your duty. She definitely doesn't hold you responsible in any way."

"Thank you, Sir. That's good to hear." A moment later the doctor came hurrying in with his nurse, arms full of charts.

At first he didn't hear the knock on the door. Then he turned his head and winced, a rich picture of pain. *Turn slowly from the waist!* he remembered.

"Don't know if you remember us or not. We saw the news. Thought we'd come by and bring you something." They stepped into the hospital room like they were entering a mine field.

Nick instantly remembered them from the gun range. The guys with the automatics. These boys could shoot.

"Sure. Jake and Larry?" *What was the name of that company? Some computer thing?* "Come on in." Nick didn't reach out to shake hands, but moved to sit on the bed as Jake and Larry stepped into the room scanning for equipment. There was nothing but the standard O2 outlet and a blood pressure cuff and tube. *Must not be too serious.*

"How ya doin'?" Larry asked, laying a three pound box of Godiva chocolates on the rolling table beside the bed.

"I'm doing pretty good. Sore as the devil. Just got a lecture from the doctor on the trapezoid muscle. He needn't have bothered. It feels like it's hooked to every part of my body except my feet." Nick sat slowly back and grinned a weak smile.

"First time getting shot?" Larry continued the questions. Jake looked out the window. It was a beautiful sight.

"Yeah. Either of you been hit?" Nick could talk to these men. They were in the hunt. Warriors with no doubt much more experience than he had.

"I got one in the butt, one in the leg in Panama, and a 22 long rifle round not long ago near the plumbing. Hit the femoral. It's okay now.

"Jake, he almost took one in the skull, but a welder saved his bacon. Hit an I-beam. His facial damage was massive as you can see." Larry tightened up and dropped his left elbow to protect his ribs from Jake's fist.

"I took a round in the web of my left hand too. Just sliced that little flap of skin. Got stabbed in the side in Iran by a goober who thought he was gonna rob a beggar. That was my cover that time. He sneaked up on me or he'd never have got me." Jake grinned. He hated knives to this day.

"After I started going to Israel, I got a little Krav Maga training. You know anything about that self defense method?"

"I sure do! Right after the Governor…" a shadow passed over Nick's face as he recalled that the Governor was now dead.

"Anyway, he sent three of us to Israel for two weeks for some advanced training. We were at a place up near Caesarea. Those boys are tough!" he laughed remembering the experience.

"That they are, but they're good. We've both been there," Jake agreed.

"We did Krav Maga until I could hardly walk. Actually I was sorer than I am now. Even when we were doing handgun drills they were pounding on us. Shoving, screaming in our ears. Stuff like that.

"I'll tell you, though, I think they may be the best in the world, and I've had some real good instructors."

"They *are* good. Did you get to see any of Israel when you were there?" Larry asked.

"I did. We took about three days and just hit the major tourist sites. That plus restaurants in Tel Aviv. It's an amazing place.

"Actually, my former pastor is sort of an Israeli guru. He's Jewish on his mother's side. Been hosting tours there forever. He lives in Jerusalem now. His son took over when he retired.

"He showed me a lot of photos and gave me a book he wrote on touring. *Traveling Israel with Your Bible.* I still get it out and check some things now and then when I read my Bible and want to know about some place."

"So your old pastor is a Christian *and* a Jew?" Jake asked with real interest.

"Yeah. Didn't know it until he started doing genealogy research on his grandmother in the mid-nineties. He was as stunned as anyone. He was actually excited about it. He already knew so much about the country. Had been leading tours for years. Loved the place. Preached the Old Testament like it was yesterday. Finding out he was Jewish was the icing on the cake for him." That Nick loved the old preacher was so evident that Jake and Larry were both touched by it.

Jake smiled, "My mother was Jewish. And a believer in Yeshua, too. That's Jesus, you know. My dad is pure Irish but my mother was born in Israel."

Larry muttered in a fake-sad voice, "I'm the token Arab. Detroit born. He only keeps me around to prove how open-minded he is," poking a thumb in Jake's direction.

"She was a believer?" Nick asked Jake while grinning at Larry and wondering if it was wise to enter such a potentially sensitive area.

"She was. It was sort of tough for her in the beginning to sort it all out. But one day she told me how she finally got it straight in her mind. I'd asked her about the differences between being a Jew and being a Christian.

"Son, each of us has to find our own way in the area of belief. There are so many traditions in the Jewish world. It's like we are all on the same side, united by our history and our catastrophes, but at the same time kept apart by the various sects and secular perspectives."

"But, Mom, you said that some Jews say you're no longer Jewish!" Jake was having a hard time grasping how someone believed they could cancel out your own personal roots.

"Yes, Jake, some people do say that. Some are very hostile toward Christians. It amazes your father. America has its faults regarding Jews, but over the long haul this country has been good to the Jewish people. The Truman government turned a blind eye to the Israel Bond drives that allowed Israelis to raise the money to buy arms and even airplanes before the War of Independence began.

"And it was President Truman who first recognized Israel as a nation.

"America has given Jewish people more of a haven than any other nation in the world. They have opened up their corporations, educational systems – all aspects of life to us."

"But Dad says lots of people around here hate Jews. Like the guy at the furniture store."

"Yes, there is a tremendous amount of anti-Semitism in this part of the country. Not just this county. Some people are very outspoken. But we have found some dear friends here too, and they know I'm a Jew. You too, for that matter. If you look at it as a personal thing, rather than regional, you won't get a chip on your shoulder. Give each person a chance, and often they'll give you the same."

"So what about being a Jew and a believer in Jesus as the Messiah?" Jake had lots of questions.

"Let me tell you, Son. Most Jewish people know very little about the Bible. By that I mean their Bible. What we call the Old Testament. They read the same passages year in and year out. Torah readings, mostly. Hardly ever do they read the whole Old Covenant.

"The rabbis have kept them away from many passages about the Messiah. Your dad and I did a study one time a few years ago. There are over three hundred different Old Testament prophecies that were fulfilled by Jesus Christ!

"The Law of Moses served to show the people that they could never be good enough to deserve Heaven. It was given as a guideline, but the New Testament tells us that it clearly shows that everyone needs a Saviour. That comes through faith.

"David was saved. He spoke of it in Psalm fifty-one when he repented of his sin with Bathsheba. He said, 'restore unto me the joy of my salvation.' He wanted his joy restored, not his salvation. He had it, sinned, but kept salvation. His joy was destroyed because he separated himself from the fellowship of joy he had when he was spiritually right. That much is clear if one just reads the Word.

"He knew he had been saved. But he also said this, 'Then will I teach transgressors thy ways; and sinners shall be converted unto thee.' He believed in sharing his relationship with the Lord.

"Your dad says that is as clear as any New Testament verse about salvation and winning the lost to the Saviour," she smiled at Harold's love for the word. He reminded her of David in that he could be such a warrior and so much love the Lord.

"You can read Isaiah fifty-two and fifty-three, or the last part of Daniel nine and see Jesus as clear as a bell." She went to the end table and retrieved her Bible. The ribbon was at Daniel chapter nine.

"Listen to this Jake. My heart soars when I read it. Here. Let's start at chapter nine and verse twenty-four.

'Seventy weeks are determined upon thy people and upon thy holy city, to finish the transgression, and to make an end of sins, and to make reconciliation for iniquity, and to bring in everlasting righteousness, and to seal up the vision and prophecy, and to anoint the most Holy. 25Know therefore and understand, *that* from the going forth of the commandment to restore and to build Jerusalem unto the Messiah the Prince *shall be* seven weeks, and threescore and two weeks: the street shall be built again, and the wall, even in troublous times. 26And after threescore and two weeks shall Messiah be cut off, but not for himself: and the people of the prince that shall come shall destroy the city and the sanctuary; ….'

"Jake, the amount of time from that the command to rebuild the Temple until Jesus walked into Jerusalem on the week before his crucifixion is exactly four hundred and thirty four years. Sixty-two weeks of seven years.

"But wait! Now listen again to verse twenty-six," She read it again. 'Messiah shall be cut off.' That means to die before one would expect it.

"There's a tombstone out at Pine Tree Cemetery that says that. A sixteen year old boy's stone. 'Cut off in his prime,' it says.

"There's more. 'But not for himself.' Your father calls that 'vicarious atonement.' It means that he died for someone else. No one can die for someone else except the only begotten Son of God, the Messiah. God would not accept it from anyone else," she was on a roll now, and the passion was strong in her voice.

"The rest of the passage talks about the destruction of the city of Jerusalem! Titus did that in 70 AD. Jake that means that the Messiah was here before the Temple was demolished. That he came as predicted in Daniel. That he died a sacrificial death, and that only afterwards did the walls of Jerusalem come down. "

As his mother closed her Bible, Jake was taken with the peacefulness on her face. It was obvious that she had fought an enormous battle within her soul over this question. Could Jesus Christ, himself a Jew, really be the Messiah of the Jews and the Christians alike?

That she had used God's own words to settle the conflict was so like her. She – like most Jews – was not one to take anyone else's opinion for much. She wanted to settle important issues on her own. And so she had turned to the pages of what she knew was God's Word in her heart first – the Old Covenant. The Tanach. That timeless arbiter in the events of mankind. Only then, when she was satisfied that, Yes, Jesus was in there, did she comfortably begin to study – indeed to devour – the New Covenant.

He'd watched her study but never really gotten involved with it. It has seemed something she and his father had shared, though they often invited him to join them. After her death at the hands of a drunk driver, how he wished he'd sat with them all those times. It was one more thing a young man learns too late.

Once he'd spoken to his father about it. Even taken notes she'd written during those many hours and studied for himself. He knew now. Without any doubt that her beliefs were also his own. And he loved knowing. He was one-hundred percent legally Jewish. And even more importantly he was one hundred percent a believer in the Jews' Messiah, Jesus Christ.

Jake snapped back to the present. Larry and Nick were laughing about a training story Larry was recounting complete with grunts and twists of his body.

" – so this old Sergeant First Class has my wrist so far up behind my back it was about to meet my skull. He lifts a bit more – I'm already on my tip-toes – and he says, 'Well, Sport, do you think you can follow my way of thinkin' about this from now on?"

Nick laughed, winced, and reached for the water glass on the table. He sipped, then ripped open the chocolates and passed them around.

"Do you know what your next assignment will be, Nick?" It was blunt and to the point, but Jake had a purpose.

Nick, back to the bleakness of the State Police reality, answered, "I won't be protecting any more governors, I know that much.

"Funny I was thinking about it when you guys got here.

"The Commandant was here a while ago. He's talking about me going to the Academy. I was there before as PT and Range Instructor.

"Truthfully, I wasn't happy on the Executive Detail. This governor was taking his toll on me, though I sure wouldn't have wished this on him.

"You know, it just occurred to me. I'm gonna get tested for AIDS. That bullet was carrying his blood!

"Sorry. That just came blurting out. Must be the pain killers.

"Not long ago two other good troopers on the detail took retirement because of him. I was thinking about doing just that when all this came down.

"Truthfully I don't know what I want to do. Probably retire. From there, who knows? You looking for a slightly abused body guard?" Nick said half-jokingly.

"As a matter of fact we're looking for someone *just* like you," Jake said.

"We're expanding and have to add some people as agents, trainers, and other duties. When we met at the range, we all liked the way you handled yourself. Dad made some calls regarding your experience. He got some great answers.

"You get out of here then we'll all have dinner with you and your wife. Get to know one another better and vice versa. That is if you're interested.

"We'll lay out exactly what's on our horizon. If you like it, then we'll go the next step and talk duties, money, and so on. From what we already know I think it will interest you. Lots more adrenaline than you're used to if you want that. And lots better pay.

"I will tell you this. We're going after terrorists. Here and around the world. We are taking the war to them. Not just killing them, but taking their organizations apart. Destroying their money men. Military strikes on their bases. Making sure that their leaders never get a good night's sleep from now on. And that's not talk. When we get together – and we can do that even while you're still healing – we can give you some of our ideas.

After they'd gone Nick's thoughts whirled at the prospects. He was sad at the loss of the Governor, that much was true. At the loss to the man's family. But professionally, things were definitely looking up.

Only a few minutes ago he'd been almost feeling sorry for himself. Now the potential promises from this catastrophe were coming full force. He liked these guys. His "people radar" encouraged him. And they were honest to goodness believers! Could this be real?

"Ready for some company?" his preacher's head poked around the door.

"Come in Preacher. Man, do I have questions for you. We need to do some talking *and* some praying."

TWENTY TWO

Savannah is an intriguing place. Located on Interstate 95 amid lakes, swamps, the Savannah River and snuggling the Atlantic's salt marshes, it is a fisherman's paradise.

Downtown the antebellum houses and Spanish moss-drenched live oaks remind one of a time when gentlemen tipped their hats to ladies in long, full dresses and danced at fancy balls. When chestnut stallions clopped down the cobblestone streets tossing their proud heads just as did their masters. That was the "Gone with the Wind" picture.

Of course the slaves laboring along the Savannah River banks back then did not share the vision and all was not propriety and gallantry. Savannah past and present is a place of great beauty and ugliness, of sinners and saints. Lookers usually find that which they seek here as everywhere. Jake and Tex went to find none of that. It was just the location of Gulfstream's business and Flight Safety's training facility.

As they flew down in the King Air 350 Tex said, "Jake, I still can't imagine just writin' off this airplane like the government did." He raised a hand as if to ward off a dismissal. "Don't get me wrong, I seen 'em do lots of crazy things over the years. It just surprised me, that's all."

Jake nodded and grinned. "It stunned me, for sure. But like Dad said, it's an investment in us. I think Don Rogers wanted us to still be able to move and respond quickly if the call goes out. Speaking of which, does it make you wonder about how quiet things are now? Nothing on the Terrorist Babe, no attacks in the U.S.?"

"Sure it makes me wonder," Tex paused for effect. "Wonder when the hammer will fall on some poor folks and ruin their lives for ever – them who survive," Tex said, watching a jet tow a white trail through the sky off to his left and much higher up.

"Does it stun you, Jake? All the changes that's happened lately? I ain't tryin' to be smart, but you guys was just government agents not long ago. Now you're rich as Midas, planning to climb up onto al Qaeda's operations and tip over their apple cart. Able to look at property, just turn over the money and it's yours, and the such.

"And I cain't believe what you did for Momma and me, not to mention how you just brought George and Helen along. Momma still puddles up when she thinks about how you guys gave us an interest free mortgage for our own house. First one we've ever owned in all our married years."

Tex was fixing to "puddle up" a bit himself. His nose grew red, and his eyes filled with tears. He was passionate about the changes in his life since he'd "got Jesus," and gone to work for Solutions. The two weren't literally connected but to Tex they were part of God's "master plan" for his life.

Jake glanced over as he heard the thickening in Tex's last words. Tex had been a government pilot all his flying career. First with Air America flying CIA agents and others around the jungles of Viet Nam, Laos and Cambodia. He'd had his planes peppered with bullet holes often enough. Getting to see the dark side of American operations and operators, Tex had been a hard-drinking, mean little man with a lot of bravado and swagger.

After South East Asia he'd criss-crossed Central America running guns and equipment to the Contras. Back to the Pacific, Tex spent a year in the Philippines island hopping – still chasing insurgents. Then he'd gone to Columbia and helped American government types fight the losing drug war.

A few choppers, mostly mid-size planes and occasionally a Cessna Citation, Tex's flying experience had been right up there with his boozing. Then that all changed when he had received Jesus Christ as his personal Saviour. The drinking ceased. He lost the swagger but not the courage. His attitude changed toward his wife – a longsuffering Christian woman that many had said "married poorly." They went to church together, and Tex worked hard to make amends for his past. He took an assignment in Florida for the FBI which allowed him to be home most of the time. He made peace with his family, and as he put it, "Didn't get religion, I got a relationship with Jesus."

When the opportunity to be a part of the Solutions.com team arose he'd flown up from Florida and interviewed. Jake's mother had been killed by a drunk driver, and Tex's face advertised his former love affair with booze. Jake's question, "Have you ever killed anyone while you were drunk?" had silenced the room and crashed Tex's hopes of working on the project.

When his answer was a clear, "No," and Jake approved him, Tex saw the Lord's hand. As things progressed he knew it was Jesus who was blessing his repentance.

Jake, sitting in the right seat of the 350, remembered the day they told Tex about the 100 percent mortgage offer complete with down payment money. He had been so overcome with emotion that he turned and quickly walked from the suite at the Willard.

Jake had risen from the easy chair near the window and followed him out the door, where he found the old pilot with his red hankie out, leaning his head against the flocked wallpaper of the hallway. Wiping tears, his face was red and his skinny shoulders were heaving with the effort to get himself under control. Jake strolled up and put his arm across Tex's shoulders, and said, "Hey man, it's only money. We gotta look after our best assets, one of which is you. Knock it off. People are going to think we're softies."

"Jake, I worked with lots of good men over the years, but you guys take the cake!" Tex said and straightened up. "Better get back in there, I guess," and with that they walked back inside and began planning their week.

What Tex still did not know was that in five years, or sooner in case anything happened to any of the principals of the team, the mortgage would be forgiven and the house would be theirs free and clear.

As they flew on both men seemed to step back inside their own thoughts. *I am amazed at how our lives have changed*, Jake thought.

Where is all this taking us? Will we be so caught up in the management of the companies that we're no longer agents? Can Dad really handle operations like Solutions and oversee Zulu at the same time? Do we need to add more agents and analysts? Is Yossi playing us for his own and Israel's good or is he being level with us?

And what about the Terrorist Babe? How can a woman that beautiful and that dangerous just fall off the face of the earth? Every government agency in the country is searching for her. They roll up these Mafia guys all the time. Why not her? Surely some of the White Supremacists have squealed on her! Maybe she's hanging out with Jimmie Hoffa! He grinned at his own humor.

Well, George and Tex are glad to be together. First time since they were young men. Jake smiled. He, like his father, had a heart for people for whom he felt responsible. He was glad when Larry had suggested that George come to work for them. It was also Larry who wanted to give Tex and his wife the interest free mortgage. "What's the sense of having lots of loot if you don't use some of it for good?" he'd asked. Obviously soft hearts were in good supply.

I wonder if I'll ever meet a woman I want to settle down with? Jake asked himself as the plane took them ever closer to Savannah. *Maybe a Southern belle. Or someone from back home. Naw. Not likely from there. I would want a wife who could share interest in international stuff. Someone who wants to raise kids and keep a home, but who would be able to discuss what is happening in the world. Most of the Patterson women are just not interested in anything outside the county*, he wrongly concluded.

Jake reached down into the open-topped saddle leather briefcase. He smiled at his negative reaction when he was buying it and the clerk called it a "lawyer's briefcase." That had almost kept him from purchasing it. But, he needed a case to carry materials in that could be strapped to the top of his rolling luggage and that could be set upright when he flew. Sorting the papers, charts and USA Today newspaper, he finally pulled out what he wanted – printed pages he'd downloaded from the computer at home. Copies of articles from the Jerusalem Post and Ha'aretz Israeli newspapers. Additionally there were some from the Washington Post and Times. Then he read Debkafile.com, a briefing website on the Middle East. Each day he read these five newspapers' internet editions. It kept him up to date on what was happening around the world, provided liberal and conservative opinion, and occasionally tipped him to events which would be of interest to the team's operations later.

To Jake, information put into his mind was grist for the mill that became one's "sixth sense." That, he believed was the subconscious filtering, weighing and finally bringing to the surface facts, ideas, hunches and causes for further thought. The same was true for sensing danger. Jake had long believed that smells, sounds, sights and other input were mostly responsible for that heightened alertness that tipped one off to imminent dangers.

He read the printouts as Tex watched the plane, though it was on autopilot. The thought entered his mind that the G V would handle different, provide different aural input, feels – everything. It felt strange to go from having to endure the lines at airports, waiting endlessly for flight schedules, explaining carrying weapons in checked luggage or occasionally onboard to airline security people. They seemed fascinated by the idea that someone was really authorized to do such a thing. It was just a hassle for Jake and Larry. One they appreciated missing by having access to their own ride.

Another bombing in Tel Aviv. The moment Jake saw the headline his thoughts returned to the one time he had witnessed a homicide bombing up close. It was only a few months ago, but seemed another lifetime. As he read the report, the smells of cordite, burning fuel, flesh and blood along with the cries of the wounded filled his mind. He recalled the school girl with her backpack. The missing arm gushing blood onto the pavement. He'd used his own belt as a tourniquet that day. *Oh, Lord, when will it be over?* he prayed.

Now Israel will blow up some terrorist in his car, destroy the homicide bomber's home, and arrest some thugs in Gaza or the West Bank. Limited response because the world's opinions are like handcuffs keeping them from seeking total victory.

I wonder how Americans would respond if our President made a speech and said, "Well, folks, France doesn't want us to strike at Al Qaeda because they fear we may upset them and cause more attacks, so we will just make a limited response to the attacks on 9/11."? There would be mass fury and he would be out of office in no time. Yet that is exactly what our government wants of Israel.

They ought to give the West Bank back to Jordan, infrastructure and all, move all the settlements out and help them with relocation, or tell them if they stay they are now under Jordanian rule and protection. Keep the Golan Heights and tell Syria "Tough Luck," and "Get on with life."

Let the UN, U.S. and EU have endless meetings and keep occupied that way. Never happen! Jake thought as he looked down at the countryside passing beneath in a slow-motion aerial map. Too simple. Politicians can't accept the simple. He finished reading the printed pages, replaced them in his "lawyer's briefcase," and said, "You want a break Tex? I can take it, if you want."

Tex did not need a break but he relinquished the flying, just changing radio frequencies as air traffic controllers handed them off one to another. Jake pulled two Snickers out of his case, wordlessly handed one to Tex and unwrapped the other.

"Now yer talkin'!" Tex said with an appreciative smile. "Airline food at it's best!!"

For the next twenty-two days Jake and Tex would be attending Flight Safety training for the Gulfstream V that would soon belong to Solutions.com.

Flight Safety is a nationwide company that teaches pilots familiarization with virtually every kind of aircraft. Since Tex was already rated in the Cessna Citation jet, his course would differ from Jake's. He would do all of his training in a simulator. Jake on the other hand, with no jet rating, would take fifteen percent of his time in a real jet and eighty-five percent of his time in the white simulators that from the outside look like a glob of silicone caulk. Inside it is every Microsoft Flight Simulator pilot's great dream.

The actual airplane cockpit is duplicated. Screens outside the false windows represent exact photo-realistic airports, scenery and skies. Operators manipulate the computers which put the student pilots through heart-thudding, sweat pouring scenarios to test their stuff. Of course much of the training is not so shocking. How the aircraft handles, pre-flights, learning instrument locations, aircraft peculiarities, and general flight rules for the specific models take up most of the time.

Completion is not a guarantee of full competence, as all pilots know. Rather, it is assurance that they can fly the plane safely during normal circumstances and have been trained for emergencies. Only piling up hours and continued training will bring real expertise.

The first day began with the introduction of their primary instructor, Constantine "Connie" Morgan. A tall, gray-haired, slat-thin guy with a checkered shirt and well worn jeans topping full quill Tony Lama ostrich cowboy boots. A sun-wrinkled face, pointy chin and Randolph Scott voice completed the idea that this was a Westerner who wasn't born out west. Tex grinned, and held out his hand, "Well you look like home to me."

"Oklahoma, but originated in Wales. My mother's country. Dad was a Yank flying there in the Royal Air Force. She worked in the flight center. One thing led to another and here I am. They lived in Wales for a while. I was raised there, then when I was twelve we came here.

After college I flew for the Marines. Nam; a couple of other places. So far I've flown 94 different planes. I'm shooting for an even 100 before they yank my ticket for old age. Gotta hurry." He grinned a proud grin. The years hadn't diluted that famous Marine pilot testosterone. "Let me show you guys around. From your forms, I see you've never been here before."

Tex and Jake's schedules sometimes coincided, but were more often spent totally apart. Jake was about finished with his simulator time – time that both terrified and exhilarated him. One day he came out of the white machine sick as a rat. The operator hid a grin behind his hand, but there was enough laughter in his eyes to let Jake know that the guy was a sadist at heart.

Jake returned from the men's room only to find the instructor leaning against the wall chewing gum like he wanted to wear out a jaw-joint. "Well, buddy. Ready to go for the hard stuff now? We got a thunderstorm cell comin' up you won't believe."

Jake stood flat footed and looked at the man. There was so much humor and good will on his face that Jake couldn't be mad at him. And bad weather *was* part of flying. It was just that the whole scenario of the simulator rolling over in the updraft, then bouncing like it was skidding down a wash board, and of course there was the garlic pasta he'd had for lunch. That was history now except for a small wet spot on the front of his shirt.

He grinned a sheepish grin and said, "Yeah, but let's keep the thunderstorm for tomorrow."

"Hey, Jake. Don't feel too bad. We had a famous U.S. Senator who happens to have gone into space twice – many years apart – on that particular flight a couple of months ago. Different plane, same storm. He re-painted the console. Couldn't move out as fast as you did. Man it was a mess! Our cleaning ladies almost rioted when they saw it. Said he would never get their vote! Hah!" He clapped Jake on the shoulder and they walked back toward the simulator side by side.

Two days later, Jake walked up to a shiny Gulfstream V. Just behind the cockpit the air steps were open. The airplane was a light tan with a wide gold stripe down the belly running below the six oval windows in the fuselage. An American Flag floated on the tail and Jake saluted it with a small movement. Connie noted the move though Jake was off to his side.

"You military?" he asked, meaning Jake's background.

"No. I spent some time with DIA though. Now I'm doing security."

"The last military jet I was in was the F-14 Tomcat. It had just come to the Navy and Viet Nam got some of the brand new ones in '74. Great plane.

"I started flying when I was fourteen. My dad had a little flight center, airport operation. He plowed the snow and mowed the infield grass, my mom handled the radio. You been to them. Small time operations, but Dad would have rather been the captain of a model plane than part of the giants. He wanted time with me and my brother and sister. Knew he could make more money flying jets but just felt that rebuilding engines and selling used planes would help us turn out better.

Flight lessons, tie down fees and a place for sky divers to operate gave us a comfortable life. My sister's a teacher, never been in an airplane. My brother is an oceanographer for an outfit in San Diego. Land, Water and Sky. We're a mix. Dad used to say we were his 'Navy Seals.'"

He laughed and began to brief Jake in the pre-flight walk around. Jake asked wise questions and Connie could see that he was serious about his responsibilities and a quick study.

Jake climbed the air stairs and looked into the body of the plane. "GOOD NIGHT! This looks like a palace!" Jake had flown in a Lear 35 once, courtesy of the Air Force, but it had been outfitted for as many passengers as possible. Nice, but nothing like this. Wide, butter-soft gold leather reclining seats. Rich, polished tables in a deep cherry hue that could be raised from the side of the cabin to provide dining and work areas. Even a leather sofa and buffet table running along the cabin wall!

There was a full galley with microwave oven, convection oven, sink, refrigerator, real dishes and crystal glasses. A washroom, head and even a bed was made up in the back! Carpeting was commercial, but attractive and rich looking. There was a full entertainment center including video and stereo systems. The wood was polished to a glass finish. Gold plated fixtures in the head (toilet) and galley topped off the luxury. The cabin was high enough to stand in comfortably, and wide enough to seem expansive. Jake looked around like Jack staring at the beanstalk.

Connie grinned. He had witnessed this before. Many pilots are accustomed to minimal space. This was a bit different. They couldn't seem to decide if they wanted to stay here in the lap of luxury or go forward to the cockpit, knowing it would lack the roominess and fine appointments.

To make up for that, though, would be the latest Honeywell Advanced Electronics System – EASy. Flat screen displays replaced many of the instrument faces. Combined readouts, terrain mapping and GPS overlays. Full color weather radar and more. It was the latest and greatest for the men and women who carried their wealthy passengers around the world. Gulfstream and other manufacturers had put not only bells and whistles in the cockpit, but the highest redundancy and safety features in the one hundred years of flight history.

"I'm not hazing you but tell, me, did you have to learn to fight with a name like Connie?" Jake asked as he was browsing in cabinet drawers, and generally becoming familiar with the cabin. "I had a buddy named Shirley when I was a kid. He regularly had to teach some big mouth that it wasn't wise to laugh at him."

Connie chuckled thinking back to his own youth. He said drolly, "Yeah, sometimes there'd be a flare up. Dad gave me some good advice, though. He said to nail the biggest guy right off the bat. Turn his lights out and the rest of them would leave me alone. Worked pretty good most of the time. I learned to make pre-emptive strikes, too. Makes me admire the Israelis and this President. Only smart way to fight. Strike first with more power than necessary then just mop up. Keep your mouth shut and let your strength speak for you. Not bullying, but not wimping around either."

Connie returned to his duties, and said, "Let's go forward and you can see the rest of the toys. You're gonna love it up front."

Jake was familiar with the instruments due to all his hours in simulators these past days, but still, the wonder of looking out the windscreen and knowing this was the real thing took his breath away. Connie spent a lot of time going over all the systems, showing Jake all the nooks and crannies of the cockpit, giving tips like where to stash stuff. "Even the cup holders are sharp," he laughed.

Finally they fired up the two BMW/Rolls-Royce BR 710 engines, contacted ground control and requested taxi permission.

They already had their weather briefing but had not filed a flight plan. They were VFR on a training flight. Savannah Tower was used to that. Requesting taxi permission to the active runway Jake said, "Gulfstream November 643 Poppa. Request taxi to the active." That was given, Connie dealt with the flaps and radios, but had Jake instruct him for familiarization. When they were holding at the side of the active runway Jake contacted the tower for take off. They immediately responded affirmatively.

Jake advanced the throttles on the two powerful engines gently and lined the jet up on the center stripe. Then he looked at Connie who grinned and nodded. He moved the throttle levers forward with his right hand and the jet burst out of the gate like a bull at a rodeo. Jake was forced backward in his seat as the speed built faster than he could ever remember experiencing. It was but a moment and they were at one hundred-twenty-five knots an hour and the nose was rising. Then the rumble of tires on concrete ceased and the plane wanted to point its nose straight up.

Jake said, "Gear," then when it was up and locked with three green lights testifying on the console, he said, "Flaps," and Connie took off the bit of flaps they'd had on takeoff. The radio was chattering about changing frequencies and Jake was pushing on the yoke to get the nose to stay in a 20 degree climb and not go to double that. He retarded the throttles a good bit and said, "Connie, I saw this in the sim, but this thing wants to rip and snort. I'm battling to keep it from going vertical!"

Connie was pushing com radio buttons and programming the next frequency. He grinned – this was common for him. Pilots who'd flown props – even turbo props like Jake's King Air were not prepared for the raw power of the G V. It usually didn't get away from them, but their juices were definitely flowing on the first flight. The simulators just couldn't provide this.

Laughing, he said, "Jake you have here the most fun you can have in this lifetime." He paused then said, "Adjust for a speed of 320 knots and go to a heading of 170." Jake made the changes, fiddled with the throttles for a while to get the speed where he wanted it, and trimmed the airplane out for smooth flying. Connie could see he worked at it. Not uncommon for pilots lacking thousands of hours. Still, he was competent and relatively smooth for his first time in this plane. He would do well, especially with a good "left seat" to help pile on more hours. There were storm clouds ahead of them.

The jet entered the cloud, was buffeted like a mildly rocky road, then popped out. Nothing to it. The ground diminished as they continued to climb to twenty-nine thousand at about 2700 feet a minute. Already they were crossing the Georgia-Florida state line as Connie pointed out landmarks. They had just been handed to Jacksonville Center's controllers, and Connie made the appropriate radio changes. He gave Jake heading changes, observed as he made the correct moves and guided the beautiful thoroughbred through the skies. *Thor should have such a steed,* Jake thought grinning from ear to ear.

Connie appreciated the joy Jake was experiencing. And too, he liked that the young man was not hiding it. Watching the honest exhilaration a pilot felt when his fast, sleek and powerful airplane complied to his control was a wonderful thing. Not feeling one had to hide or suppress it showed the love of piloting was real not just a job or burdensome task.

Connie had seen some who came to Flight Safety who were weary of the job. Sad eyed, slack-jawed and bored. Get it over so I can go back home types. That wasn't Jake. He was thriving on the experience and would be a safe, competent flier.

They flew to Daytona then turned southwest toward Orlando, where Jake did a touch and go landing. From there, they flew north to Augusta and Bush Field. They landed, went to operations and had lunch. Finally they took off again and flew over the snaky Savannah River and home.

Connie tested Jake on procedures, discussed emergencies, and had him retard one engine, then the other and deal with the changes; had him slow the plane down and "dirty it up" with gear and flaps, even spoiler, to see how it handled. They talked about icing, humid air conditions, loss of power, a number of peculiarities of the G V, and the demands of world navigation. He found Jake a hungry student, and that brought out the best in himself to teach the young man and care about his future in flying. They liked each other, and respected their mutual professionalism.

When they were on final at Savannah International, Connie coached Jake very little on approach. The landing was white knuckle for Jake – a ripping cross wind had come up while they were gone, but he handled it, bouncing a little, but doing well overall. When the nose wheel settled down and they were braking, Jake let out his breath. He didn't know when he'd begun to hold it, but it burst forth with a "whuooow." Connie laughed, reached across the cockpit and clapped him on the right shoulder. "You did fine. I was only terrified for a brief moment when we bounced, but you got it under control. No sweat."

Jake's last few days were a combination of book learning, a bit more sim time and actual flights. None of it was a drag. He loved it. Now to get that plane Yossi had arranged for Solutions! Tex felt the same way. Actually he was frustrated that Jake was in the air and he was restricted to the "glob" as he referred to the simulator.

When they arrived at the hotel, the little light on the phone was flashing. Message. Jake punched the appropriate buttons and soon the voice mail was playing.

"Jake this is Connie. Someone in the know down here says you guys are in the game. That you have a company that's free lancing or something like that. I don't exactly know how it works, but I'd like to talk to you about being a part of it. If you could call me at 555-3490 I'd like to get with you and discuss it. Thanks."

"Did anybody ask you about Solutions, Tex?" Jake replaced the phone after deleting the message.

Tex was sitting by the window sipping a bottled water waiting for Jake to get ready to go eat. "Well, one day their boss man came to me and asked if Solutions was an American or a Swiss company. Said there was some confusion on their paperwork. I said American. Didn't know what we really were, but I know me and you are Americans, so that's what I told him. He looked on his clip board, nodded, and said 'Thanks,' and walked away. That was all, and I rightly forgot about it until now. Hope I told him right." Tex waited for an up or down vote by Jake.

"Sounds okay. Yossi said it will be a Swiss registered company, but I don't know if that includes our American holdings like the farm, offices, the King Air, even."

He told Tex about Connie's message, and then called the number he'd scribbled down on the little memo pad by the phone. Tex liked Connie too, and was as curious as Jake.

"Connie, let's get something to eat." A pause. "Downtown." Another pause. "Ten minutes." And he hung up.

"Tex, we're going downtown to eat. Someplace Connie knows. He wants to talk to me about going to work for us. As a G V pilot no doubt."

Tex said, "Well we need one, and he fits the bill for professionalism. His clothes look right for the job too." Jake looked at him with raised eyebrows and Tex chuckled.

"Who woulda told him about us? But… you know, Jake, they do a security check before they allow anybody to come here for training. Since 9/11 Homeland Security is pretty touchy 'bout who gets pilot training at jet centers.

"Who knows?"

Jake nodded, changed shirts, and they were headed for the lobby to meet Connie.

When he arrived it was in a bright, lemon yellow 1959 Cadillac convertible. Fins and chrome everywhere. Wide whitewall tires. He was grinning and waving them out the door. The men grinned too. Those old Caddies just made a guy's heart happy.

The drive downtown under the big old live oak trees, draped in Spanish moss and arching out over the streets was special in the rag top. Pure fun. Connie parked in a public lot alongside the river walk downtown. He put the top up and they walked along the cobblestone street. They stopped to admire a sailing yacht that had to go a hundred feet, with teak decks and not a speck of dirt on any part. Gold lettering proclaimed it to be the "Paydirt" from Key West.

"Key West. Sunshine, warm breezes, sandy beach. Great place. Crazy, but I love it there. Nice people usually, great food," Connie said as they continued to walk down the street headed for an old three story red brick building that could have served as a cotton warehouse a century and half ago. They entered, were warmly greeted and seated by a gigantic black man in a tuxedo with a small gold earring and a diamond in his front tooth.

When the menus were dealt, iced teas ordered all around, and the waiter returned, they ordered a banquet of seafood, country-fried chicken, hush puppies, and salads. Desert would be blackberry or peach cobbler with heaps of vanilla bean ice cream.

Tex and Connie talked airplanes and destinations for most of dinner with Jake enjoying the exchanges. They had flown some of the same planes and discussed their assets and liabilities.

"I saw an old boy take a Piper cub off into a strong head wind and then set her back down sort of wallowing backwards on the runway once," Tex said. Jake's mouth fell open, and Connie guffawed.

"Bill Carpenter!" he said, and Tex's gape joined Jake. "Where did you meet him?" Connie asked amazed at how small the world is.

"Well, I was living up at Virginia Beach," Tex began his tale. "A feller who was working with me flyin' a strange assortment of men and women into and out of Camp Peary wanted to go visit some relatives up at Culpeper, Virginia. We flew into their little airport across from the Holiday Inn. Grass strip. This guy was there. Nice man. Had a Cessna 172 and this little Cub.

"There was a bunch of guys outside the trailer they used for an office. One thing led to the next and somebody got to telling how that Bill could do that stunt. He held back for a while, then, as it was windy enough, decided to try. Only took it about six feet up, but still and all. That was some deal to me. I ain't gonna try it." Tex shook his head at pilots in general. "How'd you meet him, Connie?"

"Do you remember when Audie Murphy's plane went in back in the early 70's? Near Charlottesville?"

"Sure," Tex said with a sad look on his face. "A real American hero."

"I was at Byrd Field and the CAP was flying all around there looking for the plane. I went along on one flight. We stopped at the newer strip north of Culpeper for fuel and Carpenter was there. Their CAP unit was up too, and he was refueling his plane. Had a guy from Sears flying with him as spotter that day I remember, cause he was broken hearted about Murphy too. Not back from Nam long and he loved the guy, from movies and all.

Any way, we were eating a sub and drinking a Coke together and he was trying to get Carpenter to admit that he did the Cub stunt. Carpenter was sorta digging his toe in the ground and being bashful. Finally he admitted he could do it, but said the wind wasn't strong enough. Well we had thirty knots straight along the runway, and another Culpeper guy really encouraged him, so we pushed the old Cub out of the hanger and, by golly, he did it just like they said he could. Amazing thing.

"Hey! Looky here!" Tex said as Connie finished his tale, and the waiter brought a tray with massive servings of cobbler and ice cream. A green mint sprig decorated each deep dish.

As they dug in, Jake asked, "Connie, exactly what do you know about Solutions and where – specifically – did you learn it?" He said it friendly, but there was an undertone in his voice that said the answer was very important to the continued friendship. Jake hated leaks and leakers.

"Time for me to 'fess" up," Connie said, looking Jake straight in the eye. I used to do a bit of flying for some people out of Bolling." Defense Intelligence Agency Headquarters, Jake's old alma mater.

"Apparently one of them was asked to tip me that you guys were coming here for training in a G V. That's all I knew at the time. And to be honest I was a bit doubtful when he said you guys were straight-arrows. That had not always been my experience with spooks."

"And the Solutions connection?" Jake probed for more information.

"Well, of course it's on your paperwork for Flight Safety. When I saw it, my memory was jogged. Something sounded familiar. I Googled it. A company got shot up at Manassas a couple of months ago. Some crazy broad set fire to her office and shot up the one next door. I guess it was yours?" Connie ended the statement with a question.

"It was ours," Jake said without further comment. Tex was watching the conversation and staying completely out of it. Jake was a good interrogator. Let him do his work. He'd vetted Tex well enough.

"And you want to go to work for us based on that?" Jake pushed a bit.

"No. I want to work with you and Tex. If you guys are here to be rated in a G V it means you have one or you will soon. And you are both too green to be chief pilot on one of those. Nothing personal, Tex, but you have to agree with that." He looked at the small Texan for agreement, and Tex nodded.

"Besides which, Jake, I want in the fight. Sitting in Savannah and doing this job is not cutting it. I'm still a Marine pilot at heart. I want to take it to the enemy, whoever that is, however I can. My guess is that you guys aren't just holding doors for Hollywood types. You're up to something." There was a plaintive tone to Connie's voice, but he wasn't begging. He was offering something of value to people he respected. If they said no, then he would keep doing what he was doing.

"Check me out. I'd expect that. I'm not worried about it. DIA has a file on me. I have to have clearance to do this job here, of course. And you *do* need a G V jockey don't you?" he grinned.

Jake returned the grin. "Where do I get you guys? Tex and George. Even my Dad. Adrenaline junkies! I'm glad I'm just the warm blanket and home fires type," he grinned.

"Okay. Here's how it works. I don't make these decisions alone. Tex and I are fliers, but we have a team back home. We'll discuss it and get back to you. If they say yes – and I'm pretty sure they will – when could you be in Harrisburg?"

"I'm a widower. My wife died three years ago. Brain aneurism. One day we were planning retirement, the next I'm talking to a funeral director. She was the brightest light in my life aside from my son. He's active duty in the Corps. Iraq."

Tex's eyes misted up as he thought of his own wife and what if that happened to her. He nodded understanding to Connie. Jake said, "I'm sorry, Connie."

"Thanks. Well, I actually called your hotel from my boss's office. I discussed this with him. He's a retired Tomcat pilot. Told him what was on my mind. He said to give it a try. Said when you wanted me, if it worked out, that I could go immediately. They can cover until he gets a replacement. I think he would have liked to come along," Connie smiled and looked at Jake for understanding.

"We're all sick of terror and murder and homicide bombers. All the older veterans in this country wish they could get a rifle and take them on!" There was fire in his voice and fury in his eyes. America was under attack and he was angry and feeling a little helpless.

"I want to ask you a question. How do you feel about Jews. About Israel?" Jake said it dead-pan, no indication of why he was asking.

"To me there's a difference between American Jews and Israel. Oh, I know the ethnic ties and all, but when I see 'traditional' American Jews in the media they are usually lawyers, liberals, and whining about some law-suit or injustice. When I see Israelis they are picking up bits of their loved ones, wearing green uniforms and battling terrorists who want to destroy them. I know there are conservative Jews here, but you sure never hear much about them.

"I respect the Israelis. They got guts. I think they really want peace, but they won't give their country up to get it. That what you want to know?" Connie's tone was genuine. And Jake had to admit that it was right on the button.

"Yeah, that's what I wanted to know. My mother was Israeli. We work with the Israelis some, and my uncle is an unofficial part of our team. He's in Israel. Part of their government. If you have a problem with that, I need to know it. Now." Jake said it in a friendly way, but there was that about him which conveyed depth. Some police and many military commanders had it. Men who led men into combat. A sense of responsibility that believed charging was the proper direction in war, not sitting and waiting for the next attack.

Connie saw it in Jake from the beginning, as he had in his leaders in the Corps. Perhaps that was what had brought all this about. He really didn't know specifically what had motivated him – only that he knew it was the right thing to do.

The waiter brought the check and Jake took it over Connie's objection. They had another cup of coffee while they waited for his return.

Jake signed the slip, returned his card to his wallet and said, "Well, tomorrow we visit Gulfstream. Who do you know there, Connie?"

They were given a couple of names of people in high places who would guarantee them a VIP tour, then they returned to the hotel, and Connie went home.

Two days later the Harrisburg controller gave Tex approval for landing at KMDT and he greased the King Air onto the long straight runway. Long ago and far away, this had been Olmstead Air Force Base. A SAC base with the commensurate long stretch of concrete. The old buildings had been demolished to make way for a new terminal and buildings. FedEx and UPS used the place and their jets were always about. There was a curious Boeing 747-SP sitting mysteriously on the apron.

Undesignated 747s and 777s shot touch-and-goes here. A-10s like the two the team had witnessed their first day in the area often entered the pattern. Major airlines used it as a feeder-hub, and a few small private planes were located at the airport as well. On the north end was an executive jet outfit that did time-shares and rent-a-flight operations. The largest and newly painted building on the south end had no name on it.

All the renovation was complete. The dozens of workers and trucks that had buzzed around like bees in an orchard were gone. The building has a very tall chain link fence around the outer limits, with its own private gate and security guards on duty twenty-four hours a day.

On the side facing the airport apron large hangar doors were rolling open when Tex taxied up. The hangar's interior lights and spotless white vinyl floor sparkled.

Mrs. Allen was standing in the rear of the open space smiling and gently waving as the plane turned around so it could be backed into the hangar.

"Welcome home, boys!" she called out as they descended the stairs at the rear of the plane. Momma, as Tex called her, was short, plump, with chubby cheeks. Chubby everything. She was wearing a cotton dress, still had an apron on, as if she had hurried from the kitchen just to pick them up and forgotten to untie it and toss it on the cabinet. She loved Tex more than she loved her own life and treasured Jake, Larry and Harold as God-sends.

They piled in Tex's small Rav4 and headed for Elizabethtown; about four miles by the back way. It was good to be home, though "home" was new to all of them.

A dirty white van trailed far enough behind not to be noticed by a weary Tex or Jake.

TWENTY THREE

Charlie Stence backed the trailer and green johnboat down the concrete ramp into the Susquehanna River. *Quiet as a graveyard up here*, he thought, exempting the sound of early morning traffic on nearby Route 322. Ft. Hunter wasn't one of the hot spots for fishing, but Earle Neely and Charlie liked it.

We're gonna get some smallmouth today, Earle," Charlie exulted. "Said so in the Almanac!"

Reared next door to one another, they'd been fishing and hunting pals except when they were in the military. When they returned from Korea it had resumed. For a while they fished with their kids, but now the kids were grown up and moved away. They were back to being a twosome.

Earle was standing beside the river's edge. When the boat was floating off the trailer, he raised a hand and said, "Whoa! Let me unhook her," which he did, keeping the bow line in his hand.

Charlie parked his rig then rejoined Earle. Soon he was in the stern and the small outboard was blathering a raucous, smoky discourse. With Earle ensconced in the bow, Charlie backed away from the landing, and started to turn the boat upriver, alongside a small stand of reeds.

"Oh, no! Charlie! It's… it's a man!" He then projectile vomited into the river toward where he'd been pointing.

I guess he's serious, Charlie thought. *At least he puked outside the boat*, as he rose to see for himself.

"Sure nuf," he muttered, as he noted the bloated, splotchy body. Chunks of flesh were missing, and the camouflage uniform was muddy and stretched tight as a sausage skin.

Camos were not unusual. This was, after all, Pennsylvania. Hunters, soldiers from Indiantown Gap, National Guardsmen and survivalists of every stripe wore them year 'round. Kids swapped between hospital greens and camos with the seasons.

"He's dead, ain't he?" Earle asked in a reverential whisper, as pale as the corpse.

"No, Earle, he's playing possum!" Charlie had been talking to Earle like he was a dimwit for as long as either one of them could remember. That was amazing in light of the fact that Earle had a Masters in mathematics from Penn State and Charlie had only made it through high school because Earle let him copy.

"Can't you see where a fish ate his eye out? Course he's dead, you idiot!" Without even thinking about it, Charlie was keeping the boat in place. With his free hand he dug out his cell phone and turned it on. "Hate these little tiny buttons," he griped to Earle, dialing 911.

"Me too, but if they made 'em big enough, we'd need a back pack to haul the phone around," Earle took his friend's part against phone designers. He kept glancing nervously toward the body that was buoyant, but held in place by the reeds. The higher waters in previous days had no doubt deposited the unfortunate soul there.

A few minutes passed then they could hear the sirens wailing. A Susquehanna Township patrolman rolled in first and Charlie called out to him. Soon thereafter the parade arrived. About a dozen volunteer firemen in two trucks, one pulling a johnboat, two more Susquehanna officers, a State trooper and an ambulance team. After they jammed the parking area behind Charlie's truck and trailer, a River Rescue squad from Harrisburg arrived with a dive team and another johnboat.

One of the firemen waded out into the reeds and slipped a boat hook under the corpse's belt then stood there holding him. "You boys can bring your boat in now. I got him," he called over to the fishermen.

"Yeah, sure. Like you're gonna get my truck and trailer unjammed from that mess?" Charlie mouthed back at him, pointing toward the parking area with his chin. He wasn't giving up his patrol. This was the most excitement he'd had since Lauri caught the fried chicken on fire last winter. When a cop told him to move, *then* he'd do it. Not until.

Earle was just thanking God he hadn't had the Farmer's Special at the diner before they came out this morning. He wasn't feelin' so hot. *Guess this cancels fishin' for the day.*

Seeing there was little site to secure, and nothing to do until the coroner arrived, the policemen and firemen stood around drinking coffee from shared thermoses. They told tales of other floaters and the results of the investigations they'd begun along the river.

About fifteen minutes after Charlie's call, a blue Beemer convertible turned into the small lot and Dauphin County Coroner Grant Hardwick climbed out. Trailing him was another convoy. A Coroner's van, and three members of the Harrisburg area "WE Team." With some vehicular shuffling, a pathway was cleared and they all drove in.

Channels 8 and 27 vans sprouting satellite dishes tried to daisy-chain in, but a State trooper blocked their path. Park on the shoulder, Newsies. He'd never make Colonel, they grumbled, and began to unload their equipment.

The WE Team is a stroke of genius. Like many small cities, Metro Harrisburg is comprised of satellite communities with their own police departments. Borough (town) police, township police, Harrisburg City cops, as well as the County Sheriff's Department all co-exist. Sheriffs in the Northeast do not do a lot of investigative work. They work instead as court officers, serve warrants, subpoenas, and transport prisoners.

With small budgets most of these forces lack real crime scene units. Keeping a lab and technicians equipped would break the bank. With that in mind, Grant suggested that they each contribute bodies, equipment and expertise to the pot. Sort of like the old story of making stone soup.

Once all the local jurisdictions put in their fair share, the WE (no 'I' in team) Team was born. The unit was so successful that many a plea had been copped once defense counsel got a look at the quantity and quality of evidence they gathered at crime scenes.

Grant organized the team and assigned areas of evidence-responsibility to the various members present. The dive team was asked to go downstream and work upward searching the river bed and bank for anything that might be a clue. If something was found, they would light it up, photograph it on site, and only then bring it to the surface for cataloging.

The fireman who hooked the corpse would be debriefed and his boots, along with the others on the scene, photographed so his footprints could be eliminated from any others at the scene. The weeds along the bank were beaten down into a fisherman's path leading from the ramp to the reed bed, so there might be lots of shoe prints. Time would tell.

A photo of his boat hook – in position – would be taken in case there was a puncture discovered by the autopsy. The still photographer would shoot environment. A team secretary/recorder would keep a record of everyone's activity for later investigative use. A digital video record would be made as well. If it got that far, the Prosecutor's office would like a copy too.

Grant asked one of the Susquehanna Township officers to organize search parties to work up and down stream along the bank for any possible evidence. "Remember, Mark, too much rather than discounting anything," he slapped the rookie gently on the shoulder and moved off to take charge of the corpse.

It was unusual for a "civilian" to rule the crime scene, but "circumstances alter cases," as his mother used to say, so Grant took the lead, and the various police officers worked well with it. They were glad to keep territorial bickering out of the WE Team.

The body was horrific. Turtles and fish had dined sumptuously on the exposed flesh. Gases from internal decomposition had swollen the corpse to the point that the hands and head had stretched the cuffs and collar tight as possible. The buttons had held, Grant noted.

The morning was cool with a mist rising from the river surface. It gave the whole scene a ghostly feel. Some wanted to take a peek at the body, others shivered and moved further away from the scene. A few were packing up their vehicles and preparing to return to other duties.

Beside Grant was Susquehanna detective Mike Vester. He would lead the investigation and he was good. Both men shared a U.S. Army CID Alma mater, though a generation apart. Hardwick had been to Germany and Viet Nam on his tour. Vester was in England and France, then to Brussels at NATO headquarters.

Hardwick had returned home to work with his father, George, in the family funeral business. Vester joined Susquehanna's police force when he got out. That was nine years ago. They had worked too many cases together to count.

In some states, the Coroner or Medical Examiner must be a doctor. Not so in Pennsylvania. Anyone can run for the office, and serve if elected. That makes for some interesting situations. Dauphin County had seen some of those in the past. This time however the County won. Grant Hardwick was a jewel, and every prosecutor and policeman fervently hoped he stayed on forever.

With a Criminal Investigation Division background he came to the job with the perspective of a policeman. As a very professional (read that compassionate and well-versed) funeral director he brought a sense of importance to the handling of bodies, by-standers, AND evidence. As a politician, he enjoyed media attention and was as open as practical in handing out what information he could honestly provide to the news people.

And – in spite of what some had opined when he was first elected – he dedicated himself to the task like it was all he had to do. Grant's very sharp son managed the funeral business when his father was otherwise occupied.

In younger days he'd looked like an Arian recruiting poster. Six feet tall, well muscled, blonde-haired, blue-eyed, and blessed with a strong chin, slab-cheeks, and straight nose, he was movie star handsome. And he knew it. He wasn't pompous, but had a sense of himself, and he was a leader. Reared in a well-to-do family by loving parents, neither was he insecure. He had presence and used it when necessary.

When Grant entered a room, people noticed him. Some smiled – they enjoyed his sanguine personality and charm. Others frowned or gave him a hard-eyed look – they envied him, or hated his "luck." Grant pretended to be unaware of this, and tried to treat everyone well.

It wasn't that he ran around with a Lufkin tape so he could measure them for their upcoming casket. He just enjoyed people and chose to ignore criticism. He was smart, handsome and rich. Somebody you could hate! Or love, depending on your outlook.

At his current age – sixty-two – he had changed his look from the handsome young man in custom tailored suits. Now he wore his graying hair longer and brushed back from his face, kept a small, well-trimmed beard (if he hadn't shaved it again) and small wire-rimmed glasses. It was the "wise European-born doctor/professor" persona. A political rival had grumbled one day, "I swear he'd wear tails and a pince-nez if he thought he could get away with it!"

That was probably true, some of his friends had agreed with an envious smile when they heard the *cut.* Who knew what Grant would be up to next? But with all the idiosyncrasies (he'd call them personal charm), he's the best Coroner this county has had in anyone's memory.

He'd gone back to school so often since taking office that he could write books on the various subjects any Coroner must deal with. One interesting newspaper story reported his ability as a sculptor who could rebuild facial features from the skull outward. It was more art than science but had aspects of both and Grant had studied long and hard under some of the masters around the country. The results were amazing.

A bit of personal money allows one certain predilections. Hardwick's standards tended toward excellence. Many of the Coroner's staff had learned that the hard way when he first took the reigns. Since then a new County lab facility and general sharpness in the ranks had benefited the whole community.

As the Coroner's team was preparing to retrieve the body Mike Vester's radio burst forth with more news. "Mike! Mike! This is Matt! We got another floater! Other side of the creek!"

Fishing Creek entered the river just fifty yards downstream. A small trout stream but wide enough that the searchers had had to go back toward the road to cross and then return to the river bank. It had taken them time to work their way to the area where they'd made their ghastly discovery.

"What in the devil is goin' on, Grant?" Mike asked as he raised the microphone to his lips.

"Exactly where are you, Matt?" Mike asked, a shocked look on his face. Murder in Susquehanna Township was usually restricted to drug battles, domestic quarrels and occasionally a robbery gone south. This was his first floater – set of floaters.

"We'rerightontheothersideofthecreek!" Matt was stunned and running his words all together. This was obviously new to him too. Grant smiled.

"Slow down! Take a breath." Mike was trying to get the young policeman to calm down and handle everything properly.

"Ahhhhhh. Mike, this guy is all chewed up by something. His eyes are missing, …" A sound of vomiting began then Matt released the mic button. Grant looked in Mike's eyes, but not with humor. They had both had similar experiences in the earlier days of their careers. Both knew there were still cases coming up where containing their refluxes would be difficult. Hang in there, kid.

"Ahhhh. I'm sorry, Mike. This guy is up against the bank just below the creek a ways. I'm still here. Sent the others to go on searchin'. I got some volunteers walking the banks of the creek."

"Good job, Matt. Just stay there. When we get this scene secured and recorded we'll be there with the WE Team. Keep others away from that site. Is there any possibility of the body floating on downriver?"

"Naw. He's in a bunch of river grass. Looks like high water put him in here. Now it's down, he ain't goin' nowhere."

The rest of the morning was given to recording scenes, scouring the area for evidence, then bagging and moving the two corpses to the morgue.

Grant did not personally do autopsies. That, by law, had to be done by a medical doctor. He was always present for any that were more than routine, however. These two definitely qualified.

The autopsy room was as clean as any of the local hospital's operating suites. And thanks to a staff member who had mastered the art of completing federal grant forms it was full of the very latest equipment. Television's crime scene labs had nothing on Dauphin County.

On a stainless steel table lay the still clothed body of one of the men found at Ft. Hunter. His body had not been cleaned. Dr. Pietro Colon photographed it with the camos on. He searched the clothing and exterior of the body for any trace evidence. Finding none, he then used scissors to cut away the clothing. Everything was bagged and tagged. Grant and Detective Vester watched along with the video recorder as it noted everything and Dr. Colon dictated a verbal record.

Dr. Colon was a study in professionalism. With enough degrees from the University of Chicago, Vanderbilt and Georgetown to paper his walls, his credentials made prosecutors swoon and impressed juries, when he was called upon to testify in court.

From an immigrant family who arrived from Puerto Rico when he was two, he was raised to respect three things: God, family and education. At forty-three that had not dissipated. He taught a teen boy's Sunday School class at Calvary Baptist Church in Harrisburg, had a beautiful, loving wife, four kids and the afore-mentioned wall of sheepskins. He lived in central Pennsylvania because, as he put it, "I've been all over, and there's no place better for raising kids or praising

Jesus. This is still part of the northern Bible belt, though the belt's getting' a little loose."

His courtroom testimony caused juries to listen, understand and believe what he said. "Pete" Colon was a solid six-foot-one-inches tall, bald on top, with a close-cropped fringe around the sides and back. His piercing dark eyes and full brows settled above a wide black moustache and a beautiful, white-toothed grin.

He took his work as serious as a heart attack, but not himself. He, like Grant, respected the bodies in his care, believed he was part of a system of justice that was necessary to keep a grip on a deteriorating civilization, and loved to discover forensic evidence when a crime had been committed. He was a detective in the truest sense of the word. In fact, his work had been chronicled on three different Discovery Channel programs.

Employed by four adjoining counties for autopsies due to the low necessity for that procedure, he liked working with Grant Hardwick best. They shared a dedication to professionalism and Grant had applied himself in the area of forensics far beyond what was mandated by law. "The extra mile" was part of Pete's creed and part of his measuring standard for others. Grant more than met that.

"This guy has a bullet hole in the roof of his mouth if I've ever seen one. Little bullet." Up until that point, no one really knew if these deaths were the result of a boat capsizing, other accident or foul play. Dr. Colon's statement changed the investigation. Now it was known to be a violent death and not accidental.

"Probably a .22 or .25 from the looks of it. Small enough to keep it from exiting, but large enough to spin around inside the skull stirring up the brain. I'll bet we find a mess when I get the Stryker out and remove the skull cap." Dr. Colon was tilting the corpse's head back and shining a light inside the mouth as Grant and Detective Mike Vester moved to look at the roof of the mouth.

"Well, then, I have to wonder if the other guy shot him and then himself, or if he killed the other one and then committed suicide," Mike said quietly. Autopsies were the absolute worst thing he had to do in his work. They made his stomach as shaky as young Matt's, and more than once he had made a fast trip to the nearby restroom.

"Or," Grant added, "did an unknown person whack them both and dump them in the river."

Stepping back, "Yeah, there's that," Mike agreed.

The autopsy was normal other than the bullet. Pete Colon's prediction of the brain trauma and the bullet inside was accurate. The lands and grooves were well enough maintained to be able to match it with ballistics should they find others. The "Y" incision was stitched up and the body was covered with a sheet and moved to the cooler.

"Want to do the other one now or break for lunch?" Pete asked. He was teasing Mike. The detective was an old hand, but had never acclimated to the smell of disinfectant and chilling temperatures much less what he still considered ghoulish activity. He knew it was necessary, but that didn't make it any easier to endure.

"Yeah, Right! You know there ain't gonna be no lunch for me, Doc. Let's get it over." Mike knew they liked and respected him, but that would never protect him from their verbal pokes.

The morgue attendant wheeled the second corpse into the suite and they placed him on a different table. Same procedure. A close inspection of the clothing, photographs, a verbal record, and then – again finding nothing remarkable – the camos were cut away.

"Well, this one didn't commit suicide, certainly, Grant." Pete Colon said in an ironic tone.

"What have you found?" Grant asked, missing what the doctor had noted.

"This, unless I'm wrong." With that he picked up a scalpel and sliced a one inch incision in the left cheek. Reaching in with a pair of stainless steel forceps and holding the incision open with the fingers of the other hand Dr. Colon moved the forceps around inside the cheek for a moment. Then, with a muttered, "Gotcha," he lifted his find for the coroner and the cop. A twenty-two caliber, lead bullet.

"There you are men. About forty grains of 22 caliber bullet. Most likely matching it's brother from our other body, but that's for your guys to determine, Mike."

"How'd you know it was there?!" Mike asked with a look like a kid at a magic show.

"Experience. I saw a lump under the skin, and when they brought him in, one of the technicians said he'd hit his head in the back. I looked and saw that the wound wasn't from striking something, but from a little hole. Going in from the back meant coming out or stopping toward the front. Just luck about the lump, but I knew to look for one.

"Just like all magic acts, Mike. There's the image and then the reality." Grant chuckled. Mike nodded.

"So we either got two murders or the other guy did this one and then killed himself." The detective thought out loud.

"My money's on a double murder," Grant added, as the autopsy proceeded.

They were on the head when Dr. Colon said, "Hmmm. I didn't see this in the other fellow."

That got Grant and Mike's undivided attention.

"See this dental work? Definitely not American. Not European either, unless I miss my guess. We'll pull one of the teeth with a big filling and have the amalgam checked. I have a nice collection, and a friend who can analyze it quicker than your guys, if that's all right?"

"You have any way of guessing where the dental work *was* done?" Grant asked.

"Eastern Middle East is my guess. Pakistan, Afghanistan, some other 'stan.' More than that I don't know. They use a different blend of metals. Real old fashioned. I'm surprised it stays put at all. And it has an almost black color. Definitely not cutting edge dentistry. If you see people who have one of those filling in a visible tooth, it looks like bad decay at first."

"Hey, Doc. You think he's Al Qaeda?" Mike asked. "Camos, Arab lookin' and now this. Worth a look."

"Mike that's in your court. We're going to look at him inside and out and then it's up to you and the WE Team from there on." Pete had more work to do, and a paper to write for a medical journal.

TWENTY FOUR

"This place is a pig pen!" Raquel muttered. She was stirring oatmeal with a fork, in a dented aluminum saucepan and just plain hating this farm, hating all the waiting for something to happen, and life in general.

"What'd you say?" Alex asked from the doorway as he entered across the kitchen and behind her.

He'd been outside checking warning devices. He'd set them up the first month he was here and checked them every third day. Thread strung across game trails, but thin as spider webs and high enough to keep deer from tripping them. Branches broken and placed precisely so that a man would have to either move or step on them. Rocks set in precise patterns, covered by leaves so that anyone stepping on them would disturb them. He had five or six more systems. They would not alert him to an attack, but he knew that most attacks would be preceded by surveillance and probes. That was what he wanted to know about. He had other means of alerting him to close intrusions. A couple of IR sensors, even trip wires and flash-bang grenades.

"Nothing!" Raquel felt uncomfortable by the thin, dangerous man. She had a feeling that he would kill her and then sit down to her oatmeal if the order came. He had no loyalty to her and was certainly not intimidated. Her beauty pleased him but she knew it would never protect her if he thought she was a threat. He'd kill her, dispose of her body and lie professionally to his superiors.

She pulled the saucepan from the fire, dumped the glob into a chipped soup bowl and anointed it with a touch of honey that was turning to sugar granules.

A cup of instant coffee and her meal was ready. Ugh.

Before she could taste it, her cell phone chirped. "Yes?" then a long pause as she listened.

"I understand. Send me an email with their numbers and locations."

"Thanks. Good bye."

"I'm leaving. Give me the shooter's phone number. Then close this place down. Burn it for all I care. Go back to wherever you came from and they will tell you what to do next." She was excited, Alex could tell by the flush that had appeared on her cheeks.

As soon as she'd spoken, he watched to see if she was going to reach for a gun or knife and do to him like she had those other poor slobs.

The van was still in the barn. He and Raquel had used it to drive to Middletown and do some reconnoitering. They'd driven past a farm from one direction and then back the opposite way. She'd taken photos with a small digital camera.

Afterward they'd gone to the airport and parked south of the main terminal near where FedEx and UPS had their operations. They'd sat there with him smoking and blowing it out the window because she objected to the smell. Finally, a twin engine plane had taxied to a large building. Later a small SUV had passed them heading out. A woman and two men inside.

They tailed it back to Elizabethtown. First to the farm they'd seen and then to a small house a couple of miles away.

Alex had served with a lot of men who were a bit "around the curve" in his day. Some had even "creeped him out." He wasn't afraid of much, but this broad gave him the willies. If she was who she said she was then old Osama needed a little chlorine in his gene pool.

Being with her was nice from a visual perspective. But she was jumpy. She talked about nonsense and the next minute asked him how many people he'd killed. The sun's angle and how it affected animal behaviour. The moon's pull on ocean currents. How you could focus a magnifying glass on a fuse and ignite it a day after you'd set it up. (That one he'd noted with interest.)

The next minute she'd be sounding off about "those men" who ever "they" were. She sure enough hated them with a passion. She seemed fixated on them. It was like they were the personification of everything her jihad was about.

She whipped back and forth like that all the time they were out in the van. Once she even started a high-pitched kind of keening sound way down in her throat. Like she was going to scream or cry a real broken sob from it. It went on for about twenty seconds but she never let it out all the way. When he'd looked over at her, she was beet red in the face and seemed to be holding every emotion in her spirit back. Like she was going to either blow a gasket or explode.

"Are you all right," he'd asked with genuine concern.

"YOU SHUT UP AND DRIVE!! MIND YOUR OWN BUSINESS OR I'LL KILL YOU RIGHT HERE!!" she'd screamed, letting it all loose in one long threat. Peppering bits of saliva at the dash and windshield.

"I'll leave you alone, honey, but you remember one little thing. Killing me will be an all day job, and just when you think you've got it done, I'll be burying you in one of those outhouses at the farm."

He'd said it in a monotone, no stress in his voice. Just a statement of fact like a banker telling a stranger which line to stand in.

Raquel took it in and it worked magic on her. She looked at him, nodded slightly as if to say, "Right," and looked out the window to her right. She hadn't said another word until this morning when he'd entered the kitchen.

A week with her had him leaving his holster unsnapped and staying jumpy inside.

He went to the cupboard and pulled a small spiral notebook. He wrote a number on a page, ripped it out and lay it beside her bowl of oatmeal.

"Thanks," she muttered, as she took a sip of the coffee and frowned.

An hour later she was gone. Driving down the lane without even a good bye. Alex distributed the contents of the four five-gallon gasoline cans around the barn and house. A match to each and he was driving away.

Not to New Jersey. Something told him that direction might hold too much danger. He watched his mirrors all the way up Route 15 until he reached Interstate 80. There he pointed his nose west. Idaho had some places that were way out there. He "knew people" and where he could get a name change and proper work. Perhaps it was time for him to re-evaluate his Muslim ties. Between that woman sniper and Osama's progeny he'd had a belly full of jihad.

It took Raquel only two hours to find an apartment in Harrisburg. Her cover documents were in order. The rental agent at the complex across from the big mall was only too eager to provide her a one bedroom furnished garden apartment.

Two hours at the local Wal Mart and she had everything to make her new home comfortable and supplied with groceries. And a decent coffee maker. There was a gourmet coffee shop in the mall next door. Some DVDs, two throw away telephones, and some chocolates brought the day to a pleasant end.

She dialed the number Alex had provided. It was answered quickly. After a contact verification the conversation was brief.

"We must meet." Raquel was the leader, but played it soft and gentle. She wanted this woman to like her and gladly work with her. There were big things ahead.

"Where?"

"Harrisburg."

"Name a place."

"There's an Olive Garden restaurant on Jonestown Road. Eight o'clock."

"I'll be there. Wearing a black scarf."

Click.

Maxine was on time. They acted as if they were already acquainted, requested a corner table out of the way so they could conduct some business. Just two working girls out for a bite and some planning.

After they'd ordered, had a bit of small talk, and established one another's bona fides, they were ready to get down to business.

"I have some work for you. We are going to make war on a very personal basis."

Maxine looked at Raquel with a raised eyebrow. Alex had secretly spoken to her on his cell phone before leaving the farm. He'd said she was legitimate, dangerous, and someone to take great care with.

"Go on."

"There is a group that is hunting me. I want them gone. As in gone from the face of the earth!" Raquel's eyes blazed with that old fervor that had visited her in Manassas.[6]

"And this is sanctioned by our leaders?" Maxine had no issue with taking a life, but she wanted to know that it wouldn't result in being hunted by her own organization.

"I *am* the leader in this country." Raquel said it in a deadpan way. No emotion, just a quiet confidence that she would be obeyed. "Have you not been instructed to obey my commands?"

"I have. But I believe that such a command was to further our cause, not for personal revenge. These Americans are not fools. There is a saying that revenge is a food best eaten cold."

"And the Americans leave themselves wide open to mass murderers, common criminals and borders where we and every miscreant in Mexico can come into their country! They are well armed, but they are naïve fools."

"And these people you wish to hunt? Are *they* naïve fools as well?" Maxine asked with the slightest bit of challenge in her voice. She didn't quite trust this beautiful woman with the commanding personality of a princess.

"Anything but! They are strong and wise and dangerous. It will be a desert lion hunt. We will be out in the sand with no where to run if we fail and they will devour us. Are you up for such an undertaking or do I look for another?" The challenge was thrown back at the sniper. Implicit in Raquel's voice and look was the threat that if she had to go elsewhere, there would be one more martyr in the jihad ranks. This time a female martyr.

---

[6] See *One Time Messengers* for details of Raquel's murderous activities in Virginia.

"All right. We can go on like this forever. Tell me what you want done. What is my role? Do you have a timetable? Exactly where are they?"

"In time. Do you have the appropriate weapons and equipment? Can we act as soon as I have the area of operation established?"

"I have nothing but my wits and skill. I left the second rate items at the farm. They were to be dumped down an abandoned well. I have cell phones. This one will be gone tonight and a new one used tomorrow. You know the drill, no doubt?"

Nodding, Raquel continued. She loved planning operations and was in her element. "Do you have gunsmithing skills?"

"Excellent ones. But we first must determine the best rifle. Can you acquire a professional model?"

"I cannot do so quickly. And I dare not contact my best source. I fear he will soon be eating his meals at a long table between the Arian Nation and the Muslim Brothers," she smiled at her own humor.

"Then we can purchase a Remington, scope and other items locally?" Maxine asked.

They continued to plan as the food came. Raquel forced herself to enjoy the large salad and garlic bread sticks. She wanted a bowl heaped with pasta and sauce, but knew she needed to control her appetites – all of them. This time she would keep a very tight reign on herself and the Solutions team would all be dead. Then she would celebrate.

It was decided that they would each keep their apartments as safe houses in case of emergencies. Neither knew the other's location and would not. A house in a busy neighborhood would be rented. One with a shop or garage that could be used by Maxine as she reworked a sporting rifle and in which to keep their vehicles.

The sniper worked up a list of supplies, including tools that would be necessary for the conversion from hunting to long distance work. Maxine was actually enthusiastic about that. She had loved her time in the armory. The smell of gun oil, calibrating scopes and the "snick" of parts as they clicked into place in pistols, rifles and machine guns was more pleasant than Chanel, chocolates and soft music to her.

They divided up the tasks, paid the bill and went their separate ways. Maxine drove off toward Camp Hill taking the main highway connecting the two sides of the Susquehanna metropolitan Harrisburg area. Farther back a black Saab moved in and out of traffic, the Bellamy Brothers blasting from the cd changer and the driver smiling contentedly.

When Maxine parked and entered her apartment building, the Saab found Route 15 south and headed for Warrenton, Virginia. There were some gun stores Raquel knew about near there. She still had a couple of Virginia driver's licenses and IDs. That would do for most of the lethal hardware they needed. A motel tonight and shopping for her "husband's birthday surprise" tomorrow. Piece of cake.

Solutions was about to get their ticket punched.

TWENTY FIVE

He crossed the Ohio state line still on Route 80. Alex enjoyed driving and this truck was as comfortable as the finest sedan. At the 234 mile marker he pulled off and entered the truck stop. The tales about truckers knowing where to eat was nonsense. Greasy fried chicken, disastrous cholesterol-filled buffets and ugly, poorly trained waitresses were not his idea of haute cuisine.

He grabbed his shaving kit and headed inside. A quick wash-up, shave and breakfast then he'd be back on the road. Idaho was still a very long way.

As he walked from the men's room into the restaurant he spied two Ohio State Troopers sitting at a booth. *Where'd they come from?!* He hadn't noticed any police cars in the parking lot, and he was very good at spotting even unmarked cars. Obviously they'd arrived only moments ago.

Stutter stepping then quickly recovering, Alex moved on into the restaurant and chose a booth as far from the officers as possible. He sat with his side to them. *No sweat*, he tried to convince himself.

There was a warrant out for him from South Carolina, but that was three years old and he didn't think these two would even know about that. If he kept his cool, had a meal and got back on the road he'd be fine.

Breakfast was made more unappetizing by the chill of wanting to look at the troopers but not daring in case they were looking his way.

Why didn't I just keep driving?! Relax. They are here for stale coffee and a doughnut. You aren't even on their radar. Alex smiled at his double entendre, finished up and got back in his truck. No cops to be seen anywhere.

They ate and left, he told himself.

He was forty-five minutes west, in the middle of nowhere, when he looked in the rear view mirror and his heart froze. Blue lights. Flashing headlights. Closing fast. Cops!

Alex knew that virtually every driver hated that sight even if they were not speeding, and he was not. Three miles over the limit was as safe as can be.

As the police car got within a hundred yards of his truck, he noticed that it was not one car. There was another marked car and a grey Crown Vic behind the second. Cop caravan.

In the next moment the first car was in front of his bumper. The second was beside him in the left lane. In the front passenger seat was a trooper. He poked a Ruger Mini-14 out the window. He had a very serious look on his face. Alex put both hands on the steering wheel at ten and two, just like in driver's ed class. The gray Ford was about a foot off his rear bumper boxing him in. Lights and sirens on all three.

It was certain they wanted him. He nodded once and signaled to pull off the road. When he was stopped he didn't move his hands off the steering wheel.

The next events were a blur. Strong hands opened his door and pulled him out of the truck and slammed him to the ground. That Mini 14 was a serious piece of hardware. The other five officers all had Smiths pointed at him.

The one who had grabbed him cuffed him none too gently, relieved him of the Glock inside his jeans, and stood him up against the side of the truck. They emptied his pockets.

He never said a word and they worked silently until the Sergeant finally walked up to him.

"Harley Carter? You *are* Harley Carter are you not?" Sergeant York asked. That was what his chrome ID badge said. Sergeant York.

A deep sigh, "Yeah. That's me. How the devil did you get me?"

"The trooper you killed in South Carolina? That's his brother-in-law," York said, pointing with his thumb to one of the officers who had been at the truck stop. He was now standing beside the front bumper of the Crown Vic looking like he wished Alex would make a fight of it.

Two days later some very determined gentlemen from Homeland Security, accompanied by three FBI special agents and a token Ohio State investigator were at the Federal Building in Akron. They questioned Alex for an hour and a half. At that point one of them left him in the capable hands of two US Marshals and virtually raced for a telephone. An hour later a Federal Lear 45 lifted off from Reagan National. Inside were agents from DIA and CIA, plus three FBI Assistant Directors.

Two more days passed. Alex was well treated, provided plenty of cigarettes, coffee and food. He was the star of the show. With the Silver Needle awaiting him in South Carolina he and his new court appointed legal beagle were talking "Let's make a Deal!" Once that was settled Alex was talking non-stop for as long as the Feds wanted to listen.

In Middleburg, Virginia, Harvey down shifted the Jaguar and accelerated into the curve. Folding back on itself, the hairpin was canted at an angle that allowed him to double the posted warning speed.

He hit an even lower gear and hit the gas halfway through. The tach and accelerator raced to compete for his attention.

Just as he hit the straightaway a black Saab whipped past headed in the opposite direction. He noted that the woman driver had jerked her hands to the right, shocked by his sudden appearance. Glancing in his small round side mirror he noted that the car was entering the curve, still on the road, so he returned his attention to the joyful task of pressing himself into the seat back as he went up through the gears and sang along with the tuned mufflers.

A moment later his cell phone vibrated in his shirt pocket. He pulled it out and looked to see who was calling.

"Harvey. How are you this fine sunny day?"

"I may have something interesting. You still in contact with those guys who were after Osama's daughter?"

"Hey, Tyrone! This is a cell phone!"

"Call me when you get to a land line you trust." Click.

Ten minutes later Harvey had put the black Jag into its stall, wiped the deep finish with a soft cloth and was pouring a mug of Kenyan coffee as he listened to the phone on the other end of the line ring.

"Three-eight-four-oh-oh-oh-one."

"Is the boss in, Stella?"

"Yessir, he is. How's retirement?" the lady's voice was cultured with a tiny bit of magnolias and mint in it.

"Retiring. I'm going fishing next week. Don't tell Tyrone." Harvey laughed. Tyrone Lloyd was the new DCIA, an old friend who had an illustrious career in both the CIA and at State. That was sort of like having one married parent, Harvey had teased him for years.

"Listen. The Ohio State Police nailed a guy named Harley Carter. That probably won't ring any bells…"

"Killed a South Carolina State Trooper about three years ago. They found out who did it because of new face recognition software we loaned them. Trooper's onboard camera got a look at the guy as he pulled the trigger. Traffic stop if I recall," Harvey responded.

"Okay. You're good. Anyway, this guy's pulling a Pavarotti up there. One of my guys, a flock of Feebs, even a DIA stiff are in Akron.

"The guy is now Alex something. Been baptized into the jihad apparently. He's done some jobs for them but the big news is that he just met Osama's daughter in Pennsylvania. She's apparently the real deal. Listen, let me give you the details I have so far.

"Brown hair, shoulder length, built, and driving a black Saab."

When the DCIA said that, Harvey's mind instantly flashed to the view in his rear-view mirror of a car like that he'd seen only moments ago. With a woman at the wheel.

"Tyrone! I just saw a black Saab in Middleburg! Why don't you make a call to the Virginia troopers and ask for a BOLO[7]? It might be nothing, but you know how these things sometimes work out."

"Will do. But the reason I called was to ask about the team she shot up in her last performance. They're in Harrisburg somewhere and that's where this Carter said he last saw her. What's your read on notifying them?"

"Actually I just spoke to them not long ago. I'll call right now. They're good people, Tyrone. I'd hate to see them blind-sided."

"Okay. Keep me posted if anything comes of this. See you Harvey. Enjoy the fishing." Click.

Harvey looked at the receiver. *Had Stella slipped him a note? Was he guessing? Had he tapped the phones here at the house? I think I'll get more bug catchers this week.*

He pressed the button, then looked up and dialed Middletown.

At Solutions headquarters in Middletown, Harold listened for a few moments, asked a couple of questions and hung up the phone. He looked at the notes he'd made on the pad before him.

Why was the Terrorist Babe in the Harrisburg area?

Were they now a target? Then he remembered the white van at the farm not long ago. Was that somehow connected?

He picked up the phone and dialed.

"Jake, where are you?"

"At the range. George, Larry and Nick are here. We're doing our duty and busting caps. Want to come out and show us what that new Wilson cannon of yours can do? George has so far intimidated us all with his Combat Commander but Nick's catching up. Why don't you come out?"

"Listen. Something important is happening I think. Go get Tex and then all of you come in here as soon as possible."

"Sure, Dad. But I think Tex is already heading your way. Be there in twenty minutes. Are you all right?" Jake sensed that Harold was not all right. Something serious was troubling him.

"I'm fine. But there's a chance we may be the hunted not the hunters. Keep alert."

---

[7] Be on the look out for.

TWENTY SIX

They were comfortably ensconced in a house in Highspire. Located between Middletown and Harrisburg. It was near an elementary school, had constant traffic and more importantly quick availability to every major highway that hubbed in the Capitol City metroplex. Rented furnished from a lady who had a sign tacked up on the porch and wanted to move to San Francisco to live with her daughter, Raquel had been the kind professor at Penn State's Capitol Campus who needed a place for at least three years. A tour of the house confirmed it was what they needed. A two car garage connected through the kitchen door. In the basement was her late husband's work shop.

"You may use any of the tools there. I just couldn't stand to part with them. Leonard loved to go down there and tinker with his Dremel and stuff. Just be careful with them."

The lease was signed, a check for the first year's rent handed over and a week later Miriam was California bound.

It had been two weeks since Raquel's Virginia trip. That had been successful to a degree but she wanted more hardware and had a plan to get it.

In the basement were boxes containing a Remington 700 ADL with synthetic stock, parkerized black barrel and receiver. It was a .308 caliber just as Maxine had requested. Next was a Leupold 4x12 wide angle scope, rings and base. A pair of ten power compact binoculars, two pairs of camo outfits including balaclavas, gloves and walkie talkies were in another box.

Maxine and Raquel were moved in, cars parked in the garage and dinner dishes drying beside the sink.

The dining room table was scattered with note pads and pens.

"I say we need a better rifle. That one will work but I am not able to fit a silencer on it. And we need a place to practice and test reloading equipment, which we have yet to buy. There is so much to do and every day that passes makes us more visible."

"Listen, I have a plan to get the rifle we need. We're going to hit a SWAT shooter and take his. Somewhere away from here." Raquel smiled as Maxine's mouth fell open. The audacity was part of her shock. The rest was the simple way this woman looked at problems. Of course it could be done. This part of the country was quiet. The police were not really alert.

"And I have a list of targets. We are going to war right here in central Pennsylvania." Raquel got up to retrieve the coffee pot from the kitchen. She poured both of them a refill.

"You said we were going to take down an intelligence team. Now you want a shooting war. Are you mad?!"

"Not at all. And never say that again." Raquel said it with a feral warning as clear as a cougar's growl. Maxine understood very well that the casual comment had been very close to reality. She stored that information away in a safe place.

"A sniper team already killed the Governor. We'll just branch out a bit, but first we are going to do some traveling as soon as you get your act together. And I think I know where we can shoot. Further north of here there are thousands of acres where people shoot all the time. It is a hunter's paradise. I read about it in the newspaper. Potter Country. It is God's country. At least that is what the paper said.

So the planning began in earnest. Raquel made a list for more foraging. They would go together to purchase the reloading equipment and supplies. Major gun supply companies all had stores in the area so large purchases at one location were unnecessary.

In a week the basement looked like Ruby Ridge and Maxine got to work on her part of the plan. She drank gallons of strong black coffee, hummed tunelessly and set up her reloading factory. She would work on the Remington she had as a backup gun.

The Remington was a problem all its own. Because of past accidental discharges the rifle had an eleven pound trigger pull. That was the equivalent of pulling a little red wagon with the anchor chain off an aircraft carrier. What she needed was a setting that she could whisper and set off.

She disassembled the rifle and set to work. After an hour she had it down to 2.4 pounds of pull and was satisfied. Using her clear finger polish to secure the set screws she then began work on the stock.

The black synthetic stock was lightweight and functional to her practiced eye, but it was cheaply made. Not the expensive sniper stock that she had worked with in Jordan, this one was a beginner level rifle. The stock touched the barrel at four spots. The barrel assembly was already off, but she reassembled it so she could mark the areas that needed cut away.

A rifle barrel is a vibration tool just as much as a guitar string. As the bullet is fired and passes down the length of the barrel, grooves cut in the passageway spin the bullet. That rotation adds stability to the flight of the bullet and actually gives an exact path depending on the shape and weight of the bullet, type of powder and its speed of ignition, and the "harmonics" of the barrel - the vibrations created by the bullet's progress and spin. If the stock touches the barrel those harmonics, or vibrations, are affected.

In wooden stocks moisture and temperature can swell or shrink the barrel making the harmonics impossible to predict and changing the flight path of the bullet. Inaccurate shooting.

Synthetic stocks – good ones – are not subject to any of the changes that plague wooden stocks. But cheap synthetic stocks are unpredictable based on such things as the grip of the marksman, their contact with the barrel when too thinly constructed, and in the case of this rifle, the inability to even tighten the assembly screw tight enough to stabilize the unit. Maxine shook her head at the shabby quality attached to such a fine rifle assembly.

She made her calculations, got old Morris' Dremel out with a grinding bit and went to work. Tiny bits at a time she whittled away the excess nylon of the stock. After each amount was excised she re-assembled the rifle. That screw was still trouble.

Looking around the little basement shop she spied a piece of aluminum stock about a quarter of an inch thick, six inches long, and an inch wide. Good ole Morris has scavenged everything in case he ever needed to make something from the ground up.

Maxine drilled a hole to allow the screw to pass through snugly. Then she cut the aluminum bar to the correct size. Finally grinding it on a grit wheel, she even worked a concave face on it. A few tries and it kept the rifle tight without flexing the stock.

She returned to the stock trimming until she was satisfied. Finally assembling the rifle she passed a dollar bill down the length of the barrel from the front all the way down to the assembly screw. It slid unimpaired. Perfect. She smiled at the pleasure of her own craftsmanship.

Putting the rifle to her shoulder she slipped her finger to the trigger. The firm but gentle pull rearward resulted in the click of the firing pin's release. *Maybe this will do after all.*

More coffee and then the simple job of fitting the stock to her shoulder and reach came next. She donned the camos, gloves, shirt and underclothing she expected to be wearing on their missions. Sitting in a chair, and resting the rifle on a towel on top of the electric dryer, she laid her cheek on the comb of the stock. Determining what needed taken off, she changed out of the clothes and began more stock surgery.

This time a coping saw was the tool of choice. First using a pencil and ruler she scribed the determined mark for cutting the stock. Removing the rubber butt piece that would absorb much of the recoil, she then began to carefully saw that amount off the end of the synthetic stock. A bit of work with a file and she replaced the butt piece.

Putting the clothes back on, she again laid the rifle across the dryer. She'd actually taken a bit more than necessary, but not enough to get her a scope scar. That telltale cut in an eyebrow that occurs when recoil slams the scope into one's face if he is too close. She'd seen enough rookies with bloody faces to do that. Practice with this rifle would give her the same point of contact every time.

"Practice makes permanent. Perfect practice makes perfect," her instructors had drilled into her.

The rifle was cleaned vigorously, oiled lightly then dried completely. Oil attracted dirt and dirt impeded perfection.

"Are we having fun?" Raquel stood at the top of the steps and looked at Maxine working the RCBS press. She was making rifle cartridges. Ten each with one specific weight of powder and identical bullets. Then ten of a slightly different load. Ten different loads, but the same primer, case and bullets in every one. Each scrupulously recorded and marked in plastic shell boxes. At the range each load would be fired in turn and different targets would chart which was the best for this rifle. Maxine had explained it all one evening as they ate a meal of pita, falafel, salad, and lamb kabobs. Raquel didn't appreciate it as much as the Texas Roadhouse, but complimented Maxine all the same.

"Cold zero is what we have to do," she said, and Raquel was very interested in this part.

"From what I've read on the web, most hunters fire their rifles repeatedly at the range. The barrels get warmer and warmer from the ignited gunpowder and friction of the bullet passing through the barrel. Each time the heated barrel changes the harmonics and thus the point of impact changes.

"Most hunters are satisfied with an accuracy of about three inches at one hundred yards. That is enough to hit the heart-lung area in the local deer.

"There was one discussion where a man asked why his first shot was off after he cleaned the barrel and then went to the range. The answer was probably wrong.

"The author said it was oil in the barrel. That may be, but not necessarily. My belief is that it is the difference between a cold zero as opposed to the warmer barrel. When they stopped zeroing their scope the barrel was hot or at least warm."

Raquel nodded. This was new but she was very quick and had already grasped where Maxine was going.

"For us we are going to have to have access to a range – 200 or 300 meters, or yards. And we must be able to wait the time for the barrel to cool back down after each shot. Our first shot should be the only one we fire on any given mission."

"I think I have answered our range problem and we won't have to drive three and a half hours to get there! There is a forest that is owned by a paper company about an hour west of here. It is for sale. I drove up there yesterday and hiked some of it. There's a chain across the gate, but I opened the lock and drove through. When the road stopped I hiked further in. There is a broken down cabin there and believe it or not a shooting bench. We'll need to work on it but it will suffice. And there is a clear cut area that runs out about four hundred yards if my pacing is accurate.

"When we go up we'll change the lock on the gate for an identical one but with a different key then put it back like we found it when we leave. That will prevent any surprises."

A week later Maxine was satisfied. At one hundred yards she could form a cloverleaf pattern on the target with the precise handload. This gun-bullet-scope combination would reach out to about 800 yards accurately. At least to center body mass or a head shot at that distance. She was pinpoint out to three hundred yards. After that she told Raquel she felt like one of the deer hunters – it would have to do. She really needed a long distance range.

Raquel smiled beautifully and said they were ready for a trial run.

TWENTY SEVEN

"You don't have AIDS."

"That's a great piece of news. What else do you know?" Nick Larsen was grinning with his cell phone to his ear.

After Governor Endreling had been killed and Nick was recovering from the shoulder wound it had occurred to him that the bullet which left the Governor's head and smashed into his body was covered with the man's tissue and blood. If that round had HIV on it, then Nick was in some serious trouble. He'd contacted the Country Coroner on the QT and asked him to run some tests.

"Sorry it took a while to get to back you. We fished two floaters out of the river and that has kept me busy, between autopsies, media, with them and also the Governor's case. Not to mention trying to get re-elected." Grant chuckled.

"I figured I'd hear from you when you had time. Needless to say, I appreciate your doing this for me. I didn't want to go through channels with it. Not something that would meet the PC quotient at PSP Headquarters and for Mrs. Endreling's sake I thought it best to keep it quiet.

"So who whacked the floaters?" Nick had seen the stories.

"That's the strange thing. Both of them were hit with a .22 pistol. Ruger Mark II from the ballistics. One took a round in the open mouth, the other in the back of the head.

"Who uses a target pistol to take out two men but the Mafia? The guy with the mouth wound was shot at pretty close range. There was GSR on his face but the gun wasn't inside his mouth."

Vic suddenly got a strange look on his face.

"Hang on a minute, Grant," he said and motioned to Larry. When the phone had rung, Larry had drifted away to give Nick some privacy. Now he walked back over when Nick motioned.

They'd been sitting in the yard watching the roof going on the new pool and gym building. Now Larry resumed his seat.

"What did you tell me the shooter in Manassas used on you all?" Nick asked.

Larry's antennae was on full alert now. This was no casual question.

"Ruger Mark II, 22 caliber. Why?"

Nick raised a hand in a "wait-a-minute" signal.

"Grant, I think I may have something on your shooter. I just signed on with a group of security specialists. Their offices down in Manassas, Virginia were shot up by a crazy woman a while back. She used a Ruger like your shooter. It might be nothing but I think we'll come visit you. How about this afternoon?"

"I'll make sure I'm free. I'll have the Susquehanna detective with me if you don't mind. Three at the lab?"

"The detective's fine. But let's meet at Lung Fung's?"

"Where?!" Grant lived in Harrisburg; dined out more than in, but he'd never heard of any such place.

"Sorry, that's the nickname of the Chinese restaurant on North Front. Near the Wendy's. Inside joke at the Mansion."

"Got it. See you at three."

When they all gathered in the corner booth, it was five men not three. Jake, Larry, Nick, Grant and Mike shared introductions and started with a bit of "getting to know you" conversation. Finally Larry got to the point.

"Well, since I'm the resident target, I'll give you a bit of background. First on us.

"We – Jake and I – were Defense Intelligence agents up until recently. We were given a cover as security company owners and sent out to find al Qaeda's American leadership. More teams were sent out than just ours.

"Along the way we came into some information that bin Laden has a daughter in the game.

"Then we sort of got side tracked in the Midwest with a gang of head-cases who ended up being indirectly tied to the terrorism network we were chasing. I ain't real hot on coincidences, but we caught the brass ring with this job. First with the Illinois connection, and then – get this – our office was next door to Osama's baby girl.

"About the time we were tripping to her identity she was killin' people all over the place.

"First it was messengers Pappa was sending to America. What we finally called One Time Messengers."

"Then she apparently got into some kind of blood-lust," Jake picked up the story.

"It wasn't just messengers. She was popping guys outside of bars. Even tried to kill an ex-paratrooper who ran her off his sky-diving base," Jake laughed and continued.

"That old grizzly proved a bit more than she could handle. Took a shot at her and she tore out of there like she was on fire." The others laughed. They were pulling for the old soldier.

"Right after that she really went around the bend," Larry said.

"Came over to our place, killed our young secretary then shot our electronics guy. Elvis made it, but he coulda checked out." When

Larry mentioned "Elvis" and went right on talking, the others did an eye-check around the table as if to ask, "Did he just say Elvis? And did he say Elvis is still alive?"

It was funny in spite of the comment about the secretary.

"Well, we started slamming down the stairs to find out what was going on, and 'Blam," she shoots me on the stairway. Hit me near the crotch. Everyone winced.

"I'm okay. I'm okay, but she did hit the femoral artery. Jake and his dad slowed the bleeding until the medics arrived."

Jake again picked up the tale.

"Anyway, her gun was a Ruger Mark II.

"Some other things happened and we found ourselves out of the government and in business for ourselves. Solutions.com is the name of the company. It's still a cover, but now we work for us."

"So what happened to your shooter after she plugged you?" Grant asked Larry.

"First she torched her office, shot us up, set her own house afire then disappeared to the woods down near Fredericksburg. Torched that place, too, when a park ranger came upon her. This girl loves fire!" Larry said and laughed.

"After that, we didn't hear a thing about her. I figured she was overseas someplace. Obviously not. What are the odds that somebody will shoot your two people with the same kind of piece?" Jake added this.

"That's not all of it, Jake. One of the guys she killed was from Afghanistan. I couldn't believe it, but the ME is one of the best in the country. He verified the dental work with two of his friends. One in Chicago and another at the Pentagon. They were real interested in that bit of info." Mike shared this as Grant watched their mouths dropping open. *Afghanistan*!?

"One more thing. An old farm was burned up in Perry Country. Not much of a place. Abandoned until a stranger bought it a while back. He's gone. No bodies in the ashes.

"Could have been druggies, whatever. But the curious part is that the house and the barn were both burned and they are a good ways apart. In the barn was an old beat up van. Stolen in DC."

"What color was the van?" Jake's radar was screaming now.

"Well, now it's sort of ash colored, but I think the trooper who was there said it had been white. He also told me this… a shooting range had been set up. Out to five hundred yards."

Nick's turn at bat came up. "Which brings us to the snipers who hit the Governor and me. The SUV they left at the scene was stolen in Pittsburg. There wasn't any forensics left after they torched it. The team that did it – and it was a team – was very good. Great shooter and pros about evidence. Witnesses saw two men with two vehicles. A van and the SUV. They left in the van. No report on it.

"The bullet was a 308. The shot was over four hundred yards uphill. It *was* a professional hit," Mike added.

"But there are lots of good ole boys around here who can shoot ground hogs out to five or six hundred yards," Grant added. His own father had shot a 25-06 at three hundred yards at just such targets. "And the Gov had his share of people who hated him."

"Sure, but hog hunters don't use 308s. That's a deer load, but more importantly it is a sniper round. And this one was Teflon coated, a handload." Mike was convinced that the hit was connected to those of the famous singer and liberal senator who had been murdered in the past months.

"So where do we go from here?" Grant asked.

Jake had already been considering that. "First of all, we'll touch base with our contacts. Including Homeland Security. If this woman is back on active duty they need to know it."

Nick added, "I'll start talking to PSP investigators I know. They can tap into their snitches. If the shooters were talking to anyone local they may have something."

Suddenly a chill ran down Jake's neck. He remembered that George and Harold had noticed a white van around the farm. If they were running surveillance on the farm that did not bode well for them.

Jake's phone rang. He excused himself and went to a neutral corner for his conversation.

Sliding into the booth he said, "The guy who bought the farm – no joke intended – was caught in Ohio. He is a borderline jihadist. Apparently got religion and boogied off for Idaho. Got caught in Ohio when a trooper there recognized him from a South Carolina murder warrant. That seems strange, but that's the word.

"Seems this guy was there when Raquel – Larry calls her the Terrorist Babe…"

"And she is a babe!" Larry interjected with a grin.

"That she is. Anyway. This guy from the farm apparently saw her shoot the two guys you got at the morgue, Grant. Just smooth as mercury, One and then Two," Jake used his thumb and forefinger to mimic shooting. He and the terrorist babe dumped them in the Juniata.

"Here's where we have to be careful. This guy said that they followed us from our airport offices to E'town. He didn't know who we were, but the information matches our places. That definitely puts us at risk.

"How she's tied to the sniping is something he didn't know but he did say that before she showed up there was a snake-cold sniper trainer and three teams at the farm. He didn't have anything to do with them. Said there were two male teams and one team of women!

"And get this – the sniper trainer is a woman too!"

"Man talk about black widows!!" Mike interrupted with a shake of his head.

"So, here's what we have so far," Grant took out a three-by-five card and started to make notes:

"One – the farm was an al Qaeda training site.

"Two – the guy who ran it is now captured.

"Three – there is a woman sniper on the loose along with three other teams of snipers somewhere in the States."

Nick added, "And one of those teams is likely responsible for the Governor's
shooting here." Everyone nodded.

"Four – the boss lady of al Qaeda is in our neighborhood. Armed and dangerous.

"Five," Mike offered, encouraging no one, "that's eight people on the loose who hate America, cops and can shoot flies off a horse at five hundred yards."

"Okay," Grant said looking at his watch. "I have to be downtown in ten minutes. I'll get a copy of this to you all. Give me fax numbers if you will. Also I think we should all keep one another in the loop. Should I update the WE team or not?

"For now, I don't think so. I'd appreciate it if the media didn't get this right now. I don't want the terrorist babe to take off again. This time I want a shot at her," Larry said and they all agreed.

Mike disagreed. "Look men, I know you want her, and I don't blame you, but we have to get the information out now. There is too much chance of more people getting murdered."

Reluctantly the others agreed. It was too important not to move on it. Just keep the media out of the loop for a while.

They shook hands and went their separate ways.

TWENTY EIGHT

Their roles gradually changed as Maxine and Raquel closed on the actual shooting. Maxine became the leader while Raquel, hungry to learn the fine point of the sniper trade submitted to the reversal.

They had driven to Raquel's location in Juniata County. Maxine hated it. She just felt that someone could slip up on them and the range was not clear. It just spooked her.

"I have a couple of suggestions. First this place is no good. I need to work on this gun. It is all right, but it's too light and I'm just not excited about it above three hundred yards.

"Second, what would you say to going back to the farm? The rifle range there is set up for five hundred yards, and could be extended just by driving through the brush and knocking it down. It is out of ear-range of any neighbors so we could really work on everything there. You said it was burned down. Surely once the cops look at it there should be no further interruptions."

"So do we go get a SWAT gun?" Raquel asked.

"Well, the best rifle we could get would be a military one. Second best is a police sniper's. It would be a good weapon. And the scope, all the gear would be first class I'm guessing."

Raquel smiled. She had loved the idea of hitting a cop from the beginning. Taking his gun away from him would be a gas.

"Let's go. We'll talk about it on the way home."

Maxine began stowing her gear. Raquel was impressed with the forethought that went into a sniper's work. It was detailed down to the tiniest concern.

On the way back to Highspire, it was decided that they would drive to the farm and test the area for any observers, snoopers, etc. If the coast was clear they would go down the lane and check things out. From there, they could decide.

Maxine began to teach Raquel more about sniping. It was not just hit and run or a shooting gallery. Military snipers were professional soldiers. They were not murderers. She failed to add that the latter was exactly what she had become however. Just a highly skilled murderer.

Maxine still considered herself a soldier. Her idea was exactly synonymous with a US military man or policeman's creed. The job was a necessary one, ultimately saved lives, either on the field of combat, among the enemies or in hostage situations, etc.

Raquel thought that was nonsense. Kill people, move on. But she was wise enough to just nod her head and agree visibly with Maxine. *You just hit the targets, Honey. I'll take it from there. I have plans for you!*

At the house Raquel got out a road map of the Northeast. Finally she tapped a spot with her nail. Wilmington, Delaware. Urban. Large enough to have a decent SWAT team. Far enough away to not be connected to Harrisburg.

They drove past the various police stations until they saw a SWAT step van. Then Raquel chose their location. Urban decay, crowded, rush hour.

She drove to a 7-11 and went to the pay phone in the rear. She dialed 911, disguised her voice, and in a panting whispery voice said, "HELP! My boy friend has my mom and two kids in the kitchen. He's goin' cut them!!" She gave the address of a pre-selected apartment building and hung up. They walked the two blocks and entered the bodega across the street when the sirens blared and the step van screeched to a halt.

They hurried out to the sidewalk.

"Watch for the shooter. Keep an eye on him. Be sure you can pick him out later at the police station. Don't be wrong. I'm going to get the car. When they load up, I'll pick you up right here." Maxine only nodded.

It didn't take long for the Dover police to figure that the call was bogus. They came out of the apartment building ripping Velcro tabs loose on their vests. Happy but disappointed in that adrenaline soaked way of soldiers and policemen the world over.

Just as the van rounded the corner, the black Saab purred up beside Maxine and she slid in.

At five-thirty, the officer came out of the station, loaded his squad car with the drag bag that held his rifle, added a vest and gear bag into the trunk. Then he fired it up and drove off.

Just as he stepped out of the car in a suburban neighborhood Raquel pulled up and Maxine rolled down her window. "Excuse me," she smiled.

The young policeman returned her smile and stepped toward their car. Raquel shot him in the face as he leaned down. Instantly Maxine grabbed the keys from his dying hand and ran to the trunk of the squad car. Raquel popped the Saab's trunk and kept a look out. Less than one minute later, they were out of sight and headed for the back roads from Wilmington to Lancaster, Pennsylvania. Maxine navigated and Raquel fired up the CD. Nothing to it.

The next day Maxine and Raquel drove their cars to Scranton. Raquel led the way to the Moses Taylor Hospital. She looked for signs for the free clinic. Once she found it, she sought out a parking place in an unlit location among old, beat up cars.

When she'd parked, she laid the keys to the Saab on the dash, checked one more time for any thing she might have missed when she'd cleaned the car then stepped onto the sidewalk. Walking back to where Maxine sat with her engine idling, Raquel got in and off they went.

"It's my own charity program. Give a nice car to a deserving poor car thief." Raquel laughed. "This is getting old, but I really can't sell them. Beside there isn't a money problem. Let's go."

They drove to Somerset on the Pennsylvania Turnpike. First down to Philly then west. It meant a long night, but they were young and used to late hours. Once there they checked into a cheap motel and got some shut eye. Six hours later, Raquel bought a grey Mazda with a crease in the right side and a key scrape across the trunk. But it was clean and ran well. She paid the asking price in cash with no paperwork. At the motel they bolted on a license plate Maxine had stolen downtown at a garage. They were headed back to Highspire. *Man all this driving is a drag*, Maxine thought.

Two days later Maxine was ecstatic. The SWAT rifle was all she'd hoped it would be. And there was six twenty round boxes of Lake City 308 Match quality ammo in the gear bag! She worked on the adjustable stock and comb to fit her smaller stature, re-installed the Unertl 10X military scope. This outfit was actually better than the King of Jordan's rifle!

Finally they loaded the trunk of the newly purchased Mazda and headed for Perry County. Raquel dropped Maxine at the end of the lane where she virtually vaporized into the brush. It amazed Raquel to see it.

Thirty minutes later her phone buzzed and Maxine gave her the all clear. Raquel was so impressed with this woman's skills. She had read the tracks around the place, checked the forest in all directions for any hidden watchers then gone to the back of the farm in case there was anyone stashed back there on a horse or on foot. All clear.

An hour later, they'd driven the Mazda like a brush buster and knocked down enough weeds and bushes so that Maxine could see out to 800 yards from the shooting bench. Next they moved the one and two hundred yard target backs from their locations and set them up at six and eight hundred laser-ranged spots.

Finally, Maxine set up the new rifle and fired a round. She waited for the barrel to cool and repeated it. Raquel was posted at the lane to watch for anyone to bust into their little party. No one did.

Maxine went to work in the time consuming work of cold-zeroing the SWAT rifle. It was as smooth as any she had ever worked with. The action was crisp and knocked off at exactly three pounds according to the scale in the gear bag.

Soon she was clover leafing her shots out to four hundred yards. After that she was in the 10 ring at eight hundred. AWESOME!

Next Raquel began her education. Maxine drilled her in how to spot for her. "You're left of that tree" won't cut it when a shooter needs a shot called or a target identified. So they drew range cards, lasered a variety of spots, and taught Raquel how to work effectively with Maxine.

"If you take the spotting scope and turn it just out of focus you can see the vapor trail of the bullet," Maxine told her.

"No way!" Raquel was sure Maxine was teasing. But it was true and Raquel was so fascinated by the expertise that she literally grew to be in awe of Maxine. Hero worship was a new experience for Raquel.

When enough had been accomplished for one day they packed everything up checked for wood ticks and took off to Highspire.

On the drive back down Route 322 Maxine explained setting up a hide, or shooter's nest. It could be in a building, forest or desert, or a baseball diamond that had just been mowed. That one was lots more difficult, she laughed.

Raquel then explained their first jobs. They were going to hunt the hunters. The three teams that Maxine had trained. Right after dishing up some preliminary pain to the team.

"How will we know where to intercept the snipers?"

"I'll send them to a specific place. You and I will get there first and watch them establish their shooting location then take them down when they are about to hit their mark.

"Can you figure out where they'll shoot from?" Raquel was certain what the answer would be.

"Of course. If you tell them when to hit their target there are certain set ups they will use. There will be the risk of missing them. Will they like the location we do? Things like that are always possible."

"And if I specified where and exactly when I wanted the hit to go down?" Raquel asked with a smirk.

"You can do that?"

"Maxine, my dear, I can do anything. I am god when it comes to giving orders in America."

"Then we can be certain they will cease to exist.

"But why kill them? Why not let them just go back where they came from?" Maxine asked.

"Did they see you? Learn anything about you?" Raquel looked across the seat at Maxine.

"Sure. Not my name or anything that would identify me."

"They could create a sketch and you're a hunted woman." Raquel answered.

Maxine nodded understanding.

"What about Alex? He saw me too. And he's gone away."

"Alex is a part of the jihad. He will never talk."

As they drove into Harrisburg's north side, Maxine was thinking about that last remark. Surely Raquel knew that when al Qaeda's leaders had been rolled up by the West's intelligence agencies they had sung like canaries. Perhaps they had been threatened but their treatment was nothing like it would have been if the cases were reversed. *Our people are not brave for the most part. They are soldiers, certainly, but they still want to live, except for the few who are conditioned to be martyrs.*

I'm no martyr, that's for certain. I want a back door when I shoot.

That was the moment it occurred to Maxine that she knew quite a lot about this woman beside her.

Will she decide that I am a loose end too? I must never once let my guard down. And I need a handgun and a knife. Maxine had just decided she was not a part of this team to the death.

Across the seat Raquel was watching Maxine from the corner of her eye. *She knows she's expendable*, Raquel thought as Maxine got very quiet and looked out the side window. *I will need to be very careful with this one.*

TWENTY NINE

Rain came sheeting down outside. Occasionally thunder would follow a charge of blue-white lightening. Inside it was warm and well lit. The smell of toast, coffee and fried bacon still filled the air, though the sink was now filled with yellowed plates and billows of hot soapy suds.

Helen stood at the helm doing dishes and joining in the rambunctious conversation. At the table sat Harold, Jake and Larry. George had just entered with his hat soaked and a yellow slicker draining onto a red, black and gray "rag rug."

"Man! I 'bout drowned between the tool shed and the stable. If I didn't love those nags so much I'd a let 'em go hungry this morning. He moved toward the table. Halfway there Helen handed him a steaming mug of black coffee.

In a corner near the sink a large silky-furred Labrador retriever sighed deeply and stretched. Rosalie knew what rainy days were all about. Naps followed by some food and more naps. Helen looked down and smiled. Like the men at that table, the loveable Lab had quickly worked its way into her heart.

"Okay, George! You might as well get in on this. Breakfast turned into a Bible study this morning." Larry was still new enough as a believer to be a bit uncomfortable with such discussions but enjoyed them in spite of his lack of knowledge.

Jake on the other hand reveled in them. He and Harold and his mother had discussed everything under the sun. They had a rule: No holds barred in the debates as long as it was not mean-spirited and everyone was respectful.

In the old days these forums had ranged from race relations to helping neighbors who were too lazy to help themselves. As Jake had approached puberty they touched on the more sensitive areas of dating, kissing, movies, dancing and the like.

Politics was a guaranteed issue. Jake well remembered sitting at his Grandpa Crabtree's right hand when he was the head of that old farm house in Illinois. The old man was uneducated in a classic sense, but wise in many ways. He was unbalanced in his opinions but that had never stopped him from barreling forth with a few cuss words for a wide variety of politicians. His favorite was FDR, though he respected Harry Truman. Jake recalled him saying one morning, "I could never figure a man like Harry hanging out with the likes of those *&$%@ in the Roosevelt administration.

Grandma had hurriedly interjected, "Dad, little pitchers have big ears! Dad! Dad!"

Grandpa had looked at Jake and said, "Forget that word, but don't forget the facts." He'd patted Jake on the head and ruffled his brown hair. Jake nodded.

This morning was that kind of a day around the table. Debate but not the cussing. It was melancholy to Jake who enjoyed recalling those precious times in his childhood when such subjects as homicide bombers and snipers were things beyond his youthful imagination.

Harold smiled, "Here's the premise, George. I was up reading my Bible like I do most mornings. Today I came to Luke Chapter 20. Jesus is giving forth with one of His parables.

"I thought it might be a good thing to bring it up since we need to be sure that Solutions is always on the side of the angels. We already started but let's see where you come down on this. Then I'll tell you what we all had to offer. Let me read it to you.

> Luke 20:9-18 Then began he to speak to the people this parable; A certain man planted a vineyard, and let it forth to husbandmen, and went into a far country for a long time. [10]And at the season he sent a servant to the husbandmen, that they should give him of the fruit of the vineyard: but the husbandmen beat him, and sent *him* away empty. [11]And again he sent another servant: and they beat him also, and entreated *him* shamefully, and sent *him* away empty. [12]And again he sent a third: and they wounded him also, and cast *him* out. [13]Then said the lord of the vineyard, What shall I do? I will send my beloved son: it may be they will reverence *him* when they see him. [14]But when the husbandmen saw him, they reasoned among themselves, saying, This is the heir: come, let us kill him, that the inheritance may be ours. [15]So they cast him out of the vineyard, and killed *him.* What therefore shall the lord of the vineyard do unto them? [16]He shall come and destroy these husbandmen, and shall give the vineyard to others. And when they heard *it,* they said, God forbid. [17]And he beheld them, and said, What is this then that is written, The stone which the builders rejected, the same is become the head of the corner? [18]Whosoever shall fall upon that stone shall be broken; but on whomsoever it shall fall, it will grind him to powder.

While Harold was reading, Helen quickly dried her hands and walked to the cupboard across the kitchen. Rosalie stirred enough to raise her head and keep an eye on her mistress and benefactor. Satisfied she wasn't going outside and no food opportunity presented itself, she dropped her head with an audible thud and began to snore.

Helen picked up a Bible, opened it to the passage and silently handed it to George who took a pair of reading glasses from the pocket of his bib overalls and followed along as Harold read aloud.

George continued to look at the Scriptures for a moment longer. Then he raised his head and said, "First thing is that the Lord is talking about the religious Jews who rejected him. Even they realized that according to verse nineteen."

"Right," Jake agreed.

"Then the next thing is that the parable says that God sent people to teach Israel about His Son.

"I take that to mean that the Old Testament clearly shows that the Messiah of Israel is the Son of God. I know enough to know that they believe there is a Messiah who will someday come and set up God's kingdom. They just refuse – most of 'em – to accept that He existed before Jesus came as the New Testament shows or that He will be God's son."

Larry interrupted. "Yeah, but there was one who died not long ago left a letter to be opened a year after his death. Seems he likely believed that Jesus was the Messiah according to that letter. And he was no small change. Two hundred people attended his funeral in Jerusalem!"

"I read about that too," Harold agreed. Then George continued.

"The parable says the so-called religious Jews killed the ones who came from the Father because of their own selfish reasons.

"Good." Larry said. "We hadn't even touched on that really." Harold smiled. *The boy's growing.*

"Finally they killed the Son too.

"Verses like this one feed the guys who say that the Jews killed Jesus and use it as a reason to be anti-Semitic. I heard enough of 'em in my days of actin' like I was one of 'em. Hateful, mean-spirited, racist men. Women too.

"'Course Jesus was still around when He told this so He was likely tryin' to tip off the folks there 'bout what was comin'. Didn't work. I figger some a them was shoutin' 'Crucify Him" not long after this time.

"That what you fellers were looking for?" he removed the glasses and poked them back down into the bib pocket and glanced around the table.

"Not exactly. I think all that's right, but Jake said something that sort of got us looking at another perspective.

"That there are people who are so evil that killing is the only way to stop them," Harold said.

Helen chimed in, "But God didn't kill them even though they crucified the Saviour!"

"Meaning that you don't think anybody needs killing?" Larry baited her with the remark and diffused it with a grin to let her know what he was up to.

"No I don't think that, Larry. You know better. But I do think that there has to be some real thought given to who gets killed and by whom. And I guess, ultimately, when they get killed."

"Like, did they get a chance to go for their gun first?" Jake took a turn.

"Now Jake," Harold cautioned. He'd seen the two young men get wired up on debates and really go for the jugular. They could be like two wolves at a deer, even though they were just funnin'. He didn't want them attacking Helen that way. She was too new to these guys and might be hurt.

"It's all right, Harold. I can hold my own. I've been a Baptist for a long time, and I've had some great preachers. I know how to survive against tougher pups than these two," she grinned dishing some back.

"So what about such evil people that they even want to kill the Son of God? That should be the ultimate evil in the heart of any man," Harold brought it back on course.

Helen came back, "First of all, the Jews didn't kill Jesus. The Romans did it. Individuals who were 'just following orders' as the Nazis liked to say."

"And there ain't anybody that can convince me the Roman leaders did anything to please the Pharisees or Sadducees that they didn't want to do anyway!" George interjected.

"Agreed," Jake said. It was at times like this that his Jewish roots were poignant.

"But remember this, too," Harold added. "Jesus' death was not a historical happenstance. He is the personification of the Passover Lamb in Exodus. I have a list of forty-five Old Testament prophecies that Jake's mother and I researched years ago in which Jesus met the exact requirements in every verse.

"God had a problem with man's sins that the blood of goats, lambs and bullocks would not solve. There needed to be a source of pure blood to be shed for the sins of man. Only the incarnate Son of God's veins had such blood. He came to this earth in the form of a man, born of a virgin and fulfilled the Isaiah prophecy and all those others.

"He lived a perfect life, died as it said he would in Daniel 9, and rose again – physically, bodily – from the grave. His resurrection was to prove that God had accepted the shed blood of the perfect Lamb and now man could be forgiven. The book of Hebrews says 'once for all.' I heard a good preacher say one time that the tense of the Greek words indicate that it means 'once and for all.'

"There was no coincidence, no human planning. It was all engineered by God to bring sinful man back into the fold. Jesus' life was not taken, it was given.

"Those rejectionist priests and scribes turned away from the Lamb of God because they wanted to keep their grip on power and profit. It was pure sinfulness. That's shown by the fact that people who accepted Jesus by faith were changed and others not.

"I give you the Apostle Paul who was one of those men before he met Jesus on the Damascus Road. He was miraculously changed in body, soul and spirit. Only the Lord can do that kind of house cleaning."

Larry spoke quietly, "And that's how a guy like me could pray and ask for forgiveness for my sins and God would hear me. Jake said that it was because of Jesus' goodness and purity. I know it wasn't 'cause I deserved it."

"Amen, Larry. And it's the blood of Jesus and the Holy Spirit's power that keeps you saved, not your hangin' on for dear life. You got no more to do with it than peaches in a jar keep themselves preserved," George chuckled as he said that last part.

So, then, are there people in the world who are so evil they need to be put down like a rabid dog or not?" Larry asked.

Rosalie sleeping on her cushioned bed chose that specific time to plaintively whine in her sleep.

Everyone laughed simultaneously. The coincidence of it was too much to miss.

Helen spoke softly, "I know it has to be done." Her voice cracked with emotion and her lips and chin trembled with a promise of weeping to follow.

"It's just that you men ..."

Her remarks were interrupted by a knock on the door. Rosalie erupted from her bed fully bristled and stiff-legged. She instantly moved in front of Helen and staked out that territory.

Nick opened the door a bit, poked his head in, and said, "Mrs. Allen, you better chain up that monster. I want some coffee." Then he stepped on into the kitchen.

Rosalie bolted toward him with her tail wagging her entire body. Nick immediately knelt to one knee and hugged her. "Hello Rosie."

The dog shoved her chest into his thigh with a "dog hug" nearly pushing him off his balance. Her nose then poked into the pocket of his rain jacket.

He pulled a dog biscuit out and as if by magic it disappeared.

Removing his jacket, he hung it on the rack by the door and moved to the table. Helen provided the coffee and Harold brought him up to speed on the discussion.

"And you just kept me from blubbering," Helen added when he stopped.

"So what do you say, Nick? Whack 'em or pack 'em off to seminary?" Larry joked.

"Well, this is something I think every soldier and policeman has to settle. The wiser of us do it before the facts. Some of us after they have been in their first shooting.

"For me it came after one of our troopers shot a convenience store robber near Pottstown during my first year on the Job."

"I have a friend who was a Secret Service agent and attended our church there. He and I talked a lot about it. He was a real blessing to me.

"But yeah, I think there are people who are so absolutely evil that they need to be killed for the sake of civilization. Fortunately for me I've never pulled the trigger on anyone but I hope if it ever comes to that time that I will be right in my judgment and that the Lord will give me peace afterwards.

"I'm guessing that every one of you fellows have already faced that time and gotten it settled." Heads nodded around the table.

The telephone rang. Harold rose and went to the office area. He spoke quietly for a few moments, listened, and then said, "Thank you for that. I feel better knowing it," then listened some more.

"So you have what you need, and will take care of it? How long from today?

"Thanks. I'll get back to you. See you at the lake," then hung up the phone, jotted a note and moved back to his spot at the table.

Helen looked down at her hands. A tear slipped down the edge of her nose and dropped onto her hands.

"George gave me a little handgun the other day. He said that we might be in danger from this evil woman – this Terrorist Babe.

"Larry I must tell you I hate that name. It seems light hearted. I know you did it as a joke, but I am afraid of her. If there is anyone who seems to personify this evil we've been discussing, it's her. In my mind, even moreso than her evil father.

"I know how to shoot. Been target shooting since I was a girl on the farm. But I've never ever pointed a gun at anyone. The truth is I don't like to think about it but I have been. I believe that if any of you were threatened I could shoot and never bat an eye."

Little did she know the evil that soon was about to descend upon their happy home.

THIRTY

They pulled out of the driveway at seven in the morning. The pair of Cardinals were sneaking sunflower seeds and flicking away to the ground to bite the shell off. They seemed to take turns with one sitting on the round feeder on sentinel duty. Goldfinches hung on the sack of thistle seed that George had hung in the Rose of Sharon tree not far away.

Jake noted them as he closed the car door. They were so "normal" and lately he had seemed to treasure that kind of thing more than ever. He wasn't melancholy, he told himself, but chalked it up to having Helen around the place. He had lived a large chunk of his life without a woman around. Especially one who nurtured him like she did.

Nick leaned his seat back and settled his stainless travel mug of coffee in the cup holder on the center console.

"You guys are ruining me with all the coffee you have me drinking," he chuckled.

Jake and he were going to Lake Raystown in Jake's new Escalade. Harold and Larry were in Larry's Ford F-250 Super Duty. He had a matching shell on the back. The two of them had stuffed it with gear. They were fully engaged in this fishing trip. Coolers, sleeping bags, and the like lay alongside five different rods, reels and tackle boxes.

They had already headed out to the Harrisburg Wal Mart for those last few items the two of them insisted were necessary.

For their part neither Jake nor Nick were looking forward to roughing it. But on the other hand they did look forward to getting out on the lake and having an opportunity to just sort of kick back and laze around.

They were about thirty minutes northwest of Harrisburg when Nick turned to Jake and asked, "Jake, can we talk about exactly what I'm getting into with you guys?"

"Sure. But I thought we talked that out pretty well with you and Patty before you signed on." Jake wondered what was coming next.

"Let's talk about two things. This terrorist babe, Raquel first. What do you plan to do about her? Are you going to kill her if you get a chance?"

Keeping his eyes straight ahead Jake prevented Nick from reading them, but a little white spot appeared on Jake's tanned cheek. Other than that there was no physical response.

"If she tries to take us down, of course I'll kill her. She is not to be taken carelessly. Nick, this one is a stone cold killer. Ask that policeman in Manassas, Wilson Garrity. He's got the file on all the people she just shot and moved on as if they were paper targets."

"That isn't what I mean. Are you planning to try to take her down rather than arrest her."

It was quiet in the car for a while. Just the hum of tires on the highway.

"That's not mine to decide. A policeman might arrest her before she gets near us. She could get killed by one of her own kind. If we can take her without shooting we could turn her over to the spooks. They would probably be able to sweat her for some good information.

"You know how those things happen." Jake looked across the car and Nick nodded.

"Why do I think there is more to this than you're asking me?" Jake said, holding Nick's eyes as long as he could and still drive safely.

"There is. When did you kill your first man? Do you remember how you felt? What you went through?

"Jake, we're both Christians. Not nominal ones in the sense that it means little to us. We take it seriously.

"I've never fired a shot with my weapon at a bad guy. Even on Executive Detail, we managed to take down the few threats without shooting. I only ever pulled down on two threats.

"What happens when or if I have to kill someone?" Nick wasn't speaking like there was any fear. More like he was trying to condition himself for the occasion.

"My first time was in Indonesia. I was there with a protectee. Jakarta.

"This guy was a trade delegate. He was trying to put together some deals with Indonesian shipping people. Jakarta had lots of jihadists stirring up the Muslims. Everyone was jumpy.

"There were three of us on the detail. I didn't usually pull protection jobs but there was some kind of high level orders and so I was included. Six Indonesian policemen were on outer perimeter guard. We stepped out of the hotel and had about twenty feet to the car.

"There was nothing to indicate a threat. Nobody rushing in. No crowds. Then the doorman pulled this crazy ten inch curve-bladed knife and lunged at my man.

"He had about six feet to cover, but I had a slight edge. I was about eighteen inches closer than my protectee. I shoved him with my hip as I pivoted and quick-drew. Drilled the guy. Once in the chest the other in the throat. He was going down and my piece was rising on the second shot. Either way he was out for the count. "One of the policemen ran up and kicked him about half a dozen times yelling at him in his own language. Furious about it all. Face, you know.

"We hustled our guy into the car. Away we went with sirens and lights. The next day we were on a military flight back to the States.

"How did I feel? It happened too fast to think. Training – you know this, Nick – training is the great adrenaline offset. You don't shake or puke or faint. You know how tunnel vision affects everybody. Things go into slow motion and your field of vision narrows. When you train hard and the shooting starts even the tunnel vision seems less intense than in those who don't. We've done enough debriefs to figure that out.

"That night I was finally alone. I sat and drank about a half gallon of orange juice. Couldn't get enough of the stuff. Left the lights off in my room except for the bathroom. Just sat in a chair and thought about what happened over and over. What did I do right? How could I have changed anything?"

"And what about inside your head? Remorse? Anger? Feel any guilt about taking a life?" Nick asked. Almost like he was debriefing Jake.

"Remorse? Sure. I didn't want to kill anybody. But it was what I trained to do day in and day out. I didn't even have a thought when I was doing it. Just response.

"Anger? Nope. That booger would have killed both of us if he could have. He got what he deserved.

"Larry and I talk about this some. He was a sniper for a few months in the Army. Had to take a couple of shots. He said all he thought about was that he was saving the life of some GI when he pulled the trigger. And I don't think he was making light of it.

"Like that story that went around the internet about this news chick that asked an Iraq veteran sniper what he felt when he squeezed the trigger on a bad guy.

"'Recoil. I felt recoil,'" he said.

Nick had this mischievous grin on his face at the story.

For an instant Jake had a vision of a skinny kid from outside of Elizabethtown with a dirty face getting straightened up by his mother, then flashing that grin and causing her to laugh. Then it was lost. Jake resumed his commentary.

"Guilt. Not for an instant. For a long time after my mother died I used to think about looking up the guy who was drunk when he rammed into her car. I wanted to take his hide off a square inch at a time and just repeat my mother's name with every slice.

"I talked to a preacher in the little church near our home about it one day when I saw him in town. Asked him to talk to me.

"That was when he told me what I had was mental and spiritual cancer. It was eating me up from the inside. There was a two part cure. Take it to Jesus and ask Him to help me forgive the guy. He quoted a verse about not being able to be forgiven for my own sins if I would not forgive others."

Nick nodded. "People call it the Lord's Prayer. My preacher says it isn't Jesus' prayer at all. It is a pattern prayer He gave the apostles so they could learn how to pray right."

Jake nodded understanding.

"Anyway, I walked out back and climbed up in a big old maple tree I used to hang out in when I was a little kid. Just sat on a big old overhanging limb. I prayed for the man. Prayed for the Lord to forgive him. To clean him up from the booze. To save his soul. It was probably the hardest thing I ever prayed about in my life.

"Nick, my faith is important to me, but I don't go to church like you. I don't have the Bible education you have from your years in a good church. But I feel close to the Lord and trust the Bible to have the answers."

Again Nick nodded and kept silent.

"Anyway, the guy died not two weeks after I prayed for him. Shot himself in the head with a shotgun one night when he was all alone.

"I wished I had gone to see him and told him I forgave him. Maybe it would have made a difference.

"After that I got kind of serious about telling people what's on my heart. If I love someone I love them all the way. And I tell 'em! If I can't stand them I don't let it get to hatred. I just keep away from them so I don't say something I'll have to apologize to the Lord or to them for. I ain't big on making apologies, though I do try to do it quickly when I have to."

"I understand," said Nick. "Now I have another question.

"What about the others? I know you shot a woman in Israel a while back. Were the reactions all the same when the noise died down?"

"Every one is different. Don't let anyone tell you that it doesn't matter. Every one of them affects you. Not with guilt, but it's like that woman who touched Jesus robe in the garment. I'll never forget what it said; that he felt virtue had gone out of him.

"That's what I think happens. A little bit of virtue goes out of you. I can't explain it. It's just a feeling I have.

I remember every one of the times I've killed. Every one. But don't think that I dwell on them. I've talked to a lot of combat soldiers. To a man, the well-adjusted ones – and they aren't all well adjusted – the well adjusted ones tell me that they don't feel remorse. They don't wake up in the night wanting to cry because they killed the enemy.

"Lots of them tell me that they were so cranked up getting ready for the battle that they couldn't wait to get to it.

"If you tell that to a civilian – someone who's never experienced it – they'll be horrified. And war is horrific. Personally I think that's one reason combat soldiers don't talk to civilians about it when they get back. They don't want to freak 'em out."

"Sounds right to me," Nick nodded in agreement.

"Is there any way to know if you'll freeze up when it's time?" Nick asked. In all the years in the State Police he had only asked one old veteran of three shootouts. The answer he got sounded rehearsed, theatrical, disingenuous. Jake's conversation was much more satisfying.

"Training, drills, and constant awareness. Not jumpiness. You already know how it works. You're under more stress every day you have a protectee out there than most combat soldiers do in a week, except for actual periods of combat.

"All I can tell you, Nick is that I believe there are men – and a few women, too – who are emotionally equipped for our kind of work. Mentally we are somehow able to deal with all the various aspects of danger, self control, razor sharp awareness. Even the taking of lives.

"Usually it is days or months of routine and then a half-dozen seconds of absolute response. Not terror like we've heard it said. There isn't any terror if you train. Nor fear. You just plain respond. The fear is present when you're approaching a time of impending danger. That is the natural part of the fight or flee instincts. Everybody deals with that in their own way. I've known guys that jabber like a nervous teenager. Some get surly. Others just kind of go way down inside themselves. I guess I'm somewhere between the surly and way inside. I hate people wanting to talk to me just before 'danger time.' It distracts me from my own mental and emotional preparation.

"Most of the time, though we don't have to sweat it. We never know when it will come on the job. Larry and I just hurl ourselves out into the places we go and either keep to our covers, do our recon, or take somebody back against their will. That last part is the time I was speaking of.

"It may sound like bravado but when I'm in deep cover I don't have a lot of fear or emotions. I just focus on my false identity and the job at hand. When bullets or knives come out then it's usually a fast crazy time and then it's over as quick as it began.

"Afterward you may weep or vomit or go someplace and shake like a leaf. But during the time you're in danger you just respond.

"That's why we train like we do. It saves lives."

"Nick just stay trained sharp. Be aware that killing is more a part of your job than it ever has been. Be ready. Don't hesitate. The kind of people we are up against are life takers and they won't even think about killing babies, women, or old people. They are scum.

Terrorists in the Middle East, America or any place else are pure evil and deserve getting blown away. After you see your first suicide bombing you'll know what I mean."

"Another question. What about this guy, Tortoise? Ex-CIA Director. Are you guys really going to hire him?"

"Do you mean 'are *we'* going to hire him? You're part of the team now.

"But I don't sign checks. Hiring him is way beyond my pay grade," Nick grinned.

"You know what I mean."

Jake smiled and nodded. "Yeah, I know even though it still takes some getting used to.

"Dad wants to put him on the team. We all know about the National Security Act, blah, blah, blah. Senators know it too, but Congress has more leaks than the Titanic.

"We won't be putting Harvey on salary though. That's his real name, Harvey Reid. And I don't suggest calling him Tortoise to his face.

"If he goes for our offer, we'll contract him.

"We won't put him under pressure to give any secrets away but he knows more by accident that we can use than we could ever get with outside sources.

"Dad wants him to set up a company of his own then contract him exclusively to us. Cleaner and keeps him in charge of himself. Easier than trying to manage him," Jake laughed.

At Lewistown's Route 22 exit Jake turned off and headed toward Huntingdon. Behind him a Ford Taurus followed them down the exit. Instead of following on toward McVeytown it climbed around the cloverleaf and headed back toward Harrisburg.

Jake was so involved with his conversation his mind did not even register the fact.

"Where are you?" Raquel asked as she accelerated her Taurus on Route 322 east.

"On Route 322 at that bridge over the river," Maxine answered into her cell phone.

"Clarke's Ferry," Raquel said. She had seen the signs earlier.

"What took them so long?"

"They went to the Wal Mart. Came out with some bags of groceries and stuff.

"That guy driving the fancy copper colored truck really speeds. I hope I don't get a ticket," Maxine fretted.

“Just take the ticket and smile. Be a good girl and don’t worry. They’re on a trip somewhere. Packed a lot of stuff in their vehicles before they left their house.

“Okay. Still meet at the farm?” Maxine verified their rendezvous at the burned out Perry Country location.

“Roger,” Raquel flipped the phone off and cranked up her Bellamy Brothers. *I’m hung up on this hillbilly stuff*, she grinned as she kept time on the steering wheel with her fingers.

THIRTY ONE

Dark gray clouds drifted by seeming almost to touch the top of the barn as George walked from the tool shed. He was about to begin his ride around the fence line. In the east the false dawn was painting a strip across the horizon.

As he walked into the barn the soft brown eyes of the old mare looked expectantly toward this man who fed her carrots, apples and an occasional sugar cube. Perhaps today he would choose her for his tour of the fence line.

Sure enough he walked to her stall with a bridle in his right hand. She whinnied a deep snuffling sound of appreciation. It was good to spend time with her friend. George continued the process of putting the western rig on the horse. He hoped it didn't rain until he got back.

As George worked in the barn a dark Taurus rolled past the farm.

"Lights on in the house," Maxine said looking up at the house on the hill.

"They're early risers. Maybe we'll put their lights out today," Raquel bit the words off. She was as tense and up tight as a trampoline spring.

Down the road a half mile or so were two driveways on the right. One led to a house near the road. The other to a little farmette back and out of sight. The people who lived there had moved out two weeks ago. That was what had decided the question of where to park the car.

Women dressed in camouflaged pants and jackets were unusual but with their hair up under matching hats and the bulky fit of the clothes even Raquel's stunning build was not discernable. After about fifteen minutes wait to see if anyone would tumble to their presence and come to investigate, they moved. Quietly the trunk thunked when Raquel hit the latch beside her seat. They grabbed the rifle and a pair of binoculars. The other equipment remained in the trunk.

It had been a nearly violent thing when they argued yesterday about what to bring and what to leave behind. Both were fiery and strong willed.

Maxine wanted the full compliment of gear. Drag bag, mat to place under the barrel, spotting scope, sand sock to fine-tune raising the barrel by her off hand. In the end Raquel won the debate. It is too close. *We are just going to shoot one of them and get out!*

They began the trek to the place in the woods atop the hill. Briars tugged at their clothes. One scratched Raquel deeply just above the eye when Maxine turned it loose without handing it back. She was still angry.

They climbed the wooded hill from the end opposite the farm then made their way the last one hundred fifty yards on their bellies. They'd been here before. From their previously chosen shooting spot it was only three hundred yards to the house. Nothing to it.

Maxine still recalled the argument. *Why shoot these workers and not the targets themselves?* She'd asked yesterday and still asked it in her thoughts as she crawled. Her focus was off. *This was not the proper way to do things!*

"We're going to increase their pain. Throw them off their balance. By killing their people we'll shake them up, make them furious. Angry people make mistakes. Take my word for it!" Raquel has insisted. She didn't go on to say that she hated them for some deep unexplainable reason and had since that day in Manassas when she shot up their office.

"I know these American heroes and how they think. They'll feel responsible that they left their people helpless. They'll hate us and want to 'saddle up and lynch us!'" Raquel laughed at the cowboy analogy.

"I still do not like it. We are putting ourselves at risk for no real gain!"

"You don't have to like it! You have to follow orders! Now just do your job!"

Maxine had stalked off to her room. Raquel could hear her opening the equipment box and pulling the bolt from the rifle. *Therapy time for the shooter*, she'd smiled grimly.

Now they were set up. Maxine had the rifle resting on its bipod. Lying beside her Raquel waited for something to happen at the farm. The days they had intermittently observed here the man went to feed the livestock and the woman walked to the chicken pen beside the barn and scattered some grain then returned to their house.

Sure enough, the woman stepped out into the yard. In her hand was a bag of something. Days earlier Maxine had identified it as vegetable peelings, egg shells and the like.

Today a large dog bounded out beside her. Loping toward the bird feeder where a red bird sat, the dog sent it to flight then joyfully returned to the woman. Raquel could not hear words, but imagined from the body language that the woman had mildly scolded the Labrador.

"Shoot the dog!" Raquel said abruptly.

Maxine raised her head from the rifle and looked at her like she'd lost her mind.

"Shoot the dog! Do it now or I'll shoot you!" Raquel smiled, but Maxine wondered how much humor there was in the statement. She turned back to the rifle.

In but a moment it spoke with a boom that echoed down the valley to their right. The dog dropped instantly, kicked a bit and was still.

The woman screamed and dropped to her knees beside the dog. She raised up and screamed again, something indiscernible. Her hands were covered in blood, though in the early morning light and at this distance it looked black to Raquel, who was laughing nearly hysterically.

"Let's go!" Maxine commanded, half rising.

"Shoot her too! NOW!" Raquel commanded.

Maxine looked at her like she was seeing an apparition.

Like a magic act the Ruger appeared in Raquel's hand. "Shoot!"

Maxine dropped back to her stomach and quickly put the rifle in place at her shoulder. She took a breath then let half of it out.

In the scope Helen was standing now. Looking around like a child lost in a crowd, she was crying out something but neither woman could hear her words. Suddenly she began to run toward the house.

The rifle spoke again and Helen tumbled forward onto the gravel drive and did not move.

Maxine did not wait to check her shot. She had rushed it, but knew it was a hit. She heard – virtually felt – something thudding in her background senses.

"RUN!" she shouted down at Raquel. Astonished at the burst of sudden noise from Maxine and still taken by the scene of the woman falling to the rifle, Raquel stood but didn't move for a moment.

"RUN!" Maxine shouted again as she headed back the way they had come into the woods. Briars and ground cover slowed her a little. Going back the same was as they had entered the woods broke every rule that had been drummed into her. She did not look back to see if Raquel followed – or if the Ruger was centered on her spine. She instinctively felt danger from something.

George heard the shots. One then a bit later another. Large rifle, his mind identified the sounds. He had been down on the east side of the hill by the creek where the deer congregated. With him on horseback the deer didn't spook. The scent of the horse covered his own and he could sit and watch the herd feed, drink and cavort.

He kicked the old mare in the flanks and raced directly up the hill to the patch of woods that was like a "high and tight" military haircut at the top. He sighted a blur of motion through the trees moving toward his right.

The Kimber 45 was in his right hand, the reins in his left. He wheeled the mare in the direction he'd seen the person running. As he got to the thirty foot opening between his woods and the neighbor's he caught a glimpse of someone in camos headed into the other timber.

Suddenly a woman dressed in the same way with her hair in a wild tangle burst from the patch of woods on his left. She stopped instantly when she saw him. She raised a pistol in her right hand.

He whirled toward her and reaching over his left forearm fired at the same time as the woman. George felt a blow high in his left upper chest. The horse had shied when the woman burst into view. His own shot went wild.

She reversed direction like magic and was lost inside the brush again.

He jerked the horse's neck around and galloped out of sight of where the woman had entered the woods. Experience long ago had taught him to seek cover in a gunfight. The easiest way to do that was downhill. *Helen!* George thought suddenly. He galloped back to the barn.

As he rounded the edge of the woods the farm buildings came into view. Directly ahead of him he saw both Rosalie and Helen. They were down and not moving.

By the time the mare was beside Rosalie, George was off her back and beside Helen. She was twisted and lying on her face. A large gory hole in her left side and a spreading pool of blood on the ground spoke volumes. *Exit wound,* George thought automatically. He placed a hand to her throat, but knew what he would not find. A pulse. He had seen too many of these wounds before.

Somewhere in his ears was a keening sound. Only later would he realize it was his own. He stroked Helen's hair with his left hand as her name came out in a choked cry of agony beyond belief. Then his professionalism came to the fore.

George ran to the house. Grabbing the Ruger Mini-14 and an extra magazine he headed down the edge of the hay field that ran behind a row of houses. The hay wouldn't provide much cover but that way was his best flanking opportunity.

When he'd covered about half the distance to the neighbor's wood line, he heard someone call his name quietly.

He whirled and looked down to see a neighbor. In one hand an M1 carbine. George recognized him. Retired-Marine Sergeant Major. George knew the gunfire had alerted him. In better times they had become friends.

“Larry, they killed Helen. I don’t know who. Call the police. Two people at least. In camos. One of them’s a woman. Brown hair. She shot at me too. Hit me in the chest but an overall button deflected it. I’m all right.

He sobbed then, but gathered strength from somewhere deep within and said, “Ask Gale to make the call. You get to the house. Watch yourself. They’re playing for keeps.

“Tell the law I’m out here in the woods looking for the shooters. I don’t need no friendly fire pluggin’ me,” then he quickly moved on.

Larry didn’t even nod. He just turned back to his house. George knew this was a man you could ride the river with.

At the car, Maxine was locked out. She cursed in three languages then took cover where she could watch both the lane and any approach by Raquel.

In very short order the beautiful woman emerged from the woods. Her pale and sweaty face was bloodied by the briars and her hair was flying in every direction. She had as mad a look in her eyes as Maxine had ever seen.

Raquel ran toward the car clicked the unlock with a button on her key ring and started for the driver’s seat.

Maxine emerged as she neared the door. Whirling, Raquel had the pistol centered on her nose.

“Wait! Let me put the rifle in the car.” She then moved to the trunk, which thunked open. She slid the rifle into its case. Only afterward did she lean into the car and tell Raquel, “Get out of the field uniform!”

Raquel looked like she didn’t get it. Finally she nodded and climbed out of the car. She quickly pulled the pants and jacket off. Underneath were jeans and a pullover. Both women now looked like girls out for breakfast. They sat in the car and removed their boots. Sneakers replaced them. It all went into the woods and off they sped down the lane.

That was when George stepped into their path.

He had the Mini 14 in both hands and it was pointed directly at the driver’s head. Raquel floored the Taurus and it swerved in the gravel as it leaped ahead. George fired once at her then shifted his aim and put two rounds into Maxine as he threw himself to the ground on his left side. The car brushed his feet as he left the road.

Landing with a groan he raised himself up and fired four more times at the Taurus. The back window didn’t shatter, but two holes appeared in the glass. The other two hit the trunk lid. Then it was out on the road, skidding, finding a grip and racing toward Elizabethtown.

Two miles down the road Raquel spied a man walking toward his Jeep with a cup in his left hand. She squealed the tires to a stop alongside the road.

Running up to him she fired twice into his chest. He didn't have a chance. She grabbed his dropped keys, looked back at Maxine's ruined head leaning against the side window of the Taurus, and popped the trunk lid. She grabbed the rifle and gear tossing them into the back seat of the Jeep. In less than two minutes she roared off. Twenty minutes later she was sedately pulling into her garage in Highspire.

They had fished for two days. The weather was cool in the mornings and warm almost to the point of discomfort during the remainder of the day. The stripers were biting and they had dined richly on the beautiful fish.

After dinner the first night there had been a council at which an agreement was reached. Harvey would form a company to collect and disseminate intelligence specifically and exclusively for Solutions.com. That it would find its way into the computers of Zulu and Mossad he had little doubt, but would try to see that nothing untoward went through him.

He came to see that his previously slanted perspective of the team was wrong. These were professionals of the highest caliber, even the new guy, Nick. He respected them and almost as important to him, he liked them. He could do business with them without reservation.

The beautiful boats were working a point that jutted out into the lake. Morning mist was beginning to drift upward. The fishing should be even better with the incoming low pressure front. Steaming coffee cups sat in cup holders. Two boats. Two guides. All courtesy of Harvey.

There had been no roughing it. The four bedroom rustic house not a half mile from the shore was equipped with everything from flat screen TVs to two ice makers. "Hog Heaven!" was how Nick and Larry summed it up simultaneously and without rehearsal. Jake and Harold had looked at each other, grinned and nodded. They'd have to watch these two.

Suddenly in the middle of casting his lure, Harold's cell phone chirped. He looked apologetically at Harvey who shrugged in understanding.

He spoke his name, listened, then suddenly sat down on a nearby cooler like he'd taken a hard punch to the wind. Quietly he spoke and alternately listened. Finally he hung up. Everybody was watching him. This was not good.

"Let's head in. Helen was killed this morning. It seems likely it was Osama's daughter and another woman. She's dead too, along with an innocent civilian. They shot Rosalie too."

"George?" Larry asked as Jake was forming the same word.

"Unhurt. He was fired on, but not wounded.

"I think I'll go with you if you don't mind, Harold," Harvey said as he turned the boat to shore. The other followed.

Harvey took his own phone from his pocket. "Noble pack us up. We're leaving. Please get the Sig 9mm also. We leave in twenty minutes. Thank you."

Noble, Jake knew had been in charge of Harvey's security for as long as the government had decided he needed protection. When Harvey retired, so had Noble. They were friends and confidants, as much as Harvey had one. Noble virtually worshipped his boss and took it as a personal affront if Harvey attempted to go anyplace where there might be any sort of danger without him.

He was silent as a shadow. Stayed out of the way, intuited Harvey's needs and moods in a way that was sort of spooky, but which his employer rather appreciated. At forty-five, he was as fit as a professional boxer, could shoot like an Olympic champion and kept his physique and skill levels sharp through constant workouts and practice.

Noble had once been married. That had ended badly when he was still in the military. He regretted it, and knew it was his fault. Husbanding had come too far down his list of priorities. Since he understood it now would never be otherwise he had decided not to inflict himself on another woman.

A wag at CIA had once asked a co-worker over lunch if "ole Noble was queer for the boss?" That unfortunate remark had been overheard by the subject who happened to have been sitting directly behind the questioner.

Noble simply turned his chair around to join their table, reached out quickly and broke the man's right index finger. Uttering one word, "Nope," he returned to his own meal. That had ended any such ideas on the subject.

Very few people ever knew Noble's last name. If in fact Noble was his first name. Fewer still had the temerity to ask.

At six feet two inches tall, and one-ninety-five, Noble was gray at the temples, tan in season and out, but without the standout handsomeness that would draw attention. He wore expensive, dark, double-breasted suits everywhere. Pin stripes were fine. Chalk lines were out. Muted ties, white shirts, shined shoes. He could have passed for an IBM Vice President or a top executive for a Fortune 50 corporation. Except that is, for the two pistols, a Lady Smith with rosewood grips in an ankle holster and a custom-shopped Sig Sauer 2340 on his hip.

Noble was not the staid, bully daring never to smile. Rather he minded his own business unless he was purposely included in a group or conversation. He was, Harvey often said, the perfect security, personal assistant, co-worker.

That didn't mean they were buddies. Both kept things business-like, but the friendship and mutual loyalty was there to the death and they knew it without putting it into words.

The two guides who had heard both Harold and Harvey looked across the water at each other. *Who are these guys?!*

THIRTY TWO

Raquel burst into the living room shaking like a maple leaf in a hail storm. All the way back to the house she had slammed back and forth between cursing and screaming at the absent and very dead Maxine. Could she do the shooting necessary to take out teams of professional snipers? Would she even be able to see them as they hid preparatory to doing their own shooting? Would they see her first and kill her? She was furious at the events, the increased pressure on her and most of all, at herself for pushing Maxine outside her own professional standards for sniping.

Mostly it was adrenaline. Raquel had never come so close to being shot before. The old man on that nag had clipped a branch right beside her cheek! She could not believe how fast everything had gone down!

Sitting at the table in the kitchen with a large cup of coffee before her she worked at calming down. Somewhere in her crazed mind she recognized that she was back over the edge, just as she'd been at Manassas in her meltdown. She didn't like it in herself and wanted to get a grip.

Other times I was so cool, she told herself. *Clip some guy outside a bar after working myself up. Just pop and it was done. Man this was so different!* She remembered how it was like running blindly through a tunnel as she barreled through the brush headed for the car. That was after the old fool on the horse had shot at her.

She'd been certain she'd hit him, but he didn't go down. *This 22 is too little,* she thought. She went to her room and pulled the nine millimeter Smith and Wesson she'd picked up on her weapons run to Virginia. That along with three magazines and a box of ammo. At the table she busied her hands with loading the magazines and becoming familiar with the pistol.

What do I do now? He saw me. Does he know who I am? Is he even alive?

She walked to the television and flipped through the channels. Nothing. But it was only a half hour. The cops weren't even there yet. *Right! They are like ants all over that place,* she chided herself.

Pulling a legal pad and pen from a cabinet drawer she began to write. It calmed her almost immediately. Planning was a tranquilizer to her. Unconsciously using the evil madness empowered by a devil who loves destruction, she set to work.

An hour later and with a new pot of coffee on the counter she looked over her work.

1. New vehicle. Use Maxine's to get out of State.
2. Schedule the sniper teams. Use them for practice. Get used to the rifle and remember what Maxine taught me.
3. Hit all three teams within ten days. That way the news doesn't have time to get out and tip the last one off.
4. By the time I get back here the farm will have quieted down and the men will have let their guard down.
5. Calm. Calm. Calm. Do not let your emotions drive you. Plan this like the operations you send others on.

Thirty minutes later, using her data bases, she had scheduled each sniper team to take out their next targets. She'd set them up with a specific time and place. She was confident that she could take them.

She arose and went to dye and cut her hair. A shower, then get some sleep. Tonight I head to West Virginia.

At five-thirty that evening Raquel awoke without an alarm. She spent an hour working on the gear. What had been Maxine's was now hers. She had to get it all figured out. The hours at the range in Perry Country paid high dividends and she knew what to take and what to leave.

Eight forty-five saw her in Maxine's Malibu heading down Route 81. Just over two hours later she hit exit 13 at Martinsburg. At the Days Inn she slept until six the next morning, went to the Bob Evans for breakfast and was back on the road by seven thirty.

When she came to the Winchester exits she felt like she was back home. She exited at 315 and wound her way around to Rifleman Road. Laughing at the name of the street, she parked her car long enough to get out and take photos of the park which lay to the south. Satisfied she drove to a local Best Western, checked in, then studied a map of the area before resting.

At midnight she donned the black swat uniform she'd ordered over the internet. Moving back to Rifleman Road she parked and stealthily moved to the recreation area. This time she took a dark green camo tarp, binoculars and the rifle Maxine had so lovingly placed back in the drag bag.

As a false dawn streaked the eastern sky and the hum of traffic began its crescendo on Route 81 she saw them. They must have come in when it was too dark to pick them out.

They too had a tarp or netting over them, but the rifle barrel poked out.

Hello, Howard. Where's Gerald? Raquel asked herself.

Ah, there you are, you strange one.

Then even as she thought the greeting she heard the crunch of a jogger's shoes on the track before her. He came from her right rear and on the other side of the park. The track circled and headed back toward the entrance. He would soon be heading straight for the shooters as she watched.

There was no indication that they saw the jogger. Nothing moved, not even the barrel of their rifle. Raquel kept the scope right where she wanted it.

When the explosion of the rifle sounded she flinched, but recovered as quick as a leopard on a rodent. Her rifle's report came virtually a second later.

When it settled back on the target, no one moved, but the flutter of a leg could be noticed under the tarp.

She had hit them both with her shot as planned. Unsure if it had worked or not, she had quickly worked the bolt, but it was unnecessary.

Looking for the jogger she noticed he was down and unmoving.

Quickly she threw back the tarp and headed to them. She yanked back their cover and fired a round into the head of each one with her pistol. *Insurance,* she thought.

Ten minutes later she was on Route 522 headed toward Culpeper.

By dark she was in a different car. This one came from a dear old lady she'd followed home from the grocery store. *Good! She has a garage.*

One more corpse and she was back on the road in a burgundy Buick Century with sixty thousands miles on it and no cd player.

Back to Route 29 and then 28. She ate at a diner that night.

At the back side of the Manassas Airport she parked in the lot and walked through a weed patch to an empty cargo warehouse. Just as her data said there was a steel ladder leading to the flat roof.

She climbed with the drag bag hung on her right shoulder. Once there, she set the alarm on her wrist watch and went to sleep. At dawn the insistent beep woke her. Slipping her head above the parapet of the roof she scanned with the binoculars. After about fifteen minutes she had them.

They were inside a van in the very lot she had parked in. Smoking with the side door wide open. *Careless, boys. Maybe I'll take your van when I leave,* she grinned.

This time she didn't wait for their target. There would be none. She waited until she could see the outline of the two men. First she took out the one with the rifle. The other leaped to the side and an instant later the rear doors burst open.

Run this way, Ole Juan. She watched as he raised a pistol and circled around to find a target. Seeing no one around he looked up. That was when she pulled the trigger. It seemed as if he saw her at that moment, but it was just too late. The shot hit him in the throat. She'd aimed at his heart. *Ducking.* It couldn't be that she missed.

She clambered down off the roof, lightly banging the rifle in its bag as she struggled with the steps of the vertical ladder.

Forgetting about the van, she placed the rifle in the trunk and drove the Buick back to Route 234 and then to Route 15. North again.

At Leesburg she stopped at the Wal Mart. *Be careful folks, I've killed here before!* she smiled as she walked to the entrance.

Looking directly into the cameras as if to dare anyone to notice her, she was nearly skipping with adrenaline and delight.

If I'd known sniping was this much fun I'd have begun long ago.

The joy was soon to fade. But she had more miles to go until then.

At Point of Rocks she parked the car at the little riverside park. Below, the Potomac rolled on its muddy way to Washington, DC. She pulled out the sub, chips and Snapple she'd bought at the Wal Mart.

A black bird glided in on silent silky wings and stood guard at the other end of the picnic table. A morsel for the poor bird?

Raquel broke a bird-bite-sized piece of bun and tossed it toward the starling who brazenly hopped closer. He snatched it up and retreated to enjoy his meal.

"You want some more? Let's see just how brave you are." She broke off another piece and placed it between her thumb and finger.

The bird studied her, looking directly into her eyes as if trying to read her intentions.

Finally he hopped to within six inches and just looked at the bread, rolling his head as if to see it better. He glanced at Raquel and then back to the bread.

"How bad do you want this?" she whispered. The bird didn't answer.

He just watched her and waited. Finally she moved her hand a bit. He hopped backwards. She relented and tossed the bread to him. On the first bounce he grabbed it.

"You're too anxious."

Raquel jumped straight up on the bench. She whirled around and looked directly into the smiling face of a Maryland State Trooper. Her heart leaped into her throat. She'd been so focused on the bird she'd missed him pulling in. And she was tired. So tired.

"You should have held out. He'd have come for it. I do it all the time. This beggar shares more lunches with me than my wife." It was then that she noticed he had a paper bag in one hand and a Diet Coke in the other.

"Sit down," she offered graciously. He sat across from her with his back to the river and began to unpack a Tupperware container with a thick ham and cheese sandwich inside. A two pack of Twinkies accompanied it along with a small bag of Lay's potato chips.

"Headed home?" he asked.

Raquel knew the power of her smile. *Can he hear my heart pounding? Does it shake my body?*

"Yes. I've been visiting my sister. She lives in Leesburg."

The trooper had the sandwich almost to his mouth and hesitated for the slightest instant. With that sensitivity of the truly insane Raquel picked up on it.

"You're headed home with Virginia tags and you're in Maryland? Seems like home would mean PA or Maryland tags." he took his bite then and lowered the sandwich. It was like he had seen something in Raquel's eyes but had not interpreted it sufficiently yet. He laid the sandwich on the paper bag.

"Yes, that's true, but it's my sister's car. Mine wouldn't start. Her husband will work on it tonight and they'll bring it up this weekend."

"Want a piece of gum?" she asked as she reached into her purse.

The trooper sensed trouble and his hand moved toward his own weapon but he was just too late. Raquel raised the Smith and shot him in the face. He went over backward but the picnic table caught his legs.

Leaping to her feet she raced around, and dug into his pockets. No keys. Then she heard the jingle. They were clipped to his Sam Browne belt. Yanking them free, she laid them on the table and dragged him to the edge of the nearby river bank. Over he went cartwheeling and dropping the sixty feet into the brush at the edge of the rocky shore.

She grabbed a napkin from the table and wiped the blood from her arm, snatched the keys off the table and quickly transferred her rifle and equipment into the gray unmarked police car.

She pulled onto Route 15 north with a bark of tire rubber.

Amazingly she made it all the way to Harrisburg. Once there she drove directly to the house in Highspire. When she'd shut down the engine, she just stayed behind the wheel for a moment. A deep sigh. Then she closed the garage door.

Two down and one more to go, she thought entering the house.

Inside she gathered a few clothes, her hidden reserves of cash, identities and moved to the Jeep that she'd taken near Elizabethtown. She transferred her rifle and equipment. Then returned inside, took a long, hot shower and slept between cool sheets until she woke the next day at mid-afternoon. Another shower, brushed the auburn hair and dried it, then into jeans and a blouse. Nothing to draw attention but her exceptional beauty.

She made a large country breakfast and ate it in front of the television. Brit was just coming on.

THIRTY THREE

The assuring voiced, basset-faced Brit was speaking to the panel of three columnists. Fred and Mort were joined by a dark haired woman from public television. Raquel didn't care for her. No reason. Just didn't like her.

"Finally, I'd like to get your read on some upsetting news. Pennsylvania had a another sniper shooting. A woman and her dog were killed. Then nearby a man going to work was shot, this time not a sniper shooting, though. The killer took his vehicle and left a car with a dead woman in the front seat. She was apparently a shooter as well. That was day one.

"The next day a jogger was killed by a sniper team in Winchester, Virginia. The snipers themselves were then killed by another shooter. At least that's the preliminary report.

"They were hit with a rifle. One shot hit both men then the killer shot each of the them in the head with a pistol.

"Seventy miles away an elderly woman is murdered in her home. Her car is stolen and a mystery car – no registration – is left behind."

"Well we've…" Mort started, but Brit raised a hand and cut him off.

"Wait, Mort.

"Then in Manassas two men are shot with a high powered rifle from a rooftop. Are they victims of the same killer or killers?

"Both these dead were also snipers from the evidence. They had the equipment, including a sniper rifle in their van.

"The same day a Maryland State Trooper is murdered on the Virginia-Maryland border and his body dumped into the Potomac. It didn't get to the water. A pair of kayakers found the body along the shore.

"The stolen car from the woman in Culpeper, Virginia is found at the scene. The killer took the unmarked patrol car.

"Okay Mort."

Mort was like a greyhound after the rabbit. He was nearly hyperventilating to get his piece said.

"First of all, we have insane serial killers. All the same! One massive circle. I plotted it on a map. The woman's crew are the killers and they're headed back to Pennsylvania! Maybe already there."

The dark-haired woman in the trio looked pityingly at Mort.

"First of all there have been no reports of ballistics – if there are any recovered bullets. To think that there are this many snipers on the loose – what is it, three teams? Three teams of snipers, two now dead and all killed by a third team. Can that be real? I think it's one woman. One very skilled woman." she said.

"Fred, you like statistics. What are the odds that all this is one large connect-the-dots plot?" Brit asked.

"The odds are that for some dark reason the killer in Pennsylvania is the one who killed them all or had them all killed. I know it sounds beyond belief but I know that the shooting in Pennsylvania was a sniper shooting at a long distance that killed the lady and her dog.

"Then consider the logistics. To be able to kill two sets of snipers in twenty-four hours would mean that the killer – if it's the same person – would have to know where they'd be."

"So it has to be someone with a network. One woman by herself could not do this! There's a group. Either jihadists or maybe even some criminal outfit. Do we know the identities of the dead snipers?

"Actually we do have some information on that," Brit said, looking down at a sheet of paper before him.

"One of the teams is connected to the Puerto Rican terrorist group of years gone by. Apparently the team has killed for them in New York. There are warrants out for both of them, but they're old.

"The two dead shooters at the airport in Manassas are unidentified so far."

"What about motives for the first killings? Do we know anything about the woman sniper who was killed in Pennsylvania?" Myra asked.

"Not a clue. She was apparently one of the two killers in on the shooting that began all this – the shooting of the woman and her dog," Brit answered.

"Regarding information, it's a black hole. In fact there's virtually nothing coming out on that one. One of our affiliates tried to get something from a local police contact and was told in so many words to lay off and go home. They would issue a statement when they had more.

"Our reporter said that was abnormal. She thinks there is much more than what's been reported, which is a woman and her dog killed. Woman in a car killed. Man killed and his car stolen. Dead woman and car left behind. Then the more distant murders.

"There is lot's we just don't know."

Fred summed it up well, "So we have a woman killer on the loose who is good enough to kill professional snipers and a state trooper plus cold enough to murder two women and a man - that we know of."

Raquel wiped up the remainder of the egg yellow with a corner of toast and swore quietly under her breath. Brit went on to Iraq and bored, Raquel turned the television off.

Those broads have to know they're targets now! I will have to be very careful if I'm going to get them.

Wait a minute! Why do I have to get them at all? Let them go. Get out of here and lie low for a while. Find a place where I can blend in and wait for everything to quiet down at Elizabethtown then take out the men I hate most in the world! She smiled at the idea.

That the women would be sweating her hunting them was appealing. They didn't know where she was. They were gone before she'd arrived at the farm in Perry Country and didn't know her real identity. Let them worry.

I'd better get out of here, though.

Raquel waited until around midnight. She drove the jeep to a tavern only a block from the long term parking lot at the airport. Dressed in the black outfit she walked alleys until she came to the chain link fence around the lot. Nothing more than a deterrent to kids.

She tossed a looped rope over a post and was soon in the lot. Jogging down the rows of vehicles she found what she wanted in less than ten minutes. A Jeep similar to the one she'd taken in Elizabethtown.

She soon had the license plate off and replaced it with the one off the stolen Jeep she had parked at the tavern.

Forty-five minutes later she had the new plate on her Jeep and driving south on Interstate 81. Back in her jeans and a pullover, hair tied in a scarf, with a Randy Travis cd playing she was headed for some down time.

Enjoy your safety, men. Soon you'll be bleeding! Raquel smiled at the thought as she drove through the night.

Next stop Baltimore. There she'd pick up another set of wheels, then to Virginia Beach. Sailors were sure to like a redhead.

In Wichita, two women and a Remington 700 had also just turned off the television.

"Hon, I think we'll just forget about the next target and take a cruise around the world. Whaddaya think?"

"Well, I think you are gonna start packing. Where do ya want to head?"

"Let's go to Key West. Nothing ever happens in Paradise down there but partyin'."

"Gotcha!"

THIRTY FOUR

As befitted the day rain poured down and the gutters overflowed. The funeral was over. Interment had been in Harrisburg. Grant's funeral home handled the arrangements. Nick's preacher had officiated. George, Tex and Marguerite, his wife, sat in the front of the church and Larry, Harold and Jake, Nick and his wife Patty were seated in the next row. Harvey and Noble sat in the very back of the church. Noble said someone should be there for security.

It had piqued both men's attention when the preacher said matter of factly that death was the end for "non-believers," who would face their doom in hell, but it was only the beginning of a glorious life for those who had received Jesus Christ as their Saviour.

Afterward Patty had taken Marguerite home and the men had all gone to the farm. They now were gathered around the table with full coffee cups. A war council was now under way.

"George wants to say something," Harold said. All the men except Harvey and Noble had puffy eyes and blocked sinuses from weeping. None were ashamed of their tears.

"First of all, thank you seems so insignificant for you fellers." George said, looking at each man in turn. Tex nodded beside him.

"I'm all tore up inside right now. I'm not much good for anything, and y'all know it. I also know that you're nature is to try to 'protect' me while I'm hurtin'.

"Don't do it. Oh, I'll water up now and again. You'll just have to put up with that. I'm not going to go hunker down in the stable and just be taken out for exercise now and again like them old mares.

"You know I'm an old warrior. We don't go home when we been hurt. We take it to the enemy. That's my plan. At least that's what I want to do. I want included in your plans. If there's something that I can't get ahold of, I'll tell you. I promise you, men, that I won't do anything to put a one of you in danger.

"That's all I got to say. I ain't goin' away. This is my home and you're my family, far as I see it. Outside of Tex and Marguerite I ain't got nobody else." Tex was openly but silently weeping now. Tears coursed down his wrinkled cheeks. He nodded again as George spoke and reached to the table and held his brother's hand. George squeezed it tenderly. Everybody was now wet eyed except Noble who sat near the door in a chair with his coffee beside him on the floor.

"All right, George. Thanks for that. I can assure you that you're family to all of us too. And as you wish, you'll be included in our plans. All the information we get on this you'll have too." Harold was speaking for the whole team.

The three young men nodded. Harvey, the odd man of the group simply looked around the table.

Outside a car door slammed. Noble was instantly on his feet and looking out the window in the door. “Police,” he said and moved to a corner where he was still able to cover the room but seemed out of the way.

Jake stood and opened the door before the policeman could knock.

“Come in officer. What can we do for you?”

“Good. You are all here. We need to go over a few things.” He had corporal’s chevrons on his collar points and spoke briskly as he stepped into the room.

Not a large man, he stood very stiffly as he removed his yellow rain coat and simply dropped it on the floor by the door without allowing Jake to take it from him.

“We have some problems with what’s going on here. I’m sorry for your loss, Mr. Allen. Truly sorry. But there are some things that just aren’t quite kosher.”

“Would you like to sit? Some coffee?” Harold said, rising from the table as Jake returned to his chair. They had already met the officer the day of the shooting. The Regional Police Chief and he had run the investigation. The Chief was a good man. This one had not impressed any of the men in the kitchen.

“First of all, I got a look at that Mini-14, Mr. Allen. It’s got a selector switch on the side. It can fire full auto. That’s illegal and you know it. I’ve already contacted the ATF.

“Secondly we have no record of any of you having concealed carry permits at the Sheriff’s office in Lancaster. I personally went down and looked for every one of you.

“And then there is the question of why women snipers would choose to kill a simple housewife. Too many things don’t add up.

“When I brought this up to the Chief he just said it would all be worked out. That’s not good enough for me, actually.” He spoke abruptly with his hands on his belt, one near his weapon and the other near a night stick. To say he had assumed a threatening posture was an understatement.

“Where *is* the Chief, Officer Pudroshski?” asked Larry quietly.

“THAT’S PROBLESKI!” the officer said so loudly that all the others figured he had dealt with this before.

“Whatever,” Larry said. He’d had some assertiveness training himself. That this officer did not know who he was dealing with had become quite evident.

Jake put his hand on Larry's forearm. It was like touching a stick of firewood.

"You *better* quiet that boy down. I don't like your attitude, mister." He spoke first to Jake and then to Larry. Jake took his hand off Larry as if to say, "sickem." Larry didn't move but that he wanted to was evident to everyone in the room.

Harold, who had not sat back down, stepped forward enough to be able to insert himself between the two in case Larry changed his mind.

"Officer, maybe I can explain. We are – all of us except these two men – he indicated Harvey and Noble – working with the federal government as private contractors. We have federal authority for our weapons. Full auto and otherwise.

If Harold had told the corporal that less than thirty feet from where he stood in the steel-doored armory there were three RPGs the man might have had a heart attack.

"Where *is* the Chief, by the way?" Harold asked in a much softer voice than Larry had used.

"That's none of your business, Mr. Contract worker!" Now it was Larry who put a hand on Jake's arm. Harold moved his hand out and downward as if to signal an attack dog to "stay." He had heard Jake's chair shift.

When Harold moved his hand, the officer mistook it for a threatening move. He began to reach for his weapon.

"Whoa!" Noble said it quietly as the death angel speaking to Pharaoh. The Sig was pointed at the corporal's nose. One millisecond earlier it was under his suit coat and the next it was a serious death threat to the policeman.

"Take it out of the holster, Boss." Noble spoke to Harvey and his boss replied as if he took orders from him every day. He rose smoothly from his chair and walked the two steps to the policeman.

"Excuse me, sir," he said, holding the right wrist and lifting it. With his other hand he unsnapped the holster and removed the Glock. He took it to the table and laid it on the table then returned to his seat.

"You're all going to jail for that," the officer said with a quivering voice.

"Just a minute," Harold said. He took his cell phone from his belt and after looking up a number in the directory put it to his ear.

The conversation was brief. He spoke to the Regional Chief, recounted precisely what had occurred, including the disarming. He listened a moment then handed the phone to the policeman who took it like it was a red-hot horseshoe.

"Yes Sir."

"No Sir." Head shaking in the negative like he meant it.

“Yes Sir.” Followed by some more affirmatives and negatives. Finally he held the phone out to Harold who took it and put it to his ear.

“Thank you, Chief. Yes, we will be glad to see you day after tomorrow. Why don’t we meet at the E’town Diner for breakfast? About seven.” He then disconnected the call and replaced the phone.

“Now Officer, the Chief asked us to return your service weapon. Assuming you understand our situation a bit clearer, do you believe we can do that without anything amiss happening?”

“Yes, Sir. I’d appreciate that. And I’ll be on my way, Sir.”

Noble still stood like a Stonewall Jackson statue. There was no shaking or movement in his outstretched arms. His Weaver Stance was classic. Slowly, he lowered his weapon but held it at his side rather than re-holstering it.

“Harvey,” Harold said, and Harvey dropped the magazine from its well and worked the slide. No round popped out. He handed both the weapon and magazine to the Officer. “Sorry,” he said quietly as if to an already embarrassed child.

The officer nodded, holstered the Glock and put the mag in his pants pocket.

I’ll be going now. I’m sorry about this misunderstanding, men,” he said quietly.

He reached down and gathered the slicker up in one hand and opened the door with the other. In a minute the patrol car left quietly.

Larry looked behind him. “Noble you are a wicked good man.”

Jake laughed, followed by the rest of the table. Comic relief. Every one of them was familiar with it.

Two hours later they had worked out a plan. Harvey briefed them on what he could get about the shootings in Maryland and Virginia, which was little until evidence at the scenes could be further examined.

“The dead woman in the car was a Jordanian. Interpol has her fingerprints and enough warrants to fill a briefcase. There was gunshot residue on her hand, arm and cheek. She is suspected of killing six members of various crime families in Italy, Germany and Belgium. Two members of rival Islamic groups to al Qaeda. Apparently she was trained by the Jordanian army then left them for the jihad.

“It looks like she may have entered the States from Mexico. The rounds that killed your dog and Mrs. Allen could not be found. There may be a connection between what happened here and the killing of a SWAT officer in Wilmington, Delaware recently.

“There is really no doubt in my mind that our killers are the woman who shot you at Manassas, Larry, and the dead woman she left behind. That she is Osama's daughter is also beyond doubt to me though I have no real proof. Our agents reported enough suspicions to make me believe it, but not enough proof.

"This kind of killing spree also makes me believe that her 'rabies' has returned, if you understand my meaning. I believe she has gone totally insane. Sadly it seems to be the insanity that afflicts her is the most dangerous kind. She has an almost satanic sixth sense regarding danger. She will respond to conditions and stimuli in the most dangerous of ways and without any conscious reasoning process initiating her responses. Certain people like this seem to have almost supernatural instincts. The state trooper's death might well be a case of this.

"I have…"

A knock at the door.

"Noble had stayed where he was when the police officer was there. Now he seemed to go on alert, though there was nothing visibly noticeable.

Harold opened the door. A husky black man and a rail thin oriental man stood in the rain, soaked to the skin. They were in camo field outfits.

"Sir, I'm Charlie Whitehorse. This is Gordon Allenby."

"Come in men. Please. Jake would you get some towels for these fellows, please?" Jake immediately headed out of the room.

"Harvey, I think you may know about these young men, though perhaps you've never met before," Harold said, as Jake returned with two large fluffy towels for each man. They set to work drying themselves.

"I do indeed know about them. Perhaps I should bring everyone up to speed.

"Coffee, please Noble." Noble responded, taking two cups off a rack and filling them. He brought them to the table where extra chairs had been pulled up by Tex.

"Charlie Whitehorse is a former Marine Corps sniper. He has seen duty in any number of overseas assignments, both individually and as part of two different Marine Expeditionary Forces. He holds the Navy Cross. He left the Corps two years ago and has since been employed by a company my former employer has utilized for many years.

"Gordon Allenby. His grandparents were brought to America when we pulled out of Vietnam. His grandfather was a trusted associate of our organization. He actually has the same background as Charlie. In fact they have been a scout sniper team with the Marine Corps for years. That was a few miles ago, right men?" Harvey smiled at them.

"But what are you guys doing here?" Jake asked.

"That," Harold said, "is my doing. I called Harvey and asked about an anti-sniper team when we first heard about the Potter County farm. Unfortunately, George, I fear I was too late in calling. I'm so sorry," he laid a hand on George's shoulder. George reached up and patted Harold's hand. Words were beyond him.

"I think I'd like to ask a question," Larry said.

Both men had taken seats. Their clothes were still wet, but they had silently refused a quietly asked offer of others by Jake.

"Sure," Charlie said.

"Your names. They don't ring true. I heard about the Blackfoot tribe but this is off the scale!" he said. The crowd smiled but did not laugh out loud.

At first Whitehorse seemed as if he might be upset, but then he smiled. He read Larry's eyes accurately and saw no malice or racism there.

"My name's what it is. I was abandoned at the Rapid City General Hospital when I was born. A couple adopted me. Miguel and Sara Whitehorse. Lakota Sioux. They loved me and raised me. And I love 'em to pieces. They're my parents. But you're right, Sir, I do get some strange looks when people hear my name."

Charlie was about five-nine and two hundred pounds. His skin was charcoal black with strong African American features. His hands were muscled and veins popped up clearly under the Nubian skin. He was the personification of "black" power.

The Vietnamese man grinned a toothy grin. He was as opposite as could possibly be from his partner. So skinny that his head looked like there was only skin on the skull, yet the smile made him handsome in a delicate way. Bony shoulders poked at angles and his waist was so thin and stomach so flat that Jake knew he could reach around it with both hands. No chest, no rear end, and yet, there was a sinewy, leather quality to his muscles. Like rawhide that had weathered and under constant use only became more pliant and strong.

"My family came to America, but Grandpa loved the old British Generals. Hated the French, loved the British for fighting them. His two biggest heroes were General Chinese Gordon and General Edmund Allenby. Both were believers, as was my grandfather. When I came along I got both names and my Grandpa got me. My parents were killed in Viet Nam.

"I was raised to respect the military and consider it a great career. I joined the Corps right after high school. When I didn't become a general it took a while for the old fellow to adjust, but he got over it." Another grin.

"I legally changed my name and dropped the Vietnamese. It just seemed like a funny thing to do."

"These men are going to be our first line of defense. They are going to be around. We won't know when or where they are. They will live in the woods. Build hides, stay on watch. You know the routine," Harold said it with a bit of hope in his voice.

If the crazy woman returned, he prayed these two would see her first and deal with her appropriately. He didn't care if she was captured or not. Things had gone beyond that with him.

But the idea of them all living and working inside a shooting gallery was not his idea of paradise.

"They won't be living in the house. They will find their own way. Sometimes on our land, sometimes on others." He handed Charlie a sheet of paper from atop the refrigerator. These are all our cell phone numbers. You call if you need us. Otherwise you may leave your cell phones off. If you hear three shots in a group, come running.

"Put your equipment in the barn. Come and go as you please."

George said, "There's an empty stall out there. Just put you stuff in there and if you want to, cover it with some fresh straw. There's bales in the loft."

"Thank you, sir," Charlie said, slipped the paper into a baggie he took from his pocket. The two shook hands, looking carefully at each man's face.

When they got to Noble, Charlie said, "Noble. Been a long time. Great to see you again, my man. "

"You, too, Charlie. Get one!" Noble said

"Semper fi, Noble," Gordon said reverentially, and shook hands with him. Then they both went to the door, gave small salutes and were gone.

"*Chau Ohm,* Gordon." Noble answered.

It would be three weeks before anyone saw them again.

THIRTY FIVE

The rain had moved east during the night. At five-thirty Harvey was up and showering. The house was quiet. In the dark outside a bird cheerfully greeted the coming day.

When he got to the kitchen, Noble was sitting at the table, dressed as always in a suit, though the jacket was hanging on the back of his chair. The Galco shoulder holster rig was hanging on him. Fresh coffee was in the pot and as Harvey entered Noble quickly arose and poured a cup.

For years now Harvey had accepted that Noble did not consider his role that of a manservant though certainly he was – and much more. Rather he looked upon himself as helping to equip someone that he revered for his genuineness, talent and service to America.

Once long ago Harvey had told him that he didn't expect all the extra things Noble did for him such as caring for his wardrobe and the like.

"Sir, I don't see myself as a serf. Serving you is a privilege that I consider my good fortune. What I do for you I would do for someone else who deserved it. I don't like dilettantes and I've seen my share. Everything I can do to make your life more productive and safe I consider my duty.

"If you need something done or want me to not do something tell me. Otherwise I'll just sort of figure those things out for myself. But I should tell you that my first job is your safety. Everything else is secondary."

Harvey had thought about that for days afterward. It had honestly caused him to reevaluate his own idea of duty and, he believed, improve upon it.

Now as the years passed he and Noble had become friends of a sort. They talked sometimes but never about high security topics unless Harvey asked. Noble had been a field agent in some of the most dangerous places in the world. He brought an honest perspective to the conversations that Harvey valued. Otherwise it was life, certain people, some areas of the Agency. Philosophy. Politics. Neither had family and both missed it on one level. They were like brothers and yet not.

"The old fellow, George? He's already up and outside at the barn," Noble said. He had remained standing and was watching out the window. George was headed to the corral with a bucket. Three horses had their heads over the fence awaiting his arrival.

"I think I'll walk outside," Harvey took his cup and went out the door. Noble followed with his own coffee in his left hand.

"Mornin' men," George greeted them. He walked to an outdoor manger with the bucket and poured a combination of grain and man made pellets at one end then another pile in the center and finally the remainder went on the other end. He set the bucket down and leaned on the top rail of the corral with his right foot up on the bottom rail. With his hands, he petted the cheek and neck of the mare he'd been riding when Helen was killed.

"Good morning, George," Harvey said. Noble nodded and stood near the rail but did not lean on it.

"Mr. Reid, I want to thank you for the flowers. They were beautiful. I asked the preacher to have them delivered to an old folk's home. Shame to waste them by just piling 'em up at the cemetery for the gardeners to trash tomorrow."

"You're welcome, George. And please, call me Harvey. I take it we will be working as part of the same team."

"Yessir. Got no place else to go and these fellers are special. I reckon you already figured that out," George moved to the next horse and began to pet her as well. She raised her head and softly snuffled in appreciation.

"George, I must say I think you are doing well for the intense hurt you must be feeling." Harvey spoke quietly, looking out toward where he knew the shooters had fired from.

"Mr. Reid, I ain't never experienced anything this bad since our son was killed in Nam. Maybe this is worse, I 'spect. Back then I was concerned with trying to help my wife with her own pain. It took my mind off myself some. That was bad but this is much worse." George sort of gasped and hiccupped simultaneously as he finished speaking, in an attempt to hold back the agony of spirit he felt.

"But you keep on functioning. I've seen it in very public people who have to maintain a public persona. Usually though they have a small army of people doing for them. And they are medicated beyond belief. They go through the public ceremony and then return to their bed or the gauzy fog of drugs. You are not that way. I must tell you I am impressed, but also curious as to your strength."

"Sure enough I'm walkin' wounded. No doubt 'bout that. But, Mr. Reid, I'll be very glad to tell you why I am different.

"It's Jesus, plain and simple. You know what I've been and done I'm sure." Harvey nodded but didn't answer.

"All those years my one great fear was that something would happen to me and poor Helen would find out by a call or some stranger coming to tell her. Or that I'd be like one feller they killed out in Nebraska and just caved a creek bank over him. I didn't want her never knowing.

"That would have been terrible. I prayed to the Lord to take her first. That may sound cold, but there it is. I loved that woman more than I loved my own life. More than I got words to tell you. More hurtin' she didn't need.

"I was willin' to bear the pain of separation, to not have her be faced with it. The good Lord done that for me." George moved a bit and began to love on the third horse as he spoke.

"And there's this, and it's the most important thing. I know where Helen is and that we won't be apart for ever."

"I ain't talkin' about religion. I've seen my share of religious people and they don't have peace when death comes a knockin'.

"I'm talkin' about a personal relationship with Jesus Christ. You see, I read the Bible. Been readin' and believin' it for as long as I can recall. My folks taught us. Daddy was a Texas Ranger, and Mommy faced a lot of what Helen did.

"They were good people. My father had a Masters in Electrical Engineering. My mother had one in History. Lot of people think that real Bible believin' Christianity is for the poor and ignorant. My folks was neither. And they were as saved as the Apostle Paul, that's for sure. And I took Jesus as my personal Saviour as a youngen.

"See, here's the story. And it's a true story.

"God loves people. And He's patient with them as the day is long. But God is a God of justice too. You know justice and mercy have a problem with love. They are at odds sometimes." George's country language seemed to change to a more refined manner as he tried to communicate with these men who were more of the city than he.

"So what's God to do? Man is a sinner. The Ten Commandments prove that to any honest person. And the Bible says you break one, it's the same as you broke them all.

"Well God devised a way to solve His 'man the sinner' problem. Justice demands a payment and Love wants to provide one. He sends Jesus, who is the Son of God, to earth.

"Now you know God is only one God, but He has three persons or personalities, I guess you'd say. Like an egg is one egg but three parts, shell, yolk and white." Harvey nodded. He was captivated by this, as was Noble.

"Anyway, Jesus is born of Mary. The Holy Spirit planted a seed in a virgin from Nazareth.

"That means that he ain't got the sin nature that all the rest of us have. He is a man, born of a woman, but He's God too. I know it's hard to believe. But I believe that anybody that wants to will get some help from God Himself.

"Jesus' life is spelled out as clear as you want in the four Gospels. But the bottom line is that He is perfect. Sinless. He can be the payment for man's sins. So God has the answer in the balance of sinful man versus perfect Jesus equation.

"Now don't misunderstand. I can't explain it all in perfect logic. It takes faith to get this all worked out. And faith ain't seein'. It's believin' without seein'." Both men nodded again.

"Here's the equation. Jesus died for me so I can live forever in Heaven after I die. And I believe the Bible teaches it to be with our loved ones and all saved folks. I'll see my son and my wife again. My parents – all of 'em who was saved.

"A man is not a body with a soul. He is a soul who has this body for a while. Then the soul and spirit leave this body behind and the real him goes on. Where – heaven or hell – depends on one thing. Only one thing! His relationship with Jesus Christ.

"Those who repent – feel sorrow for their sinful lot and turn away from it to Jesus, and ask for forgiveness are saved. That's a Bible word, though a heap of people nowadays mock it. Saved. Good, clean and hopeful word. Saved."

Then he stopped and looked squarely at both men.

"I gotta ask you, fellers. Are you saved?"

Noble spoke, startling Harvey he was so entranced by George's words.

"Yes, I am saved, Sir. I was saved as a little boy at my mother's knee. I believed then and I believe now." Noble's eyes were wet and there was a trembling in his chin as if the years were swept away and he was taken back to that childhood time.

Harvey looked behind him and was stunned though he showed nothing of it. He had never ever seen Noble anything but totally cool and rock solid. This was a side he had never even imagined.

He looked back at George who was still awaiting an answer.

"Sir, I must tell you that I am not. I had a friend and mentor long ago. A United States Senator. I fear he was not either. But his dear wife was a saint of God. She shared with me exactly what you have said this morning. She never asked me so plainly, but she did explain it. I have not thought of her, or of that time for many years I'm sorry to say." There were no tears in Harvey's eyes. No trembling chin. But his heart was changed that day.

"I believe I will pray and ask Jesus Christ to be my Saviour, Mr. Allen. I believe repentance is a very good idea," Harvey said and then walked away from both men without another word. He headed toward the timber up on the hill.

Noble began to walk after him, but George shook his head. The body guard saw it and nodded. For the first time in a very long time, he allowed his charge out of sight even though it was an area of impending danger. God would surely protect him on this personal errand.

"Thank you, Mr. Allen. I understand what you are saying about your faith making a difference in your life.

"Looking back I can see many things I should have done differently as a man. Perhaps I can begin to change now. Do you believe it is too late?"

"Never too late, Noble.

"What a fine name you carry. Let it stand for the Saviour. I know you serve a fine man. Same as Tex and I do those in that house," he motioned with his hand.

"Perhaps that service will be richer now that something is changed in his heart. But you both need to get in the Word.

"My suggestion is to get you a couple of King James Bibles and study them. Try to find a good Bible-preachin' church like we was in yesterday. Go when you can. It ain't always easy in our line a work but you can manage some if you want to.

"I believe Tex and his wife and I will be attending where Nick and his family go. That preacher is a fine young man. Sound as a dollar in his teachin' and with real heart."

George reached up and put his hand on Noble's shoulder. Not many men touched the large man, but Noble found it endearing and special. They walked back toward the coffee pot and left Harvey to his spiritual time in the woods with Jesus.

"Let's go get some a that Baptist gasoline you perked up this mornin'" George said.

THIRTY SIX

There is a time in every war when the tide turns. Sometimes it is for the better. At others, the momentum is lost and the advantage reverses and events roll over the previous gains.

For three weeks nothing happened at the farm. Harold, Jake and Larry began eating breakfast at a diner and though they invited George he refrained from going along. Tex came out and often rode a horse with him in the mornings. They discussed getting another Lab.

No one saw anything of the sniper team that was on the property. George would notice when their gear was a bit different than before but he never saw or heard them come or go.

Nick, Larry and Jake organized a physical training schedule for the now completed gym/pool building. They shot almost daily at the range where they had all become minor celebrities. That being the case, none of the old fellows who ran the club bothered them. They kept to their trap shooting and just watched closely as the trio worked their weapons. Occasionally George, Harold and the retired Marine Larry joined them for a few rounds of competitive shooting.

Sgt. Major Larry had become a regular on George's porch of an evening. They sat and talked about places they'd been and people they'd known. The retired Sergeant Major had seen duty in many embassies and been some of the same places George had worked in the States. There was talk of building a Kentucky Rifle from a kit when winter arrived. They enjoyed each other's company.

Supper time was a "family affair" if Jake and Tex weren't flying somewhere. They did that about once a week. Jake was gaining more hours on his "ticket" and getting so that his flying skills were much more intuitive. Tex was a good teacher and loved the time in the beautiful and powerful King Air.

"Car coming," Gordon muttered. Only his eyes were visible to Charlie in the gloom of the hide. They were located where they couldn't see an incoming vehicle until it rounded the corner into the parking area near the house.

Both men were camo-ed up with dark green and brown streaks on their faces and the backs of their hands. Bush caps covered their heads. Both men wore Ghillie suits, those burlap and brush inventions created by Scottish game keepers generations ago. Adapted by snipers the world over, they made concealment so complete that seekers could virtually stand beside a good sniper and never see him until he purposely gave himself away. Even sniper instructors were sometimes stunned by their students' abilities at hiding in the open.

Scout-sniper school was about a lot more than just hitting a target at great distances. Concealment, movement, ingress and egress, reading the elements and the ability to withstand solitude and discomfort were also chapters that had to be mastered before a graduate was congratulated at Quantico. Both men had been instructors but chafed at the routine. They loved the field.

They had served individually and as a team in many places and under a wide variety of tasks. Urban, civilian, desert and jungle combat. It was all part of the experience that made them some of the world's elite when it came to snipers.

"Larry," Charlie said as the copper colored Ford truck parked in the gravel by the house.

"They say that George shot the sniper. That means that the Terrorist Babe is an amateur." He used the name for Raquel he'd heard from Larry. It had a certain ring.

Gordon scanned the whole 180 degrees from their hide then answered. "Yeah. I listened when you called. But he also said she killed two sniper teams, a woman, a man and a state trooper. That's a heck of an amateur!"

"I wish we could take it to her. I'm sick of three weeks of waiting." Charlie liked to gripe, but he could out wait the sphinx and Gordon knew it.

"If you could find out where she's gone I'll go with you," Gordon said. "Like you got an idea.

"I wish we'd asked Larry to turn off the mercury vapor lights. They ruin our night vision goggles."

"Take the watch. I'm gonna get some shut eye. And no more beans and franks, Gordon, I mean it!" Charlie had taken the watch all the previous night. They were scheduled to do three hours stints, but he had not been sleepy and so had stayed awake while Gordon slept.

In Highspire the Swatara Township policeman knocked on the door. His partner looked around the neighborhood. Hard to believe terrorists could be in this place. Old folks, working stiffs. Kids.

Two hours earlier a neighbor lady had called and told the dispatcher that she was certain her neighbors were the killers the police had been seeking for three weeks.

"Three weeks ago?" the dispatcher asked. "Why are you just calling now?"

"Well, you haven't caught them, now have you?" the elderly lady asked with her own kind of logic and a certain amount of petulance.

"Ma'am?"

“Well, Roman and I have been arguing about this for long enough! He says they are and I say they aren’t! You just send an officer out here and settle this for us.”

The policemen had arrived. One knocked at the front door. Bored, the other went to the garage and looked inside through the glass insert. Her heart leaped to her throat.

“Oh! Crimony! Get over here! It’s a cruiser!”

Roman won the argument.

Driving a used Silverado into the edge of York, Pennsylvania Raquel heard the announcement on WHP radio. The house in Highspire was blown.

“About time!” she muttered with nothing but scorn for the law. She continued into town, crossed Route 30 and climbed up into the hills overlooking York. The house was rented through an agent. Rent paid for a year. Keys in a box on the back door with a code.

She whistled as she worked.

In Virginia Beach she had swum, walked the beach and gone bar hopping. Only once had she been tempted to pop anyone, as she referred to it. In the end, she had resisted the emotion welling up inside her. Just to see his face as she did it! But, no, she restrained the urge and a sailor lived to return from shore leave.

She cleaned her Smith, the Ruger and the sniper rifle. That took the better part of the afternoon. Finally she headed out for a box of KFC, a pound of slaw and a Diet Coke. *A girl has to watch her weight.*

At eight o’clock she was dressed in black and driving up Route 441. She turned right at the sign advertising of all things, “goat races,” *Can that be real?!* she asked herself.

Two and a half more miles and she was there. She turned left, glided down the road to the first dirt road into a field. It was hiking from here.

All light bulbs had been removed. She gathered her gear from behind the seat, gently pushed the door with her hip until it clicked and began to walk across the bean field. There was enough moon light to see by. Perfect timing.

When she came to the blacktop road she trotted over and then began to crawl up the grassy slope. It was not lawn, and the foot tall green plants, whatever they were, covered her progress. The farm lane ran parallel to her on the right as she moved ever upward.

Once she was at the edge of the lawn she rose, gathered the rifle out of the drag bag and slung it over her shoulder. The Smith was in her right had, a flashlight in her left.

She knelt beside the house. Her heart hammered in her chest. Sweat covered her face. *Nerves,* she chided herself.

Listening, she could hear voices inside, but they were indistinct. No light shown on this side of the house. Opposite there was an area light mounted high up on the barn. Another was further back on some other large shed.

Moving to the uphill corner of the house, she listened for any sign that there was someone outside with her. *I'm stupid for not coming up here in the daylight,* she thought. Then, *It wasn't necessary. It's been three weeks. No cops are going to wait that long. They all think I'm out of here for good.* She carried on the mental argument with herself. A professional would have handled this mental gymnastics before the truck ever started to pull away from the house in York.

Charlie nudged Gordon who was instantly awake. Both men searched the area below them. They had set up a line of trip wires across the woods behind them. Three in fact. If someone did manage to evade the first one or even the second wires, then the last one would have set off the flash bang grenade and alerted them. No one was coming in from the way the shooters had the first time without them knowing it. They were free to watch the field and house now.

"There. The dark side of the house." Charlie spoke above a whisper, but barely so that Gordon could hear.

Ten minutes passed and then Gordon saw it too. A shadow grew larger at the corner of the house. He raised the night vision goggles but the barn light flared them out.

At the scope, Charlie's eye began to water from the strain. He had been watching for fifteen minutes. Certainly there was something, but it never moved any more. He thought it was there and then he doubted himself. *Move* he willed it.

Raquel continued to kneel at the corner of the house facing the field. She sensed danger but could not identify it.

Finally she turned and crawled to the other end of that wall. A car went by on the road, its headlights illuminating the area around her just the slightest bit. She was out of sight of anyone except a person coming up the lane from the road. In that case the head lights would illuminate her like an airport beacon.

There were windows on this side but no doors. None showed a light. She moved around the corner of the house and upward, careful not to make a sound. Now the lane was on her right and she was illuminated by the area light on the barn.

Duck-walking along the foundation of the house, she reached the opposite corner from where she'd waited so long. A truck and two cars were parked in a gravel area about twenty feet from the house.

She moved to the side of the truck and laid the rifle very carefully on the ground. A light from a high window cast yellow on the grass between her and the house. *Kitchen.*

To the right was a door with a glass square in the upper portion. *I could kick that in and kill them all before they could move.*

She had just risen to a crouch when from behind a man's voice spoke with authority,

"Hold it right there!" He was at the rear of the truck.

Raquel spun like a jaguar. She fired at the shadow of a man, shoulders and head only above the truck's tail gate. The barn light painted him like a cowboy silhouette.

Her two shots sounded as one. Though they were but six feet apart both missed the man, who dropped from sight but not before firing at virtually the same time as Raquel.

He did not miss. One took her in the neck, grazing her. The other lanced her left ear.

Immediately the kitchen lights went out.

Raquel spun and dropped at the same time. She scrambled for the rifle, all the while knowing it was a foolish waste of time. She heard footsteps on the gravel, quickly moving up and away from her. She tried to look under the truck to find a foot or ankle for a target.

"FREEZE! MOVE AND DIE!" came the shout behind her from the open doorway to the house. Two men with pistols pointing at her stood about four feet apart. One illuminated her with a bright flashlight.

She rose quietly, hands raised, then slowly placed her left hand on her ear and neck. It came back covered in blood.

"I'm hurt," she said in a weak voice, pretending to be worse off than she actually was.

"Stay put or die!" Larry commanded loudly. Jake moved ahead two steps.

Suddenly Raquel reached up to her neck again. Her right hand was a blur.

Before it reached her hair line there was a thud-smacking sound and a mist issued from the left side of her head as it was snapped sideways. At the same moment a rifle's report echoed down the valley from the tree line. Her body dropped straight down to the ground.

Everything went a little crazy then.

Jake and Larry rushed her. "Lights! Dad Lights!" Jake shouted.

"I'm out here, men!" George shouted.

Three halogen lights blazed instantly from the eves of the house.

Larry grabbed the gun on the ground and shoved the rifle under his truck with a foot. Jake knelt beside the ruined head.

"She's down for good." He said it with intense relief.

"George, are you okay?" Harold called from the doorway.

"I'm all right. She nicked my straw cowboy hat though. I thought I hit her but I guess not," he said as he stepped into the light.

"You got her. Neck, it looks like, but that rifle did so much damage, it's hard to tell. There's a gouge here though," Jake said still looking at the body.

"Marines Incoming! Hold your fire!"

"Hua!" Larry hollered back, acknowledging the sniper team as they entered the circle of light.

"Hey! What's this?" Jake said, and rolled the body over. Strapped behind her neck in a shoulder rig was a throwing stiletto.

"That's why I took the shot," Charlie said. "I noticed the reflection in the light. Figured it for a blade. You know, I hated that barn light 'cause it ruined our night vision equipment. Guess it was a good thing after all."

"Somebody call the law," George said with weary relief very evident in his voice.

"Yeah, anybody but that crazy Pudroshski." Larry said and laughed.

EPILOGUE

At the Headquarters building Harold was sitting in his office meeting with Elvis and Sarah. He was reminded how our minds adjust to the strange appearances of our regular associates after a while. Here was Elvis in a chartreuse jump suit with fringed sleeves, rhinestones festooned the front and back. He had white patent leather boots with two inch heels. Skinny as an Ethiopian refugee and with the big, black hair of the King, he was a sight to behold. Yet, Harold had – almost – gotten used to walking in each day to a rainbow of costumes. That the man sounded exactly like Presley when he spoke was shocking still. It was like a major adjustment mentally between the visual and aural disconnects. But here they were. Elvis was the most knowledgeable electronics superstar Harold had ever met. He could bug a room, car, airplane one minute and the next wire your office with music sources that could be controlled by your own words.

Sara Longstreet was the physical counterpoint to Elvis. She was a walking fireplug of a woman. Her hair was constantly in disarray. Opposite that was a mind that was razor sharp in anything associated with computer science.

Unlike Elvis her outfits consisted of bags with holes for neck and arms, open at the bottom. They were formless, bland in color and design. Some had erratic lines of earth tones. Others brought paisleys in sand shades of gray and black and tan. All covered a body form which she had long ago given over to endless boxes – not packs – of Twinkies, Twizzlers and M&Ms of every sort, color and shape.

Between them they had devised systems to protect the house – including outbuildings, headquarters, the airplane and grounds. They built a satellite network of voice communications that would span the globe. Currently they were feeding some designs to a new company that Zulu had formed specifically to take their developments to the fight against terrorists. Included in that effort were three Israeli corporations.

On the planning board was a body implant to communicate with any member of the team at will.

This meeting was about the upcoming delivery of a Gulfstream V.

"So when it gets back here, we have two weeks to go over it for bugs, and to put our own toys in it?" Sarah pressed. Elvis nodded. He too wanted confirmation, but he would never push the issue.

"Guaranteed, assuming world war three doesn't begin and need it for bombing runs," Harold agreed with a smile.

"Okay. That's it. You're gonna love the stuff, Chief!" That unrequested moniker had sprung up the first day Sarah had walked into her lab here at headquarters.

"Chief, you are the absolute BOMB!" she'd exclaimed.

Used to student terminology from his campus days, Harold knew this would stick and so silently surrendered. Chief it was. Now Elvis also called him that.

When Jake had saluted one afternoon as he left the offices and said, "Later, Chief!" Harold had begged him and Larry not to use the name. Both agreed, then immediately forgot the promise. Still it was only utilized on special occasions.

As the two geniuses walked out Harold's secretary beeped his intercom.

"Mr. Crabtree, Ms. Frances on two." This was the former Secretary of War's Personal Assistant. A trim, tiny woman with an elfin face, coal black, perfectly coifed hair and a smile to match the sweet-tea Southern accent. She was a bird of a lady with quick steps, a twinkle in her eye, and every man's favorite aunt or neighbor lady. She favored Caspar suits and high heels – she needed all the help she could get, barely hitting 4 feet eleven and one-half inches tall.

Ms. Frances had served Don Rogers for the past twenty-five years. She and his wife Jocelyn were personal friends in a semi-professional way, and both women lived to make Don Rogers' life professionally and personally everything he wanted it to be. There was no hanky-panky. She, like her boss, was a professional and had dedicated her life to serving him. When he retired she had as well.

The life was not pleasing. Boring was the word she most often used to describe her current situation.

"Frances, thanks for calling back. How are you?"

That was the beginning.

TWO MONTHS LATER

Jake rode the pinto. On one side of him was George and on the other Tex. George was astride the brown mare. Since Helen's death there was a sort of bonding between them as if George found comfort in her company.

The three men were about two miles away along the banks of the Conewago Creek. They had not spoken except when a fox and four pups had bolted from a mound of grass in the neighbor's pasture. They had ridden here before.

As they dismounted and laid back along the high bank the only sound was the horses chomping the rich green grass. George plucked a weed stem and picked his teeth with it. Finally he spoke.

"Jake, what has all this come to? I mean the killings and all.

"Before you answer me, I need to say how much I appreciate y'all seeing that I've had company like you have. You and Tex riding with me. Larry and Nick making me go to the range with them. Your dad and I have been playing more chess than I ever have. And that Marine down the road has been pestering me to work on some landscapin' ideas he has for the farm. Man you should see his home!

"George you don't owe any of us thanks, but you're welcome. Dad and I remember how it was when my mom was killed. For the first few days folks were wonderful then it was like they didn't quite know what to do with us so they did nothing.

"They didn't do anything wrong. Don't misunderstand me. They just didn't know whether to mention mom's name or not. For fear we'd bawl like babies. And we might have. It would have been okay to just let us get it out. We did that for a while. But they just shied away from us completely.

"Everybody but the preacher at Oak Grove, Pipsqueak and Pete. They would just drop by and pick up at whatever we were doing. If we were mowing the yard they'd ask for some ice tea or something. Pip and Pete would just get into whatever work was at hand. Roofing the shop. Baling hay. They'd park their pickups and join in like they were family. And truly they are.

"When we took a break they'd visit for a while. Finally they'd say, 'Well, gotta get to work. See y'all, boys!' and they were gone down the lane."

"It taught us both the value of someone who will just let you hurt.

"George I read an article by a Dr. Davidson somewhere. He did a lot of research about how long it takes to sort of recover from losing a loved one. Even professionals like many pastors, doctors, and the like thought it was about six months. Then the bereaved person should just 'get over it and move on.'

"This professor did us the greatest service with his work. His interviews proved that the real time period is about two years. It takes that long until we are back to functioning regularly. Our emotions, our health, our attitudes. To the place where we can talk about our loved one without just breaking up. I sure appreciated that old boy's work when I read that.

"So you can thank us. We all like that, George. But owing us. Not at all. We just have a debt to pay that was put on us by Pastor Phillips and Pip and Pete. Now the shoe is on the other foot and it's time for us to try to be a blessing to you."

Tex had not said anything since they'd saddled up. He enjoyed the riding almost as much as flying. To get out here reminded him of a happy childhood with his horse.

"Did they ever catch that other sniper team, Jake?"

"Not yet, Tex. My guess is that they are holed up somewhere waiting for things to quiet down. I doubt that they were after us. I think that was the terrorist babe's deal.

"Nick talked to Grant yesterday. He says that forensics has never had a work load like this before. Not criminal that is.

"Bottom line is that the Jordanian sniper killed Helen and Rosalie. The rest of the murders were done by Raquel Linden. She was murder incorporated. I personally think that woman was evil incarnate.

"I truly do believe that she must have been demon possessed. Spooky.

"Oh, yeah, and get this. Not only did they roll up the guy at the farm where the snipers were trained up in Perry Country. He spilled his guts and they've arrested one hundred sixteen guys in New York and Jersey. Plenty of empty carpets at the mosques.

"Not to be outdone, the FBI nabbed Raquel's gun runner from New Orleans. He was hiding out in Key West. Some guy named Tomas. Harvey said you wouldn't believe the team that took him. He couldn't quit laughing on the phone when he described them," Jake chuckled at the memory.

Ms. Frances is now ensconced in a large office across the hall from Harold's. She is Executive Director of Solutions.com. It had not taken much pleading to convince her that the team needed her administrative skills. She joyfully put retirement behind her, moved to a rooftop penthouse in Harrisburg overlooking miles of the Susquehanna Valley.

Yossi Cumi, Director of Israel's Mossad is due in three days to visit his brainchild's headquarters and to request Solutions' involvement in combating Israel's challenge with Iran. There are some things that even the intrepid little nation prefers others carry out.

Reports of the nuclear potential to "wipe Israel off the map" are taken seriously. Especially in light of the fact that unrelated humit[8] sources were now filing reports of Iranian insanity at the highest levels of government.

"It's time you guys got to work. You've had enough vacation. And I have some Meshuganim to put down. Saddle up! Yes, saddle up. I like that phrase," Then he laughed. He was doing more of that since Solutions.com had come into being.

---

[8] Humint. Human Intelligence. AKA spies.

Little did Jake, Larry and Nick know that his phrase was a prophecy.

Jake, Larry and Nick couldn't wait to see his reaction when he saw Ms. Frances, Elvis and Sarah standing side by side to greet him.

FOLLOW JAKE AND THE TEAM AS THEY JOIN FORCES WITH ISRAEL TO ROLL THE PERSIANS UP IN A RUG!

THE THIRD EXCITING VOLUME OF THE JAKE CRABTREE / SOLUTIONS.COM SERIES BY ERNIE & WANDA MOORE WILL THRILL YOU!!

HERE'S A GLIMPSE

Jake struggled upward out of the deep, realistic dream. The gentle "DING" of the intercom at his right elbow accompanied a ruby red LED called for his attention.

"Yeah?" he murmured as he pressed a button, converting his bed into a luxurious leather armchair. Before it was completely upright the steward, Ace, was beside him gathering the pillow and blanket.

"We're about forty minutes out, Boss," Tex drawled from the right seat of the sleek Gulfstream V's cockpit.

"Thanks, Tex. How're you guys doing?" Jake asked as the other half of the cabin crew handed him a steaming mug of coal black coffee.

Where Ace was a Marine recruiter's dream, with the chiseled chin, wide muscled shoulders and tight abs, Karlsen was every boss's dream. She needed taught anything only once. She hated dirt and disorder like a mongoose hates a cobra. An early-forties widow with no children from her marriage to an NSA analyst who had succumbed to pancreatic cancer four years ago, she was neat, calm, and in charge of her responsibilities.

Both had come to Solutions from contacts in the Pentagon. Ace had served aboard Air Force One until all the Presidential dishes and tableware had disappeared with a change of administrations. Rather than accept his resignation outright, his bosses had moved him to civilian status and assigned him to the Secretary of War's plane. Ms Frances brought him to Harold Crabtree's attention. When the GV was delivered, Ace was there to outfit it.

Karlsen was another whispered tip. Her cooking was atrocious – Ace was the on board chef. But she could lay her hand on any item aboard the jet from charts to a safety pin the instant it was needed. Often she anticipated the need.

She knew how to set up and operate a sat phone, how to handle all the commo gear – including the crypto stuff – and she loved to fly. She was the daughter of an Air Force Lt. General and had covered more of the world than Henry Kissinger. She spoke five languages fluently, including Hebrew. And she feared no one. Tell her the same thing twice and she'd quickly remind you, "That is the same instruction you gave me yesterday. It's completed."

Jake had learned this when he gave her the special mix of coffee all the team imbibed by the gallon, one pound Starbucks Columbian mixed with one pound Elite Turkish Coffee. Brew normally. After perking, let it sit for ten minutes before decanting. When he repeated the recipe to Karlsen she had smiled a tight little grin that some said reminded them of a Paris Island DI and said, "Mr. Crabtree I got it exactly right the first time."

"Right," was all Jake could say. It sort of reminded him of Olive Cotter's conversations with him when he was in the third grade.

For a while he tried to catch her forgetting something. He couldn't even spy her writing instructions down. Regarding her first name; Harold knew it. She had informed him if it was released he was to consider it her last day at work.

Ace looked upon her as an older sister. She considered him a peer and a friend. They saw the Solutions team as people they had quickly come to love, serve, and if necessary protect. Both were unarmed self defense experts and crack shots with handguns.

The intercom did its light and "ding" thing. "Yeah," Jake said. Hidden microphones enabled him to communicate with anyone in the plane without a handset.

"Look out the port window."

Jake turned his head to the left and there off the wing was an F15E Strike Eagle with a red flag bearing the crescent and star of Turkey on the tail.

"What's up?"

"Don't know. He just showed up. We knew he was there; our radar spotted him and two others five minutes out. This one moved up about a mile away where we could see him then snuggled up to us. Then the son of a gun waved and said, "HALO SVEESS."

As Jake watched, suddenly the F15 lit his afterburner, zoomed ahead and then went vertical. The GV shuddered slightly as the air waves hit them. It wasn't dangerous, but it sloshed Jake's coffee.

Karlsen approached and handed Jake a sat phone the size of a Snickers bar. Her look said, "No idea," at Jake's questioning look.

"Hello?"

A mellifluous voice, with a touch of the grandee spoke with an almost British accent. "Hello, Jake. Did you enjoy the air show? This is Mikhail."

Mikhail was a former KGB agent. A man his father had met in the jungles of Viet Nam. On the other side. The story of how he had escorted Harold from a very dangerous ambush situation, then shook his hand and faded back into the jungle, never to be seen again was one Jake had heard a couple of times.

Then one day Mikhail had walked up to their headquarters compound at the Harrisburg International Airport and asked to see Harold. Jake's trip to Turkey was a result of a telephone call from Mikhail last week.

"Are you going to tell me how you got a Turkish pilot to do that?" Jake asked.

The raspy laugh was full of too many years of cigarettes. "My dear young man you and I both have our secrets. But this one is simple. It took only money.

"Did you enjoy it? Were you surprised?"

"Honestly, no and yes. I didn't enjoy it, but I *was* surprised. I don't like fighter jets sneaking up on us," Jake answered.

"Jake, we both know the Turk did not 'sneak up on you' what with your advanced avionics. My young friend we must learn to be more transparent with one another." This delivered almost as a reprimand.

"Perhaps you're right, Mikhail. Perhaps." Jake was giving nothing away, but he sure wondered how the Russian knew about their security avionics package.

"Ah, you are as careful as your father. But remember, Jake I never deceived your father. Quite the opposite. In fact I saved his life. Twice. Has he not shared those tales with you?" There was humor in the voice, like an older man might use with a beloved underling he was tutoring. Jake did not especially like it *or* trust Mikhail.

"Mikhail, my father has only told me of one incident with you in Viet Nam. He did tell me that he owed you a debt. That's all."

"Jake, there were two but your father knows of but one. You don't trust me, Jake? Too many stories about mad Russians?" he laughed again.

"Well fear not. I'm not a Greek bearing gifts, either. What I offer will benefit us mutually, and there will be ample opportunity for you to put your wariness to rest.

"Incidentally, your Uncle Yossi sends his regards. *Das Vidanya!"* and the call ended.

"Uncle Yossi" was Jake's late mother's brother. He was also the Director of the Mossad. Jake was a bit stunned that Mikhail would know that bit of information.

Jake sipped his now cool coffee contemplatively. *The Turkish air show and the call were not for amusement. What was Mikhail saying? That he had money to burn? Lots of the old KGB guys had Swiss or Cayman accounts. Skimmed operating funds. Extortion from marks they encountered. Outright robbery wasn't beyond belief, certainly. That he could buy favors from Turkey's military? Jake didn't need any favors from them. And besides buying favors through one means or another was standard operating procedure in the Middle East.*

Jake turned to signal Karlsen for another mug of brew. She was standing at his shoulder with a knowing smile and a fresh cup. *How does she do that?!* he wondered and smiled, "Thanks."

And was the remark about Yossi more than just notification that he knew of their family relationship?

"On final, Jake," Tex reported, and Jake could feel the change in attitude as the GV began losing altitude. He headed to the lavatory to freshen up.

Antalya, Turkey lies just north west of the western end of Cypress. It is on a large natural bay surrounded by magnificent mountain peaks that retain their snow caps late into each spring. With favorable weather, the attractive Mediterranean Sea and a location near frigid Europe, Russia and the Middle East the draw is natural. Add a generally peaceful, friendly nation (though certainly not one without crime) and Antalya is a prime tourist draw. Beloved by the Germans and Russians, it is also a vacation haven for Israelis.

Centuries earlier it was also the place where the Apostle Paul departed Turkey for Antioch, though then the name was Attalia. With spelling being what it is in this part of the world, there is no telling when the "N" was added.

On landing, the beautiful jet was directed to the apron where it joined a half dozen other corporate planes. Ace opened the air stairs then stepped back and was replaced in the door by Jake who was greeted by Mikhail Nikolay Ivanovich Lobachevsky and a Turkish Customs man. With a curt order to the Turk and, "Everyone's passport, please," to Jake, Mikhail took charge.

Jake gathered the five passports – two pilots, two attendants and his own – and handed them to the Turkish Customs officer. Jake remained between the men and the air stairs effectively blocking entrance to the plane.

On noting that all five were Swiss diplomatic passports, Mikhail's eyes darted to Jake's face, the white cross in the red field on the vertical stabilizer, then quickly away.

The officer pasted a visa stamp in each passport; date stamped each, then said something and held his hand out to Jake. Instantly, Mikhail snapped some harsh words at him, whereupon he visibly paled, came to attention, saluted Jake and, returning the documents, made a hasty retreat.

"Bloke wanted twenty bucks a head from you!" Mikhail spoke this in a perfect English upper class accent, then winked and offered his hand.

"It's good to meet you personally, Jake. I pray you had a pleasant trip. All the way from Harrisburg, was it?"

"Pray? I thought all you KGB-types PREYED, but didn't 'PRAY.'" He spelled the words. As both laughed two Ford Tauruses glided up to the airplane.

"We are going to the Delphin Palace. Your people and luggage will travel in the second car."

As Jake turned to retrieve his briefcase with a special compartment for his Glock and a spare magazine, it came out the door toward him. Karlsen's arm was just visible.

The lead Taurus made its way toward Lara, the suburb of Antalya where so many new hotels were popping up like mushrooms. Mikhail turned toward Jake and smiled a benevolent smile.

"They are building fifty – yes FIFTY – new five star hotels where we are going." Mikhail said.

Jake looked out the window just as the car turned left from a modern four lane highway onto what seemed to be a country road far from any modern development. A rough dirt road replaced their smooth highway.

"They will of course continue their highway construction as well. You'll see when we get closer that the roads improve again.

"Think of it Jake. A country with such a backward history becoming the next Riviera. But they have what it takes. Sunshine, a government hungry for outside investors and impending membership in the European Union. Beautiful beaches, clean environment, panoramic views, lovely people. And a neutrality toward – ha! Toward even the Jews, if you can believe it. Of course they prefer the Germans' marks and Russians' rubles more than the Israeli shekels. And forget Americans. If you find any English speakers at our hotel, it will shock me. Too far to travel to beaches when one has an embarrassment of riches at home.

"Still, one would think that certain wealthy companies with nearly a billion dollars in assets and over two hundred million in liquidity could do worse than to build at least one hotel of their own. Is it not so?" Mikhail smiled with that glint in his eyes again.

Jakes only nodded as he looked at the Russian and then back at the scenery as they moved onto better roads.

"You are wondering what I'm up to. Why I return to your father after thirty years.

"Before I explain, may I tell you that your likeness to him when he was your age is stunning. It is like my life has been rolled back to another time."

You're right, you old fox, but you're trying to soften me up for something, Jake thought.

"Thank you, Mikhail. I certainly take that as a compliment and not flattery.

"You're appearance still is not making sense. You arrive in a cloud, re-introduce yourself to my father and disappear. Then you call and ask me, not my father, to meet you here. I'll tell you honestly, I agreed to come because you helped him long ago. But you need to start explaining yourself. Quickly." Jake's statement was not entirely accurate. He had come because he had this instinctive hunch that he could profit somehow from the acquaintance with Mikhail.

Mikhail's eyes snapped with anger for a moment. It was plain he was unaccustomed to being spoken to this way. Then it passed, and he answered with much weariness.

"Ah, the impertinence of youth. Yes, Jake, there is much still unexplained. But be patient my friend. It will be worth it, that I promise."

They entered an area of new construction. Tall apartment buildings in white and pastels were everywhere. The telltale piles of dirt and rubble that dotted every building site spoke volumes. The four lane highway was already being expanded to six lanes. Palms lined both sides.

Mikhail spoke to the driver who nodded. "Note the next few hotel names. There on the right is the Titanic. We are in the Delphin Palace, which is a new spelling of Dolphin, but we'll go past. Now take note of this one," he pointed to the right, "the Concorde." The top of the hotel was shaped like a gigantic airliner.

"Does it amuse you as it does me that the Titanic sank and the Concord is grounded? Our Turkish friends are not very sophisticated in naming hotels," Mikhail and Jake both chuckled.[9]

Registering was simple. Mikhail handed Jake a set of 'cards' one a key card, the other for charging incidentals.

---

[9] These are not fictional hotels.

"Sometime today, Jake, you will understand the reason for your journey. In the meantime I must insist that you allow me to change your appearance. Nothing permanent, but you must not be recognized. Please allow me this one bit of trust." The last was said almost pleadingly.

"We will put a temporary rinse on your hair making it auburn,. You will instantly grow a moustache and sideburns, and don clear eyeglasses. That's all."

"All right, Mikhail. I'll play along." Jake was no stranger to sophisticated disguises.

"Come with me," Mikhail said then turning abruptly, he motioned to a desk clerk who trotted over. He spoke a few words and the clerk virtually clicked his heels in a parody of a German attention. "Your crew will be cared for when they arrive."

Sixty minutes later Jake looked at the stranger in the mirror. There was only the slightest resemblance. Mikhail laughed and touched his shoulder.

"Now we have an appointment." They returned to the main lobby with its rich dark walnut panels and gigantic thirty foot wide crystal and gold chandelier suspended above the lobby on an eighty foot chain. Three sparkling brass and glass elevators carried patrons up the back wall of the lobby. Small tables and chairs in more walnut and marble filled the area directly beneath the chandelier. Deep maroon velvet tapestries completed a look of riches befitting the palace of an Ottoman Sheik.

"We'll have coffee in there." They entered a salon the length of a football field and half as wide. Conversation groupings were placed on both sides and ran the length of the massive room. Each one consisted of two facing ivory leather couches and a brown one around a marble topped table.

Apparently Mikhail was a noteworthy patron, for as soon as they were seated a waiter arrived to take their order.

Jake looked outside and noted the arrival of his crew. They disappeared inside accompanied by a sophisticated desk manager and bellboys pushing bronze carts holding their luggage. Jake and Mikhail carried on a casual conversation about the Gulfstream aircraft for a few minutes. Jake was looking around the room, and out the windows at the same time. Then he turned to speak to Mikhail. He was met with an amused look.

The Russian was holding his right hand up, index finger signaling Jake to be still. Jake complied, then followed the Russian's gaze. In the driveway a black SEL 500 Mercedes glided to a stop. The right front door flew open and a man in a dark suit, white shirt and wrap around sunglasses was out and opening the rear door.

Security. Jake thought.

A tall, thin man with very sallow skin emerged. He was in a beautiful grey silk suit with a maroon tie. His hair was trimmed short, and he was clean shaven. Jake thought, *he resembles Osama bin Laden cleaned up.*

It is!! Jake started to leap to his feet, but Mikhail's grip was like a vice as he reached across the table and caught Jake's wrist, forcing him to remain seated.